The Darkness Within

THE SIN'S OF DARKNESS DUET
BOOK ONE

A.J. MORAN

Note to Readers

The Darkness Within is an Omegaverse reverse harem romance the first in a duet, but the story is a standalone. Each book will have their own Happily ever after, and can be read alone. Recommended for readers 18+ for adult content and language.

This is a Contemporary Omegaverse has non-shifting alphas, betas, omegas, and sigmas. Alphas have knots and ruts, omegas go through heats, but do not shift into any kind of animal.

This story includes a relationship that could be Dom/sub but is not meant to be a guide for that lifestyle and is missing a lot of key aspects. It also includes borderline non-con, dub-con, very dark elements (ie on page: torture, blackmail, crime, un-living of people, attempt of sexual abuse by non harem member). If any of this is not your thing, put the book down. Metal health matters.

It also contains the following tropes: Daddy kink, Billionaire romance, ex-mafia romance, heats, mpeg mentions, trauma healing, a/b/o/s, and physical relationships between the men.

CHAPTER 1

Audrey

A HORDE of people rushes in every direction along the busy city street. The smell of decay and trash is strong this morning as I dip between bodies on their way to high-rise jobs. I swerve and steal, all in one fluid, practiced motion. They won't know what happened until they go to pay for their fancy coffee, check the time, or try to show off the new piece of jewelry their sugar daddy gave them to their so-called friends. By then, I will be long gone.

Twirling around an unsuspecting beta, I lift their wallet from their back pocket as they brush past. With a practiced snap of my wrist, I flip through the contents, tugging out the wad of cash and tossing the rest in the nearest trash can. I am in this to get some money, not get caught with some guy's credit cards or identification.

Dodging shuffling feet, I come to a halt with the rest of the crowd at a crosswalk. An alpha shoves past me, stopping right in front of me and flashing his expensive watch. Next mark found.

Perfect.

As the crowd starts to surge forward in a hurry to start

their day and ignoring the do not walk sign, I lean forward, deftly unclipping the gold watch off of his wrist. His revolting and cloying scent of cigar smoke and burnt rubber almost makes me gag as I breathe in; it's somehow worse than the smell of the city. As he steps into the street, none the wiser that I have his expensive ass watch slipped into my pocket, I drop back, not following the crowd.

I pivot on my heel with the newly acquired Rolex safely in my pocket, putting as much space between myself and him in case he gets the urge to check the time again. Ducking my head, I pull up my hood and focus on my feet, traveling with the many passer-bys as they scurry to start their days.

It's a good morning, the Rolex alone will keep my brother, Sin, and me fed for months, and probably pay for a roof over our heads, too. No more squatting. No more sharing my nest with the local rodents. And definitely no more going to bed hungry.

Despite the pests, my nest is calling my name now that my hard work is done. I just want to relax and enjoy my favorite comfort show on my phone. I can afford the data cost with my haul today. Heck, maybe I can even afford a small TV for our new place. I'm riding high, and I'll reward myself with my guilty pleasure.

Omega in Paradise.

Do I want to find an Alpha or a Pack? Absolutely fucking not. But the fairytale that plays out in the reality show is so entertaining, as weak-minded omegas fall at the feet of rich alphas, calling it love.

Please. No such thing.

Twenty *lucky* Omegas—*heavy eye roll*—are whisked away to a private island along with a pack searching for their alpha, who also is so rich they probably have five private islands and no real need for an omega besides breeding. I shudder at the thought. Poor suckers go for love and probably become a broodmare for the alphas once the cameras stop.

Still, it is irresistible watching it on my screen, playing out like some romantic fantasy. But I know the cold hard truth of what alphas are like, even the ones that are supposed to protect you. And I had come out of the abuse better than my twin, Sinclair. He faced the darkness head-on and has his own cross to bear now because of it.

A hard left on East 42nd takes me away from Rockefeller Center and toward Grand Central Station. Hopping on the Harlem line, I tuck myself into a seat out of the way of the few tired-looking people. Only a handful of people are heading back at this time.

Quickly moving through the almost empty streets, I duck into the shadowed alley, stepping over what looks and smells like vomit on my way. *Gross.* Then, I squeeze between the old, crooked wooden slat and through the broken door.

Sin lounges on the old worn couch we found left behind by the last inhabitants. His gaze slides lazily to me through a swirling cloud of smoke. He takes another hit of his joint, inhaling sharply as he watches me. With his other hand, he dances a dagger over his knuckles, his pierced eyebrow lifting in question.

"You're back early," he comments, his tone relaxed.

With a smirk, I pull out the Rolex, watching as his eyes go comically wide, and he sputters the puff of smoke out as he leans forward.

Coughing, he covers his mouth as he eyes the watch. "What suit did you snag that off of?"

"Some high rise. He probably has ten more in a vault somewhere. He won't miss this." I shrug and drop next to him.

My finger ghosts over the initials, A.Z., carved on the back of it. Hmm. So maybe he'd miss it.

Who cares?

A spring digs into my thigh, and I shift off the errant coil that is insistent on attempting to pierce my skin. Not that the lumpy cushion beneath my ass is much better. A musty scent fills the air, clinging to the worn fabric of the couch. I wrinkle my nose in mild disgust, but it's a minor discomfort compared to the other challenges we've faced.

"It's probably worth enough to get us into our own place." I shift again. "And buy a new couch."

"What's wrong with this one, Aud?" he murmurs, his bloodshot eyes barely open. Clearly high as a kite, but who am I to judge? We've both endured the cruelty of our abusers and if this is his way of coping, I'll love him regardless.

"Uh, for one, it smells like the city—piss, vomit, and trash." I grimace, holding my breath at the offensive stench. I scan the filthy floor and walls of the abandoned building we've been using as a hideout. Even the gangs have more decent places to lie low.

"It's not that bad." He sniffs, taking another drag on his joint. He extends it toward me, but I shake my head, declining the offer. He puffs out a cloud of smoke after holding it in for a minute. His fingers absently run along the only comfort he allows himself, an old robe, a clear sign he is uncomfortable at the idea of change.

A rustling sound emanates from a nearby bag of chips, immediately capturing our attention and further solidifying my argument. A sense of anticipation fills the air as a large black rat, its eyes gleaming red, emerges from within the empty bag. Squeaking in protest, it hurriedly scurries across the grimy floor, disappearing into a giant hole in the wall as if our mere presence has greatly offended its delicate sensibilities.

"If you don't mind sharing with the rodents, some as big

as a dog." I shiver, wrapping my arms around my middle. "We can at least have a place that is safer than this for us."

As he simply shrugs, I feel a wave of disappointment wash over me, and I can't help but release a sigh of frustration. Pushing myself up from the floor, I realize we still have a precious hour before the pawn shops open their doors, and if we truly desire a substantial payout, we'll have to seek a more upscale establishment.

Determined, I make my way to my space, purposefully fluffing the pillow I had treated myself to, indulging in its softness. I meticulously rearrange the blankets, ensuring their comforting embrace surrounds me. Finally, I settle down on the worn-out mattress nestled in the corner, finding solace in its well-worn charm. It's here, within the confines of this humble corner, that I immerse myself in the captivating allure of my guilty pleasure.

***

I WALK OUT of the jewelry shop with an extra spring in my step. Bianca didn't even hesitate when she handed me nine thousand for the Rolex, and I'm certain I could have squeezed a couple thousand more out of her if I had pushed harder. But what she gave me is enough to cover at least two months of rent on the Lower East Side, a safer option compared to an abandoned warehouse. Thankfully, we face little trouble from people in Harlem; most of them keep to themselves, although, occasional fights break out. It's nothing Sin and I haven't witnessed before.

Perhaps we could even catch a glimpse of the East River from our new place. The sight of water has always had a soothing effect on me, bringing a sense of calm and grounding. The thought of leaving behind the slums, even if it meant moving just a few miles south, fills me with a newfound lightness. Plus, it's still a quick journey to Midtown and the Theater District, both of which offer great opportunities to earn some extra cash. As long as I continue finding unsuspecting suits or tourists, we should be able to sustain our new place.

The city has thousands, if not millions, of each.

My familiarity with the streets guides me along Central Park, retracing my steps toward the hideout where Sin is still fast asleep. I can't wait to share the news with him. I'm certain he'll find the idea of having bolt locks on our door appealing. After all, he always keeps a weapon nearby, ready to defend our abandoned sanctuary against any unwelcome intruders.

I know I would cherish a secure closet to retreat into during my heats. The effectiveness of my cheap suppressants has been inconsistent lately, leaving me uncertain when a breakthrough heat may strike. It's been nearly three months since my last one, so I'm certain another is looming on the horizon.

In my mind's preoccupation, I failed to register the presence of the group loitering near the alley, the route I typically use to return to the warehouse, until I was nearly upon them. But it wasn't a gang as I had assumed; instead, it was a cluster of suits. What the hell was affluent alphas doing in the streets of Harlem? Swiftly, I slipped into the sheltered entrance of a boarded-up shop, cautiously peeking around the corner to observe them.

The alpha in command sports cufflinks that hold a value substantial enough to cover rent in the Lower East Side for a year, if not more. His silver watch glimmers, drawing attention as he points toward the abandoned building we have been occupying. With his golden blond hair capturing the midday sunlight and accentuating his tan complexion, his visage exudes an air of expensive refinement. He meticulously maintains every aspect of his appearance, from his clean-shaven face to the pair of eyeglasses resembling fucking Bentleys that are worth more than the combined worth of his cufflinks. The exorbitant price tag on those glasses exceeds the cost of most homes, nearing half a million dollars.

Damn. He isn't just any suit; he is filthy rich, too.

His features resemble those of a model rather than a corporate executive. Chiseled angles and broad shoulders that could easily grace a billboard. If his neck is any sign, his abs must be equally well-defined. I can't help but focus on his fucking neck, feeling an intense urge to nuzzle into him, even from this distance. He has a way of setting my pulse racing and my breath quickening, despite not being close enough to catch his scent.

His head swivels in my direction, and it feels like his gaze is caressing my skin, leaving a tingling sensation in its wake. My legs tremble, and I hastily retreat into the safety of my hiding spot, blending into the shadows of the doorway. My hands turn clammy, and the ringing in my ears drowns out any other sound. I take slow, deliberate breaths, struggling to regain control over my omega senses that are urging me to surrender myself to this stranger on a silver platter. The very thought sends a chilling jolt through my veins. I would never allow an alpha to take control over me.

Drawing in a deep breath, I hold it, inching my head forward to peek around the corner. I observe as the men climb into their luxurious cars and the doors are slammed shut. A sigh of relief escapes me as, one by one, the vehicles pull away from the street.

I'm not sure of their purpose for being here, but it adds to my determination to secure a safe apartment. If they return, if *he* returns—I have to be gone.

CHAPTER 2

Audrey

"SIN," I hiss, nudging him once more with the tip of my shoe. "Wake up. We need to leave."

He mumbles something and covers his face with his arm, still refusing to open his eyes. A gentle snore escapes his lips, and I let out a sigh. I miss the old version of my brother, the one before everything changed and depression took over. I blink away the sadness and give him a harder kick. He grunts, sitting up and reaching for the gun that had been resting on the cushion beside him, now securely held in my grasp.

"I said get up. We need to leave."

"Where are we going?" he asks as he scrubs his hand over his face.

"The Lower East Side, grab your shit," I say. Pulling the bag containing my pillow, blanket, and a few changes of clothes securely onto my shoulder, I turn my gaze back to the broken door. "There were suits sniffing around. I bet they are going to be in here with construction any day now. We need to be gone."

"You pawned it?"

"Yeah, it was a good haul. Even if we don't find a place today, we can get a room somewhere for a few nights."

He rises from his seat and stretches, my gaze instinctively drawn to the deep scar that runs across his abdomen, a constant reminder of his infertility, ensuring an alpha will never claim him. At times, I wish it had been me instead. But then I realize that if our roles were reversed, I might also be as damaged as he is. It's as if drugs and pain are the only things that can truly reach him now. That fateful night rewired him completely, erasing any semblance of choice from his life.

He retrieves his gun from my grasp and tucks it discreetly into the waistband at the small of his back, hidden beneath his shirt. Grabbing his already packed bag, he nods toward the exit, silently signaling our departure.

"Lead the way, sis," he says, and we head back out into the sunlight.

The subway car is crammed with people as we wedge our way inside. It feels as if the ride takes forever, and I only take small inhales of breath of the dank air. The mingling scents of omegas and alphas create an overpowering odor, making me grateful when the doors finally open, allowing me to stumble out onto the platform.

How do people endure this every single day?

We decide to grab a late lunch at a nearby diner, which ends up being the most substantial meal either of us has had in days. While savoring the food, I pull out my phone and start scouring the internet for apartments to rent in the vicinity.

"Here's one, one bedroom. It has two windows–" I hold my phone out for him to inspect.

"It looks like a walk-in closet. Look the bedroom is up a freaking ladder," he replies dryly. He snags one of my fries as he hands the phone back. "How much do they want?"

"Just over three thousand and a half of that for the security deposit, but no checks," I say as I mentally count the money in my pocket. Two months and maybe some food and furniture, so we wouldn't be sleeping on the floor.

"Aud, three...thousand..." he drew the words out, and I swallow. "For a room the size of a small closet that looks like you'd have to move the sofa away from the wall to access the storage closet."

"It isn't that bad, and I can make that in a day if I get lucky." I lean back, cradling my phone in my palm as I study the picture of the small apartment. It does look like they changed a walk-in closet into a living space.

"It says the bathroom is communal," he deadpans.

He rolls his lips in, his teeth mercilessly attacking his plush lower lip. The scent of stress hormones wafts from him, and I wish, as I have many times before, that I could provide the soothing comfort he needs, just like Mom used to do.

A beta in the booth behind him twists around in his seat. "You twos looking for a place to stay?" He wags his finger between us, his Brooklyn accent strong.

Sin leans to the side, his gaze fixated on the man who interrupted our conversation. He eyes him with caution, a wariness clear in his expression.

I nod. "Yeah actually."

"I knows a place, just opened up, boss said we needs to fill it quick," he says. "I just happen to have a picture, comes furnished. No checks. Easy-peasy."

It sounds too good to be true. I lick my lips hesitantly, feeling a mixture of hope and skepticism. "How much?" I ask, my voice cautious.

"Boss says for the right people, two grand," he replies, slinging his arm over the back of the booth. He holds out his phone, showing me a picture of the place.

I study the image that resembles an advertisement for the apartment. It showcases a rooftop pool, a gym, and a doorman, and it's located in a pleasant neighborhood. My heart thumps with contained excitement in my chest. My brother, looking less enthused than I am, runs his gaze over the photo.

"Looks slightly larger than the one you were looking at and cheaper," Sin says, casting a doubtful look at me.

"We could check it out at least. It could be good for us, Sin," I say, softening my tone and dipping my head to catch his mismatched gaze. "Look, it even says there is a doorman."

"We will be living in someone's closet," he quips. It obviously takes more than a pretty picture to win him over.

"Can we just go see it?"

Sin gives a nod, and the beta says, "I'll give my boss a ring."

I hold my breath as he punches in the contact labeled "Big Boss Man" and puts the phone to his ear.

"Boss, that apartment still for rent?" He remains silent as the man's rumbling response comes through the phone. "Yeah, I gots a girl and guy that are looking."

Is it my imagination, or did he say "girl" with emphasis? A sense of unease washes over me, settling in my stomach. Anxiety takes hold, and a low whine escapes my throat. Sin's warm hand covers mine, a small comfort, and I inhale. The urge to bolt still intensifies, but the prospect of having a place to call home keeps me rooted to my seat. I grip the worn table in front of me, forcing a smile as the man glances in our direction.

"What's yous names?" He holds his hand over his phone, pausing the conversation momentarily.

"Audrey and Sinclair Taylor," I reply automatically. Taylor wasn't our actual last name, just the one we had picked up when we went on the run. Indistinct. Unrecognizable. Easy to hide with. No one is going to look at that last name and wonder if they knew them because they probably do know someone with that last name.

I pick at my cuticles as he speaks into the phone again, giving the man on the other end the names I gave him. The steady thump of my heart and the pit in my stomach have my knee jumping under the table as I hold in another pathetic whine.

He watches me, his brow furrowed as he ends the call. "He said you can tour it at two. Mr. Zade will meet you in the lobby." He turns back around and scribbles an address down on a napkin and hands it to Sin. "Don't worry, for an alpha he isn't that bad."

I release my breath in a trickle when I can't hold it anymore without passing out. "Thank you. Uh, Mr.-" I say.

"Vinny, you can call me Vinny." He gives a small nod but doesn't reach out to touch either of us. My heart continues to pound in my chest, but my anxiety spikes as he rises from his seat and places a twenty-dollar bill on the table. He calls out a goodbye to the waitress, using her name, and mentions that he'll see her later. She responds with his name, indicating that he's a regular customer. Not only that, but he leaves a generous tip for just a cup of coffee. It reassures me he has no intentions of kidnapping or torturing me. It's all in my imagination.

"You good?" Sin asks.

"Yeah, just excited."

He rolls his eyes, sensing my lie. It's hard to lie to someone who has a nose as good as mine.

After finishing our meal, I take the bill up to the register and pay, leaving the tired-looking waitress a generous tip. She's earning her money honestly, unlike me. If I could, I'd be a modern-day Robin Hood, stealing from the wealthy and giving to the poor. Though few would accept the money as pride comes with earning your own way. But whenever I can, I spread the stolen wealth in the best way I know how—by tipping big.

We make our way through the busy streets toward the apartment building. I'm eager to scope it out and check for any potential dangers. It sits on the corner of a quiet street, with flower pots framing the entryway next to the large glass doors. Just like in the picture, there's an actual doorman. It looks...normal. And that eases my fears.

With some time to spare, we duck into a second-hand shop down the street and start browsing through the racks for some new-to-us clothes. These places often hold hidden treasures. Half an hour later, my arms are laden with my selected items as I make my way to the register. I place my stuff on the counter, and Sin places his items on top. He found a couple of things, all in black, of course. My fingers trail over the leather jacket he found. It's old and worn, but the soft texture beneath my palm is irresistible.

"Nice," I say, tossing him a look.

"Mine," he replies, reading my mind. I would definitely steal it from him at the earliest chance.

I shrug and smile as the lady bags up our purchases. It is just about time to head over to the apartment.

CHAPTER 3

Audrey

AS WE APPROACH the tall building, the doorman eyes my worn-out jeans and the black hoodie I still cling to—comforts from a better life that I can't let go of. My arms are filled with plastic bags containing second-hand clothes. With a tight smile, the doorman pulls open the door, accompanied by a half-hearted bow that earns a snort from Sin. We step into the expansive lobby.

The sight is breathtaking. To the right of the entrance is a spacious common area, with high marble ceilings that likely belong to the original building. A grand double-staircase curves up to the second floor, while an old-fashioned elevator, complete with carved marble pillars and an elegant black metal door that stands at its center.

Natural light pours in through the windows, illuminating the common area where a few people chat or play chess. A smile tugs at my lips. It's perfect. I spin in a small circle, taking in all the intricate details above our heads like a kid on Christmas morning.

Just wow.

The ad boasted a rooftop swimming pool and gym, which

piqued my curiosity. Such amenities are rare for the Lower East Side, but I read about a prominent figure buying up rundown properties and transforming them into livable spaces. I bet they are making a fortune if this place is one of theirs. Maybe I should have researched more about this Mr. Zade we are supposed to meet.

My thoughts flash back to the suits we encountered in front of our previous squat. Are they somehow connected to this business? It doesn't matter; if we are lucky, we will never see them again. It seems unlikely that Mr. Zade is the same man we encountered earlier today. That would be a truly bizarre coincidence.

A throat clears behind me, and I swiftly turn on my heel to face a well-dressed beta. His vibrant purple hair, artfully tousled on top and shaved close on the sides, along with the piercings on his lip and eyebrow, create a striking contrast with his business attire. His sparkling green eyes meet mine, and a smile involuntarily spreads across my face.

He is undeniably attractive, unconventionally. I mean, objectively speaking. Not that I am interested or anything.

"You must be Audrey Taylor," he says, extending his hand for a shake.

I pause for a moment, mentally preparing myself to make skin-to-skin contact with a stranger. I reluctantly reach out, feeling his warm hand envelop mine with long, strong, and slender fingers.

None of the usual panic fills me; instead, there is this warmth that spreads inside my chest. It is the only thing that stops me from snatching my hand back the second it slides over his calloused fingers.

He gives a firm squeeze before letting go, then turns his attention to Sin. My brother glances at the outstretched hand but keeps his hands in his pockets.

Unfazed, the man continues, "I'm Felix Parker. My boss

sent me to show you the apartment. It's on the 20th floor, a pretty excellent location—only five floors below the roof. If you're interested, we can also visit the rooftop."

He swiftly turns on his heel, purposefully striding toward the elevator. With a smooth motion, he slides the metal door aside and gestures for us to enter. I exchange a quick glance with Sin before passing Felix, pressing myself against the wall of the elevator. I feel more at ease with betas than alphas, but that doesn't mean being trapped in a small box with a stranger tops my list of enjoyable activities.

Felix steps inside after us, silently closing the door. He presses the button for the 20th floor and leans against the opposite wall from me. His curious gaze travels down my body, the intensity still visible in his vibrant green eyes when he returns his gaze to mine.

"Are you two..." His voice trails off as he gestures between us, leaving the question open-ended. Sin scoffs in response.

"No."

He nods, his gaze returning to me. "Family?" he inquires.

"What gave it away? Our matching dimples? Same fine features?" Sin retorts, oozing sarcasm with each question mark. I elbow him and force a smile for the man who holds the power to decide whether to rent to us.

"He's my twin," I quickly interject.

A warm smile graces Felix's face, and his shoulders ease. As we arrive at our floor, he once again holds the door open for us, gesturing down an elegant hallway. How is it possible that an apartment in this building is being offered at such a reasonable price?

"Besides your apartment, we have a dedicated area exclusively for omegas. No betas or alphas allowed. It's a kind of sanctuary, on the floor just below the rooftop," he explains, shrugging casually. When we reach a door halfway down the hallway, he retrieves a key from his pocket.

I swallow hard as I brush past Felix and step into the small living area. It is exactly as it appeared in the picture. A plush, orange couch hugs one wall, while an empty bookshelf and one of the largest TVs I'd ever laid eyes on occupied the other. In this cozy room, watching TV would feel like being in a movie theater.

Stained, clouded glass doors obstruct the view of the small bedroom. Curiosity gets the better of me, and I move over to them, sliding them open. My heart skips a beat as I lay eyes on the full-sized bed adorned with the softest-looking blue comforter and an array of at least six pillows. It is a sight that makes my omega instincts rejoice.

I stand at the threshold of the petite bedroom, my gaze roaming the compact space that will soon become our home. It is only a closet, with just enough room for the bed positioned in the center and a dresser pressed against the wall. But to me, it holds the promise of a fresh start and newfound independence. A surge of excitement bubbles up within me, overpowering any reservations I may have had about the size.

"The furniture comes with the apartment, but if you don't like it," Felix says, his gaze sweeping across the space. "I'm sure my boss will switch it out for something more suitable."

Something more suitable? I turn back to Felix, a wide smile spreading across my face. "This is perfect!" I exclaim, my voice brimming with genuine enthusiasm, a feeling I haven't experienced in months. "Just what we need!"

Beside me, my brother stands with a more reserved expression, his brows slightly furrowed. Although he may not share my overwhelming excitement, he understands the significance of this moment for me. With a gentle squeeze of his hand, I can see the love and support in his eyes, silently assuring me he is by my side every step of the way.

In this life, we are a unit, bound together. When no one else has our backs, we have each other, and as long as we are together, we can overcome anything.

A knowing smile plays on Felix's lips, and he nods in agreement. "It may be small, but it has its charm," he says, his voice carrying a hint of understanding. "And it's in a great neighborhood, right here in the heart of The Lower East Side. Did you want to see the roof?"

I nod absently, my eyes darting around the room as I let my imagination run wild. I envision the possibilities, picturing how we can transform this cozy space into our own sanctuary—a place filled with love, laughter, and cherished memories. The size doesn't matter; it's the start of our journey, a place where we can build a home together. Even if it means I have to find an actual job, I am determined to keep this space.

This will be our home.

Felix holds the door for us, and we step out into the hallway. Heading in the opposite direction of the elevators, he says, "There is a separate elevator that will take you to the roof. Or you could take these stairs." He gestures to a door we pass by. I commit the information to memory, knowing I'll explore it later.

Silence fills the elevator as we take it to the roof, and once again, Felix studies me. The look of appreciation on his face ignites a warmth within me, stirring the omega instincts to wrap my arms around him and nuzzle my cheek against his.

What? No. We are not scenting anyone. I curl my fingers around the metal railing at my back, desperately trying to suppress the image of him pressing me against the wall. Our lips locked in a passionate kiss. Sin sniffs and raises an eyebrow at me, his knowing gaze piercing through my composure. I clench my legs together, feeling the first signs of my slick gathering between them.

Relief washes over me, pure and sweet, as the doors open to reveal a sparkling pool and a spacious deck bathed in sunlight. My eyes are drawn to the glass wall of windows showcasing the well-equipped gym. Taking in a deep breath of the fresh air, far removed from the bustling city streets, a genuine smile spreads across my face.

"My boss wants the apartment to go to someone who would love it." Felix steps closer to me, and I instinctively wrap my hands around my stomach, trying to contain the bubbling excitement within me.

"We would love it," I assert, my voice filled with sincerity and eagerness.

I quickly glance at Sin, silently seeking his confirmation. He lifts his shoulders and nods, his quiet support reassuring me, even as his mismatched eyes say he will not let my reaction from the elevator slide.

Turning my attention back to Felix, our eyes lock in an expectant gaze. "We'll take it," I declare, my voice brimming with determination. "What do we need to do to make it official?"

He offers a warm smile, his eyes shining with a sense of satisfaction. "Congratulations," he responds, his words laced with genuine happiness. "I believe you'll make the apartment truly special."

As he extends the keys toward me, I tilt my head slightly, a hint of confusion crossing my face. "Don't we need to sign anything? Fill out some paperwork?" I inquire, wanting to ensure that we follow the necessary procedures.

Felix chuckles lightly, his laughter adding a touch of warmth to the air. "Yes, to both questions," he confirms. "But

I'll give you two a chance to settle in a bit. I have a meeting with my alpha in thirty minutes. I'll return tonight, and we can sign the papers and exchange the paperwork."

My fingers instinctively curl around the keys he offers, and as our fingertips brush, a jolt of awareness shoots through me, settling low in my belly. I inhale sharply, trying to conceal the surge of reaction by quickly opening my purse and tucking the keys inside.

"Thank you for showing us around," I say.

"I assure you, the pleasure has been all mine," he says with a touch of charm, giving a slight half bow that adds a whimsical flair. He casually flips his hair out of his eyes, tugging his lip ring into his mouth, and our gazes lock in a brief but intense moment.

Why do I want to crawl into his arms? I don't have this reaction to men.

Caught in his gaze, I hold my breath, feeling a rush of unexpected emotions until he finally nods once and breaks eye contact. With a mixture of relief and lingering excitement, I turn back to Sin, my eyes wide with anticipation.

"We have a home!" I exclaim, unable to contain my joy any longer. I throw myself into Sin's arms, embracing him tightly in a bear hug, reveling in the overwhelming sense of having a place to belong.

He awkwardly pats my back, returning the hug with a touch of hesitation, before shifting back on his heels to look at me. His earlier high has disappeared, and his gaze is clear and focused as he observes me.

"Are we sure about this?" Sin's voice carries a hint of skepticism as he shoves his hands into his worn jeans, his gaze wandering over to the pool. "That guy seemed a little too eager to give us this place. It just feels off. Why would they offer us something like this, which could easily rent for four or five grand?"

I let out a soft sigh, trying to ease his concerns. "Sin, don't look a gift horse in the mouth," I say, hoping to reassure him.

He snorts and rolls his eyes. His skepticism is still clear. "Audrey, you are stranger by the day. And if this is a gift, they sure as shit are going to expect something in return." He shifts slightly giving away his next move.

Anticipating his playful gesture, I quickly step out of his reach, avoiding his attempt to mess up my hair. A carefree laugh escapes my lips, a burst of pure joy at the prospect of a fresh start for both of us. This is our chance to create something new, to embrace the possibilities that lie ahead. And I, for one, will embrace the fuck out of it.

He follows me back to the elevator, and we ride it down to the twentieth floor. I come to a stop in front of the apartment we viewed earlier, pulling out the set of keys from my purse. Inserting the key into the lock, I turn it and push the door open.

A rush of happiness floods through me as I step inside, and I can't help but let out a contented sigh as I lower myself onto the sofa. It feels like sitting on a cloud, pure comfort.

My gaze wanders around the small living area, taking in the kitchenette situated next to the entrance. The stove is equipped with only two burners, and the refrigerator is a fraction of the size of a standard one. Beside the stove, there is a small counter, barely half the size of the sink, with two cabinets mounted above it. Another larger cabinet hangs directly above the compact fridge.

I realize I haven't even looked at the bathroom yet, so I bounce off the couch and take a few steps toward the tiny room. Inside, I find a toilet, a miniature sink with a vanity, and a shower that simply drains into the middle of the bathroom floor. It's a space where you could brush your teeth, use the bathroom, and take a shower simultaneously if you really wanted to.

It's tiny, no doubt, but it's ours.

"Sin! It is clean, and it doesn't smell like trash or any bodily fluids. We can take turns using the bed, maybe even make a schedule or something. Just keep your...intimate activities to the privacy of those back rooms in the clubs." I flash a mischievous smirk at him, and he responds with an eye roll. "I don't need to know about your kinks, so keep them to yourself."

"I wasn't planning on sharing," he retorts dryly, sinking into the sofa. A soft sigh escapes his lips as he runs his fingers over the luxurious material. "I almost feel like my clothes are too grubby to be touching this surface."

"Then you should put on your new clothes," I suggest playfully.

I walk over to the windows, and we're lucky to have two of them that stretch from the floor to the ceiling, allowing ample light to flood our cozy apartment. From this height, I can glimpse the river beyond the neighboring building to the east. It feels empowering to be perched above the surrounding structures. The park is just a short walk away, and we're conveniently positioned about five blocks from the bridge.

Letting out a contented sigh, I turn back to face Sin. "So?" I venture, my eyes scanning the space once more.

"If you're happy, I'm happy. And you'll be safe here."

I sink into the sofa next to him, a wide smile spreading across my face. It's been such a long time since we had a place to call our own. I suppress the memories that threaten to resurface, swallowing hard to push them away.

This moment is too precious to be tainted by the past. My smile falters for a split second, but I quickly regain composure, ensuring it remains firmly in place. If there's a hint of glistening in my eyes, I'll attribute it to pure happiness. No need to let Sin know the memories tried to creep back in.

"I'm curious about the omega-only space," I say, hugging one of the throw pillows to my chest. "We should find out more when he returns."

"Yeah, when he comes back." Sin smirks at me, his eyes full of mischief. "Are we going to talk about that reaction you had?"

I roll my eyes, dismissing his remark. "No, we are absolutely never going to talk about it. It was just a fluke."

"Sure, if that's what you need to tell yourself to sleep at night," he teases. "But I'm pretty sure you were attracted to him."

I shake my head, feigning disinterest as I get up and pretend to inspect the cabinets. Deep down, I can feel his gaze piercing through me, seeing right through my facade.

"Aud, eventually you're going to want children," Sin continues, his tone turning serious. "Maybe you won't be able to have them with that guy, but perhaps you'll find an alpha or a pack."

I scoff at the idea. "I will never trust another alpha again."

Sin steps closer, his voice filled with empathy. "Look, I know I'm damaged goods, sis, but you aren't. You could find someone to take care of you. An alpha who would make you happy. Remember how Mom had Dad? He was always good to her."

I pause, memories of our parents' loving relationship flooding my mind. Maybe Sin has a point. Perhaps there is someone out there who can provide the stability and love I long for. Before I can push the thoughts away, they overwhelm me.

"Sin," I choke out, tears welling in my eyes. Swallowing hard, I shake my head, allowing the tears to stream down my face. "I... I can't."

His expression tightens, understanding the weight of my words. Finally, I turn to face him, my vulnerability laid bare. I know what he means. He can't protect me from my heats, only an alpha can. It's my only option, but the thought fills me with a mixture of terror and resignation.

CHAPTER 4

Felix

AUSTIN'S FINGERS tap relentlessly on the hard surface, his face a mask of passive expression. Mesmerized by the rhythmic motion, I lean back in my seat to his left. Dean—aka Saint—is still absent, unaware of the impending drama. The poor soul sitting at the opposite end of the long table seems on the verge of a nervous breakdown.

"Explain, in excruciating detail, how Nox snatched that deal right from under our noses, Edwards," Austin demands, his voice sharp as a whip crack. The intensity of his tone even makes me catch my breath. If I were in Edwards' shoes, I'd probably spill all my secrets in an instant. He hasn't even used his bark.

Edwards swallows audibly, his tie clearly feeling like a noose around his neck. He hastily unbuttons the top of his shirt, as if seeking release from its grip. Yet, it isn't physically choking him, at least not yet.

Malice emanates from Austin's violet eyes, the golden flecks barely discernible amidst the storm brewing within his irises. It's the one telltale sign that reveals the depth of his anger. If I were at the receiving end of the boss's wrath, I'd be trembling uncontrollably.

You could remove the Mafia Prince from the Mafia, but you couldn't erase the Mafia from the Prince. And in this moment, he embodies every inch of a formidable kingpin. His rage simmers just beneath the surface, held in check with a composure I could never hope to match.

Edwards stumbles over his words, his demeanor resembling that of a young, frightened omega rather than the beta he is. "I-I, uh, it... was—" His voice cracks, and he straightens his shoulders in an attempt to appear less terrified. "Nox simply had a better bid. It was something I couldn't expect."

The tapping of Austin's fingers ceases, and I hold my breath, awaiting his response. "You couldn't foresee that the bid for the building was too low? Aren't you greasing the palms of the young code official? What's the use of my money going to someone who can't do their job?" His words carry a double meaning, leaving no room for doubt. Both Edwards and the omega with the city are on the chopping block.

His mouth gapes open like a fish stranded on dry land. "Mr. Zade—"

"The time for excuses is over, Edwards," Austin declares, rising from his seat. He smooths out his jacket, effortlessly erasing any invisible creases, before locking eyes with the man. "Felix, take care of the problem."

Without hesitation, or a second thought, I stand up, my gun already in hand, and squeeze the trigger. Edwards collapses, a bullet piercing his forehead, brain matter coating behind him. I shift my gaze to Austin, and he gives a subtle nod of approval.

"The girl that Vinny sent to see the apartment. It's the one we've been following, right?" Austin glances over at me as he moves to pour himself a drink, gesturing to me in question. I nod my head.

"Yeah, and her brother," I say.

"Brother?" Surprise fills his voice. "Interesting. Omega?"

"Yeah."

I move to the body, rolling him into the carpet we just replaced last month. My stomach tries to empty its contents, but this is part of the job. Just don't make me torture someone. I can do the quick and fast kills, but I'll leave torturing to Saint.

"She's cute. You didn't tell me she was cute up close and personal."

He hums and takes a long sip of whiskey from his tumbler.

"She'll be perfect for our needs. No one would suspect an omega. The tracker on the watch was a good idea."

I straighten and scratch my neck, feeling uncomfortable with the praise. "What are our needs?"

He snorts at my tone. "Not sexual."

"Yeah, no... I didn't think that," I attempt to assure him, but he obviously senses my lie. Normally when omegas or alphas respond to me, I can ignore it, but the way the girl blushed set my blood on fire.

"Felix, we don't mix business with pleasure."

I shake my head. "Of course not. Am I counted in this 'we' you're talking about?"

A warm chuckle fills the space between us. "When she stole from me, I wouldn't have noticed if it weren't for her perfume. With the right masking, she'll be perfect."

"What if she says no?"

He puts the empty tumbler down and shoves his hands into his pockets. "She won't," he replies, every bit of confidence he feels infused in his words.

"I told her I'd be back tonight to have her sign the papers and collect rent."

"Send Reba, I need you with me. Now get rid of the garbage before it smells."

Disposing the body is simple; the cleaners take care of the hard work. I supervise. But it takes longer than expected, so I take the stairs to the lobby. At this time of day, the lift would stop on every floor. I don't have time for that.

Austin is already in the back seat of his sleek black BMW. I can just barely make out his outline through the tinted windows. The driver reaches for the door to open it for me, but I wave him off.

"I got it."

Mark nods and steps back. "Of course, Mr. Parker."

"Felix," I inform him for what feels like the millionth time.

"Yes, Mr. Parker," he replies with a half bow.

Rolling my eyes, I pull the door open and slide onto the smooth leather seats. "Where are we going, Austin?"

"The benefit for the police force. We need to show up as a unit, be visible."

"We're missing Dean," I say, stating the obvious.

"Saint will be there. He had some business to attend." Austin leans back in his seat, his head tilted toward the traffic next to us. He looks tired. Although, only Dean or I can pick up on that. The silence that falls between us is a small comfort in our dangerous world. Reaching out, I thread my fingers with his, squeezing slightly. He glances over, his violet irises void of his earlier anger, and he smiles. "Life wouldn't be the same without you, Felix."

"Glad to hear you don't regret pulling me out of the

gutters." I grin cheekily, and he playfully smirks over at me, his eyes sparkling, and shrugs.

"I wouldn't go that far."

My grin widens, and a laugh erupts. It's rare to see Austin smiling and joking. He is so busy holding the reins of the business world while keeping the mafia at bay that he doesn't allow himself the minor pleasures. So I would enjoy it to its fullest.

The drive is too fast. The BMW idles next to the curb of the expensive-ass-looking banquet center. A large crystal chandler sparkles through the tall windows. Austin smooths his tie and meets my gaze.

"Ready to charm the crowd?" he asks with a slight lift of his brow.

"It's what I do best, boss." I fall back into the role I play for the masses easily. As a beta, it shouldn't be as easy as it is, but I just have that natural charisma that people are drawn into like a moth to a flame. Why not use it to our benefit?

He moves quickly, capturing my jaw between his fingers, and drags me across the seat to him. His mouth lands on mine in an open-mouthed, promising, filthy kiss that I welcome. For only a moment, our tongues dance and our breaths mingle. Then he's pulling back, his violet eyes shining with his contained desire.

"Fuck," I say, adjusting myself, "I would rather explore this than go in there and flirt." I gesture between us, and he smiles.

"Make the chief want you, Felix. We'll reward your efforts later."

I drop my head back to the seat and pull in a calming breath. As I slowly release it, I crack open my eyes and peer at him.

"You're a bastard, Austin."

"Yet you stay."

"Of course. Where else would I go?"

A half-smirk lifts the side of his mouth as he drops his eyes down my body to my very obvious problem. "Nowhere I couldn't find you and bring you back."

A shiver runs down my spine at his possessive tone. That is one thing about Austin, don't take what is his, and that includes me in that equation. His and Dean's, and I wouldn't want to belong to anyone else. Still, I can't help pressing his buttons.

"What would you do once you found me?"

He hums and wets his lower lip with a dart of his tongue. "Let Dean punish you for running." His eyes sparkle as he thinks of it, and I would bet real cash he'd like to see me try, just so he could drag me back and enact his punishment. "Now, get your ass out of the car, and let's get in there."

Without needing another word, I push the door wide and climb out, fixing my suit and running a hand through my mess of hair. It flops right back over my forehead, and I shrug as I move to meet Austin as he comes around the car. Sucking my lip ring between my teeth, I stare up at the fancy building and steady myself for the drain the crowds would be on me. At least Austin made sure I smell a bit like him. It would keep some alphas at bay.

I follow one step behind Austin like they expect it of a beta as we enter the building and into the grand hall. Not that he would make me. He isn't like that. But I also know we need to keep up appearances. Betas are subservient, not equals, at least in our world. It would have been simpler for me to stay in the gutter and find a normal partner to have a life with.

When Austin stops, I almost barrel into his back being so wrapped up in my head. "Sorry, boss."

"Felix, fetch us a drink." He smooths his blazer out and doesn't look my way, knowing I'll do as he orders.

With a nod, I glance at the beauty he stopped in front of, Melody Lynn. She is everything an alpha shouldn't be. Willowy, tall, and fragile looking. The last part is a facade she wears well. She could match Austin in fierceness without blinking an eye. But her past is a mystery I'd rather not know anything about. Like Austin, I am pretty sure she found her roots in a Mafia family.

It is easy to slip between the partygoers, and I snag three glasses from the nearby table before heading back to Austin. When I reach them, I hold one of the slim drinks out to Melody. She smiles softly and takes the glass from me, her fingers brushing mine. Ignoring her for the moment, I turn to Austin with a smile and give him one, too. Flirting with Melody would be a big no. She would see straight through my bullshit because she knows how to bullshit.

"Melody," I say with a brief nod. We've done some jobs with her in the past, but that doesn't mean I want to draw her attention now. At the same time, I can't be rude. Fine line to walk.

"Flea," she replies.

Rolling my eyes, I look away from them as they talk in low tones again. At least the feeling is mutual.

I stand near them, as if I actually were a bodyguard, and glance around at the growing crowd. All of this would be better if Dean showed up. As it is, I will probably fall asleep if Austin and Melody continue their boring ass talk about business.

As Peter—another alpha, and my mark tonight— approaches, I lift my pierced eyebrow. The chief of police is built like a brick house. When he slaps his palm on Austin's shoulder in greeting, it almost knocks him over. Not that Austin would admit that.

"Mr. Zade, it is so good to see you at the benefit. Where is Mr. St. Cloud tonight?"

"He is on his way, and I wouldn't miss this. The city's improvement means a great deal to me," Austin replies as he shakes the man's hand.

"Your generous donation will go to good use, I promise you," Peter gushes, more like a simping omega than the alpha he is.

"It better," Austin replies.

Was it just me, or was there a bit of a growl in his tone? Maybe I am just that attuned to his moods.

"You remember Felix, don't you?" Austin pulls me next to him, and I shake the beefy hand of the police chief. I don't flinch when he squeezes, but I file it away for later knowledge. Why try to intimidate a beta? Nerves? Fear?

"Police Chief Peter, you are looking fine tonight," I flirt, allowing my gaze to drop down his large body. Melody rolls her eyes to the ceiling and excuses herself as he puffs out his chest like a strutting peacock. It makes a grin spread over my lips. I moisten them and share a look with Austin before adding, "Would you like a drink?" I hold out my untouched glass to him, and he accepts.

"Felix, it is good to see you. We could use a man like you on the force."

I hold in an eye roll and suck my lip ring into my mouth. If he had found me in the gutter, he probably would have kicked the shit out of me and left me there.

"For the right terms, I might be swayed." I wink at him, and he flushes.

"Don't try to steal my talent away," Austin warns with a friendly-looking smile.

The chief stutters over his reply, "Oh, no, of course not, Mr. Zade." But the way he eyes me makes my skin crawl. Still, I flirt some more.

"Is it stealing if I go willingly?" I ask.

"Maybe if the chief didn't offer first," Austin replies.

I flip my hair out of my eyes and wink at the man again. "Maybe we should have a *private* chat?"

He sputters, his face now redder than a tomato, if that is even possible. I hold back my laugh, and Austin taps my lower back, giving me the signal that he wants me to do just that.

"I have no fear you'll leave me, Felix. Peter have that *chat* if you'd like," Austin says. "Oh, I believe Dean just arrived. Please excuse me."

So not fair. I would love to go with him. Instead, my feet are rooted to the floor in front of the chief of police that we need to be distracted. The man leans into my space, and I hold my breath. He smells like overpowering aftershave, as if he decided that today was the day to take a shower in it.

"Felix, I think we could make you thrilled to be on the police force," he says, picking up the conversation thread. I'm sure he means 'he' could make me very happy. He is wrong, but still.

"What do you have to offer that I don't have with Mr. Zade and Mr. St. Cloud?"

Nothing. I don't need to hear him reply to know the answer.

"Job security. A steady future. Although Mr. Zade has been very generous, he is still just a *mobster.*" The way he lowers his voice and leans even closer on the last word has my act slipping for just a moment.

"Mr. Zade is my boss, so you better watch the way you speak about him or—" I narrow my gaze to the man who thinks he holds more power than he does.

The chief bursts into laughter as if he had been joking, and I had taken the bait, but I know he'd been serious. "Oh, my boy, I was teasing. I wasn't being serious. Everyone knows he has gone straight and narrow now."

Edward may disagree if he could. I allow a smile to form

on my lips as I pretend to accept his lie. His heavy arm drops around my shoulder, and he leads me out into a side room. I am going to choke on his fucking aftershave. As it is, it feels like I sucked on a bar of soap, and it now coats my throat.

"I see the way you look at me, and I just want you to know, I would be open to a little–" He trails off as he drops his arm and walks me backward toward the wall at my back. "Friendly and physical pleasure."

My stomach rolls. No, thank you. *Play your fucking part, Felix.* How much time would they need him distracted? My back hits the wall, and he boxes me in. His finger trails along my jawline, before his thumb brushes over my lower lip, catching on my lip ring. Sometimes I curse my overflowing charisma, it makes alphas lose their fucking heads like I'm an omega or something sometimes.

Now is clearly one of those moments. I try not to gag as he leans closer.

"Would you be up for that? You're pretty for a beta," he whispers, his gaze going from my lips back to my eyes. "And you smell good too."

I swallow. I could not kiss this man. It would be like frenching a fucking bar of soap. As it is, my nose is burning with him this close. I duck under his arm and put space between us, turning to watch as he slowly faces me again.

"Cat and mouse, I like that game." The huskiness of his voice sends revulsion through me. "I'll make you feel good. Come here, little mouse."

I roll my lips between my teeth as I remain silent. I glance at the exit. Did I give them enough wtime? Fuck, it would be nice if he shared the fucking plan once in a while. I know he doesn't want me incriminated if he is caught, but if I am doing this shit, he would need to start sharing.

The door bangs open, revealing Dean as if he were a

fucking avenging angel. "Felix, what the fuck are you doing in this room?"

The assertive and rolling sound of his growl settles somewhere low in my stomach.

"Saint–" I breathe.

"Don't *Saint*, me–get your ass back to the party and stop fucking around," he pauses, his attention flicking to Peter as if he just noticed him, when we both know he saw him the moment he came in. "Chief, I need *my* beta."

Have I mentioned I fucking live for the times either of them claims me verbally and openly in front of others? Because damn, it is hot.

"Got to go," I say, barely glancing at the chief before rushing across the room to Dean. He is my savior tonight. "What took so long?" I mutter as he drapes a long, toned arm over my shoulders and walks us out of the room.

"Are you questioning me?" He grins down at me.

"Yes, fuck, he almost tried to murder me with his aftershave."

Dean's deep laugh washes over me, and I inhale his familiar scent, attempting to remove any trace of the chief from my lungs.

"You did good," he murmurs against the shell of my ear.

CHAPTER 5
Audrey

WHEN FELIX ISN'T the one to return with the paperwork, it isn't exactly disappointment that I feel, but it's close. I'd be lying if I didn't say I've been looking forward to seeing him again. We sign the papers and send the young female beta, Reba, on her way.

Before she left, she explained how the Sanctuary access works and where the elevator was for the roof, even though Felix had shown us. The main one doesn't go all the way up. Once we are alone, I shove the keycard that gives us permanent access to both into my back pocket.

"Do you want to check out the rest of the amenities?" I ask.

She also mentioned a laundry area, one on the 22nd floor and another on the 12th, and I want to wash the stuff I have. I've checked and I have three pods left, more than enough to do the single load we need. And with it being Friday night, I'm positive not many people will be doing their laundry.

I sling my bag over my shoulder after collecting Sin's clothes, too. He watches me, his lips pursed. "Nah, I'll check them out another time."

A pang of disappointment washes over me. Of course, having our own place wouldn't break through to him. He's been fine living on the streets, only showing a shred of concern when my heats take over. Then he sobers up and guards me as if his life depends on it. We've been lucky so far. Even though the suppressants aren't working all the way, they at least make them shorter and less painful than I remember my first.

With a quick nod, I leave him in our new apartment. If I say anything, I'm afraid I'll cry. As it is, I can smell the acrid scent of my disappointment attempting to flow off me like foul body odor.

Pulling myself together, I take the stairs up two flights and find the laundry room right where she said I would. It's empty as expected, and I quickly start a load. The machine is high tech and can accept cards or cash. Since I don't have a card, I use the coin dispenser to get the five bucks needed to start the washer.

Once the time flashes on the screen, telling me I have at least forty-five minutes, I head back to the stairs and take them two at a time up to the 25th floor. The door for the Sanctuary looks really secure, with a thick bulletproof-looking surface and the inner mechanics showing through. I swipe my badge and watch it slide open to another smaller circular room. As I'm shut inside, a voice comes over a speaker. "Stand in the middle of the room, arms outstretched. Hold still."

I do as I'm told, even though I have no clue why. A light flashes red, and a puff of gentle air flows around me. "Omega sensed," the voice says. The light flips to green, and the door across from me slides open.

They weren't joking when they said it was really secure. The area it opens into is large and luxurious, way out of my league. An omega on one of the large, fluffy-looking white sofas looks at me over her magazine, her eyes taking me in and judging me before she goes back to reading. O-kay.

Another one looks over from the other matching sofa. She props her finger into her book and cocks her head to the side.

"You're new," she says.

"Yeah, just moved in," I reply, keeping my answers vague. I know better than to reveal too much to strangers, especially in a place like New York City. I'm not the only thief who has managed to infiltrate an apartment building like this.

She nods. "Well, welcome. Friday nights up here are pretty dead. But it's great for quiet time and being away from the constant assault of alpha hormones." She shivers, as if she deals with alphas all day long. And maybe she does.

"Right," I agree, although I keep my distance from alphas whenever possible. I don't count swiping their stuff as being around them. "I'm just going to look around."

"There are a couple of really cool pods in the back. Perfect little areas with all the comforts of home, and you can even close the door." She shrugs. "Not really a nest, but the closest you'll find outside your home."

I smile and move away from them, exploring the space. It's clearly out of my tax bracket, not that I bother filing taxes. I snort as I finger a bottle of "pure water"—whatever the fuck that is, water is water. When I reach the pods she mentioned, I'm drawn into one. It has a beautiful view of the river and a curved seat against the window. It offers a choice between admiring the river or watching movies on a small screen opposite the window. I could easily get lost in this small room.

I watch the boats on the water, feeling a deep-rooted longing to be out there, sailing on one of them. If there's one thing I miss about my old life, it's that. It was the only time I ever felt truly free from the expectations placed on me as an omega. The bow of the boat bouncing along the waves, my hair flowing behind me as I held onto the sails. There may be more yachts than sailboats out on the water, but the ache in my heart remains the same.

Shaking myself out of the nostalgic daydream, I glance at my phone. It reminds me I've explored enough for now, and it's time to switch my laundry over.

The woman who had talked to me earlier gives a wave as I head toward the exit. "See you next time," she calls after me.

I give her an awkward wave and a slight nod. I'm not great with people. Well, except for Sin. But he doesn't count. He's my twin, my other half.

As I push open the door to the laundry room, I notice a man inside. I hesitate for a moment, taking in his well-fitted suit. Tentatively, I sniff the air and catch the sweet scent of an omega. My shoulders relax as I step fully into the room. He seems to ignore me, focused on sorting his clothes between two washers: white and colors. Interesting. I, on the other hand, had just tossed all my things into one washer. I don't mind if my shirts turn pink; Sin only wears black anyway.

As if he could sense my judgment, he glances over at me. "Max will have a conniption if I don't sort them," he explains.

I nod, although I have no clue who Max is or why I should care about his laundry sorting preferences.

"He's my alpha, my mate," he adds.

I bite down on my lower lip, my teeth sinking into the flesh as I give him another silent nod of acknowledgment.

"We are on the 19th floor," he continues his over-share, and I paste a smile on my face. "I haven't seen you in here before."

I roll my lips together before parting them. "Just moved in." I gesture to the door as if my apartment was just on the other side, and his eyes follow the movement.

"Well, welcome. I'm Carl."

"Audrey," I say.

When he shuts his washers and swipes a card over the touchpad, I turn toward a dryer and open the door. Shoving some quarters into the dryer sheet dispenser next to them, I pay for a box of three and crack it open, tossing the fresh scent into the open drum. Then I turn and pull open my washer, transferring the clothes as he watches. I can see him studying me as I move, and I try really hard not to fidget. Shutting the full dryer, I drop quarters into the slots to pay for thirty minutes and then brush my hair away from my face self-consciously.

"You don't look like the normal type that rents here," he finally breaks his silence, and I tense. "No, it isn't a bad thing. We need less of the high-end omegas, betas, and alphas around here."

It wasn't his words that bothered me, not really, because once upon a time, I had been rich, or at least well off. That was before–

I suck in a noisy breath and paste a smile on my face. "Yeah. Uh, Carl," I supply his name after a brief lapse, "we got lucky. You can't beat two thousand."

His eyes go wide, and he blinks rapidly. "Two thousand?"

"Yeah, the rent."

"You are missing a few thousand to your number. Even the small one-bedrooms were going for five when we moved in, and I heard they've only gone up with demand. The wait-list is super long to get in here."

I swallow, my throat tight with nerves, and nod my head, unsure if my random motions are conveying a coherent message. "Right," I say, forcing a laugh to mask my unease. "Did I say two thousand?" I wave my hand in the air dismissively, chuckling again. "I meant twelve."

He nods, his brow furrowing in confusion. "You got one of the two bedrooms, huh?" he asks, seeking clarification.

"Yeah, right place, right time," I lie, trying to appear nonchalant.

"I'd love to see it sometime," he responds, sounding genuinely interested.

"Sure, after we settle in we can invite you over," I say, though, deep down, I have no intention of following through.

The thought of encountering him again in the laundry room on a Friday night or stepping foot on the 19th floor sends a shiver down my spine. But not because he is creepy; no, it is because I just lied through my teeth to him for no reason.

Hurrying from the room after a very short goodbye, I head straight for the closest elevator to escape.

The doors slide slowly open, and I blink once, twice, then three times. Still, the dark man is still standing in the middle of the small box, his hands deep inside his slacks. His head bowed in deep thought. His clothing is more expensive than a year's worth of rent in my new apartment. The cufflinks rival the ones from the suit outside the warehouse earlier. Of course, I would notice the material shit. My dependence on knowing how much stuff is worth is ingrained at this point.

But besides all of that, he is one of the most beautiful men I've ever laid eyes on. He styles his dark hair to perfection. Even his beard appears perfectly trimmed. He raises his head when I don't immediately enter the small space with him. As I lift my gaze meeting his, he smiles a polite smile as his eyes glint with danger, the violet color of them unlike any I've ever seen.

Except I have. In another life, before—I step back. Pushing the flash of memories back into the box they belong, I blink. It has to be my imagination. I was young. He *can't* be who I imagined him to be. Not here. Not dressed to the nines and in this apartment building.

There was no way my feet were going to move and carry

me into the elevator with him. Every single one of my senses is telling me to run the other way. That this man with his polite ass smile is faking it, and what he is really feeling is buried underneath. If I step into that elevator with him, I won't exit it as the same woman I currently am. And that is crazy, so I drag in a shuddering breath and attempt to give myself a mini pep talk.

When I hesitate, he lifts a finely sculpted eyebrow, proving every one of my crazy thoughts right. I know danger when it is staring me in the face. And this alpha was the definition of it. If it weren't for the apartment, I'd say my luck had gone down the drain, at least with strange men.

This one is almost as bad as the alpha from this morning. Was it really today? It felt like a whole different life. I couldn't scent him from here thankfully or I might throw myself at his feet and beg him to take me.

Fucking heats when they come, they really come. At least the day or two prior, I have the warnings as my hormones go completely nuts.

"You riding? Or?" He shrugs a well-defined, blazer-clad shoulder at the spot next to him without making room for me. I eye the spot; my feelings are probably painted all over my face. It is apparent I will need to squeeze past him into that small area, which would put me within scenting range. "I don't bite."

He definitely does.

Just him suggesting riding and biting has slick gathering between my legs. And I back up slowly as if he is a stalking animal ready to pounce. The side of his mouth kicks up, and I half expect him to add more, but he doesn't, he just watches me.

"Uh, I'll catch the next one. I forgot something," I say, looking over my shoulder.

There is no way in hell I am climbing into an elevator with

someone so sinfully delicious. I am turning into a fucking puddle just thinking about it.

"I'll hold it." His voice washes over me like a caress, and I hold back a shiver.

Without thought and as if the hounds of hell are nipping at my heels, I spin around and push into the stairwell right next to the elevators. I don't care if I look like a crazy person. My breaths punch out of my chest in rapid succession as I take the steps back down to my floor. They echo off of the stone walls until I push out into the hallway of my floor. Part of me expects him to give chase. Although, why would he? I am nothing but a random omega that lives in the same building as him.

Oh, God. I live in the same building as him.

Great, now I have at least two, wait, maybe three people to avoid, and I've only been here less than twelve hours.

CHAPTER 6
Saint

"SAINT–" Felix says, pure relief painted all over his face.

"Don't *Saint*, me–get your ass back to the party and stop fucking around," I order before sliding my gaze back over to the Police Chief as if I had just noticed him. The fucking man is red as a tomato and looks as if I'm stealing *his* fucking toy away. I hated this plan from the start. There are other ways of keeping the bastard out of our business. "Chief, I need *my* beta."

Felix puffs up as if my words fill him with a new resolve, and then he is at my side while throwing a half-hearted, "Got to go," over his shoulder at the chief.

As I tug him close to my side and pivot toward the exit, he hisses, "What took you so long?"

An answering grin tugs at my lips as I lower my head to him. "Are you questioning me?"

His jade-green eyes pin me with a serious look before he says, "Yes, fuck, he almost tried to murder me with his smell."

I throw back my head as a laugh erupts at the idea that a smell could murder someone. That would be a useful tool.

Felix takes a deep breath and holds it. Nuzzling the side of his head, I breathe in the scent that is only Felix. He might be a beta, but I care for him as if he were an omega. If Austin was dead set against bringing an omega into the mix, then it would just be the three of us, and I was okay with that. I guess.

"You did good," I murmur against the shell of his ear. He leans into my side with a sigh as he relaxes. "Austin said you got the girl to rent the apartment."

"Like it was hard? Two grand? I'm surprised she didn't run the other way. You know what they say about something being too good to be true? That deal was off the charts too good to be true. I was pretty sure her brother would put a stop to the whole thing, but he caved for her."

A smile curls my lips at his rambling, and I glance around at the party. God, I hate these things. But here I am, while Austin slipped out to run back to our place to grab something he forgot. My attention snags on the head of the Carmichael mafia. What the fuck is he doing here? The tension that seeps into my shoulders and the way my fingers curl into Felix's side have my beta looking in the mob boss's direction.

"Where's Austin?"

Pivoting away from the man before he catches sight of us, I tuck in next to a large marble pillar. "He ran home."

"Why are we hiding from Carmichael?"

"Last time I ran into him, he thought I was trying to fuck with his step-sister."

Felix arches his pierced brow. "Were you?"

"Austin said no omegas, so no I wasn't."

"But you would have if–"

I give him a droll stare and drop my arm to my side. "Do I look like I have a death wish? Carmichael has a tight hold on that step-sister of his."

Felix hums and glances around the pillar. "I don't know, Saint, I think if you wanted her that wouldn't stop you."

I push my tongue into my cheek and nod. "Yeah."

He was right. If my match came along, Austin would need to pry her or him from my fingers, because I would hold on tight. But if they were my scent match, that would make them his too. That is how it worked with packs. They would even attract Felix.

I lean against the wall at my back and survey the rest of the room. "Tell me about the girl."

"The pickpocket?" he asks.

Turning my attention back to him, I nod. "Who else would I be asking about?"

He laughs. "Carmichael's step-sister?"

"You'll pay for that," I reply, and he sucks his lip ring between his teeth as he attempts to hide the full-blown grin that pulls at the corners of his mouth.

"Kinda the point, Alpha," he husks his voice to the low timber that I love.

Adjusting myself in my pants, I straighten my blazer and push off the wall. "Later," I promise.

Then I tangle our fingers and tug him into the crowd that would lead us away from the Mafia boss. I wasn't afraid of him but getting his attention would screw up the entire plan. Tonight is about recon, but Austin is right. It would be easier to access things with someone that is good at stealing. And who would be better than an unsuspecting omega?

"I checked out the place our runner followed her to this morning. It was a run-down warehouse, looked like not even the gangs bothered with it. It is a good thing we had Vinny tail her. She was out of there before I even had a chance to return. Pawning Austin's Rolex like it was on fire."

"Yeah, paying off that couple helped, too. If we didn't

have an apartment to put her in, we could have lost her to the wind."

I chuckle. "Can you imagine Austin not only needing to pay to get his watch back, but also losing the girl?"

Felix shivers dramatically. "Heads would have rolled."

"You love that shit," I scoff. Well, if there isn't much blood involved, he does. Squeezing his fingers lightly, we thread toward the entrance. Austin should be back soon, and if he isn't, there is no way I am staying in my own personal hell.

"Dean St. Cloud," Melody Lynn says as she steps into our path. I come to a halt before barreling right into the alpha.

"Just Saint," I reply.

She tinkles out a laugh that I suppose is supposed to be unthreatening but is the opposite coming from her. We've worked with her in the past, but she is as dangerous as Austin. Ever since she lost her pack, she's lived life on the edge.

"Right, because you're so saintly," she laughs again and rolls her eyes before they drift over to Felix. "Flea, two times in one night, how lucky can a girl get?"

"What do you want, Mel?" I ask as Felix huffs out an annoyed breath and looks away from her.

"Conversation. Something to ease the boredom of this event. Where did Austin run off to?"

"We aren't your toys, Melody," Felix replies. "Not here for your entertainment."

"No? I suppose you are here for the same reason I am or Carmichael. The elusive Fairchild painting is said to be in the safe of Valentine's apartment. I bet Austin would love to bring that home and put it back in its rightful spot in that old mansion up north. Make sure the old man stays dead and in his grave."

I press my lips together and grit my teeth. The fact that it wasn't hard to guess why we were here meant we hadn't been careful enough.

"Is it stealing if it is his?" Felix quips. Not that he actually knows the plan.

"Who said anything about stealing, Flea?"

I step forward into her space, close enough to scent her. "His name is Fe-Lix. Say it right or not at all, understand?" The threat in my voice is heavy and true. She steps back with a smile playing on her lips.

"Oh my dear, Saintly, *Flea* is just that, a pest. Not even his parents wanted him once he disappointed them. Isn't that right?" She turns her head slowly to look at him over my shoulder, and I growl low in my chest, the sound rumbling between us.

"One more word from your well-painted mouth and I will cut your lips from your face. Slowly. And I'll enjoy every fucking second," I say, every bit of malice I am feeling thread into my words, and she inhales, pressing her lips together. "Is that enough entertainment for you?"

"You really should be more careful airing your weaknesses in public. Someone that wasn't a friend might use them against you," she replies before throwing one last look at Felix and turning on her heel.

"Fuck, that was hot." Felix runs his fingers down my arm, linking our fingers again. "You have anyone else you want to torture? We could make it a group project."

The tension lifts, and I laugh. "You'd pass out."

"Would I?"

"Yes, or did you forget the last time? The second they screamed and blood pooled beneath my blade, you were out."

"I can handle blood just fine," he replies.

"Yeah, if it is a bullet between someone's eyes. No screaming or torture, though, right?" I tease.

"You're the worst. When is Austin coming back?"

I hum. "You love me."

He holds his fingers an inch apart. "Maybe just a little."

Before I could reply or kiss him senseless, Austin is striding in the entrance like he owns the place. His gaze does a quick survey of the area in his calculated way before he heads over to us.

"Did you find what you forgot?" I ask as he comes to a stop next to me.

"Yes, and I ran into our omega," he replies.

Felix's eyebrows raise and I tilt my head, waiting for him to continue.

"The pickpocket?" I ask.

"Who else would be our omega?" he asks drolly. He runs his hands down his blazer before shoving them into his pockets, giving off the *who gives a fuck* air he is known for.

Felix snorts. "At least she is beautiful."

Austin gives him a look. "We talked about this already."

"I still have eyes, Aus." He shrugs. "Are you saying she isn't?"

He presses his lips together and glances away, a telltale sign he agrees. It makes my curiosity about the girl climb. I had hoped to run into her earlier. But it wasn't in the cards.

"Maybe we should focus on the benefit for now," I suggest. With Austin here, we are drawing some attention. The majority of businessmen here know he is still very much one foot into the 'family business' and one in this world. No matter how much he wishes to shed his old life.

"Did you learn anything while I was gone?"

"Melody is a bitch," I reply. "The chief is a predator."

"We need her for this to work." Austin shoots me a look, silently asking what I did. "And I will handle the chief."

All he's missing is the Brooklyn accent and cracking his knuckles, and he would sound like a true mob boss. He is refined, though. His mom had sent him to a private boarding school in England, so sometimes even a slight British accent mixes with his upstate New York accent. It is an interesting combination when his threats sound like a mix of setting a date to visit the horse races or afternoon tea.

"Do we really need her? Do you hear the way she talks to Felix?" I tug Felix close, my protectiveness clearly at the surface.

Austin sighs. "She doesn't really talk to him at all. Except for calling him that stupid nickname."

"She calls me a flea. You know those bugs that live on animals?"

He nods, his nostrils going wide as he pulls in a deep breath. He rubs his forehead before dropping his hand. "I'll talk to her."

His words placate me, and when Felix pulls away, I let him. He threads his fingers through his bright hair, then messes with his eyebrow ring, before shrugging his shoulders.

"I can ignore her stupid jabs. She means nothing to me. Her words don't hurt." He glances around and then lowers his voice. "But I'm going to need to know what we are doing. You have never kept me in the dark before, and you shouldn't start now."

"If we tell you and they catch us, you are less protected than Saint and me. We—no, I, can't have that."

Felix's tongue swipes over his lower lip as he shifts on his heels. "Then what is the point of me being here at all? You said flirt with the chief, so I did, and he tried to murder me."

"He what?" Austin growls.

I chuckle. "With his aftershave. But I saved him just in time."

Austin rolls his eyes and shakes his head. "Next mark is Gabriella."

"Gabby, Carmichael's step-sister?" he asks, sharing a look with me. "So, you have certain things you want to protect me from. But another Mafia boss isn't one of them?"

Another laugh pops out of my throat, and Austin sends me a pointed glare. "He isn't wrong. I was sure Carmichael was going to gut me for even looking her way before. He is really protective of her."

"He won't do anything to you."

"Just promise to dress like the grim reaper and stand at the back of my funeral," he says to me. I smile, and he releases a long breath before searching the crowd for the girl. "When I'm dead, remember me, Aus."

"God, you are so dramatic," Austin says, but he's smiling. "If Carmichael makes a move toward you, I'll intercept him. Remind him of the truce. Happy?"

"Ecstatic," he replies.

CHAPTER 7

Austin

WE WATCH Felix thread through the crowd toward Gabriella. She wasn't far from Carmichael and looked to be having a terrible time. I knew little about her, just that she was a ward of her older step-brother, and he seemed to dictate what she did most of the time. And they hated each other.

At least Felix's flirting will bring a smile to her face for a while, and it will distract Carmichael. The whole point of sending him over there. If he is watching Gabriella, he won't be paying attention to me or Saint, and I wasn't wrong when I told Felix he would be safe. Carmichael isn't threatened by anyone but another alpha, and I wonder if it is because they could scent-match her and take her away from his daily torment.

"Melody Lynn knows the entire plan," Saint says as we circle the room. His gaze is fixed on Felix as if he is ready at any moment to launch himself across the marbled flooring to save him.

"She thinks she does. It isn't just the painting though," I

reply. "And if luck continues the way it has, we will have a secret weapon."

"And how do you plan on getting the omega to help us?"

"Simple." I lift my shoulders carelessly. "We know she is a thief. I'm going to put myself in her path with something for her to steal. And then I'm going to *catch* her, and we are going to have a little chat, come to an agreement that she won't be able to refuse."

"Or you could just *ask* her." He laughs.

"But then she can decline," I reply. "I need the little omega in a position she can't refuse."

"You really are a bastard."

"How do you think I got to where I am in life?" As we pass Garrett Quinn, I slip him the envelope I returned to the apartment for. In one smooth motion, he folds it and slips it into his blazer. It is a check large enough to ensure his cooperation when the time comes. I expect he will be a key player.

"Have you thought that maybe you could buy her *agreement* with money? If she is stealing, it is probably to make a living. Maybe if you say, hey, help me and you live in this tiny ass apartment for free for as long as you want."

I come to a stop and turn toward Dean, aka Saint, his suggestion proving how he got his fucking nickname.

"This *omega* stole from me in plain daylight. She isn't getting off easy. The fact she slipped past my security and got close enough to swipe not only my wallet but a cufflink—a really fucking expensive cufflink last week, means she owes me. And if there is one thing I'm good at, it is extracting payment."

He sighs heavily, and I ignore him as we pass Jason Vanross. I slip him another envelope. Soon the painting will grow legs and fucking walk into my office. Maybe I won't need the girl after all.

"Jason? Really? That guy is an actual bastard. He's into some shady shit."

"Which is why we need him for this. Getting into the safe won't be easy. If we have Garrett, a master lock picker. The omega, our little thief. And Jason, the man that knows the layout of the building, and maybe even holds some keys to the apartments. It will be a fast and easy run."

"Fast and easy," he repeats, doubt threading through his words.

I snort and then nod at the mayor as we pass by her. "Yes. *Fast and easy.*"

He shakes his head, and I know he is dropping the conversation for now. We are really exposed here, so that's great news. As we pass the drink table, he swipes two long stem glasses from the surface and hands me one.

Eyeing Felix as he does his thing and the girl blushes furiously in front of him. I can't help but feel possessive. Had I sent him over there to do just that? Yes. Do I want to rip him away and take him home? Also yes. But business comes first.

"Did you talk to the girl when you ran into her?" Dean pulls me from my dangerous thoughts.

I poke my tongue into my cheek, remembering my first up close and personal look at her. I had been going over the plan in my head as the elevator rose to the penthouse suite, one of our many homes, but my favorite because of the view of the river. Floor-to-ceiling windows looked out over the wide choppy river.

But as the door had slid open, I barely noticed until no one came on. Then I lifted my gaze, only to feel like someone had punched me in the stomach with the force of her deep brown eyes staring at me. I pasted on a smile and said something about her getting in the elevator.

Even though my body had started to react to her nearness with her still in the hall. If she got close enough to smell, I might not have made it back to the party and that would have been a terrible decision.

Control is what people knew me for, and there is no way in hell I am going to admit out loud that when she turned and ran, I almost gave chase. Her lean form fleeing me had almost made me feel feral. I could tell she needed to eat more because she was skin and bones. A deal with me would give her security, food, and anything else she would need. And she wouldn't have to roam the streets to steal for it.

"No," I say, pulling myself back to the present. "She ran from me."

"Shit, did you glower?"

"I smiled."

He chuckles. "Even worse."

I roll my eyes but don't reply. I smile, just rarely. It isn't my fault I am predisposed to a serious nature.

"So when do you plan on putting your terrible plan into place?"

I glance over at him, but he is focused on Felix, every line in his body built with tension. But the omega isn't going to steal him away, and although Carmichael doesn't like his sister talking with our beta, he hasn't made a move to stop him.

"Monday morning if she goes out. Vinny will be near to follow her and find out where she will be. I'll make it even easier this time and be security detail free."

His eyebrows rise, and he looks at me. "Are you sure that is a good idea?"

"They will be close if I need them. But against a small omega, I'm sure I'll be fine."

THE STREET IS BUSTLING, busy on Monday morning. Vinny tracked her to Times Square. The sea of heads in the crowd does not show which one is her. Until I catch sight of one bobbing in and out, weaving like a dancer through the crowd.

The crowd parts, allowing me the perfect view. At that moment, I'm transfixed. She is beautiful as she effortlessly picks the man's pocket, coming away with a brown leather wallet. As I watch, she empties it of the cash and deposits the rest into a trash can.

She pivots around a woman and between two men in business suits, neither aware their valuables have just been lifted. The omega is fascinating, and I have to shake myself into motion as she gets near.

I step effortlessly into her path, my back to her. Flashing the loose watch on my wrist as I move my wallet into view in one fluid and practiced movement, because I did practice the flashy move in front of the mirror this morning as Dean and Felix made fun of me. Even without one of my security nodding to let me know she zeroes in on me, I would have known she was near.

Her scent slams into me, hard. Fuck. My mouth waters, the sweet smell of brownies and frosting fills my lungs, and I inhale deeper just to pull more of her intoxicating scent deeper into my body.

Then the slightest brush of her fingers against the skin of my inner wrist and a sudden lightness all tell me she has my second-best watch in her grip. Spinning on my heel, I see her already fleeing, dancing through the crowd, slowly slipping away.

"Stop," I bark. My voice carries over the busy street and unattached omegas come to a sudden stop as alphas and betas look around to see what is causing the commotion. Still she keeps moving. Couldn't she hear me? With a quick nod at Mark, I follow her.

My security closes in as I push through the people between us. Mark reaches her first and grips her upper arm. She spins on him, immediately on the defense, and chopping his neck with a flat hand. His hold loosens enough for her to dodge away from him as he sputters for breath.

But it is too late for her because I wrap her in my arms and hoist her into my waiting car. The child lock means she can't get out until my driver lets us out. She releases a blood-curdling scream, her legs kicking wildly. And I shove in after her.

I have a literal wild animal on my hands as she realizes the other door is useless. She launches herself across the seat at me. Thankfully, the dark windows make sure onlookers don't see a thing as she attempts to gouge out my eyes.

"Calm the fuck down," I snap, as I enclose her wrists in my fingers and hold them away from my face. "Jesus, you're a little spitfire for an omega."

She struggles against my hold, grinding her ass into my lap unintentionally. Between her physical body causing friction and her fucking irresistible scent, you can't blame me for having a reaction. The blood rushes to my cock, and as soon as I'm fully hard beneath her, she freezes.

Her eyes grow wide, and I am pretty sure she is seconds from launching herself off of me. Instead, she breathes out a harsh breath and meets my gaze, her tits brushing my suit jacket with each pissed-off intake of air.

"You."

It's accusing and angry and downright captivating, as if she could bark.

"You're the alpha from the elevator."

Gathering my wits before I take her right here, I slip my fingers into the front pocket of her hoodie and pull out my watch.

"I'm also the one you stole this from."

CHAPTER 8

Audrey

A FEW THINGS hit me at once. One, when I sucked in a breath just now, my breasts brushed against his chest. Two, there is a suspiciously hard rod beneath my ass, and I am relatively sure it isn't a flashlight. Three, his violet eyes have flecks of gold in their depths you could only see sitting on his lap. Four, he smells like a fall day. The scent of spice and chilly rain practically urges me to nuzzle into his neck. And five, definitely not least. He is the fucking alpha from the elevator Friday night. And up close and personal, I am pretty sure he is who I thought he was at first.

A Mafia Prince that had come to see my dad when I was a teen. The one that didn't give me away as I hid behind the curtain and listened to my father's deals.

"You. You're the alpha from the elevator."

I don't mention that I know who he is.

Anger hot and bright flames through me. Is he following me? Waiting until the right time to kidnap me? He will have the surprise of his lifetime with me. I am no meek omega ready to roll over and be tortured. Mafia Prince or not.

He reaches forward, and it is too fast for me to jerk away,

even though his hold on my wrists has loosened. He comes away with the watch I stole, holding it out like a prize. Or proof of my crimes.

"I'm also the one you stole this from."

Dawning horror washes over me as his words hit me square in the chest. *I'm also the one you stole this from.* They repeat in my head as my eyes drop to the silver watch between his fingers. I got cocky. I should have taken the money I snagged and called it a day. But did I? No.

I put myself right in his path. My blood runs cold and air freezes inside my lungs.

Shit. How am I going to get out of this?

"We need to have a little chat."

I scrabble off of him, my ass finding purchase on the seat situated across from him, the privacy window still firmly in place. My attention drops to his slacks. The clear outline of his cock runs down the left side. Heat floods my cheeks as I tear my eyes away, and they slam into his sparkling violet orbs.

It had definitely *not* been a flashlight molding into my skin. And I undoubtedly had his DNA beneath my nails, because he had four perfect scratches down the right side of his previously flawless face. At least if I died, they could trace it back to the bastard.

"About that chat." He quirks an eyebrow in question.

Slick floods my center, and I clench my legs together. God, I hate being an omega. Folding my arms over my chest, I watch him. Which might be a bad idea because the more his pheromones fill up the car, the more likely I am to throw myself at his feet.

"Are you turning me in? Or taking me some place to torture me?" That has to be it. I glance out the darkened windows, but it only appears as if we are doing a lap around Central Park.

He chuckles, low and deep, and a stupid whine answers him from my throat. Can I disappear?

The corner of his mouth kicks up. "No, my little omega, I have a proposal for you. You are a skilled pickpocket, and I need a thief."

"I don't–"

He waves his hand in the air between us as if my objections are merely a fly he can shoo away. "I know your situation. Until a few days ago, you and your brother were living in a dirty warehouse. But then, as luck would have it, you stole this watch." He draws out a Rolex that looks exactly like the one I pawned. No, it can't be. Without thinking, I snatch it from his fingers, flipping it over to see A.Z. engraved in the metal at the back. What are the odds? "And the tracker inside? Vinny trailed you until an opportunity arose. Then you were exactly where I needed you."

As he speaks, the blood drains from my head, and I feel dizzy. Sin knew it was too good to be true. Any remaining anger flees like the coward it is, as a mixture of anxiety and untimely desire spikes through my veins.

My throat is parched as I whisper, "What do you want?"

"I thought you'd never ask." He pauses, tapping his fingers on his leg, bringing attention to his hard-on again.

My scent is blooming between us, and I am transfixed as he inhales deeply and holds it as if savoring the smell. My head feels like I have put it on backward because this reaction to him could not be normal.

"I'm not sleeping with you." The words come out threaded with the need to do just that.

"I don't bed omegas."

His reply hits me in the gut, leaving a sick feeling behind. Licking my lips, I swallow. "Good."

He smiles, that fake one from the elevator, the one that says I have you where I want you. "You will have to act like my omega in public, for appearances and to get you into the places we need you."

"If I refuse?" Because *that* would be such a bad idea for my current state.

"You won't."

That's it. He is so sure of himself. He doesn't even look at me as he says it, his eyes instead focused on the park passing on our right. His jawline pulses as if he is clenching his teeth, yet he gives off the air of being unbothered and sure of himself. It is so at odds, I narrow my eyes on the tendon as it jumps again. He is for sure clenching his pretty white molars together.

Slowly, he pins me with a look I can't read. "You see, I imagine that since you are the one out on the streets each day, stealing your way through life, that your twin is important to you. You protect him. Let him go out and party each night with the money you steal. Come home in the wee hours after doing God knows what in those clubs. Only for you to support him."

He leans forward across the space, bringing his tantalizing scent closer, enveloping me like a hug. My mouth pops open, but not even a whimper comes out. And thank fuck for that.

"I can help you with that, and you won't need to steal to keep that little slice of heaven you've found." He inhales, and his eyes drop shut as I catch a glimmer of something that looks like desire. "Well—you won't have to steal on the streets, that is."

He shrugs like that makes all the difference, and it probably does to him. A high-class thief is better than a pickpocket in his eyes, I am sure. I wet my lips again, and his attention drops to them, making my pulse thunder through my ears.

I don't know what to ask. My vocal cords feel frozen. Butterflies dance in my empty stomach at the idea of spending more time with this alpha. I slide my clammy palms down my jeans to my knees and lean forward.

Can I do this? He doesn't know who I am. That is apparent.

"How would we fool anyone into thinking I was your omega if I didn't smell like you?"

He smiles, but this time it is authentic, and it reaches his eyes. There is something about it that says he doesn't do that often enough. "You will smell like my pack. I'm sure Dean will nuzzle you."

"Dean?" My voice cracks.

"Part of my pack. Don't worry, Dean has the nickname of Saint, and it isn't because he's nefarious."

"So not like you?" I lift a brow, and he scowls. It sends a thrill through me to poke at him, probably not the best reaction since he is an alpha that the omega in me is ready to surrender to, and I'm not even in a heat.

"Baby girl, you don't know the half of it," he says, his voice dropping to an almost whisper that makes my tummy flip uncomfortably.

The car comes to a halt outside an expensive-looking office building, and he leans back into his seat, his eyes fixed on me.

"If I'm supposed to act like your omega in public, I should probably know your name."

My ears ring as I wait for him to confirm his identity.

Surprise filters across his features. "You don't know who I am?"

I widen my eyes at him. "Should I?" A half laugh follows the question.

"Austin Zade," he says. He stretches his hand between us as if I'm going to shake it. I look from him to his long fingers.

"Well, Austin Zade, the first thing you should know is I don't touch people."

It's him. A Mafia Prince acting like a high-class suit. Am I in some kind of fever dream?

His fingers curl in, and he withdrawals the offered hand, reaching for a button on the armrest next to him. He lowers the privacy window a crack.

"You can let us out. Audrey has agreed to my terms." His violet gaze rests on me, daring me to contradict him. But why would I? He is going to pay for my rent and make sure we have a roof over our heads. Sure, I have to steal for him and pretend to date him, but it is honestly a better deal than running the streets every day. And if he just doesn't realize who I am, everything will be perfect.

The door pops open, and Austin climbs out before extending a hand to me that I ignore as I climb from the darkness out into the bright morning light. He easily drops his hand again and slides it into his blazer pocket. Once I'm on my feet, he turns and heads into the building, the doorman addressing him by name as I hurry to keep up.

He really is sure of himself and his plan on having me steal for him. But he is right. It is an offer I can't refuse. One I don't want to refuse, even if it means being around his unique pheromones. He's all business now as we pass people who incline their heads at him, almost in a bow. Do they know who they are dealing with?

As we enter a hall lined with elevators, he punches the call button, leading the way into the tiny box once the doors slide open. Everything in this place looks like they coat it in marble or gold. Except for the mirror at my back. I press against the far wall as he hits the button for the top floor. The silence should be unnerving, but it isn't. He doesn't feel threatening or dangerous at the moment, maybe because he is clearly getting what he wants.

After we exit the elevator, every single person we pass greets him, and by the time we reach a conference room with floor-to-ceiling windows facing the park, I am pretty sure I have confused him with the Mafia Prince from my memory. It will be the first search I do as soon as I get back to the apartment. Which, after this, will really be mine. I tamp down on the building excitement as he crosses the room and opens a folder that was sitting on the long table.

He slides a thick packet of paper across the table and gestures at the seat in front of it. "The contract."

I swear my eyebrows reach for the sky as surprise runs through me. He really had this whole thing planned. It is a little awe-inducing.

"Do you want me to sign it in blood, too?" I ask as I flip through pages and pages of words.

He rolls his eyes and settles at the head of the table. "I want you to read it. Understand it. Ask questions you might have about your duties and responsibilities listed. And then sign it."

With a sigh, I settle in and start reading the thick packet. This would take me all day, maybe longer, with his eyes boring into me and awareness of him spiking each time I feel the caress of his gaze along the side of my face. Is this what it feels like to scent match someone? An intimate awareness of them even if you aren't looking directly at them? Or maybe it is my oncoming heat forcing an attraction to an alpha that it knows could ease the symptoms.

Whatever it is, it makes me fidget. "Can you stop?" I brush my hair behind my ear but don't look directly at him.

"Stop?"

"Yeah, stop watching me."

I sense it as he averts his attention to the folder in front of him. A sort of relief of pressure eases from my chest and I am able to focus on the words on the paper. It is a lot of legal jargon I will never understand. I flip through the pages looking for my *duties and responsibilities*.

"You should read the whole thing."

"We both know I'm doing this, no matter what is inside these pages." I flip to the last page and scrawl my signature across the bottom. Why waste time?

"Audrey, you should never sign a binding contract without reading it first. You can't negotiate terms if you agree to them."

"You basically told me everything I need to know. You need a thief. For some reason, you think I can do the job. I'll pretend to be part of your pack when in public. Doesn't seem to be much more that needs to be said."

He inclines his head and presses his lips together. "Very well, I'll have your room made up in our apartment in the city. It is the same building you reside in now, only the penthouse. It should be easy to move your things. Of course, your twin is free to come with you or stay in the apartment. Either way, he will be close."

When my eyes feel like they are about to pop out of my damn head, he sighs.

"But then you would know all that if you read it."

I reach for it as he snags it away. "I'm not doing that. I didn't agree to *live* with you."

"My pack lives with me. You need to have the appearance of being a part of my pack to the public. I'm in the public eye. The magazines will run stories about you as soon as they realize we now have an omega. The elusive Zade and St. Cloud, settling down with not only a beta but a beautiful omega."

Something about the way he says Zade and St. Cloud reaches some part of my memories. It feels like something just out of reach, right there, yet slippery enough not to be able to grab hold. "Give me the contract."

"Baby girl, my sweet little omega, what would you do if I gave it to you? Rip it in half?" He flicks his eyes at the corner of the room. "You signed it on camera, destroying it now won't change that fact."

I growl, and he chuckles. Another one of his sinfully delicious and elusive smiles spreads across his face, making me think maybe he smiles more than I thought.

"If you don't give me the contract back right now. I'll–"

"You'll?" he ventures when I stop talking as the man from in front of the abandoned warehouse strolls into the room as if he belongs here.

My heart leaps into my throat as it attempts to flee my body. My eyes ping-pong between the two of them. It was a setup. The whole thing. It is finally sinking in. They were bringing me in one way or another.

The new alpha is tall and as toned as I thought when I saw him on the street. Sunglasses don't block his eyes and they are the deepest caramel brown I have ever seen. The same undeniable magnetism flows off of him as if it seeps from his pores.

He comes to a halt when he notices me, his caramel orbs gliding from my head to my toes. I quickly stand up and face him.

"Oh, my apologies. I thought you were alone," he says the words while staring at me, but he meant them for Austin. I can not pull my attention away from him.

"Saint, meet our omega." He holds up the contract and grins. "Audrey, this is Dean St. Cloud."

I can literally feel my pulse in my clit as he steps closer, extending an open palm to me. "Audrey, Felix mentioned your beauty, but seeing it myself is like staring into the sun. Dazzling and bright."

I snort at the corny one liner. Rolling my eyes, I focus on Austin.

"He's not joking," he says as soon as our eyes connect. I'm

not sure if he means I'm beautiful or that his flirting is just that bad, and there is no way in hell I'm asking.

When I continue to ignore Dean's outstretched arm, he drops it.

"I don't do touch," I explain, feeling a need to ease the confusion on his face. The lines only deepen on his beautiful face as he looks to his friend.

"I'm surprised you agreed so quickly," Dean says, bringing his dark and warm gaze back to me.

"I didn't. I signed it by *accident*, but Austin refuses to give it back and let me actually read what I agreed to."

Austin scoffs. "I told you to read it fully before signing. You are the one that is impatient and signed it anyway. So it is valid."

Dean's eyebrows raise higher on his face. "If he warned you—"

I take it back. His eyes aren't warm. He is an alpha and not someone that will help me out of this. He wants this as much as Austin does. But I can't help trying one last time.

"He said I have to live with you," I say.

His lips press into a tight line as he nods. "That is the only way the public would believe Austin has an omega after—" He snaps his mouth shut, and I suddenly want to know *after what?*

I grip the back of the chair as I'm sure I perfume my curiosity for the both of them. Dean inhales deeply, his nostrils going wide and his pupils following, erasing most of the caramel color. He steps forward, and he was already close.

"Your scent is—" he inhales again, "it's delectable."

CHAPTER 9

Audrey

THE CONTRACT IS BINDING, and now that I've read the whole thing, dread settles in the pit of my stomach. It clearly states that he has proof of my pick-pocketing, which he will hand over to the police chief if I don't comply with his demands. I'd go to jail and Sin would be out on the streets, with no one to help him.

But if I do everything, including move in with them, we will both be safe. Sinclair is out when I return to the apartment, resigned to my fate. I empty the small dresser of my clothing, shoving as much of it that will fit into my backpack, and putting the rest into plastic bags.

The door opens and my brother strolls in without a care in the world, but at least he doesn't look high. He stops as soon as he catches sight of my packed bag still sitting on the bed.

"What's going on?"

I sag into the plush couch as tears gather in my eyes. Crying is useless. I've learned that lesson in life already. But they come anyway.

"Aud, are you okay?" The concern in his tone has the tears cascading down my face as he drops next to me and gathers me into a tight hug as if he can put the pieces back together. As if he could rescue me again. Because that is where Austin was wrong. I wasn't his protector, he was mine, and I couldn't do enough to pay him back for the sacrifice he made to protect me. So this is another thing that I will do for Sin.

I sniffle against his chest. "Yeah. I'm fine, Sin. I got caught by a suit. But he offered me a job in exchange for not turning me in."

"Why the bags?"

"Part of the condition is pretending to be the omega in his pack."

"What kind of job is it?" I can hear the censor in his tone, and I bristle at it. As if he doesn't do things that are better left unsaid during the light of day to chase away his demons.

"It isn't sex. He needs me to steal something for him. But I have to be able to get into places he goes, so the only way is living with him."

He mouths my last words, attempting to let them sink in. "Who is this guy?"

I knew that for sure too now. He is who I thought he was. A very dangerous man. I'd looked him up, and there is only one Austin Zade. Rolling my lips between my teeth, I pull away from him and sink back into the couch. He is going to lose his mind.

"Aud," he warns. "Who is he?"

"Austin Zade and Dean St. Cloud, and a beta I haven't met yet," I admit.

He shoots off the couch like his ass is on fire and spins to face me. "You just made a fucking deal with a Mafia boss?" He stomps across the room into the tiny bedroom and starts throwing my stuff back into the drawers I had emptied them from. "I did not get you out of that fucking life for you to just go right back into it. No, Audrey, this isn't happening."

I bite down on my lip as I watch him. He really isn't going to like this next part.

"I signed a binding contract, Sin. I have to do this or he will turn over physical proof of my pickpocketing. I'll go to jail, and you will be on the streets. He said you can come too."

He pales like I knew he would. If I had suffered the same extremes he had at the hands of the men that had worked for our father, I would feel the same; he almost lost his life, and some days, I wonder if he wishes he had.

"You can stay here in the apartment, too. His place is in this building. I'll be close. Just a few floors up. It was part of the conditions. We keep this place for as long as we want it."

"Aud," he pleads, as if I had the power to do something different. "The Mafia is dangerous."

"The papers said he's out of the business. He's legal now."

He slowly blinks at me, my backpack hanging off his fingers. "*Legal now*? Maybe the shady shit is all done under the table, but a Mafia Prince doesn't go straight and narrow even if he wanted to. You know that as well as I do."

I do. Being a deposed Princess of the Mafia, I know that too well. But it's a lie I have to tell myself to leave this safe haven and move into a viper's nest.

"What if they see you in the papers? What if they come for you? For us?" His voice cracks and so does my heart.

I never would have signed that contract if I had followed my instincts and looked him up before so I knew who I was dealing with. I just want to curl up and lose myself in the fantasy of *Omega in Paradise* and pretend none of this horrible day happened. But it isn't a luxury I have.

"I'm sorry, Sin."

He nods. "Yeah." He drops my empty backpack on the bed, defeat clear in the lines of his shoulders. "Me too."

My emotions are a mess once I repack my things and pull my bag onto my back. Sin doesn't look my way as I open the door and head into the hallway. He hadn't said another word while I moved around the apartment. I wish I could say he would get over it, but I knew my twin and putting myself into danger after we almost died getting out was something it would take a long time for him to *get over*.

On wooden legs, I approach the elevator. I press the call button and my heart thunders in my ears, anxiety a heavy ball in my stomach. The elevator doors slide open almost soundlessly, either that or I can't hear over my pounding pulse. The interior is empty, and I breathe a sigh of relief for that small gift. My finger hovers over the 24, and I force myself to light it up while twisting the key Austin gave me in the lock.

Seconds later, the doors open, a small open area greets me. A planter with a miniature tree stands to the left of the closed door in front of me. I curl my fingers around the straps of my backpack as I take a step onto the floor. To my right there is a floor-to-ceiling window with a pretty view of the river and bridge. The door swings wide before I can take another step.

My breath stutters inside my chest as I stare at Felix taking up the doorway, a welcoming smile on his face. His long bangs flop over his forehead in disarray, and his green eyes sparkle.

"Audrey, come in." He steps to the side, holding the door open for me.

The room beyond him is huge. More floor-to-ceiling windows line the entire wall that faces the river. The whites and grays of the furniture and the fancy sculptures on the end tables come together to make for an expensive-looking room. A plush rug lays beneath the coffee table, and there is not a television in sight. Instead, the couch faces the windows. Arm chairs flank the large sofa facing each other.

My gaze flicks over the open looking floor plan, and I glance over at a large dining table that is both elegant and rich, matching the rest of the furniture perfectly. The kitchen is viewable past the open island between us. With the best appliances money can buy filling the space. The fridge looks like one of those you just tap a screen and view what is inside without opening the door. Our cook back home hated that I never used that function, preferring to release all the cool air as I searched for a snack.

The memory brings with it a familiar pang of sadness for a life that was destroyed by the most terrible of betrayals. I shove it back where it belongs, in the blackest depths of my mind. My hands shake, and I wrap my fingers around the straps of my bag again. Felix notices the movement and gestures toward the hall.

"I can show you your room. But you might not need any of those clothes. Austin has a flare for the dramatics and bought you a whole new wardrobe that was delivered earlier today."

He pushes open a door that reveals a room that is bigger than four of my apartment combined. The soothing view of the river greets me, and when he catches my attention on the windows, he moves over to a control panel on the wall.

"You can lower the blinds so the sun doesn't shine in and wake you in the morning. Or if you want it to be dark in here." He demonstrates and hidden blinds unfold from the ceiling and slowly spread down the glass. "This also controls the air, heat, and lights."

When I remain silent, he moves over to one of two doors and opens it. A light turns on automatically, and he steps inside the largest closet ever. Even bigger than the one I grew up with. There is a large window at the end, adding daylight to the space and a fancy-looking bench in the center of the open space. They lined a wall with places for shoes, and there are some already in place of my exact size.

I fold my arms over my stomach and press my lips together as I take in the rows of clothes. Most still have plastic covering them. A single dress cost more than I pawned the watch for. I recognized the designer's name when I peeked at the tag. I couldn't imagine how much everything else cost. On the other wall, there is a safe. Felix moves over to it and punches in a code, and when it opens, I can't help the gasp that comes out of my chest.

Jewelry. Sparkling diamonds, gems, and gold catches in the interior light of the safe. My lips part on another breath. I could pawn all of that, and we could run.

As if he could read my mind, Felix glances over. "The jewelry in here looks nice, but it all has trackers in them. If more than a single set is removed at the same time, an alarm will alert Austin on his phone. So I don't suggest taking them to pawn."

"I wouldn't–"

He laughs. "I would, so I know you would."

A smile tugs at my lips. "Do you work for them?"

He turns to me with a look of guilt on his face. "I'm pack, actually."

My mouth forms an 'oh', but no sound comes out. I am doomed.

"Hey, it won't be that bad. They are good guys."

A sarcastic laugh pops from me, and I shake my head. "Yeah, Austin is a charmer. Set me up, kidnap me, make me sign a contract…"

"When you put it like that," he says, rubbing the back of his neck; his cheeks darken with embarrassment as if Austin's actions reflected on him. "I'm sorry. He's pretty focused on this."

"That's putting it mildly," I grumble.

"Right," he breathes and moves past me. "You have your own bathroom, and your bedroom door has added security on it if you go into a heat. You'll be able to lock it from the inside, only you will have the passcode."

"Can I use it when I'm not in a heat?"

He looks surprised at my question.

"You're safe here. Austin says, hands off, he's the boss. And even if he didn't, we aren't that type of pack to force ourselves on an unwilling girl."

"Reassuring," I say drily. It's not. His *boss* has already backed me into a corner. I am positive he gets what he wants, when he wants it.

"Here, let me show you how to set this so you'll feel better."

I shift my arms, hugging myself tighter. My emotions are so raw I want to cry again. I am just glad he's a beta and has no clue I don't have my scent under control. When I step next to him, he goes through the settings and gives me his back as I set my code. It makes me feel marginally better, so I smile as he turns back around cautiously.

"All set?"

I tuck a stray curl behind my ear and nod. Then I slide my backpack off of my shoulders and set it on the floor next to the wall before tugging the sleeves of my hoodie over my fingers. I guess I am really doing this.

"Want some food? I'm not much of a cook like Saint, but I can make a mean grilled cheese and tomato soup." He winks before leading the way back into the kitchen. He gets to work pulling the ingredients out, intent on making me something even if I refuse.

I lean against the marble island and finger the string on my hoodie. He might not be a chef, but he moves like he cooks more than a little.

"Where are the other two?" I ask, my curiosity getting the better of me.

"Working." He sets a pan on a flat burner, flipping it on to warm the metal. "They work late some nights."

He doesn't seem bothered by being left alone, and it's probably normal for him. The omega in me would hate it. If this was real, at least.

"So, are you just the designated tour guide?"

He grins, flashing straight white teeth my way. "Guess I'm just lucky that way."

In that moment, the reminder of what Dean said earlier crashes into me. Felix told him he thought I was beautiful. My cheeks heat as a blush spreads over them, and I duck my head, hit with a wave of nervousness. Even my stomach joins in as it flips over.

When I manage to lift my eyes from the swirling gray and white marble, I find him staring openly at me.

"You're stunning when you blush." The compliment is almost more than I can handle, and I drop my gaze again.

It is nice to realize I can still react to flirting without running away screaming. Not that I am completely myself, or who I used to be, at least. For a while, I was sure the damage ran too deep and I would never respond to a man again. But there is a softness to the beta before me, almost like he knows what it is like to be damaged. A kindred soul.

"Thank you."

"No need to thank me for telling the truth. But you should be prepared to blush more, because I'm certain I'm going to become addicted." His green eyes twinkle as he sucks his lip ring between his teeth. And I find that maybe I might be looking forward to his flirting and that his lip ring is giving me bad, bad ideas.

CHAPTER 10

Austin

I'M bone tired and ready for a nightcap as I ride the lift to our penthouse. It's after eleven, and I'm sure everyone else will be asleep.

So when I unlock the door and find Felix and Audrey laughing together on the floor in front of the sofa, a game of Scrabble spread out on the glass coffee table, I think I'm hallucinating. I stroll into the living area, making my presence known because neither of them even glance over when I come in.

Felix looks up first, a grin on his face that is so happy it is hard not to return, even though I'm not sure exactly how all of this came to be. It is the last thing I expected, and I almost forgot the omega would be here at all. But even if I couldn't see her, her scent is infused in the very air.

"I didn't expect you to be up still," I say. Did the words come out a little accusing? I'm not sure. But Felix's brow creases, and he flicks his gaze at Audrey before bringing his brilliant green orbs back to me.

"We both have a love of Scrabble, and you two are sore losers, so I talked Audrey into playing a game. But we are running out of letters and board. I'm not entirely sure who is winning."

"I'm winning," Audrey says confidently, and Felix laughs, giving her his full attention. They *smile* at each other like they are falling in love or some shit.

I don't like it. And I'm not even sure what I don't like. But jealousy is a beast, and it has a grip on me right now.

"Where's Saint?"

Felix rolls his eyebrow ring between his fingers as if he can sense my emotions. I know the omega can because she has gone tense. Maybe it is my scent. It has turned sour since I entered to find them so cozy together. "He was wiped out when he returned and just went to bed."

"We have an early morning, you two should go to bed too."

Audrey pops to her feet like a jack in a box, not needing another suggestion to vacate my presence.

"Good night, Felix," she says before turning on her heel and fleeing to her room like she ran from me in the elevator the first night I really saw her.

"Be up by six," I call after her.

I have a sudden need to show the world she is a part of my pack. The plan was to let her settle in a few days first, but plans change, you have to stay fluid to survive.

She flips me off without looking back, and Felix chuckles. As soon as the door clicks shut, I can hear the mechanics that secure it from the inside whirling into place.

"I like her."

"Hands off, Felix. The pack thing is only for show." I open the liquor cabinet and pour a tumbler of bourbon. I don't bother offering any to Felix because his vice is not drinking or drugs.

"Does that mean I'm supposed to treat her like shit while she is here? I was trying to make her comfortable in this fucked up situation. What do you even need her to do?"

"Of course not," I say, answering his first question. "I'm sorry, it's been a long day."

When I sink into the armchair, he shifts on the floor over to my feet and lays his head on my knee. It soothes me to run my fingers through his silky hair, and he sighs happily.

"Whatever it is, it's not going to get her killed, right?"

"No. I won't let anything happen to her," I promise. But it is dangerous, I just happen to think she will be able to manage it.

"Good."

He trails his fingers up my slacks, over the seam in the middle, and I gently remove his hand, placing it on my other knee before my body could react.

"Not tonight."

It wouldn't be right, because I have been semi-hard all day just from the reminder of the omega pressed against me this morning. If I accept Felix's touch, I can't guarantee I would think about him while fucking him, and that isn't a line I am crossing.

He rubs a circle over my knee before lifting his head to look up at me. "You can tell me what you need her for. I know it has something to do with stealing something, and if you think the police chief won't pretend I know something just to get his hands on me, you haven't been paying attention to the bastard. So just tell me. I can help protect her."

I press my lips together. Saint and I have talked about this. We are trying to keep Felix out of it. But he is right. If Audrey is caught, all of us are going down. It wouldn't hurt to have him informed, at least not now.

"We are going after the Fairchild painting."

His eyes go wide, and he sits straight, falling back on his heels. "In the Valentine's safe?" He sounds like he is repeating something he heard. When I nod, he inhales. "Melody Lynn knows you are looking for it."

"She thinks she knows. She was fishing the other night, attempting to get a reaction. But it is a race to see who can get it first. I've hired both Garrett Quinn and Jason Vanross. Garrett will handle the lock, and Jason used to be employed by the Valentines. He knows the layout of his apartment."

"Jason Vanross, can you really trust a guy that is turning on his old boss?"

I take a sip of the bourbon and shrug. Probably not. But we only need him for the layout and then, after that, I couldn't care less if he helps Melody or Carmichael.

"Valentine will gut anyone that is caught. This is dangerous."

"With Saint on the security cameras, our secret weapon Audrey in the vault, and Garrett Quinn the best lock pick on the East coast, we will be in and out faster than he could respond." Felix glances at the omega's shut door, and I can read the worry on his face. "She's tough. She almost took out my eye today before I could get the upper hand. Our omega isn't like other omegas."

"That has a nice ring to it. Our omega."

"We're not keeping her."

"Good thing she's a person and not a dog then," he quips and stands up. "I'm going to bed. Six in the morning comes fast."

I can't help the feeling that he is upset with me. And he proves it when he turns away without a goodnight kiss and heads to his room. He'll get over it. After his door shuts, I stand up and lower the lights so I can look out of the windows into the dark sky beyond and settle back into the chair with a new pour of bourbon. I'm lost in my thoughts as I finish the drink.

Is the painting really worth all of this? My dad would

think it was. My mom insists it is. I would leave it where it is if it were up to me. But this last thing, if I do it, can break me free of that life. My mom's new husband will take over the reins. And he knows what needs to be done. He had been my dad's right-hand man.

My head lulls back as I relax, the city lights blurring out the stars. I miss them sometimes, while we are in the city. But the country house reminds me of her. The omega I thought I loved and who I thought loved me in return. Sidney. Even the thought of her name sends a pang of regret through me. The betrayal still felt fresh, even though it happened over ten years ago.

I finish my drink, setting the tumbler on the end table before closing my eyes as I attempt to forget the haunting memories of a girl that cared more about money than pack, than me. I had been a stepping stone for her in her climb to the top. A minor fish in the sea of hunters. Young and stupid.

Light blinds me as it rises over the horizon. I blink blearily, squinting against the cheerful sun. My blazer is wrinkled from a night sleeping in the armchair, and my shoes are still on. Stretching out my sore muscles, I meet Audrey's defiant gaze. So that is how this is going to go.

"You said six."

I glance at my watch. Six-thirty. A yawn works through my jaw, and I shrug. "Six, six-thirty, same thing, right?"

She crosses her arms and glares. It is then I notice she is wearing her old clothes. The ratty hoodie sleeves pulled over her fingers.

"You need to change. You are not wearing that."

She glances down, her brow furrowing. "These are my clothes."

"I'm not taking a street urchin to breakfast at The Clocktower."

Her eyes go wide, and she flushes in embarrassment. "The Clocktower?" A swallow works her delicate throat as she looks back down at her old rags.

"Yes, I bought you clothing appropriate for my omega, and you will wear it when you are out with me. I would prefer you to wear it at all times. We can burn that."

Her fingers curl over the ends of the sleeves of the hoodie, and I know I've misstepped before she says a word.

"You are not touching my things. This might be your apartment, but this is mine. I will murder you in your sleep if you damage even a single thread of this shirt."

I chuckle at the threat, and she glares at me. "Get changed," I order.

"I don't think I will. I guess you're taking a street urchin to breakfast. Call it charity work. The press will have a field day."

Grinding my molars together, I stand up and close the distance between us. I lean forward and grip her chin between my fingers. She lets out a little squeak, and I almost ease the pressure on her skin.

"I said, get changed," I say threateningly.

Green fire is shot at me from her eyes, and if looks could kill, I'd be dead. I drop my hand and straighten.

"You have until I'm ready to be presentable." I stalk away to my bedroom, passing a bleary eyed Saint on my way. The satisfying slamming of my door between us eases some of my anger. She presses my buttons in a way no one has in a long time.

Showering and dressing in one of my suits, I exit the bedroom in a slightly better mood that sours as soon as I catch sight of Audrey. Her legs curled beneath her, a book open on her lap, still in the same clothing. Felix and Saint sit in the armchairs while she is in the sofa's corner.

"You aren't dressed."

"I am."

She doesn't even look up, and a growl rumbles in my chest, low and threatening. "I told you to get changed."

"And I decided that free will *was* a thing, and I might be your *omega* outside these walls, but in here, I'm my own person." She folds the book in her lap and lifts her gaze to me as she basically tells me to get bent with her expressive eyes.

My ears ring and rage makes me feel hot. Before I even know what I'm doing, I'm scooping her up from her comfortable seat and stalking into her room. Once in her closet, I deposit her on the bench in the middle and turn to survey the clothing. Snapping a yellow dress that would look good with her skin off the rack, I turn back toward the stunned omega with a threatening smile.

"If you won't get dressed, I'll help you."

I know I'm crossing some lines here, but I can't stop myself as I tear her hoodie off of her small body. Revealing a pale lacey bra that is almost the same color of her skin. I pause, taking her in. She needs to eat. I can see her ribs. That's the first order of business: getting some food in her. She attempts to snag her hoodie back, and I toss it away from us both before I dress her like a rag doll as she releases a growl low in her throat that would rival one of mine.

Stalking across the closet, I pick up her hoodie and ball it up in my arms and say, "You can have this back after you behave at breakfast."

Her perfume in the air is at odds with the scowl painted on her face, and I know I need to put some distance between us before my hard earned contract is broken.

"Asshole," she hisses, as I leave her to finish dressing on her own.

"At least you have one thing straight," I reply over my shoulder. Saint and Felix watch me, both in a state of stunned shock as I cross her bedroom back to them. "She will be ready soon," I tell them, making sure I'm loud enough for her to hear me. Her answering growl brings a smile to my face, and I realize I enjoyed that. Maybe I really am fucked in the head.

CHAPTER 11

Audrey

THE YELLOW AND silky hem doesn't feel long enough as I emerge from my bedroom. I briefly entertained the thought of locking myself inside the confines, but Austin would have broken down the door to drag me out.

Which should *not* make slick gather between my legs. Hell, the way he manhandled me should have me running from the penthouse—contract or no contract—not ready to strip back down to my underwear for his eyes to devour me again.

Yeah, I am screwed. When three sets of intense eyes land on me, two with concern, the other with triumph, I smooth down my dress and cross my arms over the barely there fabric.

"Happy?" I practically spit the word at him, and he grins.

"Ecstatic," Austin clips, his violet orbs running a trail down my bare legs to my boots. His face tightens as he takes them in, but he doesn't say a word about my worn footwear.

"You look breathtakingly beautiful," Felix murmurs, and I feel my cheeks pink.

"The car is waiting," Austin says and spins on his heel.

I follow, because what else am I going to do? But as they fill the elevator, I come to a full stop, my eyes going wide. My mouth works around words that don't come out, and Dean stills, his sharp gaze alert as he inhales.

"You two go ahead. I forgot something. I'll come down with Audrey." He steps out, hitting a button as he does, and the doors slide shut before either of them can voice an objection. "Are you going to be okay riding with me?"

I shake my head to clear it. He just lied to his pack to make me more comfortable. I am going to melt into a puddle of feelings right here in front of him. He may be an alpha, but he may be a different sort, and that is dangerous.

"Yeah. We should go before he comes back and holds me down to change my shoes."

I toe the floor and look down at my boots that don't go with the cheerful yellow dress he put me in. Small victories, but at the moment, it made me feel like a silly child. My defiance would have embarrassed my mom if she were alive. However, she always aimed to please my dad and wouldn't have understood my need to disobey an alpha's orders.

Dean grimaces. "He isn't usually like that. I'm sorry."

"Don't apologize for him," I reply. This is the bed I made, and now I'm going to lie in it. "I'll play this role, but I'm going to do it on my terms."

When the elevator opens up again, I resolutely lift my chin and step inside. Dean follows me and leans against the opposite wall. His presence isn't overbearing, but I am very aware of him as an alpha. My perfume seeps from me, filling the space. His fingers turn white as he grips the banister at his back, but he doesn't react besides that, which is probably for the best. I should probably mention to Austin that my heat is close and being alone with them is a bad idea, because my body is not connecting with my brain at the moment.

Once we reach ground level, he pushes the iron gate to the

side and launches himself from the space. I follow slowly as his chest moves to inhale a deep breath of non-perfumed air. Pressing my lips together, I try not to blush, but I can feel the heat spreading up my neck, anyway. My fingers curl in, looking for the hem of my hoodie that Austin had confiscated from me like I was a child.

I should replace it. He is right. It was old and more of something that should be trashed than worn. But it is all I have left. And I know it's silly, but even though I lost my entire world when my father was betrayed, having it made me feel like I haven't lost it all. That I'd wake up and it would be all some horrible nightmare.

Shoving the intrusive and depressing thoughts away, I step next to a now relaxed-looking Dean. He holds his arm out for me, and I suck in a deep breath. I knew touching in public would be a thing, but my stomach flips over as I gaze at his suit covered arm. It isn't really touching if it is fabric, right?

Forcing my hand on his bicep, I swear I can feel it contract beneath my fingers, as if my small touch is making him as aware of me as I currently am of him. He leads us through the lobby, a friendly smile on his face. Wide eyes follow us, and I swallow. I am not ready for the spotlight.

As we push out into the bright morning light, he shields his eyes with those expensive ass sunglasses.

"Why do you wear those?"

He looks over at me quizzically and arches a blond brow behind the frames. "What do you mean?"

"They cost as much as a fleet of cars or a few houses," I say.

He chuckles. "When you have so much money you don't know what to do with it, you buy expensive shit."

"You could help people with the cost of those." It isn't my place to judge, and I'm not, not really. It is just an observation.

"Well then, it is probably a good thing that I help people too." He winks behind the darkened lens, not taking offense at my comment thankfully.

"Yeah? How do you help them?"

He waves the doorman away when he attempts to open the waiting car door for us. As he holds the door open, I climb in, waiting for his answer. Austin glowers at me from across the seat, and Felix smiles. I slide across the soft leather beneath me, attempting not to flash either of them my panties in this short dress. Dean slides in right after me.

"I build tiny house villages. Some of them give the homeless a chance at getting their lives back, a place to lay their head and shower so they can get a job. We dedicate others to domestic violence survivors and their children. A haven for them to hide and find their feet again. It is something that is close to my heart." He shrugs like it isn't a big deal. "I was looking at a place in Harem the other day that I want to turn into an apartment building to do something similar in the city."

My heart flutters. Could this man be more perfect? He is fine as fuck and cares about the less fortunate. A smile plays on my lips as he watches me. I'm sure I'm making the whole vehicle smell, but none of them say a word about it, and honestly, all I can smell is the combination of them. Leather, fall, cinnamon, lemon, and an almost fresh scent of an ocean breeze. Together it is almost intoxicating in the same way it tantalizes the sense when I'm only around one of them at a time.

Felix is very much the ocean breeze, and I'm not sure if it is a rare beta scent or body wash. But it is nice. Dean is a mixture of leather and lemon; the earthy and citrus smell combines into the perfect mix that I just want to nuzzle into. It seriously does things to me that are better left unsaid. And of course the fall leaves and cinnamon are comforting in a way the man isn't. It reminds me of home in the country and safety. Almost fooling my brain into thinking I am actually safe with these three.

"And that is why we call him Saint," Austin says dryly.

"I suppose you don't help the needy?" I ask, giving him a look that says I already know you don't.

He pokes his tongue into his cheek and eyes me. "Sure I do. I have a charity case sitting right across from me."

I roll my eyes at the jab and wiggle my feet just to highlight the fact I still won. "I was doing just fine before you came along."

"Okay, play nice," Felix says, attempting to be the peacekeeper. "You are going to love The Clocktower. They have the best pancakes with berries."

I've been before, in another life, and I have to agree that it is the best dish on the menu. My dad loved the British offerings, said it reminded him of being in England for school.

"Sounds amazing," I say instead. They don't need to know my past for me to do this job. And it is probably better the less they knew. If Austin picks up on the fact that my dad was the De Luca Kingpin when he was alive, I'm not sure what he'd do about it.

The drive over is fast and, as soon as we pull up outside, Dean opens the door and climbs out, followed by Felix. Before I can slide over the smooth leather, he shuts the door and jogs around to the door closest to me, holding it open for me and offering me his arm again. Right, public appearances. I'm their omega out in the world, so they are going to treat me like a cherished one.

My fingers wrap around his bicep easily this time, and I smile up at him as if he is my world. It is easy to fake. Austin climbs out after me and walks on my other side, his hand guiding me. As we approach the door, Felix rushes to grab the door for us, while Austin's warm palm burns a hole through the fabric at my lower back.

Once inside, the woman at the podium eyes the men with me. I know what she sees. They are all off the scale of hotness. When her attention turns to me, she looks me up and down, her attention pausing on my boots.

What felt like a win in the penthouse doesn't feel that way as the corner of her lip rises with derision, and she brings her attention back to Austin.

"Mr. Zade, what a pleasure to have you this morning. Do you want your usual table in the back?"

"No, today, I want to be seen. Do you have something near the windows?" He presses into my side. "I want the world to know we found our omega," he adds after she gives me another nasty look.

Then he fucking nuzzles my neck like he has a right. A low rumble that sounds almost like a purr comes from his chest and ghosts across my skin. And I whine. In public. My face flushes hot, and I'm sure it is as red as the velvet seats.

My fingers curl into Dean's bicep as I hold myself in place. The woman snaps out four menus and practically stomps across the room to a seat near the windows. Her friendly demeanor evaporated like a puddle in the scorching sun. When her eyes land on me again, I straighten and give her a smile. That's right, these men are mine.

Whoa.

No, that isn't what I meant. I am playing a part. That's all. Right?

Austin leads me onto the bench seat and sits closely next to me, while the other two pull out the chairs across from us. His fingers wrap around my upper thigh beneath the table, and I don't call him out. I should. There is no reason for the touch and I *hate* touch.

Don't I?

The longer his palm presses half against my bare skin and half on the silky fabric, the more his fingers rub soothing circles, relaxing me.

Once the tension seeps from my shoulders, he removes his hand, and the cool air on the spot is a harsh reminder that I want him to touch me more.

I get my wish almost immediately as he tosses his arm across the bench behind us and then tugs me to his side as the waitress approaches. He drops his head and inhales at my neck again, and I shudder as my nipples pebble beneath the thin fabric, poking obviously hard past the two layers I wore.

"Can I get you something to drink?" This new woman is all business. Not a shred of desire is in her tone, and it eases something inside of me as I smile up at her. Omega's order first. I knew that, but my heart rate kicks up as nerves make my palms clammy. This is silly.

"Orange juice, please," I say, almost tripping over my words in my haste to get them out.

"I'll take the same," Austin rumbles, his breath caressing my skin.

Dean clears his throat, and my gaze snaps to his. His brow furrows, but he says, "Water and coffee, please."

Felix looks up from the menu and smiles at the waitress. "Cola, light ice. I can't do the breakfast drinks."

She smiles politely and jots it down before leaving to retrieve our drink orders.

"Austin, you are going a little overboard," Dean says.

"Am I?" he asks. "Gregory Chase is across the room. I'm sure this will be in the papers soon. And Valeri Underwood is right there." He nods, and my gaze lands on an older woman who is watching us with a keen eye. "If there is no PDA, then there is no proof for them to write about."

Right. Head on straight, Audrey, pretend—that is what it is.

You can not lose your damn head on the first day of the first outing. Just channel Omega in Paradise, you can do this.

"Is that what this breakfast is about?" I ask. "You want the papers to write about your new romance?"

He grazes my earlobe with his teeth, and I almost launch myself out of my seat in surprise. If he wasn't holding me down with his arm draped over my shoulders, I would have made sure they really have something to write about. "Yes."

My cheeks heat again, but this time because I can feel the slick gathering between my legs. Not good. Abort.

Shrugging his touch off, I say, "I need to use the restroom."

I scoot out of the booth on my side and flee them into the safety of the expensive powder room. Damn, I didn't remember how expensive everything was in here. But then the last time I had been here, I didn't know what living on the streets was like.

Experience changes everything. Gripping the porcelain sink, I stare into my doe brown eyes that look as bright as leaves changing color in the fall, and my cheeks that look rosy and happy. I was enjoying this. I am so screwed.

CHAPTER 12

Felix

"YOU SCARED HER," I accuse the second she practically runs away from the table. "We will be lucky if she doesn't sneak out."

"She was enjoying it," Austin replies as he unbuttons his jacket and smooths the blazer out.

"She looked terrified."

"No, Austin is right, she was perfuming like crazy," Saint replies. "But she smells unattached, so you might want to tone it down unless you want every alpha in this place clamoring to claim her."

The waitress appears with our drinks, and we fall silent as she places everything down. She excuses herself, saying something about returning once our omega is back. *If she comes back.*

Austin leans back against the backrest, his gaze fixed on the exit for the bathrooms. I may not have the super sniffer my alphas did, but I am sure that Austin was enjoying himself, too.

"We need to fix the scent issue," Austin says.

"You said," I start, and he cuts me off with a look.

"I know what I said. But there are ways of marking someone without claiming them. Lots of alphas and omegas court each other, and they smell attached while they do it."

"But that would require a shit ton being around each other," Saint murmurs.

Austin shrugs, a smile playing at his lips. "Then I guess she should get used to it until this is finished. Because that girl is going everywhere with one of us."

I suck my lip ring into my mouth and roll it between my teeth. "She's really sweet. I like her."

"That hellcat is anything but sweet." Austin takes a sip of his OJ, dismissing my comment.

Saint chuckles. "Maybe if you treated her like a person and not a possession, she would show you that side of her personality."

"Maybe I don't need to see it to get the job done."

"You're being stubborn," I point out. He scoffs and rolls his vibrant violet eyes. The gold is darker, and I'm not sure if it is the lighting in here or if Audrey is getting to him, too. Maybe we'll ask her to really stay after all of this is done.

"He's being an ass," Saint replies drolly. Then he lifts the creamer and pours the small container into his oversized mug.

"I'm doing what needs to be done. If you think you can do it better, be my guest."

I don't like the tension between them as they stare at each other. Why are alphas so high-strung?

"You can whip them out right here, but I think it would trump a story about a new girl in the papers...and I could tell you who's bigger and solve the whole thing for you," I say. I suck down half my coke as I wait to see who would break first. As always, Saint smiles first, which in turn makes Austin crack too.

A light chuckle rumbles Austin's chest as he shakes his

head ruefully. "Who's bigger?" He lifts an eyebrow, and I grin.

"I said I could tell you, not that I would."

Saint laughs loudly, his head thrown back. "You know that means it's me," he says.

Audrey slips back into her place next to Austin, but he only looks at her as she unfolds the napkin and spreads it into her lap. "What were you talking about?" She looks up at me before glancing between the other two.

Opting to change the subject, even though seeing her blush is tempting, I point at one of the many pictures hanging on the walls.

"You see that picture right there, above the golden frame?"

Her attention tracks to the picture of a blond boy sitting atop a Clydesdale horse. His mop of curls and the almost devilish glint in his dark eyes, so much like the Saint I knew and loved, only now he held more caution in his gaze. He doesn't allow himself to be that free now.

"The boy?"

"That's Saint when he was just a baby."

She smiles, which is almost as addictive as her blush. "You were adorable."

He snorts and ducks his head. "Ouch. You really know how to hit a guy where it hurts."

"I didn't mean–"

"He's just fishing for a compliment. Ignore him." Austin lays his arm across the back of the bench, his fingers playing with one of her curls.

"I'm sure he gets them all the time. I'm sure you all do." She straightens and shoots Austin a look when he inadvertently tugs on her hair.

The waitress returns before he can utter the apology I can

see on his face. After we order and she strolls away, Audrey leans back into the bench.

When Austin's fingers brush her bare shoulder, she tenses momentarily, so minute I'm not sure anyone that isn't hyper aware of her would notice. But the three of us take notice and share a silent conversation. Whoever made her fear human touch would find something to fear themselves when we find out who it was.

Was that why her brother and she were living on the streets? Were they running from something? If I am feeling protective of her, I can only imagine what's running through Austin's and Saint's heads.

The brunch turns to light topics and, by the time we are at the end, I wish we didn't need to leave. It barely felt like pretending as Saint offers Audrey his arm, and we exit into the bright sun.

The smile slips from her face as the paparazzi descend. Fucking vultures must have been tipped off by Gregory or Valeri. Because the flashing of cameras and shouting as they attempt to get a look at the omega with us tells the entire story.

Audrey buries her face into Saint's chest, and he tucks her closer to his side as he pushes through the throng. A soft whine comes from her, and his other hand comes up to smooth over her hair. Mark pulls open the waiting Rolls-Royce door and, somehow, Saint climbs in without releasing her. Austin and I are right behind them. The dark tint of the windows keeps their invasive eyes off of her.

"Shit, it's like they smelled blood in the water," Saint says, Audrey is now draped across his lap, her face still hidden.

"I imagine that yesterday's headline, 'Did the Mafia Prince crack?' with a photo of me shoving her into my car stirred them up."

Austin straightens his blazer before pulling out his phone and swiping through to an image of Audrey being forced into his waiting car. Her dark hair blocked her face, so you can't see who she is, but it is clear that someone took a picture of an omega that literally could have been being kidnapped, and they only wrote a story about it. Not to mention that it actually was a kidnapping.

"You knew about that photo and thought it would be a good idea to go to brunch where we would be seen?" Saint asks. Something in his voice is dangerous, and Audrey pushes away from him, her eyes wide. She scoots into the seat next to him and straightens, her face a different kind of flushed as she peeks at him from the corner of her eye.

"That is the entire point of this," Austin replies, his tone dry and sarcastic.

"And you didn't think you should warn us?" Saint asks. "Did you ever think how that would affect Audrey? Someone that isn't used to being around the paparazzi should at least get a heads up."

Austin rolls his eyes and sighs, his gaze darting to the omega as he rubs the bridge of his nose. "If she read the contract before signing it, she would also know that was part of the deal."

"I read the contract, and my face plastered on magazines wasn't part of the deal." Audrey smooths out her dress as she glares across the space at Austin, in a way that no one but Saint and I would get away with.

"Page thirty-two, *Being seen in public to ensure our ruse is accepted widely.* What exactly did you think that meant?"

"Um, being seen in public?" She sounds defiant and a bit angry. "I can't have my face on magazines or tabloids. That–I just can't."

"Well, sweetheart, you don't have a choice."

"Take me to the police station. I would rather go to jail."

"Whoa, no one is taking you to jail," I say, finally breaking my silence. When Austin doesn't immediately agree with me, I toss him a look. His face is stoney, and he looks like he wants to throw our omega over his lap and spank her until her cheeks are red. "Austin, tell her," I hiss.

"He's right, you aren't going to jail. The wheels are in motion now, and you are seeing this through."

CHAPTER 13

Audrey

AUSTIN REALLY DOESN'T UNDERSTAND how much I can't have my picture taken and plastered all over the place. If I did–God, I don't want to think about what would happen. I suck in a breath that is *filled* with the three of their scents. And after basically throwing myself at Dean, aka Saint, the need to do it again just keeps growing. He definitely is a Saint that is for sure. He's saved me twice now.

No, we would not think that way about a fucking alpha. They are all bad–even the ones that protect you. Especially those.

Staring unseeing out the window, my memories go to Jason. He had been kind and caring. At one point, I thought he loved me. I hadn't realized he was using me to get close to my parents. He'd gone through all the courting, romantic picnics, walks beneath a starry sky, and planning of a future that would never happen.

He'd fooled me. The same way those girls are taken with the fantasy on *Omega in Paradise*, I had been taken with him. My father told me to stay away from him, that he wasn't good enough for his princess. If I had listened–

Blinking away the moisture in my eyes, I push the thoughts away. I can't change the past, but I can change my future.

"You okay?" Felix's way too kind voice pulls me all the way out of the past, and I glance over at him, attempting a smile. His forehead creases, and he rolls his lip ring into his mouth, his teeth capturing the barring holding it together.

"Never better," I force cheer into my voice. Dean tenses next to me, and Austin focuses out his window as if the three of us aren't even in the car. "Who wouldn't love to be kidnapped and paraded in front of paparazzi like a prize horse?"

Austin slowly turns his head to look at me. The fire in his violet eyes tells me exactly what he wants to do with me. Violence is barely leashed inside of him. And a part of me wants to push him to do whatever it is I can see burning in the depths of his gaze.

"Where to next?" I quirk my eyebrow in question.

"I have to go into the office. You're coming with me today," Austin says.

Apparently, he wants to torture me some more. Although, during the brunch, I'd grown accustomed to his touch. Part of me wants him to touch me some more. The stupid part of my brain that definitely isn't understanding that alphas are dangerous.

The little hussy part believes that being dominated before cuddling is good. She'll be perfectly happy that way. I am going to stuff that part of myself into the same box my memories are in, because that will never happen.

"How fun. I get to go to work with Daddy Zade." I clap like a child, but get the response I crave, so I'll probably do it again. A low growl rumbles in his chest, and I'm sure he's seconds away from launching across the small space at me.

"Daddy Zade." Felix chokes on a laugh, easing the tension that had grown. "Fuck, that is priceless."

"You're not an orphan, and your name is not Annie. Knock off the Daddy shit," Austin snarls.

I lean forward, asking for trouble. "I am an orphan actually and maybe my name really is Annie. Does it bother you to be called Daddy?"

He moistens his lips, a smile playing on them. "I enjoy being called Daddy, princess, but only in the bedroom."

Heat travels through my body and into my cheeks as they flame to life. Okay, I had walked right into that one. Retreat.

"But that isn't in the contract, so don't call me Daddy," he growls. His door swings open a moment later, and I realize we have come to a stop outside his office building. Massive letters spell out his last name over the doorway, and I swallow. How had I missed that? When I don't follow him, he ducks his head back into the dark interior and says, "Come out willingly or I'll drag you out."

Scrambling over the seat and to his door, my heart in my throat, I attempt to exit the vehicle with some sort of composure. Before following his orders, I glance at Felix and Dean, both of who have been nice to me so far, and grin. They both look like I am walking into the gallows.

"Don't worry, I'll be home soon. Just have to go to work with Daddy Zade," I quip.

Dean chuckles, the serious expression on his face evaporating while Felix shakes his head as a smile forms.

"Give him hell," Dean says.

"Oh, I won't just give it to him. I'll take him there for a visit." With my parting words, I pop out of the vehicle, my gaze landing on an impatient Austin. At least there are no cameras taking pictures here. Forcing the thoughts of what would happen if paparazzi got a good image of me, I smile for the alpha glowering down at me. "Ready, Daddy Zade?"

His jaw clenches, and I know the absolute torture I'm going to put him through. He wants me. I had that proof yesterday. But I also know the contract will hold him back. So I'm going to perfume to my heart's content and push all his buttons. What can I say, playing with fire is one of my favorite pastimes.

HE HAS ATTEMPTED to ignore me all morning, and honestly, it is boring. I spin in a circle in my chair, my head angled back to stare at the plain ceiling above. Still, Austin solely focuses on his books. He has an expert skill at ignoring people when he is engrossed in something, and I wonder how it would feel to be the center of that focus.

Am I wishing for a pack or an alpha? No. But to be the single intense focus of a man like him would feel like you own the world.

With a sigh, I stop spinning and stare at him. His wide broad shoulders remind me of my guards growing up. Some of those alphas were reassigned when they realized I was an omega, and I started perfuming around them to get attention.

His black hair appears to be silky soft and part of me wants to run my fingers through it. While his violet irises are lowered beneath long eyelashes that fan his cheeks as he reads silently. The dark stubble over his jaw would feel heavenly against my skin. Not that I would allow it. But I can imagine what it would feel like. A muscle pops along his jawline before he drags his attention to me.

"What?"

My eyes widen. "What do you mean what?"

"I can feel you watching me. What do you want? Are you hungry? Thirsty?"

I snort. "I'm not a dog."

His lips part, and he blinks slowly. "Did I say you were? Last time I checked, humans eat and drink too."

"You have a whole fridge of drinks right there." I point at the mini fridge. "And snacks, there. I think if I was hungry or thirsty, I would just get up and get something."

"Then why are you watching me?"

"Does it bother you?"

"That doesn't answer my question," he mutters.

I laugh. When his gaze meets mine, I bite down on my lip. Time to take him to hell. "Well, *Daddy*, you are beautiful for an alpha. I was admiring it. You have it down. The dark looks, the intensity, that small bit of chest hair peeking out from your currently unbuttoned shirt; it is all alluring. But I'm sure you know that."

"I told you not to call me Daddy."

"Or you'll what? Spank me?" I'm being bratty, almost like a child really, but there is something about him that drives me. He pushes my buttons as much as I press his.

"Something like that," he says almost too low for me to catch, but I *do hear* him, and I can't help the flush to my skin as slick gathers between my legs. "Do you know what a dom is?"

My lips are suddenly dry, and I sneak my tongue out to moisten them. My heart rate picks up, and butterflies come to life in my stomach. I thought I was playing with fire, but I am pretty sure I just jumped right into the flames.

"Do you, Audrey?"

I nod. Of course I know what a dom is. Doesn't everyone?

"Tell me what it is," he says, his voice low and dark and definitely not boardroom friendly.

"It is–" I swallow hard. "A dom is someone that takes over control of a submissive to give pleasure. Usually with express permission. There's a misconception that subs don't have any power, but they have all the power. With a single word, they can take away everything." Textbook answer for the win. I release a breath as I stop rambling and watch him for his response.

He grins wide, flashing straight white teeth at me. "That's it, princess."

My stomach flips at the praise as he stands to his full height. Towering over me. Igniting many fantasies I didn't know were locked inside me. Instead of turning my way, he strolls over to a standing desk and slides open the wooden drawer. The wood-on-wood glides, sending a shiver down my spine.

My full attention is on his broad expanse of shoulders as he shrugs out of his blazer, and I'm absolutely transfixed as he rolls up his sleeves, exposing tanned and toned forearms as he turns back to me.

"I suppose you know what a bratty sub is, too?" He quirks an eyebrow beneath the flop of styled hair on his forehead.

I press my lips together and shake my head.

He chuckles, and the warm sound spreads through my chest, forcing me to clench my legs together. "Oh, I'm betting you do, princess. And if I'm correct and you fall into that category, you crave what a dom could give you. Spankings and all that come with it."

"You're wrong." It's automatic and, from my gut, a defense against something I can't name. *You're so right.* I shake my head and stand. My boots firmly on the ground, I move to the mini-fridge like I'm thirsty, putting some distance between us.

When I stand back up, he's behind me, and I squeak in surprise. His dark tan arms cage me against the countertop. I can feel his warmth, but he's not touching me.

"Am I?" he whispers, and a not entirely unpleasant chill runs over my chest and down my stomach to my core.

"What are you doing?" I'm breathless, my chest tight with anticipation. This is all wrong.

His hand drops, and I suck in a harsh breath as his fingers land on the mini-fridge's door. "You didn't offer to grab me something to drink."

When his other palm lands on my hip and he moves me out of the way, opening the door in one smooth motion. Something in me wants to turn around and press against him. His overwhelming scent has filled my senses, and I want more. I clench my teeth together and find purchase with the drawer handles at my back.

He twists open the water bottle he grabs out and takes a long swallow. When his violet eyes land on me, I hold my breath. My water is unopened in my fist, and his eyes drop to it.

"Drink your water, princess." The underlying command is explicit in his tone. He's used to being listened to, and I challenge that.

I step to the side and place the bottle on the counter. "I actually decided I'm not that thirsty."

In my stomach, I knew what that response would get me, but he still caught me completely off guard as he closes the distance and boxes me in. His thigh settles right between my legs, and he leans forward, exchanging bottles and opening mine. Then he looks at me, like seriously pins me with the hungriest gaze that has ever been given to me, and I just might melt. He lifts his empty hand to my face, settling on my jawline. His thumb brushes my lower lip as he urges my mouth open.

"I said drink your water," he says. There is no true alpha command in the words, but when he holds the open bottle to my lips and lifts, I listen. This is a dangerous dynamic, and I'm falling head first right into it. "That's a good little princess."

My heart pounds beneath my ribcage as my throat works to carry the water to my stomach. It's too late for my panties as I soak them with my arousal, my perfume effortlessly strong between us. His hard length grows even bigger against my thigh, and it takes everything in me not to mewl and press myself against him. Fuck. I am not this needy little omega. Yet, he makes me this way with only a few small actions, and I am not sure I hate it.

When he backs up, I feel the loss of his heat. He eyes me and sets the bottle back down. "Let me make one thing clear. The contract promises no intercourse, but there is a really fine line I intend to walk. If I cross one you don't want crossed, you need to stop me."

I swallow but don't say a word as I wait for him to add the rest.

"Tell me your safe word, princess.Then we'll talk about hard limits."

"What makes you think I'm okay with this?" It doesn't come out angry or demanding; no, the questions are completely breathless and the corner of his mouth kicks up.

"Safe word, or I'll assume you have no limits."

I part my lips. My tongue sneaks out to wet them, and his eyes drop. Am I doing this? Fuck. The idea of holding power over him is intoxicating, because that is what a sub is, powerful. They hold the control and only accept what they want. My palms are clammy as I flatten them against my yellow dress.

"Mango." The second the word leaves my mouth, he grins widely.

"Hard limits?"

"Torture," I croak, already ready for anything deals out.

"The one promise I can make is you'll only feel pleasure with me, and the kind of pain that leads to pleasure, like spanking," he says. His lips quirk up at the corners as he watches me.

Shit, I am crazy. This is crazy. Instant regrets slam into me, but when he closes the distance again and tilts my head up to his with his large hands framing my face, I don't utter my safe word, because I want to know what this feels like.

It is electric. When his lips touch mine, fireworks go off behind my eyelids as he claims my mouth with his demanding tongue. A purr rumbles in his chest, and I press closer, my arms snaking around his neck. He nips my lower lip, soothing it soon after with soft kisses. Then he is nibbling his way along my jaw and down my neck. My head falls back as I stare sightlessly at the ceiling. This is a bad idea. With my heat so close, I should stop him. But I don't.

He palms my right breast through my thin dress, his thumb flicking over the hard nipple poking through. His large hand massages and squeezes it until it feels heavy and achy. When he sucks on my flesh just above my collarbone and to the left of the place he would bite me to claim me, I whine low in my throat. A craving for something I never want is like a rock in my stomach, and I push at his chest.

He doesn't listen to my insistent pawing at him, attempting to shove him away. And my body is growing heavier with desire, slick, making my thighs damp now that my wet panties are no barrier.

"Mango," I gasp, and everything stops.

He puts distance between us, his irises blown wide, his breathing harsh, rapid puffs. He tugs his fingers through his hair, giving me one last scalding look before he leaves the room. I feel like a melted puddle of feelings on the floor as I sink to my weak knees. What was that? I was going to climb him like a damn tree.

I gulp lungfuls of air, my attention on the door he exited. We filled the entire room with the scent of our lust for each other. It is the most perfect smell I'd ever smelled. I run my fingers over my swollen lips and down over the sensitive skin of my neck. Gathering my feet beneath me after a few minutes, I push to my feet. And I thought I would take him to hell. I couldn't have been more wrong.

CHAPTER 14

Austin

I AM seconds away from saying fuck the contract. Seconds away from making a terrible decision. I suck at her throat, next to the place I wanted to bite. My hands are full of her perfect breasts.

She is enthralling, and I am under her spell. I don't want an omega. I don't need an omega. But this one in my arms is making me break all the rules. I don't even need a sub. Felix plays that role anytime I need him too. Just the idea of having Audrey on her knees, begging for a taste of me, or me between hers and her begging for release. Fuck. I grind against her. Holding her tight.

Distantly, in some part of my brain, I recognize she is attempting to push me away. That is part of it, the struggle, the dominance. It excites me as her perfume floods my senses.

"Mango." It is like a gun going off.

I shove away from her, stumbling away. My restraint hangs on by a thread as I stare at her. She's perfect. Her chest rises and falls with her panting breaths, and her lips look deliciously puffy from my kisses. A small love bite darkens her skin on her throat. I want this woman, more than I've wanted another woman in a very long time, possibly ever.

Shaking myself out of the clinging desire to spread her out on the boardroom table and feast on her, I tug my fingers through my hair, causing pain in the process just to bring myself back into myself. If I stay in this room, no safe word is going to keep her actually safe from me. Without a word, I flee the room like the hounds of hell are on my heels.

I drop into my large office chair and spin to look out over the city. If I look toward the boardroom, I will be back in there with her, convincing her she didn't really mean to say mango. My dick throbs in my slacks, and I rub my palm over the hard length. I don't stop myself as I unhook my belt, undo my pants, and slide the zipper down. Then I reach inside, freeing myself from the confines, thankful as fuck I went commando this morning.

Fisting myself, I take my time with long, slow strokes. My thoughts return to the omega in the boardroom. The first to tempt me since–Squeezing my knot hard, I let out a low groan as Audrey's perfect lips take center stage in my imagination. My head drops back as my pace increases. Thoughts of her mouth wrapped around me.

Pre-cum leaks over my fingers, only aiding the image. The sounds of my harsh breaths filling the office and my hand stroking my dick fast enough to start a fire, I shot straight toward release.

"Fuck, yes," I gasp, lifting my hips up as my balls tighten, and my cock jerks as I explode. I ride the after effects of my hand job for as long as they last. Urging the last of my cum to flow from the tip with a few more strokes.

Staring unseeing out at the cityscape as my breathing evens out. At least I feel in control now. The door latches behind me, catching my full attention. Wide brown eyes meet mine before she can hide. I had been so far gone I hadn't heard her come in. Or leave apparently. Had she watched the whole time?

The little voyeur stares at me through the glass door of my private board room that separates us. Dipping her gaze to my spent dick, she blinks as her cheeks turn a pink that rivals her lips. It makes me wonder what else is flushed. Without tearing my eyes from hers, I take out my handkerchief and clean up the mess she caused, then tuck myself away, even though I can feel the blood flowing in that direction again.

She backs up when I stand, her eyes growing wider. I stalk across the room and tear open the door before she can think to run. A sane person would run.

"Your turn," I growl.

Mute, she shakes her head, backing until she hits the table. Easily boxing her in, I lift her onto the surface and lift her dress, cascading it around her hips. What a good fucking idea that was. Her panties are damp, and I'm tempted to swipe my fingers over the fabric. But I don't.

"You're so wet, *my* little omega. Is that for me?" My hands clench around her upper thighs, spreading her wide. My nostrils flare as I breathe in her intoxicating perfume. "Fuck, all of this is for me."

My fingers flex into her soft flesh when she remains quiet.

I order softly, "Touch yourself."

Her legs quiver, and I know she wants to. Her pupils are blown wide, making her eyes almost black. And her chest rises and falls with heavy breaths.

I lick my lips as if I can taste her. "Do it."

When she doesn't move, I release one of her legs and snake up to grip her wrist, dragging her hand closer to her pussy. She swallows and her fingers curl into her palm, little crescents form on her skin from her nails.

"Come on, princess, touch yourself," I coax her.

Slowly, her fingers uncurl over her soaked panties, and a

groan slips out of my chest. She runs them over the fabric, not quite touching herself the way I want to see. My fingers tighten on her wrist, and she slips a finger beneath them.

"That's it," I murmur, completely entranced as she runs her long fingers through the dark patch of curls.

Her knuckle moves beneath the slip of fabric, and she moans. Her head drops back and her eyes shut as she gives in to what I want.

"Pretend it's me, my little omega."

Her lips part as her breathing becomes harsher. Suddenly, the tease of fabric blocking my view is too much. In one swift movement, I tear them off of her. She gasps and attempts to shut her legs. Her dark eyes pin on me as I shove the destroyed panties into my pocket with one hand and keep her spread wide with the other.

"Did I say stop?"

"Austin," she moans.

My name on her lips has my eyes dropping shut for a moment in pleasure. I need to hear it more. Moaned from her perfectly pink lips, as she gives herself an orgasm.

Her fingers dip into her folds, and she swirls her thumb over her clit. Her slick glistens on her sex as it prepares her for something that isn't coming. And my dick throbs painfully in my slacks, a knot already forming. Fuck. I thrust my hips into the edge of the table, seeking something that I can't have.

"Faster, omega."

I drop to my knees to have a better view, is what I tell myself. But my mouth waters and all I can think of is tasting her nectar. My fingers curl over her legs, tugging her to the edge and close to me. Inhaling deeply, my eyes drop shut again.

Sweet.

Tantalizing.

Tempting.

The worst idea I've ever had.

I lick my lips and lean forward. Her fingers halt as my breath puffs over her heated flesh. But I don't put my mouth on her. I imagine it. I tease myself with it. And I definitely have put myself within range, but I made my restraint of unbreakable steel.

Her legs shake on the edge of the table, and I run my fingers down her calf to her booted foot and place it over my shoulder before doing the same with the other. She is literally vibrating with need.

Ever so slowly, her fingers pump in and out of her. The sound of her wet pussy and the heavenly scent inches from my face have me pressing an open-mouthed kiss to her upper thigh. She arches her hips, as if asking for my mouth some place else, and I smile against her skin.

"Not today, princess."

"Austin, I'm going to come." Seconds after she moans the words, she tenses, her fingers pausing and her pussy pulsing around her fingers, leaking more slick onto the edge of the table.

My gaze tracks the moisture as it rolls over the side toward the floor, and I don't know what possesses me but I dip my head forward, catching it with my tongue. My fingers flex uncontrollably into her legs as I attempt to pull myself away. I licked the table to taste the omega despite her being in front of me, all because of the fucking contract I wrote.

Sure, I could walk this line and fuck her pussy with my mouth, but that would definitely lead to my dick getting involved. Now she isn't the only one shaking.

"Just a taste, *daddy*," she says, and I feel my restraint snap like a weak ass twig, bending and breaking with just a few words.

Daddy.

She is trying to make me feral.

In punishment, I lift my head and meet her steady and lust-filled gaze, then lower my head like I'm going to put my mouth where she wants it, turning at the last second and sinking my teeth into her upper thigh again. She gasps and arches, and I realize my mistake, because this close to her center, her skin tastes like her slick. I soothe the bite with my tongue, licking up every bit I can reach. Then I move my head to her other thigh and repeat the process. Like a man possessed, I clean her skin of any trace of her taste.

Her fingers thread into my hair and tighten just before I pull away. She lifts my head back, staring at me. Something glitters dangerously in the depths of her irises.

"Put your fucking mouth on me," she growls. When I hesitate, she dips her fingers into her folds with her free hand and pushes the wet digits into my mouth. "I know you want to taste me, Alpha, so do it."

I suck and lick her fingers clean, and when I'm done, I yank my head away from her hold and stand up, her legs dropping from my shoulders. Backing away from the temptation she is, I suck in a deep breath of her sugary sweet scent. My dick reminded me that my hand would not cut it the second time around. It almost feel like I am entering a rut, but that isn't possible unless I'm around an unattached omega going into a heat.

My gaze travels from her booted feet up to her flushed face, pausing on her exposed sex, still as tempting as ever. I want this woman. More than I've wanted any woman, including the one responsible for me swearing off omegas. She is dangerous.

"Fix your dress," I say.

She lifts an eyebrow, ready to be a brat again.

"I'm serious, Audrey. Fix your damn dress."

"Do it for me." She challenges me with her steady gaze,

leaving her sex exposed and still fucking tempting. The curls damp with her juices and still begging for a knot. "Are you afraid?"

I roll my lips between my teeth and shake my head once. My heart pounds in my chest, attempting to break through my ribcage, and I step forward quickly and cover her up with the bright, cheerful yellow dress. Then I pull her up to a sitting position and frame her face with my hands.

"I'm not afraid of anything, princess. Don't challenge me, or your ass will be perfectly pink like your lips."

CHAPTER 15

Dean

"COME GET THE FUCKING OMEGA. I don't want her here anymore," Austin barks through the line. Felix shoots me a look that makes it clear he could hear him, too.

"Did she do something?" I ask.

"Just come get her before I do something I'll regret."

I push off the sofa and grab my blazer from the chair at the island I had left it at. "I can be there in twenty."

"Make it ten," he orders, and the line goes dead.

"Make it ten?" Felix laughs. "He knows this is New York City, and he'll be lucky if we make it in twenty, right?"

"Come on, something has gotten under his skin." We head for the elevator as I send a quick text to one of our drivers to meet us out front.

"I'd say she is brunette, dark eyed, five-foot something omega, with a knack for pressing his buttons."

Felix punches the main floor button, and the door slides close. Somehow, the driver reaches the front before we arrive, and we are at the office in record time. The mid-day traffic benefits us, and in fifteen minutes, we are pulling up outside Zade enterprises.

The security guard nods us through the metal detectors, ignoring the fact that they both go off. We are the only ones allowed to carry within the building. It is a safety measure Austin insisted on. And with his background, I suppose he isn't wrong.

After getting off the elevator on the top floor, we head for his office. He is behind his desk, a scowl on his face and papers spread all over the surface. Although he doesn't look as if he is reading any of them. He glances up when we enter and points to the door of the boardroom.

"She's in there."

With a nod, I take three long strides to the door and pull it open. I'm hit immediately by the smell of sex. Of an omega on the verge of a heat. Audrey spins slowly in a seat near the window, one foot on the ground moving her. Her brow lifting when she catches sight of us, and she comes to a stop.

I try not to inhale deeply, although every sense inside of me wants to. Felix passes me, oblivious to the fact that Austin may very well have crossed some pretty hard lines. His restraint would have to be superpowered to ignore the perfume coming off of her.

"Hey, we came to get you, break you out of this prison."

Her gaze flicks to the doorway, and she licks her lips. "That's probably for the best, actually."

She uncrosses her legs and stands. With purpose, she strides across the room and into Austin's office. I follow, watching curiously as she moves across the space to stand in front of his desk. He looks up at her, and she leans forward, her hands on the cherry surface.

"I want my panties back," she says.

My eyes unwillingly drop to her skirt. The fact that she doesn't have her underwear on and she thinks he has them. Oh God. He did it. He crossed all the uncrossable lines. A muscle ticks in his jaw as he looks at us.

"Get her out of here," he orders.

"I said I want my panties back," she says again.

He huffs out a laugh. "That won't be happening. Now be a good girl and go with Dean and Felix."

"Don't you dare patronize me with your good girl shit."

He stands up slowly, planting his palms on his desk and closing the distance between them. "Unless you plan on being *claimed* by me, you better go. Do you understand, my little omega?" He caresses the side of her face and runs his thumb over her lip as if he wants to kiss her, and she pulls back with a hard swallow.

"Fine, keep them. Do what ever perverted shit you plan to do with them. Enjoy jacking off into them."

Felix chokes on a laugh as she spins on her heel and stomps across the room toward the exit. I pause as he follows her, my gaze on Austin.

"We will talk about it later," he sighs after she exits the room. "Go before the little devil has a full-blown heat in the middle of the city."

I nod and turn to go.

"Saint–" he calls after me. "Don't fuck her."

I snort. "I have control of myself, I'm not impulsive like you."

"You haven't faced anything as tempting as her. You have to be strong."

His words tell me three things. One, he's tempted. Two, he is afraid of falling. Three, he thinks that if I fold, he will have no other option but to follow.

THE CAR RIDE back to the apartment is silent. As soon as we enter the elevator, she presses the button for the nineteenth floor. I share a look with Felix and lean back against the mirror.

When the doors slide open, she steps out, and we follow. "What are you doing?" she asks.

"Visiting your brother, I assume," I reply.

"No, that is what I'm doing."

Felix shrugs and falls into step next to her. "Rules. Austin wants someone with you at all times. So, here we are."

"You aren't coming in."

"I'm hurt. I thought we were friends," Felix says.

She stops and faces both of us. "You both are perfectly fine. But I need to talk to my brother. Alone."

"We will stay outside." I tilt my head to see if she is agreeable.

She says nothing but turns and starts heading down the hall again. When she reaches the door, she knocks loudly. In a few seconds, her brother is swinging the door wide. He smiles when he sees his sister, but tenses when he spots me.

"Sis?"

She pushes past him and pulls him out of the doorway without answering him and shuts the door between us.

"Austin really riled her up," Felix says.

"I think her heat riled her up. Austin was just there."

He takes a second look at the shut door and leans against the wall across from it while I take my position next to it.

"Heat? Fuck. Austin picked a stellar time to reel her in."

"She is going to need an alpha if she doesn't want to be in pain for days."

He knew that, but I felt like I had to voice it. The idea of her in pain doesn't sit well with me. If not for the clause in the contract, I would offer my *services*. I wasn't one for casual sex, but I also would not force her to go through that.

"Austin will not risk his plan and allow her to find relief with some random alpha."

I blow out my cheeks and kick my foot up on the wall behind me. "I know. But it won't be a random alpha, it will be me."

An unexpected laugh pops from his mouth before he doubles over, laughing like a lunatic. He glances up, shakes his head, and devolves into even more laughter.

"God, Saint, you really are trying to take one for the team. I bet it feels like a real *sacrifice*," he gasps out the words between chuckles, tears streaming his red face.

I cross my arms and pin him with a glare until he stands straight, a wide grin plastered across his face.

"Jesus, you should see your face." He chortles out another round of laughter, swiping at his cheeks.

"Are you done?"

His back presses into the wall, and he suppresses more laughter. "Yeah."

"You're a prick."

"Better than pretending to be saintly," he replies. He sucks his lip ring into his mouth, rolling the ball between his teeth.

"One, you two gave me the nickname. Two, I've never claimed to be."

Before he can respond, the door swings open and her brother comes storming into the hallway and stomping down the hall. The acid scent of anger heavily coats my tongue, and I move before thinking, barging into the apartment to make sure Audrey is okay. Felix is right behind me.

There is a noticeable disparity between the fresh, baked scent of brownies that usually clings to the air around her and the pungent, sour aroma of her sadness that envelopes me as soon as I come to a stop. She sits at the edge of the couch with her head bowed, eyes on her boots, and fingers curled into her palms.

"Are you okay?" I ask. The words hang in the air between us, and I share a look with Felix.

CHAPTER 16

Audrey

AS SOON AS the door snaps shut, closing out the men in the hallway, I lock it. Not that a simple lock will keep a determined alpha out. With a deep breath, I lean against the surface. Sin watches me with a quizzical expression.

"What are you doing here, Aud?"

He crosses the small room that looks like a closet after moving into my new room that is bigger than this. In fact, I am positive that my walk-in closet *is* bigger than the whole place. The coffee table has a few takeout containers open with old food in them.

"Sin, you have to clean up after yourself. This isn't the warehouse." I automatically stack the styrofoam and push them into the almost full trash. "You are going to end up with flies, or worse."

He shrugs when I turn back around. "Worry about the shit you have gotten yourself into. Have you seen this?"

He holds up *The Star* and on the front of it is a blurry picture of me being forced into Austin's car. I know it's me and Sin knows it's me, but the men we ran from wouldn't know unless they had a clear picture.

"If there is a blurry picture out there of you, then there is a crystal clear one. That will place you *with* Austin Fucking Zade, one of the easiest men to find in the city of New York because his name is on a fucking building. Do you know what that means, Aud?"

I swallow and lick my lips. I didn't come here to be lectured. Even if it is coming from a place of worry.

"It's fine." I don't tell him about earlier today outside The Clocktower. He would lose it.

He paces to the window. "Your fine and mine are two different things. I went through hell and back to get you out of there," his voice rises, shaky with his anger. The acid scent flows off of him in waves, and I sink into the sofa.

"Sin, I know. I'm sorry. I told him to take me to jail and turn me in after–" So much for not mentioning this morning. Fuck. I drag my fingers through my hair.

"After?"

I sigh. "Breakfast this morning. The paparazzi were outside."

"Shit. They could have a clear picture of you already. We have to run." He moves to the bedroom and starts filling up his backpack. "We can get lost in Chicago or maybe go south to Atlanta."

I fold my hands into my lap. "I'm not running."

He stops mid thrust and stares at me like I've grown another head. "What do you mean you're not running?" he asks slowly, like the words are unknown to him.

"I can't." *I don't want to.*

"You've been with them for one night. One. Night. And you are brainwashed?"

I cross my arms over my stomach, curling my fingers into the soft fabric of my dress. "I'm not," I say weakly.

"Aud, look at yourself. You are in a fucking dress like a grown dress-up doll, because I know it wasn't your choice to put that on." He shoves his fingers through his hair and swears under his breath. He comes over and kneels in front of me. "Please. Don't make my sacrifice be for nothing."

"Sin," I breathe, tears gathering behind my eyes. "I didn't ask you to do that."

"You are my twin sister. You didn't have to ask me to do it. I'm going to protect you. Running. Now. That will save you and me."

I drag in a shaky breath, my sadness coming off of me in waves. "I can't run, even if I wanted to. My heat is almost here. There is nowhere we could go to be safe in less than a day. I'm safer here. The room they gave me has controls that will keep me secure and away from alphas as I ride it out."

He shoves to his feet, staring down at me like he doesn't know who I am, and it tears something inside of me wide open. Sure, we've fought in the past, but not like this. If I said we needed to run, we ran, and if he said we needed to, we did. It has kept us safe. Away from the men that took over our father's empire, the men that won't be satisfied until we are both dead.

"Fine," he spits. His anger is back, a force that feels almost physical in the intensity. "Stay, but don't come running to me when they find you, because I'll probably already be dead."

"Sin," I say pitifully as he storms across the room and almost rips the door off its hinges in his haste to get it unlocked and open before leaving without a backward glance.

My lips press into a thin line, and I drop my head, defeat filling my very being. Sadness leaking from my eyes and dripping down my nose toward the floor. I curl my fingers into my palms and squeeze, attempting to cause pain to pull me out of this downward spiral. What if he's right and they come for me but find him?

A sob works its way from my throat. I didn't even talk to

him about why I came. We share everything, and now…it felt like I lost a part of myself.

"Are you okay?" Dean's rich voice washes over me.

He makes me feel safe in a way I've never experienced before. Which is absolutely insane because he is an alpha, and after my experience with Jason, I don't need another one. Although I had been close to begging Austin to take me, consequences and contracts be damned. Maybe Sin was right, and we should make a break for it. I press harder into my palms, wincing as pain breaks into my sadness.

Dean is on his knees in front of me, his large hands touching me, forcing my nails from my flesh. The tips of my fingers are red, and little crescent-shaped wounds bleed on my palms, four on each hand. Maybe Sin knew something I didn't about pain and its ability to remove your thoughts.

His large thumb runs next to the self-inflicted injury, the skin sensitive. "Felix, wet a paper towel. We need to clean this."

I blink up at him, tears hanging on my lashes. "You really are the savior type, huh?"

His face softens, and he brushes a stray tear from my face, leaving his warm palm against my cheek as he stares into my soul. "Only for those I care about. And you, little omega, have just added your name to that very short list."

My heart thumps, and my breath catches. There is *something* about him and Austin calling me a little omega that reaches inside some hidden part of me and makes me crave more. It makes me *want* to be *their* little omega. I am so screwed.

Felix holds out the wet paper towel, and Dean releases my cheek, taking the towel and bandage supplies he had grabbed from the bathroom. My skin cools with the air, and I almost need his touch again. He purrs deep in his chest as he cleans up my wounds. Taking care of an omega must fill some sort of need inside of him, too. Because I'm pretty sure he doesn't even know he is purring. It makes me want to nuzzle into him and wrap myself in the safety of his arms.

"Your brother was really mad. Did he hurt you?" Felix asks as he sinks into the cushion next to me.

I shake my head, my brow furrowing. "No, but I'm pretty sure I hurt him." I press my lips together as another tear sneaks out. Sin was my world. It was me and him. A team. But now, it felt like something shifted and he wasn't the one that had changed.

"Sometimes those closest to you can cause the deepest wounds," Felix says softly. "But I'm sure you can fix it."

He spoke from experience. I could see it in the depths of his green eyes. A sadness that seems to lurk in their depths, beneath his laughter and jokes. Someone hurt him. Reaching out with my now bandaged hand, I wrap my fingers around his. How could I touch the three of them so easily? Why do they each feel like a piece of my soul that has been missing? Even Austin and his bossy, dominant behavior felt like a missing puzzle piece to my heart. It is too fast, yet not fast enough.

"Thank you," I say with a watery smile.

"Anytime." He squeezes my fingers gently as Dean finishes up his work on my other hand.

CHAPTER 17

Audrey

THAT EVENING, I am curled up on the couch, watching the city lights and a boat out on the water twinkle under the full moon. Dean is reading in one armchair, and Felix stretches out on the couch, his feet tucked next to my ass, sound asleep. Soft snores come from him, and I smile. It is all so…domestic.

It reminds me of what home used to be. Sure, my dad was a big mafia boss, but it didn't come home with him. Our home was a sanctuary.

Which brings my thoughts right back to the man I am not thinking about. Austin Zade. He hasn't returned yet, and a part of me knows it is because of what happened at the office. My cheeks feel warm as the memories of it all washes over me. I had gone to his office to give him a piece of my mind, only to find him stroking himself.

It had rooted me to the spot, only released when he came. Then I moved. And he–well, he became a man possessed, and I loved it. The absolute possession in his gleaming violet eyes, the way his fingers flexed into my skin. Even the fucking way he licked my slick from the edge of the table. Damn, it was everything. The only thing that would have made it better was feeling his weight on top of me, or…

"You okay?" Dean asks, pulling me back to the present.

I clear my throat and nod. He is so sweet. I am probably stupidly half in love with him already. But Dean's kindness puts me on edge at the same time. I've been lied to in the past and am not getting caught up in that fantasy a second time. At least with Austin I knew he wasn't trying to get anything from me other than what I'd already agreed to.

"Yeah. I'm fine. Tired, I guess."

I stand and stretch, my comfortable sweats and t-shirt hug my curves in ways I'm aware of. There *are* two mirrors in my closet alone. But Austin still has my hoodie, so it is all I have. I couldn't bring myself to take the tags off the new silky pajamas that were folded up on a shelf in my room. Dean's eyes track my movements, making me feel warm.

It's the heat. It's influencing how I see alphas, and Dean is one fine man that I am already drawn to. Not to mention his scent feels like a match.

He inhales, his nose flaring as he catches my perfume. "Sleep well."

I stare at him for a full minute, part of me wanting to climb into his lap and cuddle with him. Pressing my lips together, I nod and turn away. Taking a few steps away, I pause, a thought occurring to me. They might have access to better suppressants than what I've been using. I'm not fully in a heat and part of that honestly could be the fact that I had an orgasm today. Those are supposed to make it easier to handle, but only if given by an alpha. Could it be considered given by an alpha if I was the one to touch myself?

Apparently.

"Dean?" I turn back around. He lifts a brow and closes his book. My teeth sink into my lower lip, and I almost say fuck it and run for the safety of my room. "Can you get me suppressants? The ones I have are cheap, and I don't think they are working."

He clears his throat, and I can tell I've surprised him with my question.

"You know what? Forget it. It's okay," I say, waving my hand in the air between us in a dismissive motion.

"If it was okay, I'm sure you wouldn't have asked," he replies. "We can make a trip to Doctor Stephens in the morning. She is known for her research into heats and suppressants."

Relief spears through me, and I almost sag to the floor. I'll be okay until tomorrow. I'm sure of it.

MY BODY CONVULSES, and pain spears my abdomen. I curl into a ball, holding in a scream that wants to come out. Sweat coats my body, and I feel like I'm having a hot flash, even if I'm too young for one. I whimper, pressing my face into my pillow. Slowing my breathing and attempting to get my heart rate under control.

I should lock my door. Secure it. But I can't move. I feel needy and wanton. My breasts feel heavy and full, while slick makes my thighs wet in a way that tells me I'm out of time. My pheromones are strong in the air. Fresh baked brownies with a hint of vanilla tell me my perfume is in full bloom.

At least, I shut my bedroom door. But just the slightest brush of my legs pressing together is enough to send a dose of lust through me. If I got up now, I'd walk through the door and offer myself up. I am screwed.

It is as if my body knows there are two alphas on the other side of that door and wants me to go find them.

I need a toy, that is what I need. Practically crawling to my backpack, I unzip the front pocket and fish out my tiny bullet.

With a sigh, I lean against the wall, not bothering with going back to my bed. Curling my fingers around the vibrator, I press the button on the end and something eases in my chest at the low rumble. At least it will be some relief.

Although, one of those alpha dildos would do a better job at fooling my body.

Not bothering with removing my sweats, I snake my hand beneath the waistband and under my panties. Then press it against my clit. A moan comes from my throat as I drop my head against the wall. Circling it in slow, easy circles. It is seconds before release washes over me, and I gasp out a breath. As soon as I come back down, the need is there like it never left.

I've never had a heat start out this strong before. My skin is feverish as I push to my feet, my legs weak as I stumble to my bathroom. I take a cool shower that does nothing for the lust building like a storm inside me. As the air hits my skin, I shiver, not even bothering to dry off before I move back to the bed. I lay on top of the covers, drops of water still clinging to my body, goosebumps forming along my arms and legs. Even so, all I can think of is searching out one of the alphas in the apartment with me.

How stupid would that be?

I'm not sure how long I lay there like that. The light from my windows tells me that dawn is breaking. And normally I would be there looking out over the water, watching the sun greet a new day. But today I am an achy mess.

A soft knock on the door breaks through my daze. "Audrey? Dr. Stephens has said we can come before the first appointment."

Dean.

My pussy clenches around nothing, and I groan. Fuck. Being an omega is a fucking nightmare. Why couldn't I have been born an alpha? Or a beta?

"Audrey?" he calls when I don't answer him.

I can't because if I say a word it would probably end up being, *'Please come fuck me. I need your knot.'* Just the thought of saying that has me ready to take him.

"Aud? Are you okay?"

In slow motion, my doorknob turns.

Anticipation builds in my stomach.

My core clenches again.

He could make it all better. Need, strong and pure, floods me as my perfume blooms.

To say he is shocked by me naked on the bed, spread out, ready for him to shed his clothing and enter me is an understatement. He inhales and chokes, his eyes going wide, his knuckles around the doorknob bleaching white with his grip.

"Fuck," he groans.

I see the fight inside of him. The tense way he attempts to shut the door. But his internal alpha won't let him, and I smile. His attention on me easies some of the ache that had taken over my whole body, and I slide my hand down my stomach and into my folds, circling my clit with my middle finger, then I slip it further down and press it inside. He watches, the bulge in his pants growing larger. His other hand is gripping the wood on the doorframe so tightly I'm sure he is going to rip it from the frame.

But none of that matters. The only thing that does is his eyes fixed on me.

"Dean, I need an alpha," I whisper.

He breaks at my words, slipping into the room and shutting the door behind him. Tingles of awareness shoot through me, down to my toes and out to the tips of my fingers, like electricity. The bed dips beneath his knee as he crawls over the surface.

He pauses, his deep caramel eyes tracing my face, memorizing it. Then he pulls my soft comforter over my body, wrapping me up in the warm and plush blanket. Cocooning me away from him.

"I'll hold you," he says, his voice smooth like a shot of whiskey sliding down my throat. Infusing heat into my very soul.

Then he does just that. He lays down next to me and gathers me into his arms, still wrapped in the blanket. He tucks my head into his neck, and I inhale his unique scent of leather and lemon. My mouth waters, my instincts urging me to lick him.

His palm rubs over my back, and I cuddle closer, nuzzling into his neck as if I could climb inside of him. The tip of my tongue darts out to taste his skin, and he purrs low in his chest. The rumble of approval spreads through me. It doesn't make the cramps ease up any, but it is a comfort I didn't know I needed. It calms something inside of me, makes the needy and lusty feeling lessen. Probably because my body thinks it is going to get what it wants.

And my feelings for him expand in my chest like a sponge soaking up as much water as it can. What sort of alpha sees an omega in full-blown heat and resists the urge to rut? I saw the impressive bulge in his pants and can feel it still pressing into my stomach through the comforter, but he's just holding me.

I feel his lips press against the top of my head, and his fingers slide beneath my hair and to the nap of my neck, gripping me gently.

Is it possible to fall for a man you only just met? Or is it the heat talking? A trick to get me to mate. I'm not sure. But I've never felt this cherished in my life, and I want to hold on to it with both hands.

CHAPTER 18
Felix

IT'S BEEN an hour since Dean went into Audrey's room. I am not jealous. I don't think I am, at least. But curiosity has my attention glued to the door. Austin is still asleep. He would blow a gasket if he knew where Saint is. That he is probably helping her through a heat, at least that is my guess. Why else go into her room?

Cracking an egg into the pan, only half my focus is on cooking, the other half is firmly on the omega's bedroom. I've never wished to be anything but the beta that I am, until now. Being an alpha in this situation would have its benefits.

And I'd be a liar if I didn't admit that she had captivated me. Even now, there is an urge to just be close to her. I've never felt that with anyone but my alphas. Didn't believe it was possible.

Austin's door swings open. He scratches at his jaw as he yawns, bleary-eyed, coming into the kitchen. I am not sure what time he came home, but he looks as if he had less than four hours.

"Where were you last night?" Did the question sound like

an insecure omega? Possibly. Especially with the thready way it came out.

He stretches and strolls into the kitchen. When his hand comes down, it is on my hip with his warmth infusing me from behind. "Late night at the office."

I roll my eyes. "You do know who you are talking to, right? You don't have to lie. Besides, you smell like you stepped out of an alcohol cabinet."

He drops a kiss on my neck. "The omega got to me."

"She is getting to all of us." I glance at her shut door. At least there isn't moaning coming from inside.

"Where is Saint?"

I clear my throat and focus on my hopeless egg. The yoke is broken and no longer able to be dipped. Bummer.

"Felix?"

He nips my neck, and I yelp in surprise. Although I shouldn't be, I had ignored a direct question from him.

"He–" I start, my gaze landing on Audrey's door again.

Austin follows my line of sight and swears. "Are you fucking kidding me?"

I roll my lip ring between my teeth and play with the barring. He isn't looking for an answer.

When he storms across the floor to her bedroom, I follow. The door rattles on its hinges as he tosses it open. A growl so fierce it rumbles the floor beneath my feet erupts from Austin like a dormant volcano getting ready to blow its top.

"*What the fuck are you doing?*" His question flows over me, making me shiver.

Saint's answering rumble comes from inside the room.

Fuck. They are going to get territorial over the omega.

Her room smells so bakery sweet, it makes my mouth water, so I can only imagine what they could smell. Saint bundled Audrey into a blanket burrito and wrapped her in his arms. He tugs her closer to his chest, and she snuggles into his neck, eliciting another possessive growl from Austin.

"Get out of the fucking bed, Saint." Austin's command makes us both tense.

"She's in heat," he replies, like it isn't obvious that is what is happening. Although I did honestly think there would be sex. Lots and lots of sex.

I can't give her a knot, but I could give her orgasms, and I've heard those help with the pain. I step forward, and Austin slaps a firm hand to my chest.

"*No.*"

My feet root to the spot, and my sweats tent. Need slams into me. My breath catches. What the fuck was that? Even with Austin's command echoing in my ears, I take another step. The sweet perfume of her pheromones is like a hit of cocaine to my system, and I want more.

I inhale, filling my lungs to the brim with her. Mixed with my alphas, it is intoxicating. Leather and citrus, a crisp fall morning with spice, and her fresh from the oven sweet scent of brownies. All of it is enough to make me feel as if I'm home.

"Need…" she murmurs, and it forces another step toward her from my legs that are so confused they don't know who to listen to.

"*Felix.*" It is all warning and command.

And I try to listen to the meaning behind my name. *Back off, do not engage.* But fuck, I'm only a beta. How the fuck am I supposed to resist the plea in her voice?

His hand lands on my shoulder as he follows me into the room. A scent cloud of a crisp fall morning in an apple orchard spreads around us, making me light-headed.

Austin clenches his jaw and his tendon pops, while his nostrils flare to breathe in her pheromones like the drug they are. I'm sure my irises are as blown as wide as his. The violet and gold are nearly nonexistent as he focuses on her.

"Saint, get your ass out of her bed. *Now.*"

I give him credit as he tries, but she's like a spider monkey, clinging to him through the blankets. Her arms are secured around his chest, and I'm pretty sure she has at least one leg curled around one of his. Saint's low purr fills the room when she whines. He settles back into the mattress, and she drapes herself over him, breaking free of the blanket just enough to flash us her bare leg to the top of her thigh as she wraps it around him.

He groans, and his hands land on what I assume is her ass beneath the covers. His fingers flex, and she grinds into him. She is completely a being of need and lust. We aren't very far behind, if I'm honest.

"Kitten, shhh, we can't," Saint says. He brushes a strand of hair that had fallen over her face. He presses his lips to her forehead, and she whines again.

It sure looks like we can with the way she is dry humping him. I glance at Austin, and his face is so stoney I think his jaw is going to break.

"Felix, call Dr. Stephens. Tell her to bring the suppressant injection." I don't want to. I want to climb into the bed with Saint and Audrey and encourage actual sex. "*Now.*"

The command finally yanks me out of the haze of lust that had descended, and I pull out my phone, dialing that doctor. Injections aren't the best way to avoid a full-blown heat, but it suppresses them until the time is *better,* as if there is a better time to go into a need-filled, sex driven, heat.

"Keep her calm," Austin commands, and then he is tugging me from the room and shutting the door between us. An alpha not giving into their baser instincts is unheard of, but two? I'm pretty sure, until today, it was a myth.

When the door shuts between us, I drag in a breath that is

only Austin, fall and spice. It always reminds me of cold fall days spent next to the fire or the impossibly sunny fall days that are perfect with the stunning blue skies that go on and on. And the lazy picnics at an apple orchard that are just so cozy. Just crisp enough that your cheeks are pink but not so chilly you need a jacket. It centers me, like it always does.

"Fuck, that was—" I trail off. I'm not sure what it is, but I am pretty sure betas shouldn't react the way I did.

"We are screwed. I don't normally have destructive plans. But this omega in our apartment, that was a terrible idea." He looks on edge. The bulge in his pants is near to splitting the seam and springing free. Even his knot is growing.

"The doctor is on her way."

He grunts and paces across the living room floor. Tension is thick in the air, and he is in full-blown rut. I'd seen him like this a few times, when he got too close to an omega in their heat. It is an unavoidable problem when you are an alpha. The control your baser needs have over you is insane. But it has led to some amazing nights.

"We have time, I could—" I suggest. He pauses like he is considering my words and the unvoiced offer of release.

"Too dangerous." He waves the suggestion away and stops in front of the large floor-to-ceiling window, his hands clasped behind his back. He stares sightlessly out at the city and river beyond.

After twenty minutes, a sharp knock at the door signals the doctor. She made good time. It probably helps that she is only a few blocks over. I stride to the door and swing it open. She inhales deeply and shakes herself out of whatever it does to her as she steps into the apartment.

"Where is she?" She looks around as if someone should splay Audrey out on the living room floor, begging to be knotted.

"In here." I lead the way to her room and knock once

before swinging open the door. Austin remains next to the windows, not even acknowledging the doctor.

Audrey's perfume hits me square in the chest, and I'm positive I will never forget it, even if I never smell it again. She is further gone now. Completely oblivious to the two of us entering as she writhes on top of Saint, blankets and his clothing separating them.

Saint's sharp pants and unwilling moans fall from his lips, and I know he is losing the fight. His head is pressed against the pillows, his eyes on her moving over him, and if they were both naked with nothing separating them, she would be riding him like a cowgirl riding a horse. The blanket is puddled around her hips, and her nipples stand at attention, begging for touch. She grinds against him. Little mewls fall from her parted lips as she seeks what she needs.

The doctor brushes past me and strolls into the room like she's attending tea, and she's late. Saint's low warning growl rumbles from him as he sees the woman, his possessiveness red hot, shining from the depths of his eyes.

"I know, Alpha, but you're the one that set up the appointment," she replies all business as she draws out a syringe. In one smooth motion, she has it pushed into Audrey's arm, the suppressant traveling through her veins.

A gasp of pain, definitely not pleasure, bursts from Audrey, and I take a step toward them. Ready to do what? I'm not entirely sure. But the need to protect her thrums through me like someone beating steadily on a drum.

"She's fine, Felix." I'm not sure how the doctor knew I moved.

"I can't–" Audrey cries, and it tears something inside of me. I shift so I can see them, and Saint is holding her to his chest, a rumble of a purr coming from him. But tears stream down her face as the medicine burns through her system.

"Shhh, little omega, it will be okay." Saint runs his hand

up her bare back and, without thinking, I move and cover her up.

Before I step back, she reaches out and tangles her fingers with mine, tugging me down. Her scent has lessened, but it still makes my mouth water.

The doctor murmurs something from behind me and then leaves the room. I don't hear the words, because I'm caught like a fly in a spider's web with Audrey's bright green eyes.

After another twenty minutes of helplessly watching her face the pain, the drugs infuse her system fully, and she brushes tears from her face and scoots off of Saint. The brownie smell is stronger when she shifts, and I try not to look at the wet spot her slick made. Part of me wants to bury my face in it and lick it up. While the other half wants to wrap her up and hold her.

Her face flushes as her eyes fall to the spot I'm focused on. She swallows. "You can go, both of you."

CHAPTER 19

Audrey

PAIN WRACKS my body as the cool water falls over my skin. I am sitting beneath the spray of the shower head, washing away my slick. I don't know how long I've been on the ground, but it's been long enough for the water to run cold. Shivers vibrate through me, and I hug my knees. I'm not sure which is worse, a heat or being yanked out of one artificially.

It feels like the flu. My body is one big ache, and the sad part is I still want the men that are now my roommates. Reaching up a weak hand, I turn the spray off. As the water runs off me and down the drain, I sit there staring at the fancy tile. I should dry off and get dressed.

Eventually, I pull myself to my feet and wrap a towel around my body. Exiting the bathroom, I stop. They have stripped my bed down to the mattress, and even now I can smell my pheromones strong in the room. It won't surprise me if they infuse the entire apartment. But what stops me is my hoodie, the one Austin had taken from me. He neatly folded it and placed it on the foot of the bed.

I cross the room and tug it on. He had it washed because it

smells like freshly washed clothes and him, fall and spice. Giving in for a moment, I bury my nose into his scent; it is mouthwatering. It probably helps that fall is my favorite season.

Discarding my towel beneath my hoodie, I cross to the closet and search out a pair of panties and leggings.

Since my bed isn't an option, I leave my room. The three of them are in a deep conversation in the living room, none of them realizing I'm out of my bedroom. I curl my arms around myself, feeling a little uncomfortable. All three of them had seen me like a wanton omega, throwing myself at Saint. Can the floor swallow me whole now?

I want my nest.

This is the ultimate embarrassment. And I should be thankful that Dean didn't take full advantage of what I so willingly offered. But part of me really isn't. A deep down part of me wished he wasn't so saintly. In the darkness of my soul, I crave the knot he can give me.

I clear my throat and three sets of eyes, from intense violet and gold to summer green, all the way back to the warmest deep brown of coffee, settle on me.

My mouth is bone dry, and I swallow, my face heating. "I wanted to say thank you, for, uh–"

Words.

We can do words, right?

Austin rakes me with his violet orbs, and I straighten my shoulders even as my fingers are curling into my sleeves. "I see you found the hoodie. It really is ratty, we can buy you new ones."

"I like this one," I reply. I hug myself tighter, burying my fingers deeper into the fabric.

He snorts and dismisses me as he turns back to his pack.

"My parents are dead. It is the last thing I have from them," I say, feeling raw. I don't know why I shared that, but maybe if he knew, he wouldn't look at me like I was a lost cause. Maybe he would understand.

His shoulders stiffen, but he doesn't turn back. Asshole. My emotions are too raw for the dismissal of an alpha, even one I don't want attention from. I don't want attention from him, right? I'm a mess.

I shift on my bare feet, my eyes drifting to the bright afternoon light. It shimmers on the river in the distance, and I focus on that as I determine to thank Dean.

"Thank you for just holding me." I tear my gaze away from the water and look at Dean. He nods, a small smile on his face. "And uh, letting me, um–"

Grind into you? My stomach flips as the hazy memory assaults me. The noises he made, the encouragement his hands on my hips gave. A flush of warmth spreads between my legs, and I shift again, my scent blooming around me.

"How long is the drug supposed to suppress my heat for?" I ask.

"Doctor said you should be good for a few days at least," Felix replies. He sucks his lip ring in and ruffles his hair as he looks away. "But your next one will be stronger. You'll need an alpha to ease it." His cheeks pink, and the other two avoid looking at me.

I lick my lips. "Will we be done with the mission by then? I can visit a center, sign up for—"

I don't get the words out of my mouth before Austin is in my face, gripping my shoulders. His face is like stone as he lowers it to mine, pinning me with his fierce gaze. "I don't want to hear those words come out of your mouth. You are not signing up for some random alpha to ease your heat. End. Of. Story."

I shake my head to clear it. He just barked at me as if he had a right, and the omega in me wanted to roll over and give him my belly. What the fuck?

Closing the space between us, I breathe him in, the sharp bite of his anger filling my nose like a late fall storm with a touch of winter infused. "You don't own me."

He smiles, a cruel smile, one that makes my heart race in my chest like a thousand horses running from a fire.

"Say that again," he breathes, danger infusing each syllable. The puff of air from his words gives me another hit of his anger, and it is almost as intoxicating as his normal scent.

"You. Don't. Own. Me." One word at a time. Clipped. Fuck him. Or maybe fuck me? Damn.

"That is where you'd be wrong, princess."

"How about we deal with that when the time comes?" Dean pops to his feet and tugs at Austin's sleeve. I'm sure he won't back down, and then he does. He steps back, and Dean blocks my view of him with his large linebacker shoulders. "I think you need to go work out some of that aggression."

A growl rumbles in Austin's chest, vibrating straight to my clit. Are they really sure the drug worked? Because I am needy as fuck. And some of his promised spankings sound fantastic right now.

"Come on, Aud, let me get you something to eat," Felix says. He moves me away from the pair like they face off all the time and settles me onto the stool at the island before he pulls items from the fridge. "You had my grilled cheese already, so what about some tacos? It is Tuesday somewhere, right?"

I laugh. "Uh, no, it isn't."

"Right, yeah, that doesn't work, does it? Because then it would mean that it would have to be Monday or Wednesday here and only at certain times." He chuckles. I try to ignore the alphas in the room and focus on him as he pulls out a pan. "I think I'm going to make brownies too. I really have a craving for them for some reason."

A blush blooms on my cheeks. I know I do, because the

sparkle in his eyes tells me that is what he is aiming for. Dean joins us in the open kitchen as Austin stomps across the room and out the door.

"He is going to work off his aggression."

Jealousy pierces me as I imagine him working it out with a random girl. I want to wear his hand necklace, and the idea of someone else getting that pleasure makes me feral. I grip the counter in front of me, attempting to keep it under wraps, but even I can smell the bitter bite of jealousy as it rolls off of me.

"At the rooftop gym, there is a punching bag he's friendly with," Dean says.

"I didn't–"

"You didn't have to," he replies. "Audrey, you have to know something. I might have the nickname of Saint because I choose the right path most of the time, but if you ever spread your legs and offer yourself up like you did this morning again… I won't resist."

My breath catches in my throat, and I blink, his words sinking in.

"I resisted this morning because I hadn't made that clear before. So if you don't want that, keep your door locked, especially when you feel a heat coming on."

"Or maybe you could not come in if the door is closed?" I suggest.

"She has a point, *Saint*." Felix looks up from chopping up a tomato and winks at me.

CHAPTER 20

Austin

SWEAT DRIPS from my brow as I land another blow to the punching bag. Images of Audrey spread out before me play in my head like some sort of carousel I can't get off. Her mouthwatering delicious brownie scent clings to me.

If I am not absolutely wrecked when I go back to the apartment, I will do something I'll regret. *No omegas*. It's a rule. One I plan to keep. Even if I can barely remember the face of the one that made me put it into place. No, each time I try to bring it to mind, I see Audrey's wide innocent eyes and her defiant pouty lips.

Fuck.

I slam my fist into the bag; my knuckles split under the force, but I keep going.

It isn't until I'm hanging on the bag to keep myself upright that I stop. I push back to my feet and wobble on exhausted legs.

Perfect.

Rut avoided.

The other people working out ignore me as I swipe my

face with a towel and head out. Even my sweat smells like spice and fallen leaves. I haven't had a rut hit me so hard in my life. It is the omega. There is something about her scent. It feels like she belongs to me. Like she is mine.

I shake off the feeling as the elevator closes to travel a single floor because my legs will not carry me down a flight of stairs. The apartment is silent when I enter. No cozy scene of Audrey and Felix playing a game in the living room. Or cooking in the kitchen.

Just *silent*.

It works for me.

Sinking into the armchair, I stare out at the night sky. A whole day has passed. I'm not even sure how. The clock on the wall reads just after nine.

It should make me anxious that someone else will get to the painting first. Losing a day of planning to the haze of rutting was not in the plan. And we would have lost more than that if we hadn't called the doctor.

That is possibly what haunts me the most. I could have given in, and no one, including Audrey, would have blamed me once the heat was over. Hell, she may have even thanked me. But I would have known that there was that moment of choice, that sliver of ability to walk away. Even knowing what she tastes like, I did it, and my dick had reminded me of that fact all day long.

I'm not sure how long I stare out the window. The soft snick of a door unlocking and opening comes from the hall-way. Still, I keep my eyes on the bridge, sparkling with lights in the distance. Her brownie and ice cream scent washes over me, and I can feel her eyes on me like a physical touch.

"Your hands," she gasps.

"Are fine." I curl my sore fingers in, cracking the dried blood where it started to form a scab. I should have taped them, but I was too far gone. Over this girl.

I *feel* her putting space between us. I don't even have to look to know that she's moved to the kitchen. Water running tells me I'm right. Then she is back. Standing in front of me in that damn ratty hoodie and a pair of leggings that draws my attention to her legs. She drops to her knees and reaches for my clenched fist. I pull back, and she gives me an irritated look.

"Let me," she commands. A bit of her own growl infuses her words, making her seem like an angry kitten.

When she reaches for my hand again, I let her. The soft touch of her fingers on my skin sends an electric current straight through me. She brushes the wet paper towel over the wounds, removing the excess dried blood before drying it with a different one. I watch her through hooded lids. *She is perfect.*

Her lips part as she works, her full attention on making sure I didn't damage more than the few split knuckles. A purr works its way through my chest. Is this what it's like having an omega take care of you? It isn't normal. Alphas take care of omegas, that is how it is supposed to be.

But here she is, looking like a fucking angel on her knees between mine, and she is making sure I'm okay.

Something snaps inside my chest. Fuck the contract. This woman is mine. She doesn't know it yet, but nothing will take her from me.

"Why are you looking at me like that?" She gazes up at me, her cheeks pink, perfume blooming.

I swipe my tongue over my lower lip, attempting to taste her from the air alone. "You look good on your knees."

She rolls her eyes and moves to push to her feet. But I'm faster. My hand shoots out and wraps around the back of her neck, holding her in place. I run my thumb over her pulse point, the rapid pace of her blood flowing and the excited scent of brownies and sugary sweet frosting washes over me.

Her eyes dilate as she brings them to mine. And ever so slowly, I move my hand from the back of her neck, stroking the pad of my thumb over her parted lips. I'm pretty sure her tongue peeks out to taste my skin. In a fluid motion, I tug her up to me, not standing but up, the type of encouragement that can be ignored, but she is up on her knees fully between my legs when I lower my face to hers, capturing her lips in a heated kiss.

She lets out a soft breath against my mouth, and I slide my tongue down the line of her perfect lips. This time, when she darts out to taste me, I deepen the kiss with a possessive rumble. She submits, and something grows in my chest. A need so strong, it almost knocks me over.

I thread my fingers into the hair at the base of her scalp and tilt her head for better access. She tastes like sugar, a pure shot straight into my bloodstream. I feel high on her. Drawing her even closer, I tug her into my lap. She straddles me, pressing her warm core against my straining length.

The excuse that she is in a heat will not work for either of us now. Yesterday, I could blame our play at the office for it coming on. But now, with it temporarily suppressed, we are solely attracted to each other, with no hormones trying to deceive us. It makes it sweeter.

I'm flying.

Floating with the clouds. Drunk on her kisses.

She is purer than any bourbon I could drink, the same drunken effect, loosening my muscles and lowering my inhibitions. Exploring her body with my free hand, I flex my fingers into her hip, asking for her to move. Some sort of friction.

When she rubs against me, a half growl, half purr rumbles from my throat. I arch into her, wishing our clothes weren't a barrier.

"That's it, princess, show me what you want." I press kisses along her throat. Following the goosebumps exploding beneath my lips.

I wrap my fingers around the base of her hoodie and lift it up and over her head. She lets me, and I'm greeted with her bare chest, nipples fully erect. With a groan, I lower my head and capture a tight peak between my lips. Her soft moans encourage me as she rocks into my lap.

"Austin, I'm going to come."

Her pace picks up, and I suck harder, rolling her other nipple between thumb and forefinger. When she shudders in my arms, her head dropping back, a whimper of pleasure falling from her pink lips, I know she has reached her climax. Our pheromones mix, creating the perfect home for the holiday's smell. And that is what it feels like, having her in my arms, like I'm home.

Sure, I'm throbbing in my pants, straining for my release, but as she draped herself across my chest, all I want to do is wrap her up and carry her to my bed for the night. Even if I only hold her. My dick pulses, not liking that idea, but it is true.

But before I can act on any of it, she is out of my arms, on her feet, and tugging her hoodie back over her head as if nothing world-shattering just occurred.

She tugs her fingers through her hair and looks out the window. Her throat works a swallow down her throat. She doesn't look at me.

"Thanks for the, uh, orgasm."

I hate it.

My inner caveman wants to throw her over my shoulder and carry her to my bed where she belongs. The more rational part cautions me that the hellcat standing in front of me wouldn't take that well. She isn't like other omegas using a fake personality to draw an alpha in, attempting to trap them in her web.

"It's not in the contract."

CHAPTER 21

Audrey

"IT'S NOT IN THE CONTRACT."

The words somehow pierce my heart. Which is stupid. I just threw myself into the lap of the man who displayed so much restraint that he wouldn't kiss me when I was laid out in front of him like a dessert after Sunday dinner. Of course, he would think of this as transactional. He is a businessman with a dark past.

I bite the inside of my cheek to keep in my cutting response that would give away too much of my true feelings. Next time I get thirsty in the middle of the night, I'll get some water from my bathroom's faucet rather than repeat this, whatever it fucking is.

Bringing my gaze back to him, my eyes drop to his very obvious problem, and my pussy clenches around nothing. Of course, the hussy would want his knot. Greedy little bitch can't be satisfied with a mind-blowing orgasm that was created by literally dry humping and his mouth on my tits. I almost snort, holding in the hysterical laughter.

I lick my lips, my face probably glowing from the heat

that is rushing to my cheeks. I'm really going to offer to get him off. It's only right. One orgasm for another. It has nothing to do with the fact I want to see him. If the length and width look impressive trapped in his sweats, I can only imagine what it would be free.

"I could," I say, gesturing at his issue.

He blinks, his palm cupping his cock through the fabric, then he shakes his head.

No.

He said no to a blow job.

I pull in a shallow breath, attempting not to drag more of his insanely appealing scent into my lungs. If I do, there is no telling what I'd do. Drop to my knees and pitifully beg for a taste? Nothing says needy bitch like begging. Or maybe climb back into his lap and ride out another orgasm?

Pushing my hand through my hair, I press my lips tightly together and give a nod. Then I practically run back to my room. Locking it behind me, if I could set it to unlock at a certain time, I would, just to keep myself in the damn room. His pheromones cling to me, and I shed my clothes as I head for my third shower of the last twenty-four hours.

WHEN MORNING ARRIVES, I groan and bury my head beneath my pillows, blocking out the happy music coming from the other side of the door and the blinding sunlight. I slept late apparently. After a moment, I sniff my wrists and armpits. At least I am not perfuming now.

Putting off getting out of bed for as long as my growling stomach and full bladder will allow, I kick off my blankets and climb out of my bed and makeshift nest. Then pad over to the bathroom and take care of the morning routine of using the toilet, washing my face, and brushing my teeth. If I had some descenting lotion, I would use that, too, just for good measure.

Moving the purchase of the lotion to the top of my list, I go into my closet and grab new underwear and leggings before coming out and grabbing my hoodie from the floor where I had left it. I pull it over my head and freeze. Late fall nights sitting in front of the fire wash over me with Austin's scent that is clinging to my hoodie.

I rip it from my head like it burns and suck in a fresh breath to clear my senses. The fact that I want to pick the sweatshirt up off the floor where I threw it and bury my head into his scent is crazy. Still, I scoop the hoodie up and fold it while holding my breath, placing it on my bed. I should wash it. But something holds me back from throwing it in my hamper.

Going back into the closet, I eye the section of shirts on hangers. A black hoodie I don't remember from the first day hangs at the very end, and I tug it out of the place it is stuffed and hold it up. It looks almost exactly like the old one I just folded up. Same size, same brand, and super soft. I absently run my fingers along the velvety soft interior as I decide to put it on.

It is the same comfort as my old one, and the fact that someone obviously tailored it to be the same made my heart thump painfully in my chest. Had Austin done something so thoughtful?

As I curl my fingers into the sleeves out of habit, my thumb pokes through pre-made holes. *It has thumb holes!* Pure joy at that simple fact spreads through me. It is small and insignificant, but he noticed my habit and made sure the shirt accommodated that.

We are not falling for the dominant alpha. We are not falling for the dominant alpha. It is my new mantra as I head for the bedroom door.

The music is vibrating the hanging lights over the kitchen island as Felix bounces around, dancing to his own beat. It brings a smile to my face. He doesn't see me. The rest of the area is empty, so it looks like he is my babysitter for the day.

His hair is now a bright blue, and I'm not sure when he dyed it. The sides are newly shaven too. I glance at the clock, and my eyes widen. Eleven? I slept that late? He could have done all that and gotten back this morning.

He startles when his eyes land on me before a smile spreads over his lips. Then he is bounding over to me like an excited puppy and drags me into his happy dance. I laugh and let him. Some kind of tension leaves my shoulders.

After last night and offering *more* to Austin before being rejected, I wasn't sure I could show my face again.

"Did you sleep well?" he asks over the music.

"Like a rock."

I smile as I bounce around with him. Our hands intertwine, and our bodies bump every once in a while. It is at that moment I realize I didn't flinch when he came at me, or when he touched me. And even now, with our fingers tangled, I don't feel like I need to escape. Unexplained moisture gathers in the corners of my eyes, threatening to make a river down my face.

Maybe my mantra for not falling for the dominant alpha needs to expand to include the other two, because my heart is in danger.

The second song ends, giving a lull to the happy beats. And if he sees the emotion gathered at the corners of my eyes, he says nothing. Instead, he releases my hands, and my fingers curl in with the loss of his touch before he lowers the music.

"You must be hungry," he says as he opens the refrigerator door and peers inside.

"Starving," I admit. My stomach loudly agreed with my words.

He sighs and shuts the door. "Not much breakfast food. Want to go out?"

The last time I was out for brunch, there were cameras. I wince.

"Nothing fancy. And the paparazzi don't care about me, so they will follow the other two around, hoping for the perfect shot."

And he read me like a book. How did he do that?

"Okay," I agree.

In less than a minute, we had our shoes on and were in the elevator, riding it down to the main floor. It stops and when the doors slide open, the dismissive omega from the sanctuary on the first day steps inside. She eyes me like I'm gum on the bottom of her shoe before her gaze catches on Felix, and she preens, like a bird attempting to get the attention of a mate.

"Felix," she purrs. "How have you been? How are your alphas?"

When I tense, he steps closer to me and drapes his arm around my shoulders in a familiar way that says, *this woman is important*, without needing to say a word.

"We've been good. Happy now that we have our omega." He gives me a blinding smile, and *I* almost believe his words, and I know the truth.

She deflates, her eyes flicking over me, assessing me all over again, but this time like a threat.

Fucking great. A jealous omega.

"Omega? Wow. How–When did that happen?" Her voice is sugary sweet, but not the good kind, and her perfume smells like radioactive acid.

My nose crinkles at the stench, and I tuck myself further under Felix's arm. At least he smells good. Angling my head into his chest, I breathe him in. Full-on nuzzling him in public.

"I had the pleasure of showing her and her brother their new apartment. I was captivated from the first moment I laid eyes on her. Who wouldn't be? She is beautiful. And smells fucking amazing. I've always been a sucker for the omegas that smell like something I could eat. I'm not into that flowery scent." He presses his face into my hair and inhales deeply, as if he can't get enough.

I hold back a smile as her scent sours more, smelling like day-old funeral home flowers. Felix knew what he was doing because she sniffed and leaned against the far wall, her arms crossed for the rest of the ride.

When the doors slide open, the omega almost rips off the iron gate blocking the exit out of the way, and then she is gone. I laugh and attempt to pull away from Felix. But he tightens his arm around me.

"I enjoy having you in my arms," he whispers.

Then, with his arm wrapped around me, he leads us across the lobby, oblivious to the stares we are gathering, and out on the thankfully empty street.

"Want me to call a car or are you good with walking a couple blocks?"

"Let's walk." I didn't need to say more before he calls a goodbye to the doorman and guides me down the sidewalk.

We walk in silence, our hips bumping comfortably, and me soaking up his warmth and fresh ocean breeze smell. Which I've decided is entirely him, not some body wash he picked up. And it is almost stronger today, like he is musking. Betas don't musk, so that isn't possible and is entirely in my head. Still, I inhale, enjoying it.

He navigates the streets like a pro, and before long, we are standing outside the Coney Island that led me and Sin to the apartment. He holds the door for me. The jingling bell announces our arrival, and the same waitress from before smiles and calls out a greeting as we seat ourselves like the sign says to do.

Felix hands me one menu from the napkin holder, and I open it even though I'm sure I'm getting strawberry topped waffles and bacon. My stomach rumbles loudly at all the food smells, and he chuckles, looking at me over the menu.

"Sounds like you are starving. Order whatever you want," he says.

The fact that I've had more food in the last few days than the previous two months combined means I could survive longer without eating. But I am not looking a gift horse in the mouth, and I'll eat as much as they let me while I'm working for them. Like a squirrel getting ready for the winter, I'm planning on putting on some weight.

Closing the menu, I grin. When the waitress comes over, he greets her by name, like Vinny had. She fusses over him like he is her kid, before she turns her smile on me.

"What can I get you? Some of those waffles you had last time?" Her pen hovers over her notepad as my mouth falls open.

"You remember me?"

She waves her hand. "I remember all the good tippers." She winks. "Now, what can I bring you?"

Ordering, I splurge and order the waffles with bacon and a western omelet with toast. Felix has the widest most cat that caught the canary smile on his face that I flush, which makes him grin wider.

When she turns to him, he orders enough to feed an army of alphas. Once she walks away, I eye him. "You are going to eat all that?"

"Maybe. But maybe I just got it so I can feed you."

I laugh. "If I ate that much, I would burst."

He shrugs. "I ordered all my favorites, sometimes I can't decide."

CHAPTER 22

Felix

AUDREY'S little moans of pleasure do things to me, things that I'm glad are hidden by the table between us. Still, I encourage her to take another bite of the biscuits and gravy on the tip of my fork. Feeding her is a physical need. Something feels like it is shifting inside of me. I am not sure what it is, but it feels big.

All the changes have roots with the omega across from me.

She takes the bite and falls back against her seat with a groan, holding her stomach.

"Mercy," she cries. "I'm stuffed. If I eat another thing, you are going to have to roll me out of here like Violet from *Willy Wonka and the Chocolate Factory*."

I snort. "I doubt you are going to blow up like a blueberry."

Her eyes light up when I catch the reference. "You never know. My life is already a lot like *Pretty Woman*, only I wasn't a prostitute when you guys found me. What is one more movie?"

"You really like your movie references," I say.

"I like TV, but yeah, old movies were something I would do with my mom and Sin." Her smile turns a little sad, some of the sparkle leaving her eyes.

"I didn't mean to bring up something that drags up sad memories." I shift in my booth.

I knew what it was like to have memories that brought emotions and regret with them. If only I could have been what my parents wanted. Forcing a smile, I say, "Have you seen the TV that comes down from the ceiling at the apartment? It is huge. We could watch some old movies today."

She bites down on her lower lip, looking adorable as she holds back a full-blown smile. "That sounds amazing."

I pull out my wallet and lay down two one-hundred-dollar bills on the table before sliding out of the booth. "See you next time, Margaret!" I call to the waitress.

"Be good, Felix," she replies with a wave.

I hold my hand out to Audrey, and she barely hesitates before placing her palm on mine. "No promises."

Audrey laughs, her cheeks pinking again. I sniff her hair as she turns toward the door. She is the first omega that I could smell like this. Even though I am stuffed, she smells good enough to eat.

We walk down the street, the foot traffic picking up with lunch time arriving. Our pace picks up without an audible decision to move faster. And we are almost back at the apartment building when a familiar voice calls out.

"Flea, where are your alphas?" Her silky voice drapes over me like an unwanted blanket, and I shrug as I turn toward Melody. "Sorry, Fe-lix," she draws out my name, a cat-like smile playing on her lips.

"They are busy."

Her eyes drop to my hand, still holding Audrey's, curiosity brightening her gaze. "Who is this?" She shifts her attention to Audrey.

"A friend." I try to tug her behind me, but she doesn't budge as she sizes up the alpha.

"You smell divine, dear," Melody says with a sniff of the air. "But also as if you've been rolling around on Austin and Saint's beds. Are you the omega the papers are raving about?"

I suck in a breath, my fingers tightening on Audrey's. "I'm pretty sure that isn't your business."

She laughs as if I give her endless amusement. The wind changes, blowing the scent of lilacs directly at us. "When will you understand everything is my business? Besides, I don't need an answer. I can smell the three of you all over her. Dear, if you need rescuing, my name is Melody Lynn. You can find me on the 20th floor of the Empire State Building."

We are silent as she passes us in a whirlwind. I'm not sure Audrey breathes again until she is gone. "I've never smelled an alpha that smells so–floral."

"It is probably a masking scent. Because I could smell it too."

Her nose crinkles as she looks at me. "No, that was definitely all her."

There is no way it was her, but it isn't worth even talking about. Melody Lynn is the last person on this planet that I'd want to talk about, well maybe not the last person because the chief of police takes that spot.

***

THE *BREAKFAST CLUB* ENDS, the credits rolling. The living room is as dark as night with the shades down and the TV blocking most of the large floor to ceiling windows. I glance over at Audrey, and she wipes a tear from her cheek and grips one of the ten pillows she pulled from her room.

"Do you think John and Claire end up together? They

come from such different backgrounds, it almost feels hopeless. You know?"

"They definitely do," I say. "You want popcorn and we can watch another one?"

"Yes to the popcorn, but..." she pauses. "Can we watch *Omega in Paradise*? There are two new episodes, and I haven't watched them yet."

I stand up, a smile tugging at my lips. "I didn't peg you as the type to watch that show."

She shrugs and tugs her blanket higher on her lap. "Guilty pleasure. It is just such an unattainable fantasy, and I'm sure it is all scripted and fake. Or those girls don't know what they are actually getting into. But for the entertainment factor alone."

I hold up my hands in the universal sign of surrender, but I can't help the grin that tugs at my lips. "Not judging."

"Shut up. Where's my popcorn?"

I laugh. "Bossy."

"Austin says bratty," she quips.

Tossing the popcorn bag in the microwave, I lean against the counter as she twists on the couch to look at me. "They are sort of the same thing. Two sides of the same coin."

"Well, when you grow up spoiled, I guess that is the byproduct. You know what you want and mostly how to get it."

"What happened?" I ask before I can stop myself. "I mean, you were living on the streets and stealing to eat before you came here. Again, not judging. I was doing the same when Austin dragged me out of the gutter."

She swallows and smiles sadly. "People that my dad trusted, they weren't very trustworthy and they–uh–they–" She wets her lips and blinks rapidly. "They killed them. My parents. And then they came after Sin and me. We survived, but we have to stay low. If they ever find us–" A shiver wracks her tiny body, and she clutches her pillow closer. "We would be dead too."

The microwave beeps, announcing that the popcorn is done, but I can't tear my eyes away from Audrey. No wonder she didn't want her picture taken. She'd been a mess the morning we had brunch, and the paparazzi were outside.

"We will protect you," I promise. Because even if Austin and Saint don't, I will. No one will hurt her or her brother ever again. The need to wrap her up and keep her safe builds inside of me like a hurricane, gathering strength the longer it brews.

Ocean breeze envelopes me, blocking out the buttery popcorn. I inhale, sniffing myself. What the fuck? I smell like the fucking ocean. Salty and fresh.

Audrey tilts her head and studies me. "Felix, you're musking."

Musking? Only alphas do that. It wasn't possible. I'm a beta.

I chuckle and reach for the popcorn. Taking down a bowl, I pour the bag into the container. "That isn't a thing."

Turning back to the couch, I almost drop the bowl when I find her standing right behind me.

She leans in and sniffs deeply. "It is now."

When she inhales again, I can't help but draw in her perfect sweet cocoa scent. It is so strong I want to roll around in it. My body feels as if I've stuck my finger in an electric socket after ensuring it was wet. A wildfire courses through my veins, the blood raging like an out-of-control forest fire. My jeans tighten over my growing problem, and I shift on my heels, attempting to put some space between us.

"You smelled amazing before, and now this is. Wow." She closes her eyes, breathing me in, and every fiber of my being *loves* the attention. I *crave* the attention.

Then I feel it. My breath catches, then becomes ragged. It

isn't like I can whip my dick out right here and see if what I'm feeling is my imagination or not.

"I–" I drop the bowl on the kitchen island and bolt past her before I gather her into my arms and kiss her until she wants me to stop. "I'll be right back. Get the show started. I'll join you in a minute." I shut the bathroom door between us. Looking down at the bulge in my jeans, I hesitate. Tugging my lip ring between my teeth, I pop the button and slide my zipper down. Releasing some of the tension on my dick.

I snake my fingers beneath my briefs and down my shaft, and my heart stops. I'm pretty sure I've died. A knot. I have a mother-fucking knot, like I'm some alpha or something. And the musk is rolling off me in waves, the storm building inside me and crashing into my very soul. It isn't possible. I'm beta. I know I am. Unless–No, that's rare, almost an urban legend.

Shoving my jeans down to my knees, I push my briefs out of the way, seeing with my own eyes what I felt. My cock is throbbing, a knot forming at the base, pre-cum leaking to the floor in a larger quantity than I've ever seen coming from my body.

Fuck.

I can't deny the proof of my body. The knot tells me every-thing I need to know, I'm a sigma, a switch–I am all three designations. *Holy shit. I'm a fucking unicorn.*

I lean against the door. The driving urge to shed my clothes and strut back out into the living room is insane. The need to *claim* the omega that is *mine* rides me hard. Her scent clings to my clothes, and I lift my shirt to my nose and inhale. Then I do the only thing that is sane, and I grip my cock and stroke while breathing her in.

My pace quickens as I smother myself with my shirt. I squeeze my knot and roll my palm over my head, lubricating my hand as if it is enveloped inside of her. Closing my eyes and imagining her mouth on me.

When I shoot my load, ropes and ropes of cum fly across the bathroom, hitting the glass shower door and sliding down the surface as I catch my breath. Still, I'm hard. I don't know what to do. Kicking off my pants and toeing off my socks, I tug my shirt off and turn on the shower. Cold water sprays from the showerhead, and I step under the frigid temperature, hoping to shock my body out of this driving lust that has taken over.

I stiffen even more, half growling, half groaning as the water flows over my heated skin. It is too much to bear, and I stroke another one out. Even more cum shoots from me this time. I'm like a fucking machine or the energizer bunny, I just keep going and going.

Eventually, I'm able to dry off and put my clothes back on. Sans briefs because I can't bring myself to put them back on. I duck out of the bathroom, my shirt in my hand, briefs hidden in the balled up material. Audrey glances over, her eyebrows lifting in a question she doesn't voice, and I head to my room without a word and toss the shirt and underwear into the hamper before grabbing a fresh shirt and joining her again.

"What did I miss?" I ask, dropping onto the sofa next to her. Closer than I had been earlier. Was that an alpha instinct?

She sucks her lower lip between her teeth, and I track the movement. My fucking dick twitching in my jeans. Down boy, you've just had like four orgasms. He isn't convinced, and I can feel blood pumping to him as he wakes up. I grab a throw pillow and shove it in my lap.

"Everything okay? You were in the bathroom a long time."

"Breakfast, not settling," I say. Grimacing, I look away from her. Sure, tell the beautiful omega that you were shitting in the bathroom for that long. That is so attractive, I'm sure.

"I can start the episode over," she says, drawing my attention back to her. Her hand is wrapped around the controller, exactly how I'd like to see it wrapped around–*No. No. No. We are not going there. Get your fucking head on straight.*

"No, it's good."

She smiles and looks back at the screen. "Trisha is the front runner. But I also think that Felicia has a chance. The pack seems to like her. Grace is so elegant though, she would make a great match. And this episode is the start of the one-on-one dates. They are the best part. Each guy picks a girl and takes them on a date to some exotic location, then the pack comes back together and compares notes."

I watch her, not the screen. I'm transfixed. The way her eyes light up as she watches the story play out. The way a soft, wistful smile plays on her lips as the helicopter takes off to whisk one pair away on one of their dates. We have a plane. I could take her on a dream date and see that look on her face again.

The plans unfold as the episode ends. And I know exactly what I need to do to make it happen.

CHAPTER 23

Audrey

HOW CAN you unhear someone *pleasing* themselves? Because I need to do it, stat. Instead, I'm over here making stupid conversation about *Omega in Paradise* like I was watching it and not giving the bathroom my full attention.

My hands are clammy, the blood pumping through my body gives my clit special attention, and I'm not even sure what Trisha is saying on the large screen. There is something about his scent, even now, that makes me want to climb into his lap and nuzzle his neck.

He shifts beside me, the pillow in his lap. Not that I look directly at him, but I can feel his eyes on me. Sure, the dream dates are my favorite part of the show, and I can't help but imagine one like it, especially in an apartment like this. But that will never happen. I'm here for business, not pleasure.

Inhaling, I catch a whiff of his musk. The things it does to my body feel off. He doesn't *feel* like a beta anymore. Something shifted. Either that or my omega self has decided it doesn't care if he can knot me or not, because the slick that is gathering between my legs should be illegal when I'm not in a heat.

My skin flushes at his continued attention, and my perfume is making itself known. Well, it would be if he was an alpha. It smells as if I opened a bakery, and the only thing I make is brownies.

Space, I need space. As the forced commercial plays, I practically leap from the couch and put much needed space between us. Maybe some fresh popcorn will drown out the scent.

Taking the box, I prep a fresh bag and toss it in the microwave. I attempt to get my perfume under control as I tap the counter, waiting for the time to tick down.

"You okay?" Felix asks, and even his voice has me wanting to turn into a puddle.

Before he had an impact on my hormones, but now it feels as if he has tuned into my exact frequency with every single breath he takes.

"Yeah, fine–" I pull the steaming bag from the microwave and pour the popped kernels into the bowl. "I just–" A yelp explodes from my throat when I turn to find him closer than expected. "Jesus, you scared the crap out of me."

The corner of his mouth kicks up in a half smile. He drops his eyes to the bowl, but it feels like he's checking me out as he does it. Then he reaches over and takes a piece of popcorn and pops it into his mouth.

"Sorry, want a water or soda? Beer?" he asks as he passes me and opens the fridge.

"Not really a day drinker, so water is fine."

"Austin would be disappointed." He reappears with two bottles of water, and I head back to the couch.

He sits back down beside me, and I swear there is the clear outline of his dick running down his leg. Either that or he has a really large cucumber stuffed in his pants. I can not tug my eyes away, even as *Omega in Paradise* plays on the TV.

And he doesn't hide it. He sucks his lip ring into his

mouth as he watches me watch him. The air is so thick with tension it feels like we could slice through it with a knife.

I'm not sure who moves first.

Does it matter? No.

Because the end goal is the same, his lips on mine. I whimper. Seriously fucking *whimper* as his tongue slides over my lips, asking to stroke inside. Parting my lips with a soft breath, his rumble of approval has my nipples pebbling as it vibrates through his chest to mine.

I've been so on edge the last few days that I dive headfirst into whatever this is. Because a beta isn't dangerous. They can't trap you. Not the same way an alpha can.

"You taste fucking divine, Audrey. Shit, I will never get enough," he murmurs against my lips. "Austin is going to need to fix his fucking contract."

Austin? What does he have to do with this? It takes a minute to sink in. His lips drag more tiny moans from me. I'd be embarrassed if I wasn't so into it. His mouth searing my neck as he runs his tongue over my pulse point.

"Your name wasn't in the contract," I gasp. Was that a loophole? His teeth graze the base of my neck, and I arch into him. *More of that, please.*

I clench around nothing, needing to be filled up. It has been a long time. All my choice, but I was ready, and I am taking that step with Felix, the flirty, harmless beta.

My fingers work the button on his jeans as I swing my leg over him, straddling him as I free him. His length is hot against my ass, the fabric between us a thin barrier.

"I need you, Felix." The words come out pleading as I rock against him and lower his zipper at the same time. He's bare beneath, and the electricity of my skin against his has me breathless.

"I'm yours." He burns a path along my neck, up to just below my earlobe. His breaths are ragged. His musk, because it is musk and not body wash, makes me feel like I'm about to have sex on a sunny beach rather than a sofa in a highrise apartment building in the middle of New York City.

My fingers wrap around him and tug him free, as his lips claim mine in a soul deep kiss. He is the perfect girth, the tips of my fingers brush as I stroke him. My thumb rubs over his slit, gathering the moisture and working it over him. Rubbing my hand all the way down his shaft, I feel it, a growing knot. The breath stutters in my chest, and he continues to kiss me as I freeze.

Alpha.

Not a beta.

Abort.

One second, I'm kissing him, and the next, I'm scrambling across the floor like a crab on cocaine. I stare at him. At his dick, really. It is jutting straight up, ready to impale me, the knot as undeniable as the pre-cum leaking from the red, swollen head. I blink. Still, I can't tear my eyes away.

"You're an alpha," I say with a hard swallow. It is obvious. Why hide it? "Is it a game? Pretending to be a beta? Have you been using descenter?"

Anger burns a line straight through my haze of lust. The fire it ignites in me should scare him. But he only stares at me helplessly.

"Audrey–"

No.

No. No. No.

I clamber to my feet, putting more distance between us.

"I didn't know." His voice sounds broken, but alphas, they lie to get what they want. "I think I'm a sigma."

My heart pounds in my chest. "You didn't know?" I laugh. Right.

"I swear, it happened today," he says.

His mouth works around more words that don't come

out. I can't have this conversation, especially with his dick just standing at attention like I'm going to submit any second and sink down on him, giving him a velvety hug. My traitor of a pussy pulses at the thought.

I snort. "What did you think this would accomplish? Bite me? Mark me, so I'm more compliant? I already said I would do the fucking job. I signed the contract. I know what is at stake. Was this all part of the ruse? Send the beta to show us the apartment, have him flirt and unarm me, make me think he's harmless, then seduce me."

"You kissed me," he sputters. "And I know you did way more with Austin in his fucking boardroom. Don't you think if that was the plan, he would have claimed you?"

He doesn't sound angry, more confused or hurt that I would say those things. My heart gives a pathetic pang as a just as pointless whine builds in my throat. If I could tear the omega from my soul, I would. I'd rather be anything but this mindless, wanton thing.

"No, because it would make the contract void. But you… you could." I'm backing away like he is going to pounce and hold me down to have his way with me. And the sad part is I would fight, but I'd enjoy every second. I am fucked up.

"Audrey, please, let's talk about this."

I shake my head. Five more steps. He shifts, watching me, finally covering his dick with a pillow. Four more steps. He inhales, probably dragging the bitter scent of my anger into his lungs. Three more steps. I see him move before he does, the tiniest way he leans forward. As he pushes to his feet, I turn and bolt into my room. Locking the door behind me and flipping on the security system he showed me.

"Audrey, open the door!" He knocks on the door, but it feels like he is pounding, as if he would break it down and claim me. "Open the door!"

Pressing my fingers to my lips, a soft whine escapes, and

the pounding stops. Footsteps retreat. Muffled swearing reaches me, and then a low conversation. He is probably telling Austin and Dean that it didn't work. I am never leaving this room again if they are here. They will have to drag me out.

CHAPTER 24
Dean

THE MEETING LASTED way too long. With a sigh of relief, I settle back into the plush leather of my BMW. The city passes by in a blur, the darkened windows barely held at bay, honking horns and random voices.

I miss the country.

Sending a quick text, I let Austin know I'm heading back to the office. Then my thoughts turn to Audrey. The omega that is quickly worming her way into our lives. Every single one of my instincts wants to make sure she is protected, and I know this plan to steal the painting back is anything but safe. It feels like angry bees are circling in my stomach, stinging me in an attempt to be released.

Austin is so set on the plan, he won't see reason. Our pack works because I allow him to lead us. But if I start challenging him, we'd fall apart at the seams, because if I know anything about Austin, it is that he can't handle not being in control. It is ironic that we came together with Felix in the first place because we never wanted an omega. Now here I am, unable to pull my thoughts from the one currently in my apartment.

I don't want to go back to the office. I want to be with Audrey. Insane? Probably. I've never claimed not to be. On the surface, I was a saint, but in the deep darkness that lives inside, I'm anything but that.

Would the omega run from me instead of cuddling my chest if she knows what kind of man I really am? Sure, I help the homeless and omegas that are in dangerous situations. I set them up with the least I can give them. But if they squander that kindness, they will find themselves right back where they started. I don't tolerate the ones that take advantage of what I offer.

Live rent and board free, find a job while you have a roof over your head and food coming in. Save enough money to get your own place and move out. Six months. It isn't unreasonable. Hell, it is beyond generous. But there are those that take advantage and expect the handouts to keep coming.

Hank is one of those men. I took him in because he was living on the streets in sub-zero temperatures. He's used the time in the tiny house to lounge around and be lazy. I should have kicked him out after the second month of no attempt at getting a job. Now I have to go through the fucking red tape of evicting him. Tying the place up for someone else that would actually do something with their lives.

Shaking myself out of the nightmare the single man is going to cause me, I stare sightlessly out at the city passing by. The need to pound my fists into someone builds inside of me.

While Austin made his money with the mafia and is attempting to make it all legal, I made mine in the fight rings. And I am itching to get into one. It is either fuck like I'm fighting, or actually fight, and since the only person I want to put my dick into is currently an omega I can't have, the fight rings it is.

Sure, I could go home and Felix would try to take care of

the need brewing inside of me, but since Audrey's heat, it is like the alpha inside of me only wants her. It is fucked up.

Although, now that I think about it, he hasn't come to Austin or me since she's moved in. Maybe he feels the same. I guess that is the good thing about our pack. We love each other, and the sex is a bonus if we feel the itch, but often we each search for that outside of our pack. It is a longstanding agreement. No hurt feelings.

The wrench in the whole thing is Audrey. Because I know we all want her. The whole *want what you can't have* syndrome, I assume.

The car pulls up in front of the office, and I climb out before Mark can come around and open the door for me. Long strides carry me into the building, past security, and into the elevators that will take me up to Austin's office. The pleasantries go in one ear and out the other. I am not in the mood for the boot kissing that the betas and omegas in the building do every time they see me.

"What's wrong?" Austin asks as soon as I step into his office. "You look like a storm is rolling in."

I tug my fingers through my hair and sigh. "I need to fight."

He gives me a sharp look. "If you want to beat someone, I have a guy I need taught a lesson."

"No, I need to *fight*."

"The last time you did, you ended up in the fucking hospital. Because you just kept going like you thought you were a force of nature, unstoppable and untamed. But just like a fucking hurricane, you lose power the longer you fight. If I knew it would be just one fight to get it out of your system, I'd say sure, but you don't stop."

"Austin, I don't need your permission." I pace the space in front of his desk. Already I can feel the tape on my knuckles, the flesh giving beneath my punches, sweat dripping down my back. I need it.

His jaw sets like he is going to fight me on this.

I hold up a hand. "Three fights, tops. Bring the girl, it will be a good show of her being in our pack. She can wear a mask like the other omegas that go. Pictures for the tabloids."

He narrows his eyes at me, but I know I have him. He wants to get in the newspapers. And the idea of fighting while her eyes are on my every move makes me hard with anticipation. I am so screwed.

"Fine, go home and let them know. Tell her to be ready by seven, or I'll help her get dressed."

I grin. "You'd like that."

He shrugs. "Possibly."

With a foreboding eagerness zipping through my veins, I call the car back around to take me home.

"Seven," Austin says just before the elevator doors shut between us.

A GROWL RUMBLES in my chest as I push open the apartment door. *Alpha.* In our space. All I can smell is their musk. I slam the door shut, making my presence known, and Felix shifts his eyes to me, like I am throwing a tantrum.

"Where are they?" I demand.

"Where is who?" he asks.

"The fucking alpha," I say. After scanning the open area, another thought occurs to me. "Where is Audrey?"

He releases his lip ring, his eyes shifting to her closed door. I'm across the space beating on her door before I can think better of it. If she is in there with another alpha, they are dead.

"She won't open the door."

"The fuck she won't. If she thinks she can sleep with another alpha in *our* home, she is going to learn that lesson today."

He sighs. "She isn't in there with another alpha."

That stops me. I turn slowly to look at him. He is standing now, looking nervous. In fact, I'm sure the musk I'm smelling is all over him. "I thought we had an agreement, no alphas in the apartment."

He shifts on his feet and swallows. He looks guilty.

"Felix–" I warn. I'm already on the edge. Almost all of my 'Saint' persona completely shed like a snake sheds its skin.

"Saint, it isn't–"

I'm across the space, in his face, breathing in the fucking ocean coming off of him in waves like he rolled around in the alpha's cum. He lets me grab onto him, his body going limp like a rag doll.

"It's me, Saint. It's *me!*" he says. "I'm the alpha you smell. I'm a fucking sigma, I switched."

I rake my gaze down his bare chest. He zipped his jeans but didn't button them. I don't know why he would lie, but it makes little sense. He was a beta this morning. People don't just change who they are, at least it isn't common. Sigmas are unusual.

"I think it is Audrey. Since she's arrived, I've felt different. Like something is waking up inside of me. Then this morning, I could smell her. Really smell her. And my body...it reacted. We, uh–"

"Jesus man, you didn't..."

"No," he says and swallows. "Well, almost, but she," he pauses and licks his lips. "She thinks we've been lying to her, using me to tie her to us. Austin didn't put my name in the contract as off limits. So now, she thinks it was on purpose so I could get close and claim her."

"Fuck." I really need to get in a fight ring. I have a lot to work out and three fights may not do it.

"Yeah." He looks at the shut door like a lost puppy.

"She's been in there since?"

He nods.

I rap on the door, calmer now. We need to hash this out. Let her know it wasn't some diabolical plan to trap her. Just the thought makes me feel sick.

"Audrey," I say softly. "Open the door. We need to talk."

No answer.

"Please open the door. I can override the system and use the key, but I don't want to do that."

The lock clicks, and if anger had a body, it would be wrapped up in her. Her eyes are like liquid fire when she pins them on me, setting my soul on fire with a single look. "What is the point of a security system to keep me safe if you can override it when you don't think I should be in here?"

"It was a bluff," I say, and she tries to slam the door in my face. But I'm faster. My foot jams in the door before she gets it shut. "But we need to talk."

"Your plan failed."

"Plan?" I chuckle. "You mean Felix attempting to do something Austin would castrate him for? He was definitely thinking with the wrong head, and I'm not sure him waking up a sigma would deter our fearless leader from the conse-quences."

She narrows her eyes at me and crosses her arms, releasing the door in the process. I nudge it open, so I can see her entire face. When she shifts, I smell Felix all over her. He wasn't lying when he said they almost did something. And she is right in thinking she would be claimed because a new alpha wouldn't be able to help themselves, even one that was a switch. But how do you tell an angry omega all of that without pissing her off more?

"I thought he was a beta with the rare ability to scent."

"He was a beta when I left this morning," I reply.

"I'm standing right here," Felix says.

She shifts her gaze to him and flushes. Perfume fills the space between us. Yeah, they were into something really deep, if even in her anger she was reacting. She moistens her lips and looks back at me.

"So, if it wasn't a plan to get me to do what you want, he just turned alpha?" She sounds as disbelieving as I feel.

"It has been known to happen. The sigma trait stays dormant until–" I clamp my mouth shut.

Nope. Not saying that out loud. *Until they match.* She is all of our scent matches if she is his. If she heard that, she would bolt, gone with the wind. And I'm not losing the only mate I would ever have. Fuck the no omega rule. We are keeping her.

"Until what?" She steps out of her room, and I want to capture her in my arms and hold her to my chest. A purr rumbles from me, and she tilts her head at me. "Dean? Until what?"

"Until they find their mate," Felix says, finishing my sentence while looking at Audrey like she hung the fucking moon.

She tenses but doesn't retreat. Then she forces a laugh. I know it is forced because it sounds brittle and breakable.

"That is not possible." She shakes her head, denying his words.

"Why?" he asks, stepping closer. "I've felt a connection to you from the start. Like a puzzle piece clicking into place. A part of my soul returned after a lifetime of loss. I finally felt whole. The world became vibrant, where it used to be gray and dark. You, Audrey, are my light. Another piece of me born into a different body. I know you feel it, too. I bet you feel that with each of us. We complete each other because we really are a pack. You are what was missing all along."

I've felt everything he is saying from the start. He's just the one to say it out loud and put a voice to it.

"No, I don't want a pack. Especially one with three alphas. Do you think I'm crazy?"

Her rejection spears straight through my chest, twisting something inside of me as if she shoved a knife in and twisted.

CHAPTER 25

Audrey

"THAT IS NOT POSSIBLE." My own words echo in my head like I'm in some sort of alternate reality. A pack? No. I can't. The need to flee hits me hard. If I could, I would run as fast and as far away as possible.

"Why?" Felix asks. He takes a hesitant step closer, and it takes everything in me not to bolt. "I've felt a connection to you from the start. Like a puzzle piece clicking into place. A part of my soul returned after a lifetime of loss. I finally felt whole. The world became vibrant, where it used to be gray and dark. You, Audrey, are my light. Another piece of me born into a different body. I know you feel it, too. I bet you feel that with each of us. We complete each other because we really are a pack. You are what was missing all along."

Shaking my head in denial of his words, I hug myself tighter. I can't rely on anyone but Sin. Only my brother truly has my back. Not these alphas with their pretty lies.

The fairy tale of love and happiness. Of a future where I never have to hurt again. That isn't life. That isn't real. It is as fake as a mirage of water on hot cement in the summer, always there just out of reach but disappearing when you go toward it.

"No, I don't want a pack. Especially one with three alphas. Do you think I'm crazy?" My perfume has a metallic scent, like metal melted in with the brownies. It turns my stomach.

My gaze shifts to Dean, and he looks pale, as if I physically hurt him with my words. As crazy as it sounds, I want to snatch them back from the air. I don't want to hurt any of them, because it feels a lot like hurting myself.

"We would never force our bite on you," Dean utters the words, and they sound hollow, like he is only a husk of himself.

"Good." I want to retreat into the room, but I don't. Instead, I face them both as if waiting for something else. To what? Tell me I'm wrong? Force me to submit? Is that what I want?

"Audrey, I know you feel it, too," Felix says. "You can't run from a match."

A shiver racks my body, and Dean steps forward to steady me, but I dodge his touch. "No."

"Felix, drop it. We will force nothing on her." Dean steps back, putting an ocean of space between us with the single movement. "Austin wants to take you out tonight. You can wear a mask to conceal your identity. He's requested you be ready by seven."

He didn't have to say *'or else'*. I knew Austin now, and he would get pleasure out of dressing me like a doll.

"Where are we going?" I'd need at least that information to be in the right clothing.

"A fight ring." He sounds dead inside, and it twists my heart in my chest the same as if he had reached inside and done it with his fingers.

"He agreed to that?" Felix turns wide eyes on Dean.

Without answering, Dean presses his lips into a tight line

and retreats to his room. Leaving me alone with Felix. Who hadn't tried to trap me after all. I curl my fingers into the sleeves of the hoodie as we stare silently at each other. Shifting my weight, I'm not sure what to say.

Felix toys with his eyebrow ring, while sucking his lip ring into his mouth. He doesn't look like I devastated him. He looks a lot like he is trying to figure out how to get me to see his point of view. I can see the wheels turning.

"I'll give you time to adjust. But once Austin realizes, all promises are off. He doesn't want an omega any more than you want three alphas, so at least you'll be on the same page of denial. But once he is all in, he will get what he wants." The way his voice lowers in promise sends a tendril of excitement straight to the pit of my stomach. Not that I want to be trapped, no that isn't it at all.

Instead of answering him, I hug myself and nibble on my lower lip. "I'm going to get ready."

He nods but doesn't move a muscle, so I back into my room and shut the door between us. I don't know if he stays outside the door, but I can almost feel his presence on the other side. Entering the walk-in closet, I eye the racks of clothing. It is probably more clothes than I had even when my parents were alive.

Designer jeans in the perfect size and in every shade imaginable line one full rack, and I tug a black pair off. I have a feeling that a fight ring isn't a cheerful place. Sin would love to go to one, but he'd want to be in the ring, not watching.

Completing the look with a soft navy t-shirt and another hoodie, I lift my shirt over my head. Getting a face full of Felix. After pulling my hair free, I press the old hoodie to my nose and inhale deeply. Just the smell of him fills me with warmth. I am so screwed.

There is something about his scent that calms me. And I am sure it is because he is a scent match. I'd pegged that as a fairy tale, only on *Omega in Paradise*, but the feelings swirling in my stomach don't feel like something that is fake.

Tossing the hoodie on top of the one that still smells like Austin, I hesitate before pulling that one out and sniffing it. The same calm when Austin's spicy fall scent hits me. Because insanity is obviously my middle name, I pick back up the Felix hoodie and shove my face into it, bringing Austin's hoodie to my nose at the same time.

My whole body tingles. Can you have an orgasm from smell alone? I am pretty sure if I had Dean's scent in here, too, I'd be in heaven. Since, apparently, I am embracing the crazy, I carry both hoodies back to my bed and put them on my pillows.

I can fantasize about each of them. It doesn't mean I have to accept their bite. Do I realize I am headed down a dangerous path? Yes. One-hundred percent. But this train car is out of control, and there is no stopping it now.

Once I change and apply new make-up, I am as ready as I'm going to be. Felix is on the sofa, staring out the darkening window. He has thankfully found a shirt. Instead of dropping next to him like I would have prior to what happened, I take up Dean's armchair. I know it is because it smells like him. Enveloping me in a hug that is a sharp bite of lemon, followed by the soft leather.

A sigh slips out as I curl up into the large chair, and Felix eyes me knowingly, but keeps his comments to himself. I wonder if he can tell I want to climb into his lap and nuzzle into his neck too. Stupid hormones.

At almost exactly seven, the door swings open, and Austin strides in. His suit jacket hangs open and his hair is slightly disheveled, as if he ran his fingers through it during the day, and sunglasses block his violet eyes. It is full on dark, and he has on sunglasses. I snort, and he pins me with a look.

"What are you wearing?" he barks.

I shift in the chair beneath his intense attention. "Jeans and a hoodie–" I say, trailing off as if it is a question instead of what I am actually wearing.

"You are not going to the club in that."

"Club?" I squeak. I thought we were going to an underground fight ring. Silly me.

"Did you tell her what to wear?" Austin turns to Felix, who shrugs. "And why does it smell like another alpha was here today?"

He slowly looks at me, as if I am the one that smuggled an alpha into his space. I lift my eyebrows, a little shocked neither Felix nor Dean spilled the beans.

"Felix is a sigma now," I say as I push to my feet. Dropping the bomb like I am a Night Witch bomber from World War II. While he is still absorbing that fact, I stroll over to my room, putting an extra sway in my hips, knowing they are both watching. "What should I put on?"

When Austin doesn't answer, still in shock obviously, Felix says, "Omega females wear slinky dresses. They are more arm candy than people."

That is how Austin wants me to dress? Like arm candy?

CHAPTER 26

Audrey

I **WANT** to say when I re-emerge fifteen minutes later in the shortest black dress possible, without flashing everyone my ass cheeks with each step, that a thrill doesn't shoot straight to my core at the three matching hungry looks on the guys' faces.

But I'd be lying.

Dean changed into a pair of gray sweats and a loose fitted t-shirt, while the other two are dressed as if they are attending a cocktail party. Actually, seeing Felix dressed earlier should have given me some sort of clue, but I was too in my head.

All three of them are eye candy regardless of what they wear, and I can't help but check them out. Austin looks like he stepped right out of *Omega in Paradise*, and he's ready to sweep me off my feet. While Felix is the bad boy that has tried to clean up, his piercings and hair are at odds with his expensive suit. And Dean, he is the furthest thing from a Saint in those gray sweats that make him look like he has a fucking baseball bat running down his leg. *That* has to be in my imagination. I tear my eyes back up and put them where they should be, on their faces.

Austin holds out a mask as I approach. There are silver beads that line the eye holes, embedded on a black velvet, with soft black feathers that come off the edges. Silk strings allow it to be tied at any tightness around my head. His expression doesn't look like he noticed my appraisal from a moment ago. Thank goodness for small blessings.

"Put it on before we leave. The paparazzi were downstairs when I came home."

At his soft words, I pause, my fingers curling over the mask, my heart rate spiking because he knows the cameras upset me, and he cares enough to protect me in his way. Is this what people were talking about when they would say that alphas expect the needs of their omega and meet them without being asked? It makes me nervous for reasons I would rather not examine.

After fumbling with the tie for a few seconds, Austin releases a heavy sigh and circles me, taking the ties from my fingers and deftly tying the mask securely. A shiver of awareness skates through me when he leans over my shoulder and inhales, his warm palm searing a hole right above the swell of my ass on my back.

"Is it too tight?" His soft question catches me off guard, and goosebumps explode along my arms. He trails two fingers along my skin over the gooseflesh. "Are you cold?"

I suppress a shudder as I shake my head, not trusting myself to speak. While Felix catches my gaze and tells me with his expression, he knows exactly what is wrong with me.

"I don't want to miss the first fight. Let's go," Dean says. He is still distant, broken.

"Wait, why aren't you in a suit?" I ask.

His jaw tenses, and he ignores me. What in the world

happened to the sweet alpha? It knocks me off my axis. I thought I had them figured out. But I don't.

They have layers that would take months to peel away. I've entered a topsy-turvy reality where Austin is sweet and caring, and Dean is distant and hurt.

Austin doesn't answer either as he follows Dean out. But Felix pauses, looking at me fully. "Saint is fighting."

The air punches out of my lungs in a surprised whoosh. Fighting? Austin seems more the type to hop into a fight ring than Dean.

"Don't look so surprised. He's good. There is nothing to worry about."

"I'm not...I wasn't worried."

He chuckles, seeming more like himself for the first time since I locked myself in my room. And I want to keep him smiling, make him laugh some more. Find that place we had been in before everything. It is an unexplained impulse, but when I say everything inside of me wants that, I mean *everything*.

"Come on," he says, holding his hand out for me to take as if he senses the need growing between us, too.

Hesitating only a moment, I wrap my fingers around his, and he leads me out of the safety of the apartment. The other two are waiting for the elevator, and when the doors open and they step inside, I follow. Because what are they going to do to me in the elevator that they couldn't have already done to me in the apartment? It seems silly now, the first morning's hesitance. The danger is greater inside the apartment, as I've learned on two occasions. Three if you count just now.

Once inside, they form a 'v' around me. Dean stands in front, where I can't see his face, and Austin and Felix flank me. Their scents mingle in a pleasant mixture that makes me want to breathe them all in. Or roll around on each of them so I can carry them with me. The thought had barely formed when Austin steps closer, his hand falling to my lower back again as he dips his head closer.

"I forgot one thing," he murmurs. "You need to smell like you belong with us."

I swallow. "Okay." I curl my fingers in, wishing for my hoodie to hide under and wait for what he had in mind.

"Come here," he whispers. The intimacy of the elevator as his palm wraps around the back of my neck and he bares his throat to me, urging me to nuzzle into him, is almost too much, but I go. "Wrap your arms around me, brush your wrists along my back. Rub against my neck. That's it. Just like that, princess."

I run my fingers over his expensive suit, gliding my wrists over the fabric, my pheromones making it really easy as they seep from my pores being this close to him.

"Good, now rub your cheek over mine." The words are a purr, almost a soft rumble of sound.

Running my cheek over his, where day-old scruff grazes his skin, feels like tracing the edge of a rugged, unexplored terrain. Each bristle is a whispered promise, a tactile connection to his raw masculinity.

The sensation is a gentle dance between texture and tenderness, a subtle friction that ignites a spark of intimacy, reminding me of the untamed allure that lies beneath his exterior. It's like tracing the contours of a whispered secret, a tangible symphony of vulnerability and strength that leaves a lingering imprint on my senses. I pull away with my heart in my throat, and my breath frozen in my lungs. What was that?

Touching someone like this is personal and intimate in ways I haven't allowed myself to hope for or want since my parents were murdered. His palm falls away from the back of my neck and, with his sunglasses in place, I can't read his eyes. I blink rapidly and move back to between the three of them.

Felix reaches for me before I can find my center. "My turn," he says.

My perfume blooms as he pulls me into his smaller frame, but he runs his face along my neck. His breath ghosting over the shell of my ear, his cheek nuzzling me as his fingers hold my hips like a lifeline. My fingers thread into his colorful hair as I arch my neck, allowing him to mark me with his scent.

Need, strong and pure, pulses between my legs as he sets me back into my spot between them. I can no longer distinguish where my perfume ends and their musk starts. We really smell like a pack.

"Saint, your turn," Austin says.

Dean tenses before he turns slowly around. As I look into his eyes, I glimpse pain, like a fleeting shadow clouding his gaze. His brown eyes hold the raw ache I've unintentionally triggered, and it tugs at something deep inside me.

Remorse tightens my chest as I witness the impact of my thoughtless words from earlier, a silent connection passing between us. The weight of his hurt presses down on me, igniting an urge to mend what I've unknowingly damaged. I had meant my words. I didn't want a pack, but the way he took them–that I somehow thought they could force themselves on me, it made my heart ache.

"Dean–" I start.

"No. Let's get this over with."

He isn't soft like the other two. He lifts my wrist and drags it over his face, the prickle from his not yet visible blond scruff scraps across my skin. Then he lifts his shirt and rubs my skin against his sides.

"I won't have my shirt on fighting," he says without looking at me as my fingers curl tighter into my palm instead of along his skin.

He's all flame, and I am catching fire. Then he drops my

wrist and raises his arm, running it over my neck, leaving a trail of his leather and lemon scent.

The air carries a tantalizing fusion of rugged leather and zesty lemon, creating an intriguing olfactory dance as he steps back. The rich warmth of leather intertwines with the bright zestiness of lemon, forming a harmonious symphony that awakens my senses and makes me want to climb him like a tree.

I suck in a shaky breath as he turns back toward the door of the elevator and punches the stop button back into the wall like it offends him; the elevator starts its descent and I'm left wondering how I didn't even notice they had stopped it. That had been the furthest thing from my mind. And now that I am practically vibrating with need, they could probably convince me that sex in an elevator is a great idea.

When the door slides open, Dean almost tears the decorative iron door that blocked us from the lobby off as he pushes it away. Then he is stalking across the long expanse of marble floor to the doors. Paparazzi converge just outside the door in a mass I have never seen before. Except on the TV.

"Saint, wait. We exit as a pack." Austin's command stops him, and he holds himself still until we are a step behind him, and then he leads the way without another word.

I straighten my shoulders as the doorman holds the door open for us, and the chaos of voices descends on us. Shouted questions similar to the first time echo in my ears as Austin's palm lands on my lower back, and he leads the way to the waiting car. My mouth is dry, and I hold my breath, a fake smile plastered to my face as fear grows inside of me. What if they see me and know it's me? They will come for me and Sin. A mask won't hide their identities from me. I'd know them even with half their face covered.

As the door shuts between us, muffling their shouts and blocking off their line of sight, I suck in a breath. Swallowing hard, I grip my knees and hug the other door as the others settle into their seats.

"Fucking vultures," Felix mutters.

"They are serving a purpose," Austin replies. "No one will blink an eye when Audrey attends the party thrown by Valentine next weekend."

"Shit, next weekend?" Felix's eyes go wide as he looks at me.

"Yeah, if we can get it done during the party, our little omega will be free." He looks out the window, and the only eyes on me are Felix's when I flinch. That is what I want. To be free. Right?

CHAPTER 27

Austin

STRAIGHTENING MY JACKET, I glance over at Audrey before putting my hand on her back and leading her into the warehouse. The ground is uneven, and even though I despise the boots she has on, they are probably for the best with the pits and puddles left by the rain the other day. When my fingers curl into her dress, she doesn't even tense this time, and satisfaction spreads through my chest.

I've found a sort of enjoyment in the omega. Caring for her does something to me. The more I do, the more I want to do. It is like an obsession. And when she accepts it without question. God, that really presses my buttons.

"Princess, while we are here, remember your safe word, okay?"

"Safe word?" she asks, looking at me with her wide brown eyes.

"Yeah, tell me it, so I know you remember."

She licks her lips as her cheeks turn pink. And I know she is remembering what I am. "Mango," she breathes without looking at me.

"Good girl."

She tenses beneath my touch before relaxing again. "So do I call you daddy?"

The question is unexpected, and I shoot Felix a look when he chokes on a laugh. At least Dean had left us already. I poke my tongue into my cheek as I think of my response.

"It depends on how you want tonight to go," I say. It is meant to sound like a threat, but that is not how it comes out. No, I mutter the words as a purr fucking rumbles in my chest.

"Okay, Daddy," she says with a smirk.

My fingers tighten on her back as I tug her closer to me. "Stay close."

With her smelling like us, there is very little danger to her tonight, but I will not admit that out loud.

"Fight is soon," Felix says, and he practically bounds over the gravel to the entrance.

I am positive he enjoys watching Saint fight as much as Saint loves to beat people into the ground. When Audrey attempts to pick up her pace to follow him, I curl my fingers around her side and pull her into mine.

"We have a reserved spot, no rush."

"You come here a lot?"

I shrug, her body rubbing against mine as I do. "Saint gets an itch every once in a while. And this is where he made most of his money, so for him, it is like coming home."

She shivers and hugs herself. "Aren't you afraid he will get hurt?"

"It is always a possibility. He pushes it too far, and we have had a few visits to the hospital from his fights. But he's good, and he promised three fights and done tonight."

Her eyes go wide again, an innocence in their depths that is tinged with darkness. She has seen things. Bad things. Yet, she is still innocent in ways I want to protect.

I tuck her head under my chin and pull her further into my chest, making it harder for both of us to walk, but I don't care. It is a need to have her close. And she fits so nicely against me.

Eyes track our path, and I know that news will travel fast about *Austin Zade and the omega he brought*. And that was part of the plan, right? So why does it make me want to hide her away from all the other alphas watching her? As if they would swoop in and take her from me. A growl builds in my chest at the thought, and she lifts her head to look at me.

"You okay?"

"Perfect," I say. Then I lift her into my arms, cradling her against my chest in a way my inner alpha is demanding. She squeals and grabs hold of my neck instead of fighting me.

"I can walk."

I purr. "But I want to carry you."

"Austin, I can walk."

"It's daddy, and I'm going to carry my princess, my little omega." If my voice came out a bit gruff, I'm ignoring it.

I expect her to fight me, so when she settles her head onto my shoulder, one arm wrapped securely around my neck and the other laying against my chest, I want to shout to the entire room that she submitted. Threading through the crowd and ignoring the looks, too, really relishing in them, if I'm honest. I want them to see that she is mine. At least for tonight.

When we reach the edge of the cage, she shifts in my arms, silently demanding to be set down. Relenting, I slide her down my front before tugging her back into my chest. Fuck, if this isn't a sweet torment I am engaging in.

Still, I have a part to play.

Everyone in attendance tonight needs to believe I'm completely gone for this girl.

Felix joins us after placing his bets for the fights I'm sure. He leans against the cage and drags his green eyes over us. I can read him like an open book, probably as well as he can read me.

He wants Audrey. Join the fucking party. After next week-end, and the job is done, she's fair game. Not that she realizes that.

Melody catches my attention from the other side of the ring, and I hold in a sigh as she heads our way. In what feels like seconds, she is in front of us, leaning next to Felix on the chain link.

"Austin, is this the delightful omega that was with Felix this morning?" Her smoke voice wraps around us as she openly studies *my* omega.

Her musk of lilacs makes the air feel almost unbreathable.

"I can't believe these three brought you here," Melody addresses Audrey with a smile. "Blink twice if you need rescuing." Her tinkling laugh flows around us as she throws her head back.

"She's fine," Felix barks. The full impact of his newly enquired alphaness is put on display with his annoyance.

The fact that he's now an alpha doesn't matter to me. We've always treated him like one, anyway. Only now it's true. But Melody gives him another look as her laughter dies, the grin on her face growing and her eyes going wide as if she's just learned a secret.

"Oh, Felix, how lucky you must feel finding the one to awaken you." She shifts her gaze back to Audrey and her meaning clicks between two beats of my heart.

Involuntarily, my fingers flex into her soft stomach, ready to shield her. *Mate? No. I don't want a real thing with an omega. They only betray you in the end.* Despite that, the look of interest shining in Melody's eyes makes me want to put Audrey behind me, out of her view.

"Anyway, sweet omega, remember what I said earlier. If you need *anything*, I'll help you."

"My name is Audrey. I'm more than just an omega." Audrey shifts beneath my touch, her muscles bunching like she is going to throw herself at Melody and claw out her eyes. "Even if I wasn't exactly where I wanted to be, you'd be the last person I'd run to."

When her hand settled over mine, keeping my touch on her, accepting it with her actions, I want to carry her out of the warehouse and back to the apartment to show her exactly what that does to me.

"Oh," Melody laughs. "Austin, you have a type, don't you? No meek little girls for you."

"Did you need something?" I ask. "The fight is about to start."

She follows my gaze that has locked on Dean as he strolls into the cage. All of his contained anger bleeds from him with each step. He had been on edge earlier, but this is something more.

"Just a friendly warning. Valentine knows." Her gaze dips back to Audrey for a moment, but I am still stuck on her words. *Valentine knows.* How? As if she can hear my thoughts, she answers me. "I don't know how. But I overheard him talking with his bodyguard. There will be added security next week. Maybe it isn't your omega that needs help." She tilts her head, but I can't acknowledge that she hit the nail on the head.The tension in my shoulders doesn't lie. I just have to hope that she doesn't notice.

The manager of the fight club walks into the ring, and Melody sighs, her eyes running over Saint's opponent. "How long do you think Oscar will last?"

"Not long knowing Saint," Felix replies.

She hums and nods. Then walks away without saying goodbye.

"That alpha is crazy," Felix says as soon as she is out of range.

I smile. "Yeah. But she has her uses."

CHAPTER 28
Saint

THE RELENTLESS IDEA that I would or could force my bite on Audrey hounds me, like I'm being hunted. The faint echo of her words in my head. *I don't want a pack. Especially one with three alphas. Do you think I'm crazy?* She doesn't want us. Who am I to make her stay? I would be no better than my asshole father.

Yet every single part of me wants to lock it in. Claim her. Deal with the fallout later.

Fuck.

Yanking my attention back to the present, I try to focus on the fight to come. The crowd outside the chains is already growing loud. Some pounding on the stands, demanding that fists fly now. I bounce on the balls of my feet and shake out my arms.

I know my pack is to my right, and that Audrey is with them, but I don't look. I can't.

Sweat already ghosts down my spine as I warm up my arms by throwing punches that cut through the air. I know the procedure, come into the ring, put on a show to get the crowd betting. Then beat the living shit out of my opponent.

Eyeing the larger alpha, I size him up. He throws his punches, but his left jab looks like he holds back. Impatient to begin, he hops lightly on the balls of his feet. Clearly showing which side he favors.

If my opponents knew how much they gave away before we even started, they would stand like a statue until the bell.

Garrett steps into the ring and roars over the crowd, gathering attention and listing the rules. Knock out equals a win. Down for ten seconds, another win. Twenty minutes with neither and it is a draw.

Five rounds of four minutes each, with a minute break. Immediate disqualification if there is any gouging of the eyes, groin strikes, strikes to the back of the head, biting, hair pulling, and striking the throat or spine.

His words become noise in the background as I watch the man I'm going to take down. I know the rules. This was my second home after I escaped my father's harsh rules. Often, I would picture his face while I took my opponents down. It was a release for my anger, and I'm hoping it does the trick tonight.

Garrett steps out of the ring, the chain-linked door clanging shut behind him. I approach the center and touch knuckles with the alpha I'm fighting. The bell sounds, and the crowd surges, the noise level becoming deafening. The ringing from the screams and the absolute silence as they break the sound decibel makes my ears pop.

I fake to the left, and he follows. His punch hits air, before I jab him under his ribcage, forcing the air from his lungs. He grunts and stumbles before coming back at me. More frantic, less in control. Off kilter. I grin and slam into his other side, following him as he retreats. He grabs my head, attempting to control my movements. But I'm smaller and faster. I pound into his stomach until he collapses. His weight pressing me down. I kick out from beneath him, and he bucks as I straddle him.

I lean forward, already seeing the win. I hold him to the mat as he struggles. When he attempts to grab me again, I shift so my knees pin his shoulders to the ground, and my groin is in his face. The ding-ding-ding indicating the ten seconds sound, and I release him. He grunts and gets to his feet.

Effortlessly, I push to mine. When we meet in the middle for the next round, he doesn't smile, and he barely touches my knuckles. Guess he doesn't like to be smothered by my dick. I grin. It is a feral twist of my lips, and nothing like my practiced and well-mannered one I use in polite society.

"The next one is mine," he mutters.

I laugh, a toss of my head, an exposing of my throat. A complete lack of fear. Or maybe I'm just that damaged.

"You're going to need to be faster on your feet to take me down," I reply.

The bell rings, and he lunges. No skill. His training is thrown out the window with his anger. He lands a hit to my jaw, and the pain that cracks through me is welcomed. Yes, this is what I need. I let him hit me again. My head snaps back, and I slam against the chains as I twist away from him. As I push away, my eyes land on Audrey's horrified gaze. Her hand preses over her mouth, and her large brown eyes dwarf her face.

I grin and straighten out. Turning, I duck his next punch before hitting him hard just beneath his ribcage again. He'll be lucky if he doesn't end up with internal bleeding. This is the one place my anger can be fully on display. Everyone expects it.

In seconds, he is back on the mat. I lay over him, holding him down with my weight. When the bell sounds, I spring to my feet and offer him a hand that he slaps away. Oh, have I pissed him off?

When we meet in the center again, I say, "You favor your right. It is easy to slip in. Once I'm in, you've lost. You need better defense of your sides."

He growls. I grin and spit out some blood that gathered from my teeth cutting into my cheek.

"Take it or leave it, just trying to make the fight more challenging." I shrug.

As soon as the bell sounds, he is dropping his elbows, protecting his sides, and jabbing at me when I get close. Complete defense mode. I bounce on the balls of my feet and circle him, looking for a new opening.

With an upper cut, his head jerks back and his elbows drop for a fraction of a second. Enough for me to slice right through his defenses. He topples to the mat as my fists slam into his chest, breaking a rib. He cries out and stays down. His hand grips his side as he takes shallow breaths. Garrett unlocks the cage and strolls back in. He grabs my wrist and holds it high, announcing my win.

"Find me someone harder," I say as he drops my arm. Then I stroll past him, back out of the cage, without looking at the roaring crowd.

CHAPTER 29

Audrey

IF I THOUGHT the first fight was bad, the second topped it. And the third is planning on taking the cake. I tug out of Austin's arms, my fingers cut into the chain-link fence as Dean's opponent lands hit after hit. My stomach churns at the blood dripping off of his chin as he shoots a bloody grin at the larger alpha and charges.

He pounds his fists into the guy's sides, the impact of his punches loud even over the uncontrolled and rowdy crowd. The man falls like a dead tree in the forest. Dean follows him down like a man possessed. He is primal and violent, obviously relishing every moment. While my heart is bouncing between my throat and ass as it decides what way it is planning to escape.

Dean climbs to his feet and circles the cage, his arms in the air, taking the win before the man is down for the count. I see the alpha twitch in preparation of springing back to his feet, and I scream out a warning that I'm sure he can't hear over the crowd.

"Dean, behind you!"

His eyes snap to me, as if he can actually pick my voice

out of the clamouring crowd. An electric current runs between us and feels like it lasts an eternity before it shatters. The man lands a punch to his kidney. The pain on Dean's face slices through me as if it is my own, and he stumbles for the first time. He hits the fence right where I'm gripping it. We are inches apart as he gathers himself to return to the fight.

His fingers fist into the chain links on either side of my hands as he stares into my soul. My heart is in my throat, and I want to beg him to lose the fight, not to get hurt anymore. But he winks and then pushes off the fence, right back into the fight.

He looks like his legs are spent, his arms are sloppy, and his punches aren't as precise as they had been. If I can see this with an untrained eye, then the alpha he's facing can see it. I watch in horror as the man slams his fist into the side of Dean's face, snapping his head to the side, blood spraying from his slack mouth before he is falling in slow motion to the mat.

"No! Get up! Get up, Dean!" I rattle the fence, joining in on the chant of the crowd. Forgetting my thought of moments ago that wanted him to quit. His head lulls in my direction, and he takes a breath and blinks. He's done. I can see it in his face. But the other man is almost done, too. "Saint, don't quit!"

He smiles a bloody smile before the massive alpha is on him. Before the ten seconds are up, the round ends, and my heart can finally beat again.

Dean climbs to his feet. He swipes his arm over his mouth, smearing blood down his forearm and across his cheek. The purple bruise surrounding his eye is dark. He'll be lucky if his eye socket isn't fractured.

He moves to us, three fingers lace into the ring's chain linked wall. As he leans his forehead against the metal.

I can feel Austin at my back. "Stop fucking around and

knock him out," he says.

Dean laughs. A tangy burst of lemon fills the space between us, weighed down with the scent of iron as it seeps from a serious-looking wound over his eyebrow.

"Don't worry, I won't let Felix lose his money." He winks and presses even closer, lowering his voice. "Keep cheering for me, hellcat. I like it."

I suck in a breath as my eyes bounce between his. "I only cheer for winners." Really, I don't cheer for anyone in a fight ring, but for Dean I would.

He grins. "Well then, I guess I better win."

When he pushes away from the fence and saunters back to the middle of the ring, Austin runs his fingers up my side, sending little spikes of pleasure to mix with the anticipation that had filled me. It is a heady mix that makes me feel like I've been drinking.

"He'll be fine, princess," he whispers. The ghost of his breath dances over the shell of my ear.

I watch as Dean shakes out his arms, flexing his taped fingers. He looks like he has gained a new purpose. He throws another wink our way, and I can't help the responding smile that spreads over my lips. The feathers of the mask brush my cheeks, making me feel secure in this crowd. Almost as good as my hoodie.

Casting my gaze around, I take in the entire space. Part of it reminds me of what happened to my brother and me, just because it is a warehouse. But the energy here isn't the same. It is primal and bursting at the seams. The freedom to embrace a violence that is contained.

This is the kind of place that I'm sure my brother would come to. Having free rein to beat on an alpha that can't control him would be appealing to him. I could picture him in the ring, circling one of them, just waiting for the bell. It would probably be a better outlet than what he has now. Drugs and drinking, possibly some kinky sex that includes pain of some sort. Not that I'd want to watch him get beat up.

Austin's fingers curling into my hips in the most delicious way brings me back to the present. Each moment around these three is dangerous, because I fall a bit more without even meaning to. I soften to them. I can feel it. And it isn't even taking much to make it happen. Touch. The one thing I avoided like the plague is actually something that I crave with them. And when I'm around them, one of them always seems to find reasons to brush their hands against me.

Like now. Felix is next to me, his arm brushing mine, not willing to push it further because of what happened earlier. While Austin is very much pressed against my ass, making it known to me at least, that he is very aware of my body. I'm sure my perfume is surrounding us in a haze, but I can't smell anything but the three of them, since they marked me with their scents.

The bell rings, and the fight starts. And I cheer for Dean, but only with his nickname because he seems to like it best and that matters. If I can't soothe the pain I caused earlier, I can at least bring him some kind of happiness now. Right? Is that a fucked up way of thinking about it? Possibly.

He only lets the fight go on for less than a minute. His opponent steps into him, attempting to take advantage of a fake stumble, and Saint slams his fist into the alpha's jaw. His head snaps back before he is out cold, falling to the mat.

I'm as loud as everyone else as I cheer. Part of me is embracing the fantasy that I can never actually have. The strong alphas that will protect me from anything. The safety and security that I crave at my fingertips. All the things I know are lies or feelings encouraged by hormones. I let them in and give them free rein. Because for the next week, I would live the life I could never have.

My breath catches in my throat as I think of what it would feel like to take their knots and their bites. Because I would do both, even if it killed me to leave, for a single week I would be their omega in every sense of the word.

Am I insane? I think at this point that is a given. Either that or I'm being so driven by the scent match that I've lost my head. At least this way, it is on my terms. I don't have to wait for them to turn on me or throw me away. I can enjoy them and then walk away.

Excitement surges inside of me at my thoughts.

The world moves around me, and the next opponents enter the ring, circling each other, as Austin pulls me away from the fence and moves us through the crowd. We enter a back room, and I see Saint sitting on a stool, bruised and bleeding, while a simpering omega tends to his wounds on her knees in front of him. A rumbled growl vibrates my chest. She looks over, startled, but doesn't put up a fight before scurrying away without a word.

"Awe, princess, you scared her," Austin says, amusement threading through his words as he holds back his laughter.

"She is a hellcat, so it is no surprise," Saint murmurs.

Felix scoffs. "The omega knows who we belong to." No one disagrees, and it does something to me, something warm and fuzzy, like burrowing down into a soft fluffy nest with my favorite snacks and a romance playing on the TV.

I've never looked at a pack in that way before. That the alphas belong to the omega and not the other way around. I like it.

Saint watches me like he can see into my soul, because he is Saint now, fully and truly—I can't fathom calling him Dean when I know he likes his nickname. His left eye is almost swollen shut, and his eyebrow looks as if it needs stitches.

"I'll tend you," I inform him as I drop to my knees in front of him.

"Is this the reward I get for winning?" Saint asks.

"You could have won with less blood and bruises, but I think you like the pain in the same way my brother does."

I hum as I brush the wash rag over his forehead and along the side of his face, taking with it sweat and blood before rinsing it in the bowl of water. Slowly, I clean his entire face, avoiding the seeping wound on his eyebrow.

"You need stitches," I state as I sit back on my heels, clamping my teeth into my lower lip. He is still the most handsome man I've ever seen; only now, he looks like he's gone through battle and came out the other side a little worse for wear. "It is probably going to scar."

Austin calls over someone, and as I get to my feet, they take my place in front of Saint. As the needle pierces his skin, I feel woozy in a way I didn't while cleaning up the blood. I shake my head to clear it, but it doesn't go away. I'm going to pass out.

I mumble something about needing a bathroom and head for the backroom entrance and toward the bathrooms I saw when we arrived. The crowd is still loud and intense as I thread through it. It is one I wouldn't go into willingly if I didn't smell marked by a pack of alphas already.

A few stray hands brush me, and if I was really claimed by a pack, they'd lose those fingers. But I am not, so I ignore them as I reach the freedom of the bathroom. Locking myself in a stall that is surprisingly clean, I lean against the painted yellow wall. The emotions clamoring inside me for attention are demanding little devils.

Other women come and go as I hide from the men that cause these feelings. My head clears of the dizzy feeling but fills with unanswerable questions. Can I really do this? Offer myself to them and then leave? I swallow as my head drops back against the wall. The darkness inside of me wants to rise up and tear me apart, but I won't let it. I push it away.

For one week.

I would taste the fantasy, I would live it. No one will take the memories from me after it is all said and done.

CHAPTER 30

Audrey

FINALLY, leaving the safety of the stall, I wash my hands before leaving the washroom. I'm single minded as I head back to the backroom, and excitement courses through my veins. Cutting along the back of the crowd, I don't see him until he is on top of me.

One of the alphas of my nightmares, Luther, pins me against the wall behind the bleachers. "Oh, little thing, where are you headed so quickly?"

I freeze.

He's stepped right out of my living nightmares and terror holds me immobile as he leans in close and sniffs. The acid and metallic scent of my fear washes over us, and I'm sure it drowns out any marking the guys had done.

His hand drops to my leg as he drags up my short dress as I try to press myself into the cool wall at my back.

Using his body to pin me in place, Luther works the button of his jeans free. There is no way he knows who I am. He wouldn't be trying to fuck me if he did. I'd already be in some van as they ship me away to some dark and dank warehouse to torture me some more. For the sins of my father, as they often told me.

My heart slams against my ribcage as I hold back a whimper of fear. If I scream or yell for help, he will know who I am. He will recognize my voice. The choice between two horrible outcomes is not a choice at all, but at least with one of them I'm still breathing after.

Squeezing my eyes shut, I breathe in through my nose. This is better than being cut open, better than having my uterus removed, better than–

I don't finish that thought before he is ripped off of me; the force tearing my dress that is still gripped in his fist. A dark blur is on top of him, pounding him into the ground ruthlessly. While Felix wraps me in his arms, tucking my head into his soothing ocean scent. I sob. I can't help it, they wrack my body, and before I know it, I'm snotting all over Felix's suit. The feeling of safety opening the floodgates.

Feathers are stuck to my cheeks as I pull away from him. The mask is lopsided, but still mostly covering my eyes. But the whole reason for the mask is to keep the man on the floor away from me, and the other men from my nightmares at bay. If Luther is here, are the others?

"I have to go," I say. I attempt to stumble away from Felix, but his arms turn into steel bands and hold me in the circle of his heat.

"Saint is getting the car. But we need to take out the trash before we go." Felix nods toward Austin, beating the crap out of Luther. I'm pretty sure he is out cold, but Austin doesn't stop, and I don't stop him. If he's dead, it is one less monster to worry about. "Austin, I'm pretty sure he won't be waking up anytime soon."

"Or ever," the deep growl rumbles from Austin as he pushes off of the monster come to life and then huals him to his feet enough to drag him to the exit.

There is a deep satisfaction at seeing my dad's ex body-guard being beaten so ruthlessly. Especially knowing what he put Sin and me through. Luther deserves more pain. I want him woken up and beat again. But by me.

Felix comes to a sudden stop, his eyes on me. "You really are the perfect omega for me, aren't you?"

The admiration in his eyes throws me off before I realize I must have spoken my thoughts out loud.

"Because I'm violent?" I really want my hoodie. I need to hide.

He smiles softly. "Because I was thinking the same thing."

A shiver vibrates through me, and he immediately shrugs out of his jacket and drags it over my shoulders, cocooning me in warm sunny days and salty water on the breeze. I duck my head and bury my face in the blazer as I pull it up to my face and inhale at the same time. Comfort.

"Austin, we need to bring this one back to the office."

Austin looks back at us. He is one-hundred percent primal alpha right now. And it is a turn on in ways I didn't think were possible. Especially after what just happened. But he saved me, and I wanted him before, so I don't resist the feeling building inside. I won't let Luther ruin the one bright spot in my life. The next week is going to be everything.

"Sounds like a plan."

"Office?" I ask. I'm so confused. Why would we take him to the office?

Felix shrugs slightly. "We have an interrogation room. It has a drain."

I absorb his words as he tucks me closer to his side. Our hips bump as we walk. The constant contact is nice, and I slip my arms around his middle. Making it almost impossible to walk. He fixes that issue by sweeping my legs up and carrying me. In one fluid motion.

A surprised squeak pops from my mouth, and he grins down at me. "I've got you."

———

THE ROOM HAS gray metal walls, a host of tools that I wasn't sure what they did, a long exam table I am sure was for torture, and chains that hung from the ceiling in the middle of the room. And a small metal sink with a large hose hanging on the wall next to it, I would assume, is to clean up messes. Austin and Saint hung Luther from his arms, his legs limp against the smooth floor.

Saint unhooks the hose from the wall and twists the knob to turn it on, then sprays Luther relentlessly until the man wakes up. My heart is in my throat even though I know I'm not in danger with him in this position.

He sputters and flops around like a fish attempting to get out of the spray. Saint cuts it off, and the monster blinks, looking at each of the guys before his gaze settles on me. The moment I dreaded is here, but I hold the power in this room, not him. I had removed the mask and Felix's jacket, ensuring he would know me as soon as he opens his dead brown eyes.

I hold myself still as I watch it hit him. That I am the one he just attempted to rape. He had been so close to the person they were searching for and hadn't known it. None of them would be satisfied until they tortured information out of us that we didn't have. Would we be living on the streets or half a world away if we knew where my father held his assets? I'm pretty sure I would have been on some beach without a care in the world if I had the money.

"You!" he growls. "You are going to pay for this, bitch." He struggles against the chains, and they clang together musically.

I step forward, picking up a knife as I do. "I think you have that backwards."

"Even if you kill me, they will find you. Your brother is sloppy and was spotted at a club. What will you do then?"

The spike of fear hits me in the gut.

"We will kill anyone that comes for her or her brother," Saint says.

Austin shifts against the wall. He examines his knuckles. "We may just come for them first."

Felix steps up behind me, giving me strength. His arms circle my waist, his fingers curling over mine that are gripping the knife. "Let's get some names out of him. What do you say, Audrey?"

I don't tell him I know all the names. Instead, I let him guide my hand. Red blood oozes from the thin line we cut into his skin.

He arches away from us, swinging on the chains as much as he can. Pain contorting his face. Blood thinning as it soaks into his already wet clothes.

But it isn't enough. I want to slam the knife into him over and over again, until I know he is dead. That he will never hurt me or my brother again.

"Who is coming for Audrey and her brother?" Felix murmurs, contained fury laces each word, but I can feel it vibrating into me from his chest, the barely audible growl as it rumbles against my spine.

Luther ignores him. His eyes pin me in place. Making me relive the hopeless fear I had felt back when I was chained to the ceiling. "You crazy bitch, you are going to die a very painful death. They have big plans for you."

"Too bad you won't be there to see it," I say.

I don't need urging to cut him a second time. I slice a long line from his collarbone all the way to his belly button. His shirt falls open, and his skin parts. His gurgled cry as his insides become outside is music to my ears. Why haven't I gone after them? It feels like taking my power back. Maybe I don't have to run and hide. I step back into Felix's arms as his intestines plop to the ground.

Revulsion should be what I feel, but all I feel is satisfaction that one monster from my nightmares is dead.

"We have to work on your torture techniques. There are ways to keep them alive a bit longer." His breath fans through my hair, and I sag against him.

"We have to talk about who is after you," Austin says. His arms are crossed, and his face is serious.

"It doesn't matter," I say.

Saint snorts. "If they are connected to that man, you have some dangerous men after you. They have a reputation. None of it good."

"I've never hidden that fact."

"You haven't shared it either," Felix replies. The tips of his fingers slide up my bare arm, sending little spider webs of pleasure straight to my toes.

Setting the knife back down, I turn away from the mess I made and face Austin. "Is it a requirement to know with the contract?"

His lips turn into a flat, displeased line as he narrows his eyes at me. "No."

I cross to the sink next to Saint and wash my hands as he stares down at me. I can feel all of them watching me, actually. But I ignore them as I lather the soap and silently sing the happy birthday song in my head. When I finish, I grab a paper towel and dry my hands as I turn back to face the stony face of my alpha.

My alpha. I like the ring of that, not that I'd ever say the words out loud. My heart kicks my ribcage with a painful thump, but I ignore it.

"It isn't your problem."

CHAPTER 31

Saint

I'M PRETTY sure Austin is going to explode. When Audrey turns off the water after ignoring him for over a minute and then faces him, I can see the urge to bend her over his knee and spank her. Not that he'd get very far with our little hellcat.

"It isn't your problem." The words are soft but feel like a gun going off and tearing straight through my soul. Of course it isn't. She doesn't want us.

Has Austin pieced it together yet? Felix's change and her in our life... there really is only one thing that could have *woken* him up.

When he vibrates with barely contained rage and crosses the room slowly, like some sort of slasher flick villain, backing her into the metal wall next to me, I'd say he has.

He grips her chin, lifting her face to his. "That is where you're wrong, princess. You are currently an asset to Zade enterprises. If something or someone is threatening our asset, we will handle it."

She swallows, her throat working as her perfume blooms.

"You don't own my life, Austin Zade, and I said it isn't

your problem. Asset or no asset. I won't fuck up your mission."

A smile tugs at my busted lip at her bravery. No one talks back to Austin except for Felix or me. As it cracks, I smother the grin that would piss off both the alpha and omega glaring at each other next to me.

I glance over at Felix, and he is shaking his head, not bothering to hide the grin. But he likes fireworks, and there will be a few going off shortly.

"Say that again, and I will bend you over my knee and spank you," he threatens.

She clamps her mouth shut as her eyes repeat her words. Then she ducks under his arm, brushing against his body, and crosses the room to Felix.

"I'm not a child, *Daddy*," she says.

When he slowly turns to look at her, I know how this is going to end. "Call the cleaners and meet me in my office. Apparently, our little omega needs to learn a very important lesson."

Felix side steps as she attempts to hide behind him, and Austin descends on her, eliciting a little squeak as he tosses her over his shoulder. She slaps his back and squeals in outrage as he pushes out of the room.

Silence falls once they are gone, and I look impassively at the dead guy that Audrey obviously had a history with. I call the cleaners like Austin instructed. Leaning down, I snag his wallet from his back pocket and flip it open. I know the name. Rumors suggest that the man was involved in the De Luca take down, but there are also rumors that they eliminated the entire family. I'm not so sure that is the truth now. When I hang up, Felix meets my gaze as the pieces click into place.

"You did good. I'm surprised you didn't pass out as soon as the blood appeared and that man's insides fell to the floor." I cross the room and press a kiss to his lips.

"Yeah, well, he deserved it. I wanted to cut him into pieces. But you're right, I didn't faint at the sight of the blood. Progress."

The memory of the last time we tortured someone flashed a reminder of him out cold in this room. I had to stop getting the information we needed while I made sure he was okay. When he came to, I was positive he was going to pass out again. So tonight is a complete one-eighty.

I shake my head and focus back on the present. "I think we just learned a very important fact about our girl," I say.

"What's that?" Felix pulls open the door, leading the way to the elevators up to Austin's office.

"The De Luca twins. They aren't dead."

Felix stops and turns to face me, his eyes wide. "As in the De Luca Mafia? The same one that Austin's father tried to create a merger with before they died?"

I nod as we step into the elevator. Pressing the button for Austin's executive floor. "I'm pretty sure they were in the final stages."

"Do you think Austin knows that is who she is?" He leans against the wall, completely wrapped up in the mystery of our omega.

"I think if he did, he wouldn't have involved Jason Vanross in the planning." I wonder if it will matter to him now? Sometimes Austin can be hardheaded and so focused on what he wants that he could push forward with the plan with promises to protect Audrey. "Don't tell him just yet. Let me talk to Audrey."

The doors slide open, and we enter Austin's large office. Where the fireworks are going off. It doesn't appear that we missed much, as he firmly drapes Audrey over his knee, and he runs his hand over the swell of her ass. Which is half revealed in that position with her short dress.

"Do you know what bad girls get, princess?" he asks.

She stills and stops fighting. "Austin, if you spank me, I will do worse to you than I did to that man in your torture room."

He glides his fingers along the spot her dress meets her skin and hums. "It smells like you want me to."

I inhale, taking a deep whiff of the proof in the air that she is as turned on as him, as us, because I'd be lying if I said that the sight of her bent over his legs didn't do something to me.

"I don't," she replies, denying his words. But her ass arches into his touch, and he chuckles.

"Oh, little omega, maybe in another world you could lie to me and yourself. But in this world, you can't." His hand lifts and then drops to her ass. Her body jerks in surprise, and she whines with a low, needy sound. "Yeah? You like that, my bad omega?"

He doesn't give her a chance to reply before he slaps her ass again. Her hands are pressed to the floor, and she curls her fingers in, lifting her head to look up at him.

He meets her gaze, his violet eyes more like an incoming storm than I'd ever seen before. He smooths his hand over her right ass cheek, then smacks the exposed skin. It pinks, and he soothes it with his touch, all without breaking eye contact.

"I've been a very bad omega, *Daddy*."

At her words, my fucking cock swells. I'm not into the Dom and sub shit Austin is, but that she is, and it is clear she is enjoying it even if she is playing a role, and denying it turns me on so much that I might spank her if she looks at me like that. I adjust myself, riveted at the sight of the two of them.

That contract might be destroyed and null and void right here in this office, and I'm not sure Austin will care one bit as long as he gets to knot her.

"You have," his gruff reply betrays the desire he is feeling too. "I think I need help to teach you your lesson."

She licks her lips before biting down into her lower lip and glancing over at us. If I didn't know that she had her heat stopped, I would think she was far gone into one with the glazed look of pure lust on her face. I would hang a man up every night and let her gut them if it brought this side of her out. Fuck, let's hunt down every one of those bastards that hurt her and her brother and let her destroy them.

"I'm going to have Felix make you come. All over his face and my desk, so I can smell you on it tomorrow. But first, you are going to beg for it." The resounding smack of his fingers on her bare skin has her pushing into his hand and pre-cum seeping through my sweats.

CHAPTER 32

Audrey

"DO you know what bad girls get, princess?" he purrs. His hard dick swelling beneath my stomach as I'm draped over his lap.

I know what's coming, and I want it. I want it so fucking bad that I don't move in case he changes his mind. But I say, "Austin, if you spank me, I will do worse to you than I did to that man in your torture room."

He glides his fingers along the hem of my dress, and it takes everything in me not to whine and wiggle for his attention as he hums low in his throat. "It smells like you want me to."

It is automatic and from the gut when I mutter, "I don't." But I do. I really fucking do, and I can't help arching my ass into his touch just to make it clear that I want him to spank me. My pussy clenches around nothing, and he chuckles as if he can sense what he is doing to my body.

"Oh, little omega, maybe in another world you could lie to me and yourself. But in this world, you can't."

Butterflies erupt into chaos in my belly, and then he smacks my ass. The needy fucking whine I can't hold back when the sting of his hand spreads through me would embarrass me if I wasn't so ready for all of this. He is lighting me up in the most delicious ways.

"Yeah? You like that, my bad omega?"

He doesn't wait for a reply before he is spanking me again. I look up at him, prepared to beg for him to keep bringing me that pleasure that is just on the edge of pain. And without looking away, his palm lands directly on my bare skin.

Fuck yes.

The flood of moisture between my legs would give away the fact that I want this more than he knows. But he doesn't touch me there. No, he smooths his fingers over my stinging skin, the soft touch a contrast to the spankings.

"I've been a very bad omega, *Daddy*." I need to pull out the big guns, and I know that calling him daddy works him up. It is my secret weapon. And now that I am all in on being claimed at least for a week, I would use it as often as I could.

His next words almost give me an orgasm just by him uttering them.

"You have," he replies. "I think I need help to teach you your lesson." The almost growl of his words has my stomach doing somersaults. It's become an acrobat all for him.

I wet my dry lips and look at the other two that I hadn't heard arrive. But the more the merrier. Fill me all up. Let's void that contract. My nipples pebble at the desire shining back at me from each of their eyes. Saint's hard-on tents his sweats, showing off his impressive size. It makes me pause for a moment. Would he even fit?

"I'm going to have Felix make you come. All over his face and my desk, so I can smell you on it tomorrow. But first you are going to beg for it." Austin drags my attention back to him, as if he is greedy for it, and smacks my ass again. I moan low in my throat and accept another round of spankings.

Each one burning through me. Then his fingers stray between my legs, and I spread them for him, giving him access to the needy part of my body.

He dips his fingers beneath my panties, and I'm pretty sure I'm going to die of anticipation because he doesn't curl them into me; no, he grips the fabric and tears it from my body. Leaving me bare to the room. To all of their eyes.

"Felix, come here," he commands, and I watch through hooded eyes as Felix approaches. "Our omega wants to feel your fingers inside her. And I want you to tell me what it feels like when I spank her, while you have your long fingers deep inside her cunt."

He drops to his knees next to me, and I spread my legs further. "Is that what you want, Audrey?"

When I remain silent, I'm rewarded with another smack. I moan as another flood of moisture drips from me onto Austin's slacks. "Words, princess. Felix needs you to tell him what you want."

"Touch me, Felix."

His fingers glide up my inner thigh and pause. "Where, Audrey?"

"My pussy. I want your fingers deep inside me while Austin spanks me. I need to learn my lesson," I pant.

Need takes hold of my soul like a living being inside of me. I am clenching around nothing, needing a knot more than fingers, but everyone has to start somewhere.

His touch is like liquid fire as he parts my folds and presses first two fingers, then three inside of me. He pumps them in and out, drawing even more slick out into the open air. Then Austin's palm slaps down onto my bare ass, and I clench around his fingers.

Felix groans and presses deeper. "Do that again, Austin, she likes it."

Austin smooths his hand over the sting with a gentle

touch before lifting and spanking me again. I'm sure my eyes roll into the back of my head, and I'm on the verge of an orgasm just from three fingers working inside of me and Austin making my ass cheeks glow.

"Tell me what it feels like–" Austin rumbles.

"Tight, slick, warm. I think we are too big for her."

A purr vibrates through Austin, pressing his knot and length into my stomach, and I'm pretty sure Felix is right. From what I saw of Saint and what I feel beneath me right now, I'm going to be a goner. But at least I'll die happy.

"She can handle us. Saint, join us. She needs to know that rejecting us isn't an option. Isn't that right, princess? Are you learning your lesson? If we ask you a question, we want to know the answer. While you are with us, everything about you is our concern, including your safety."

Right. That is how I got here, bent over his knee, so close to an orgasm I am pretty sure I will beg for it. But it still isn't his concern, so none of this will change that. But I will say nothing that makes him stop all of this.

"Yes, Daddy," I murmur.

He hums his approval. A second later, Felix's touch is gone, and Austin has lifted me into his lap, my back to his chest, and my legs spread wide. Saint steps forward, his melted chocolate brown eyes burning into me. I can see his hesitance caused by my earlier rejection.

"Saint," I say and curl my fingers toward him. I am going to enjoy all three of them. And with only a week to do it, time is ticking. "Please."

Those two words are the only thing he needs to hear before he is on his knees next to Felix. It is like being worshiped with them between my legs and Austin holding my thighs open.

"Taste her," Austin commands, and I'm positive I'm going to turn to mush right here in his lap. The almost feral way his words rumbled through me is better than my best vibrator.

Saint's touch is as hesitant as his gaze, as his fingers touch my knee before running up the inside of my leg. A whimper drags from me as he lowers his head and presses a soft open-mouthed kiss to my thigh just above my knee. Apparently, my omega is a needy bitch, but that is fine with me.

My perfume mixing with all their perfect musks makes me feel like they have transported me to the perfect end of summer vacation. With fall creeping around in the early mornings, but the summer sun still reigning during the day, full of swimming and horseback riding. And nights ended with sugar and melted sweets by the fire, while embraced in my favorite hoodie.

Tears prickle at the edges of my eyes, but I blink them away. Crying will not get me what I want right now. If I know anything about these three, safe word or no safe word, if they see tears, it all stops. It wouldn't matter to them that they are happy ones. The kind that is shed when you have found your way out of the dark after being lost in it for so long.

In a week, I might regret every moment I give them. But right now, I'm going to pretend it never has to end.

"You smell like sweet, melted chocolate drizzled over a brownie sundae," Saint says, his husky words uttered against my skin as he mouths his way toward my center. "And you taste just as fucking good, hellcat."

He sucks at my thigh, leaving love marks as he slowly makes his way to where I'm dripping. I'm pretty sure I'm going to combust when he inhales sharply seconds before his tongue is swiping up through my slick, a moan vibrating from him as he tries to smother himself in my folds.

When a groan falls from my lips and my head drops to Austin's shoulder, he murmurs his approval, the low rumble of his purr adding to my pleasure. "That's it. Work more of those sounds from her."

The brushing of fingers along my upper leg has my eyes popping open as Felix drags my dress higher. His palm flat along my stomach, as he pushes it up. My nipples pebble in anticipation of the attention they are about to get. As Saint sucks my clit between his teeth and runs his tongue over it as he grips it. An unintelligible sound chokes from my throat as I press my hips into his face at the same time Felix rolls my nipples between his fingers. I've never been so thankful for my past self and choosing not to wear a bra tonight.

My thoughts scatter as the dam breaks, and I give Saint a fucking shower in my juices, as my orgasm clenches my stomach tight and crashes over me. Rolling me in the relentless waves as they force more pleasure from my body, not letting up for a second as I am tossed straight into a second climax before the first has ended. I'm wrecked.

Eventually, I come back into myself, their soft touch leading the way. They haven't finished yet, and when Austin clears his desk by sweeping his arm over it, he places me on top. I plan to ensure that he can't stop thinking about me while he's working by leaving my perfume ingrained in the wooden surface if they continue.

"Princess," Austin says, a question in the single endearment.

"Get the fucking contract, and I'll sign the clause. That giving me orgasms doesn't mean the contract is void. Just don't stop."

I breathe deep as I hold his violet gaze until he relents and finishes undressing me. I'm in nothing but my boots, with three sets of eyes devouring me and making me feel like I own the fucking world. Because with their attention on me, I do.

I lick my dry lips as Austin steps back and motions for Felix to take his place. "Felix, take care of our omega."

Fixing my full regard on Felix, I watch as he unbuttons his fly, and the soft sound of his zipper lowering fills the room. Then he is pushing his slacks and boxers down, revealing his already thick cock. This time his knot doesn't send me running as anticipation melts through me like a burning hot lava.

Saint takes one side of the desk while Austin takes the other. They shoved chairs out of the way to make room for them, while Felix steps up between my legs. My breath is coming in short little pants that halt altogether as his fingers run along my thigh, and he spreads my folds teasingly. His fingers dipping between them, his full concentration on me.

"You're sure?" he asks.

Without thinking, I lift my legs and wrap them around his waist, using them to tug him closer to where I need him.

"Positive."

It is just the two of us. As he sucks his lip ring into his mouth, all the emotions he's feeling painted across his face for me to read freely. The tip of his cock nudges my folds, and I adjust my hips until he is at my entrance. Then I tighten my legs around him, urging him forward.

The stretch of his head entering me gives me pause. His knot is at least twice that size. He is going to tear me in half. Slowly he works his way into me, having a patience and determination not to hurt me that I threw out the window twenty minutes ago.

Short teasing thrusts have me groaning in protest. "Fuck me, Felix."

"Listen to our omega." Austin's gruff command brings my attention back to him. He's freed his cock and is stroking it in long slow strokes, matching the way Felix is moving. It is erotic, and I want to taste him. But it will have to wait, I want to enjoy every second of Felix inside of me.

As his knot touches my entrance, teasing me with more fullness, I half whimper, half moan. Fuck. Oh God. I could live off of this feeling. He folds over me, and I run my hands over his back as he thrusts into me. Dragging my nails over his skin seems to urge him faster, so I do it repeatedly. Instinct has me arching my neck for his bite as he kisses along my collarbone.

Every part of me belongs to him, to them. And because of that, every single part of me wants his mark on my flesh. Even if the pain that will come later will make me regret it, now, in the present, it's what I crave.

I gasp as his teeth sink into the base of my throat. The most intense orgasm of my life makes me explode into a million tiny pieces as he pushes his knot inside of me, locking us together, before he explodes inside of me. The pulsing of his cock as he releases every bit of his seed into my body sends shockwaves through me. Pure bliss spreads from where he marked me, making me limp and thankful I have the hard wooden surface to lie on.

Austin and Saint say something, but I'm so far gone I can't hear a word. If I could, maybe I'd be concerned. But right now, I don't have a care in the world. I am where I'm meant to be.

CHAPTER 33

Felix

MY CHEST IS tight as I stare down at Audrey. She is the most beautiful woman I've ever seen. And knowing she is accepting me right now has me second guessing everything. Her slick glistens on her folds, telling me more than any words that she is ready for me. Still, I hold back. Sucking my lip ring between my teeth, I clench the ball, keeping my lip trapped as I watch her.

In one fluid motion, her legs are around me, urging me closer. My dick bobs against her, nestling into her folds, ready to sink into her. She shifts, and my head enters heaven, and it takes everything inside of me not to thrust into her up to my balls, knotting her until she can't walk ever again.

Instead, I give her short measured thrusts, teasing the shit out of myself. Her tightness is almost too much, and I almost spill my seed with the small contact. Need is seeping into my bones and soon, holding back won't be an option.

"Fuck me, Felix," she moans. Sweeter words have never been spoken, and I don't need Austin's command to do what she says for my body to listen to her.

As my knot nudges her entrance, our moans mix, and I

thrust into her, my hands propping me over her body on the desk. I know that both Saint and Austin are getting off on the vision of us, but at the same time, it feels like it is just the two of us.

Pleasure and need are a lethal combination as I kiss along her collarbone. Her skin is sweet, just like her perfume. A perfect match. A scent match. I can't let her go.

So I do the only thing I can think of to keep her. I thrust my knot into her, locking into her body as I sink my teeth into the base of her throat. The mating bite sends me rolling into my orgasm, and my dick jerks inside of her as I soothe the bite on her neck. The silver moon mark already forming, as her skin heals the way it should after a mating bite.

I empty my seed into her, part of me hoping it creates life, while another knows that it is unrealistic outside of a heat. It is only the newly awakened alpha inside of me that has me thinking that way anyway. So I push it away as I let my climax wash over me, as she grips me so tightly in her folds, I am positive I will never leave.

"What the fuck were you thinking?" Austin drags me back to the present, my vision just barely clearing enough to know he is talking to me.

Audrey looks like a vision beneath me, my mark on her neck, where it belongs. I run my fingers along her sides as I straighten up to look at my alpha. Anger is burning in his eyes, but I think it is probably at the fact he wasn't first. Not that he'd admit that to himself.

"Fuck," Saint says. At least they both reached their own climaxes before getting pissed at me.

Ignoring them both, I press my hips into hers as firmly as I can, and she pulses around me. She smiles up at me, a blissed out look painted on her face. Not ready to leave her heat yet, I gather her into my arms, still firmly inside of her, and carry her over to the black leather sofa. She curls into me as I settle her in my lap. As we cuddle, I can feel the blood returning to my dick, and I can't help flexing up into her warmth.

She lifts her head and grins down at me. "Mmmm, Felix, I think we are on the same wavelength."

As she moves on me, riding me in slow, easy strokes, I glance over at the other two. Neither one of them can bring themselves to pull her from my arms where she clearly wants to be, but I can see the same need inside each of them that built up inside of me. Now that I've claimed our scent match, I'm sure they won't hesitate to do it, too. I'm just curious if the contract will win out over instinct.

As pleasure builds at the base of my spine, she moves faster, bringing us both to our climaxes faster than the first time. She drops a soft kiss to my neck as the orgasm subsides and nuzzles into me, scenting me like she can't get enough.

Then she pulls back, looking over her shoulder at the other two. I know what she is thinking, because I am thinking it too. They should join us. She licks her lips before pressing them together, and I know she must be thinking about something that arouses her because she clenches around me again, tugging a groan from me at her folds tightening around my sensitive dick.

"If you keep doing that, it will just be you and me all night," I say.

She brings her deep brown eyes back to me and sinks her teeth into her lower lip as if she really has to decide if that is what she wants. And if it is me, who would I be to say no? But sharing is caring, and we tightly strung my alphas even with their release.

"You're right, I should give them attention, too." She pushes off of me as my knot loosens, her slick coating me in the cool air once she is on her feet.

Hunger shines in their eyes as she turns toward them. When she approaches them, she walks her long fingers down the front of Austin's shirt, to just above where his dick bobs, leaking pre-cum to the floor.

"What's next, Daddy?"

She blinks innocent eyes up at him, and he growls before crashing his mouth into hers in a punishing kiss. One that releases all of his pent-up frustrations. She melts into him, her hands going around his neck and threading into his hair as she mewls into his mouth. Then he pushes her away, harsh breaths puffing out of his chest. And a burning desire flaring like an out-of-control forest fire in his eyes.

"Take your boots off, princess, Daddy doesn't fuck with *your* clothes on."

She lifts her brow before doing what he orders and turns around to face away from him, bending over. Her ass and puffy pink folds are on full display as she unties her boots. *Slowly.* I grin as I watch her tease him. As she kicks off the first boot, he slaps her ass.

"Stop taking your time."

She moves as slow as a sloth as she pulls on the lace of her other boot, shifting her weight so her legs are slightly open, and anyone in the room could smell her perfume. He growls low in his throat and smacks her other cheek. She arches back into his touch with a moan.

"You like that, princess? How would you like my knot while you touched your toes?"

If possible, she moves even slower. I huff a quiet laugh as I watch her toy with him. As the other boot flops off her toes after she's untied it and lifted her foot to kick it away, she reaches for her low black ankle sock. But stops and runs her hands flat up her legs until she is almost standing. Austin growls at her disobedience, and I'm sure he is seconds from taking the socks off her feet himself. Her fingers smooth over the curve of her back and over her ass as she looks at him through hooded eyes.

"The socks too."

She smiles slowly like a cat that's caught the canary and is full of satisfaction at their actions. "The floor is cold," she says. A fake pout crosses her face for a second before she is smiling again.

"You won't be thinking about the floor when I'm deep inside of you," he replies, sure of his abilities. And he isn't wrong. You think little with him buried inside, at least I don't. "Socks. Off. Now."

The corner of her mouth kicks up, and she leisurely bends at the waist, her fingers walking down her legs. She looks at him as she reaches for the first sock, and unhurriedly, she tugs it off and tosses it on top of her boot. He closes the distance as she works the other one off her foot. As soon as it is off the tip of her toes and her foot is back on the floor, he slams into her, knot deep.

They both groan, and his fingers hook onto her hips to tug her back to him with each thrust. The room is full of skin slapping and pure sounds of sex. Then he runs his hand down her back and tangles his fingers into her hair, lifting her head from where it dangeled near her toes.

"Do you want to taste Saint while I'm buried deep inside you? I think he would like that."

She hums in response, her eyes falling on Saint. He honestly looks like shit, all purple and blue, one eye half swollen shut, but if she sees any of that, she is ignoring it.

"Words, my little omega," he utters.

"I want to taste him," she confirms.

Austin pauses his thrusts and urges him closer. As soon as he is within reach, Audrey curls her fingers around his length, guiding him to her mouth. Then she licks the pre-cum from his tip and sucks just his head between her pink lips. Saint's hand drops to her head, and his fingers tangle in her hair, finding purchase, but he doesn't force more of his dick into her mouth.

"That's it, princess, take him as deep as you can," Austin encourages her, his hands back at her waist.

The three of them start a rhythm I knew well. Austin thrusts, and Audrey takes Saint deeper, then they both withdrawal almost completely before filling both holes again. Audrey is smart, she has her hand firmly around Saint's dick, just above his knot so he doesn't choke her out with the full length. I don't like deep throating either, and I think the omegas that say they do are lying.

After what feels like both an eternity and mere seconds, they all find release. It is erotic, and I love watching, being the silent observer of something I'd done hundreds of times. But it doesn't end there. Saint steps back, and Austin withdrawals long enough to have Audrey lie back on his desk. He props her feet on the edge and pulls her to the edge before pressing back into her warmth.

He moves slower this time, his mouth giving her breasts equal attention before he sucks at her neck. But he doesn't bite her; it is a little disappointing. Especially after he pauses over my mark, his tongue flattening against the silver moon shape as if he can taste me on her. She arches her neck, practically begging for his bite, and he still resists.

He is a stronger alpha than me.

CHAPTER 34

Audrey

WHO KNEW orgasms could make your blood sing and your body hum? Because damn, even back in my room, I can still feel the strokes of their knots inside of me.

I trace the mark on my neck. It sends a strange sense of calm through me. Like belonging to someone is what I crave. But it is a trick of omega hormones, because being a possession is not on my list of things to do.

Still, every part of me wants to find Felix in his bed and nuzzle into him. As if the closeness is a craving that only he can ease.

How would it feel to have all three mate marks? Would I need a bed large enough to fit all of us? Would it just become one never ending sexcapade? I'm okay with that. At least for the next week.

Bliss does strange things to a person. For one, it makes you crave more of it. And it makes you come up with different ideas that would create it again. I'm like a junkie planning my next fix.

I stare at the ceiling, but I don't really see the ceiling fan or the plain white of the surface. No, the previous night is just on replay at the front of my mind. I haven't even taken a shower because it would wash their scents off. How pathetic is that? If they were my actual pack, it wouldn't be a worry, because I'd shower and then be back in their arms.

Groaning, I press my head back into my pillow and flop onto my side. This is stupid. I seriously have moon eyes for the three of them. That is dangerous, and I need to quit that shit now.

As my irritation builds, I toss off the blankets and practically stomp across the room to my bathroom. I turn on the water as warm as I can without scalding my skin and slip beneath the flow. Washing off their scents is the only way I'm getting any sleep tonight. After scrubbing them off of me, I towel dry and pad back into my room.

The entire space smells like them. My blankets are infused with musk. An ache spreads inside of me, and I glance at my closed bedroom door. If I went to Felix, would he send me away? Tugging on a t-shirt and shorts, I make up my mind. I would go to him. The worst he can do is say go back to bed.

Right?

Heart in my throat, I crack open my door as if one of them will be waiting on the other side to order me back inside. Then I creep out into the hallway and glance at the other doors. It is the first time I realize that I don't actually know who sleeps in each room. Have they told me? I don't remember.

Capturing my lower lip and punishing it ruthlessly with my teeth, I study the doors as if they would give me some sort of clue. Forcing my legs to move, I pause at the first door. Felix would be in the door closest to the exit, wouldn't he? Or would Austin be in there?

Pressing an ear to the wooden surface, I strain to listen for anything on the other side. It is silent. Moving to the second door, I do the same, not a sound. Although, my pounding heart makes it unlikely for me to hear anything. The final closed door earns the same results, so I move back to the first.

Sucking in a deep breath and holding it, I turn the knob slowly and crack the door open, peering into the darkness beyond. Leather and lemon hits me as I release the air in my lungs and inhale.

Saint.

I go to tug the door shut. Hopefully, I didn't wake him.

"Wait," he calls from the black room. "You don't have to go."

I blink wide-eyed into the darkness. Then it hits me. I knew this was his room. I watched him go into it less than twelve hours ago. Does that mean I want it to be him?

I lick my dry lips as I debate.

"I just need to cuddle," I say lamely. I hold back the cringe as I wait for his response.

"I'm pretty good at that. Just be careful of my ribs. I think I broke one," he says, and then a bedside light is flicking on, and his black silk sheets puddle around his waist as he half sits up, grabbing on to my attention with both hands.

Even black and blue, he draws the eyes. Like a freaking magnet, I drift across the room to him, to his bed. He gestures to the surface next to him, and I chew on my lower lip some more. A soft smile tilts his busted lips. It looks painful.

"Did you put anything on your eye?" I ask, my gaze running over his face.

"I'll be fine, just a black eye for a week," he says, shrugging away my question. He pats the bed again. "Are you joining me?"

"Just for cuddles, right?"

I am pretty sure anything more would destroy him unless I was the one in control. And that thought right there twists my stomach and clenches my core at the same time. As much as I love to be bossed around and told what to do sexually, being the one to call the shots appeals to me way more than it should as an omega.

"No wandering hands, promise."

Relenting, I climb up on his bed and crawl into his arms. Resting my head on his shoulder, I snake my hand across the expanse of his abs. A sigh puffs from him, and he adjusts the covers to tug me beneath them with him. He flicks off the light, his arm tightening around me. As soon as we are situated, I relax into him. I keep my touch PG as my omega drives me to run my palm over his skin, soaking in as much of his warmth and scent as possible.

I am surrounded in the comfort of him. It is the best feeling in the entire world. I knew from his fighting that he could protect me, and something deep inside of me desires that as much as it craves all of their touch.

"I'm sorry for what I said," I whisper into the darkness.

He stills. Not that I can see him. But I can sense it, as if he stops breathing altogether.

"If I wanted a pack, it would be yours."

"Audrey, you don't have to say that."

I curl my fingers around his side as I attempt to get closer. "No, but I want to. And it is the truth."

A soft purr vibrates through him, soothing my rough edges even more.

"Dean–Saint, I've been through a lot. And it is hard for me to trust."

"I know."

It's my turn to freeze. He sounds so sure of knowing something.

"You are one of the De Luca twins. Everyone thinks you're dead."

What is air? I can't breathe. Panic attempts to take hold, and then he runs his fingers down my spine and presses a soft kiss to the top of my head.

"You're safe with me. I won't let any of them hurt you again."

I want to scoff at his words, let them roll off of me, and shrug them off as inconsequential, but part of me wants the opposite. I can't hide my perfume as it blooms. All of my emotions in the betraying scent.

"We will hunt each and everyone of them down until you have nothing to fear."

"Saint," I sigh.

"No, I promise. Even if you reject us in the end, you'll be safe to live your life."

My chest tightens. I want that. Safety. No fear. Home.

His arms tighten again, as if he can merge us into one person with sheer strength. I welcome it as I snuggle closer, embracing the dream of living a life like that. Maybe it could be with them. I drift to sleep feeling lighter than I have in years, the soft press of his lips to my forehead the last thing I remember.

CHAPTER 35

Austin

THE CONTRACT IS VOID. All of my work to ensure I brought the painting home where it belongs scattered like leaves in the wind. The omega had broken me. I am still reeling from being between her legs. Hell, I want to do it all over again.

Her pretty mouth calling me daddy and submitting to me. Fuck. It is a dream. There is something about a strong woman handing over their care. The memory of her giving me all of her trust at that moment is a heady drug I can live on. As if I have all the answers and will make all the correct decisions.

And I don't regret any of it.

My mind keeps creating scenarios where she stays. Where she is really part of our pack. My very soul wants that. And I don't think I can fight it.

If it wasn't eight in the morning, I'd pour a drink. Instead, I pull open the refrigerator door and peer inside, ignoring the fact I could just tap the door to see the contents. Even the quiet in the apartment feels full of unfulfilled expectation. Selecting the O.J., I get a glass down and fill it to the top before returning the bottle to the fridge. As I turn back to the living room, I notice Audrey's door wide open.

I'm not sure if it was like that when I passed it earlier. But she isn't out here, so I take a few steps toward her room. The bed is rumpled but empty, and the bathroom door is open with the light off. Even her scent is weak in the air, as if she hasn't been in her room all night.

Has she run? Did she take the first opportunity to leave? A sick churning twists my stomach, turning it over. Of course she would. There is no reason to stay.

A flash of Felix's bite on her neck runs through my thoughts. The urge to add mine had been strong, but I resisted. Now I wish I had marked her.

I already know that you can't trust omegas. That they take what they want while they fool you with pretty words and promises. Not that Audrey has done either. She never uttered a single promise to stay.

My mood turning, I stalk over to my armchair and sink into the cushions. My gaze fixes on the storm on the other side of the glass. It matches my energy and makes me feel at home.

Felix joins me after a while. He drops to the couch, rubbing his hand over his face and through his hair.

"What's wrong?" he asks, his voice gravely from sleep.

"Nothing." My fingers tighten on the untouched O.J. still in my grip.

He hums.

"She ran."

"What do you mean?" He glances toward her open door. "She is our scent match. She won't leave."

I huff out a laugh that is anything but amused. "They all leave, Felix. Omegas only want two things, power and money."

He chuckles. "Then why would she leave after last night?

She'd be on her way to both with very little effort. Not that I think Audrey is like that. She probably has a ton of money that she could have if she wanted and power if she took her rightful spot."

"In our pack?" I scoff.

"No. At the head of her family."

I cock an eyebrow.

He shakes his head. "Saint, put it together last night. She is a De Luca twin."

The world stops. My father had tried to match me with one of the twins to ensure the future of our families. But I'd been in *love* with Sidney, and I refused to even meet the girl. Maybe the future would have been different if I had. But I can't change the past any more than I can change the fact that she ran.

"None of it matters, because–" I start as Saint's door swings open, and Audrey slips out. A skimpy tank top and even smaller shorts cover her.

Her cheeks are pink, and she ducks her head behind her hair before disappearing into her room.

"You were saying?" Felix grins over at me, wiggling his eyebrows.

Saint emerges from his room in a pair of sweats, hanging low on his hips. He scratches absently at his chest as he comes into the living area. Her scent is all over him, marking him as hers as clearly as his scent would mark her.

"She stayed in your room last night?" Did the words come out accusing? Yes. Because she should sleep in my room. Irrational. Possessive. Unhinged. All the above. I can't fight it.

He glances at her closed door, a soft smile on his bruised face. "It was the best I've slept in years."

"Did you bite her?" I threw the words out as if they were a venomous snake ready to strike.

He laughs and brings his brown eyes back to me. "No. All

we did was sleep, you possessive asshole. Not that I should tell you the truth with how you're acting."

"He thought she ran," Felix supplies, unhelpfully I might add.

"I wouldn't blame her if she did," Saint says with a shrug. "She's been through a lot. Speaking of that, Jason is out. He can't run the mission with us."

Jason Vanross. The bastard who is rumored to have taken out the head of the De Luca Mafia. Audrey's father, if she really is one of the twins.

"Jason?" Felix asks.

The door to Audrey's room cracks open, and she appears dressed in a hoodie and leggings as I reply to Felix.

"Vanross," I murmur.

She freezes like a bunny ready to flee. Her fingers curling into the cuffs of her hoodie as she crosses her arms, practically vibrating with contained emotion. It is all the confirmation I need to know it's true. She is a De Luca, worth as much as me and twice as powerful if she took over her father's place with her brother. She never needed to be stealing on the streets in the first place. Living like a waif. It makes me irrationally angry with her.

If Sidney had tried to take everything from me, Audrey lived that life and lost literally *everything* she was entitled to. All because of the betrayal of her father's inner most circle.

"Did he hurt you?" I ask. Setting the O.J. on the table as I stand up, straightening to my full height.

Something flashes in the depths of her eyes, and she presses her lips together, her forehead creasing with whatever she isn't saying.

"How do you know Jason?"

The familiar way she says his name has a growl forming in my throat, rumbling like a threat from my lips.

"He was part of the plan to steal the painting back. He knows the layout of the Valentine's place."

She abuses her lower lip with her teeth as she absorbs what I admitted. "Was?"

"Now he is a dead man walking," Saint says.

Audrey shifts on her heels, looking over at him, a softness on her face that wasn't there last night, only for him. Jealousy for Saint spreads through me like a poison. I need her to look at me like that.

"The contract is void. You can leave. You can keep the apartment with your brother." Three sets of eyes slam into me, and I straighten my shoulders. The words might have come out clipped and slightly angry, but that isn't how I meant it. I just want her to know she is free. I can't hold her here.

Instead, a tenseness straightens her shoulders, and she swipes her tongue over her lips before looking at the other two. They don't say a word, but I can read their expressions. Neither one of them wants her to walk away, but they would let her.

"Oh," she says, her fingers curling deeper into her sleeves. "I–"

She sucks in a breath, and suddenly, I can't breathe until she does. She's going to leave.

CHAPTER 36

Audrey

WHIPLASH.

That is what I have. Of course, an alpha would toss me away after they got what they wanted. It was a lesson I'd already learned in the past. I bet Austin is only sad he didn't get his painting first. The pretty lies Saint whispered in the dark last night meant nothing. And his promise of eliminating Jason is just an empty one.

I blink, praying any telltale wetness from their rejection doesn't show. And I focus my thoughts on the strength I had to have to get this far, hoping against hope that my perfume doesn't betray me as I get my stuff and leave.

"I'll be gone before you know it," I say, ducking my head.

I don't risk looking at any of them as I turn on my heel and flee into the false safety of my bedroom.

In a haze, I toss my stuff into a bag. After gathering it all, I slip the clothing that still smells like each of them into the top. My heart hurts, and the fucking ache between my legs reminds me of my stupidity, while the tingle of the mark on my neck promises pain as it fades with my next heat.

This is exactly what I get for trusting an alpha. They are all rotten. Every. Single. One. Of. Them.

Looping the backpack over my shoulder, I look around the room that had been mine for only a few nights really but still felt like home. What a pretty lie. One I would have held onto until the bitter end.

Pasting on a bland look, I turn back to the door, finding Felix in my way.

"Don't go," he says. Emotion shines in his eyes, and I blink as mine tries to rise to match his. I will not cry. Not for him. Not for any of them.

"You heard Austin, the contract is void. I have no reason to stay."

His mouth opens and closes. "He wants you to stay, too."

I laugh, little humor in the sound. "Does he? I'm pretty sure saying I can leave means he doesn't want me here."

"Audrey, please, you are our scent match. You belong with us," he pleads. It breaks my heart because they are empty words. None of it means a thing. He just wants to own me.

"I belong to myself, Felix. Now, please move," I say, gesturing at his whole body blocking my way.

"That isn't what I meant. I'll prove it to you. Audrey, you are going to break me if you go."

My heart thumps, and I blink, forcing the fucking useless tears away. "Move."

He folds his lips between his teeth and runs a frustrated hand through his bright hair, but he moves, and I slip past him like a ghost. Without looking at the other two watching me, I head for the door. The need to be away from all of them before I collapse and give into every single emotion battering inside of me. I'm in the elevator headed back to my brother's apartment, no, my apartment, in less than thirty seconds.

As the doors shut, I slump against the mirror at my back. Memories of the previous day and them marking me with their scent invade my thoughts, and I don't have the strength to push them away, so I embrace them. The little things, like the way Austin's eyes dilated as he made sure I smelled like him, or the way Saint's hard face slightly softened as he reluctantly touched me, and the absolute adoration that was in Felix's gaze.

Fuck.

Tears fall, rolling down my face and dripping from my chin as my heart breaks. How have I fallen so quickly? Swiping my hand roughly over my cheeks, I push off the wall as the doors slide open on my floor. When I reach my apartment, I try to compose myself before I slide the key into the hole. It is so early that Sin was probably asleep, so I shouldn't have to worry about him seeing me like this.

Pushing the door open, I find the apartment empty. I'd worry if I didn't know he could take care of himself. Well, kind of. He is still messy as hell, and I use it as an excuse to ignore the emotions and shove them into the box I keep all the unwanted shit. Hours later, when the door swings open, I've cleaned the whole tiny space from top to bottom.

Sin eyes me and then the apartment. He looks sober.

"What are you doing here, Aud?"

"They voided the contract. I'm free." I rub the orange couch cushion and don't look directly at him. "We can keep the apartment."

He sighs. "What did the fuckers do?"

I lower my brow and pick at a stray thread on the couch. "Nothing."

"For fuck's sake, Aud, you look like you've been through a fucking hurricane of emotions. It doesn't look or feel like nothing. Do I need to beat some ass?"

I choke on a laugh as I bring my eyes back to him. "Beat some ass? Really, Sin?"

"I can fight. I might be an omega, but that doesn't make me weak."

Nodding, I give him that. "You don't need to do anything. They did nothing to me I didn't consent to."

"Aud," he breathes as he drops to the couch next to me. He tugs his leg up and faces me. Then he is comforting me in a way he hasn't in a very long time.

It's all it takes to unleash the storm of pain, and I cling to my brother as I sob, releasing every bit of my broken heart.

He murmurs soft words that mean nothing and rubs my back, letting me get it all out. When I release a hiccupped breath, he pulls back and brushes a strand of hair away from my wet face before wiping away the shed tears.

"What happened?"

I huff, a half laugh, half almost sob. "I fooled myself into thinking I could handle leaving after a week and jumped headfirst into a fantasy I could never have." My shoulder lifts in a half shrug and fall back on the couch cushion with a sigh. "But the week ended sooner than expected."

"Did you finish the job?"

With a twist of my lips, I shake my head and glance out our small floor-to-ceiling window. Images of the last night play in my head like an old movie. I finished something. It just wasn't the thieving they had wanted me for.

"I found a loophole, and it turns out the Mafia prince turned billionaire business man has a code. He told me the contract was void, and I was free to leave."

Sin's forehead creases as he watches me. "It sounds like you could have stayed, too."

'The contract is void. You can leave. You can keep the apartment with your brother.' Austin's words spring fresh in my head. A fresh wave of tears threatens. He had sounded so angry, as if I had done it to trick him and be free.

"It was a dismissal." I blink back at him, dragging myself back to the present.

"There is nothing wrong with wanting happiness, Audrey, just because a few alphas–" he breaks off; he can't even say it. And what would he say? *Just because a few alphas tortured us doesn't make them all bad?*

"I don't *need* or *want* alphas or a pack," I say stubbornly.

He scoffs. "Is that why you watch *Omega in Paradise*? Because you don't want to be swept off your feet and treated like the princess you are?"

"I watch it to remind myself of how fake it all is."

He laughs and runs his fingers through his dark hair. "Then it is the perfect remedy for your current state. There was a new episode last night. Want to watch it? I can put it on."

My stomach drops as he calls my bluff.

"It was the meet the family one. That one is always full of drama."

I watch silently as he flips on the TV and brings up the show. He looks over at me and lifts an eyebrow as he starts the episode, daring me to stop him. To admit that I was full of shit. I bite my tongue and stare up at the screen. Of course, I'm dragged into the fantasy and clutch a throw pillow to my stomach as I watch.

Grace is with the pack on a private date to meet her family. That is something I would never have, introducing my pack to my parents. Not that I had a pack. But even the thought feels like a lie as Felix, Saint, and Austin's faces fill my head like a haunting dream. I have a pack, I just can never keep them.

I fall into the fantasy, imagining it is me and the guys, and my parents aren't dead. By the time the episode is over, I want to curl into a ball and sleep away the nightmare my life is currently having. But I don't. Instead, I push to my feet and force a fake smile for my brother, who is way too perceptive when he is sober, and pick up my purse.

"I'm going to treat myself to ice cream for dodging the pack bullet. You want to come?"

"Nah, I have plans."

I smile and hope it doesn't look as brittle as it feels. "Oh, okay, I'll see you later then."

As I start to pull the door shut, he calls out to me, "Aud, just remember it is okay to go after things you think you don't deserve."

CHAPTER 37

Saint

THE DOOR SHUTTING behind her sounds like a bomb exploding. And we stare at each other in the aftermath. Our lives destroyed by the omega.

It feels as if I am in a wind tunnel as the blood rushes through my ears, drowning out everything else.

Felix tugs at his hair, his eyes locked on the door. While Austin adds Vodka to his O.J. and downs it in one go. He carries the bottle over to the fridge where he pulls out the bottle and adds the Vodka directly to the remaining O.J. and takes a swig.

He can't be serious. He pushes our girl away, and now he is going to have a pity party for one over it?

Stomping back to my room, I pull out the first pair of jeans and boxers I find and change into them. Then pull out a dark green henley and tug it over my head. Wincing at the pain my ribs radiate as I pull the shirt down my stomach. I have shit to do, and it doesn't include moping around. Slipping on a pair of shoes, I head back to the living room where Austin has settled into his chair, his eyes on the window.

Fucker.

Without a goodbye to either of them, I leave, punching the elevator button with more force than I need.

I could never stop Audrey from walking away from us, but I can do everything possible to make sure she is safe. And I just happen to have connections into that world thanks to Austin. My plan is simple: find every single monster that is associated with Jason Vanross and the De Luca Mafia and take them out.

But I'd have to play a part to do it. I am familiar with pretending to be something I'm not, so it should be simple.

I send a text to Jason, with the ruse of talking about the job that no longer mattered. He agrees to meet me in Midtown at two. It is only twenty blocks, so I choose to walk, and I have a few hours.

With plenty of time to kill, my long legs cover the distance, and soon, I'm standing outside the sushi place he suggested. He isn't here yet, of course. But I go in and check the exits. They only have the front door and probably one from the kitchen. I check out the bathrooms. Windowless. That means no quick escape that way. After I'm satisfied that I can defend myself if needed, I head back out and walk the two miles to Central Park to eat up some time.

When I return a few hours later, the sight of the man makes my blood boil. Rage turns my vision red, but I have information to gather, and I need to use my wits, not my fists, in this situation. Not even my walk worked to calm me.

I slide into the booth across from him. At least I am facing the street and entrance. He probably doesn't want his back to the room, but I like to see the exits.

"Vanross," I say in greeting. It is all I can get out without wanting to beat him senseless right here.

"Saint," he replies. "What is so urgent?"

"The plan is changing. Our thief backed out."

He chuckles, a greasy sound that makes my stomach turn. "So you need one of mine?"

"I know you have connections to the old De Luca Mafia. I'm sure they had someone on the roster that could do it." I attempt to relax back into the seat, one hand flat against the table and the other laying on my thigh.

His eyebrows go up, and he grins. "De Luca Mafia," he says. "Yeah, I know a few trust worthy guys."

"Can I get introductions?"

He shrugs. "Depends. What's it worth to you?"

He means money. Of course he does. The slimy bastard probably believes money makes the world turn. He doesn't realize that without class, you could have all the money in the universe and still not be able to buy your way into society's circles.

"It would be worth your time," I say, draping the arm that had been on the table across the back of the booth.

"I'll reach out to my contacts and be in touch," he replies.

I nod and stand. I offer the snake my hand to shake and as his fingers curl around mine; I catch sight of Audrey staring at me with wide eyes from the street. Her eyes drift to Vanross, and she shakes her head as if she doesn't under-stand, and then she darts. Like a startled cat, she disappears into the busy street.

She read something else in that handshake, and I wonder how long she stood there for. Does she think I made a deal with him to turn her over?

With barely a goodbye to the asshole, I run after her. She is able to weave through the crowd as if she is an expert dancer and each of the bodies is her partners.

"Audrey, wait!" I call over the busy street. Shit, is everyone flooding the streets so I can't catch up to her? Finally, a wide opening yawns in front of me, and I dash into it, covering lost ground and reaching her just before she flees across a crosswalk. "Audrey, it isn't what it looks like."

She looks back at me, her eyes dipping to my fingers around her arm with venom. I release her as if I am burned, but she doesn't run. "What does it look like, Dean?"

Dean. Not Saint.

I can't decide on an expression, and my lips twist between a smile and a frown. "It looks bad, but I just need to make sure you're safe."

"By shaking his hand?" Her voice breaks, and I see the crack in her anger at the hurt just below the surface. "Do you even know what those fingers did to me? What he used his hands for? What weapons he dragged over my skin to cut me open?" She swallows hard and inhales a shaky breath. Then she takes the hand that shook his and spreads my fingers wide, her total attention on my palm as she says her next words. "He is the worst of them all and a reminder of why I don't trust alphas. Why I shouldn't crave a pack."

When she drops my hand, it feels like goodbye. More final than this morning. And I panic. She can't go. She can't leave me. Not now.

As she attempts to slip away, I wrap my fingers around her biceps and tug her back to me. She folds into my chest as if she was made to fit perfectly in my arms.

"Don't," I say. Don't go? Don't do this? Don't break me? Don't think the worst of me? All the above.

Sending a clumsy text to a driver to pick us up, I hold her to me, because I am not letting her go. I'm not Austin, I can't let her walk away. I am a selfish bastard, and she will be happy, eventually. Felix and I will make sure of it.

"Dean," she says.

"Saint, call me Saint, spitfire," I murmur into her hair, pressing kisses against her scalp as her scent calms me in a way nothing else can. I need her. I will die without her.

"Dean—Saint, let me go," she says.

"No."

"No?" she chokes.

"No," I repeat. That is all she needs to know. No.

When the car slides to a stop on the curb, I scoop her up into my arms and carry her to the door that Mark is holding open. Then I fold us into the interior. She doesn't fight me or make a scene, and I'm not sure if that is a good or bad sign.

I settle her on my lap, my arms around her like a band, as Mark navigates the streets back to the penthouse. He pulls into the darkened garage, and I slip out of the car with her still in my arms and head for the elevator. She hasn't said a word and is silent as we ride the elevator up to the apartment.

I push in the door and stride with her across the living area and directly into her bedroom. I drop her to her bed, a squeak popping from her lips as she bounces and stares up at me wide-eyed.

"Don't come out until you understand that this is where you belong," I order, and then I stride to the door and shut it between us. I don't bark the order, because if she comes out sooner, we will discover other ways to convince her.

Her wide surprised eyes are the last thing I see before I'm turning to face my pack.

"What the fuck did you do?" Austin says. His gaze darting to the shut door behind me.

"I brought her back home." I pass him to the kitchen, a need to cook for her driving me. Pulling out pots and pans, I search the fridge for items to cook, while ignoring my pack.

Felix clamps down on his lip ring and eyes the door, a smile wanting to play on his lips. "She didn't fight you."

"She didn't have a choice."

"You kidnapped an omega and are holding her hostage in

our penthouse. Do you know how insane that sounds?" Austin asks.

Slowly lifting my gaze to his, I blink. "At least the reason I'm doing it is that she is our scent match and belongs with us. We aren't whole without her. When you did it, all you wanted was a fucking old ass painting you don't even care about."

"I didn't hold her hostage," he grumbles.

I laugh, loud and deep, as I throw my head back. "Is that the lie you tell yourself? A contract doesn't mean shit when you had to blackmail her to have her sign it."

"It was business."

"This is business, too. Personal business. Audrey isn't going anywhere until we convince her she belongs with us."

"We don't need an omega," Austin protests.

"You know that not every omega is Sidney. Not all of them are out to get your money or control you. And if Audrey was doing that, she wouldn't have left earlier. That is all the proof you need. If you make me choose between pack and her, I'm choosing her, just so that is clear."

Felix joins me in the kitchen and pulls out sliced cheese. "She likes grilled cheese," he says, his words making it clear that he would choose her too.

Austin paces on the other side of the island, his fingers tugging through his hair. "I know Audrey is nothing like Sidney. I've known it from the start when she wanted to walk away from money just to be away from an alpha." He inhales deeply, his gaze fixing on the closed door. "I didn't mean for her to leave earlier. I only said that she could go because I wanted it to be her choice to stay with us. This isn't giving her that choice."

"If you think for one second that hellcat wouldn't be out here tearing me to pieces for bringing her back here, if she didn't want to be here, you haven't been paying attention."

CHAPTER 38

Audrey

HOODIE up over my head and hands shoved into the pocket, I take in the fresh air. It doesn't help. My brother, with his perceptive words, echoes in my head like an awful song. *'Aud, just remember, it is okay to go after things you think you don't deserve.'*

Who says I don't deserve happiness? I do. But why does it have to be with a pack?

Walking aimlessly, I head toward the food places in Midtown. Not in the mood for ice cream or celebrating something that hurts. Maybe I can find some comfort food to drown myself in.

There is a small diner over on 34th I used to go to once in a while on my own. They have some suitable home cooked food. Maybe one of everything on the menu would soothe my soul. At least now I have the money to buy it if I want.

Passing a brightly lit sushi place, I catch sight of Saint in a booth facing the window. A familiar head of hair across from him. My feet root to the spot as I stare at him through the window. Saint stands, offering his companion a hand to shake, and I watch as Jason reaches out with his ringed fingers and touches him.

And all I can see are the things Jason did to me with those hands. Not while he was trying to woo me, not when he was still gentle and playing pretend. My stomach twists, and I am positive the leftover breakfast will attempt to escape.

But I'm stuck in the past. Chained to a metal table in the middle of a clinical room, so the blood can be washed away. So similar to Austin's room that I'm surprised I didn't fold as soon as I stepped foot inside it. Jason and his terrifying smile stepped up, blocking the bright light shining down on me. It glinted off the scalpel he had between his fingers, and I struggled, attempting to get away.

It was no use, and he sliced it into me. No request. No demand. Just to cause pain that he enjoyed. I screamed. My voice gone and throat painful from the act over the last few weeks. I was losing hope that I'd survive this. That we would survive this. Sin had been missing since they cut the body parts from his body. Since I had begged for the opposite. The only promise I had that he was still alive was the single video feed that they fed into my prison.

"Oh, look at that pretty red blood welling up just for me," Jason said. He dipped his fingers into it and ran them down my cheek, spreading my blood over my face. "You sound so pretty screaming."

Saint looks up, his eyes landing on me. My eyes drift to Jason. I shake my head to clear it. Panic, bright and hot, spears through me. I have to go. I need to get away before he sees me. Standing here will only get me strapped back to a metal table.

"Audrey, wait!" Saint calls after me. I dodge an elbow and twirl around a lady walking her dog. I can see freedom. If I can make it across the street at just the right moment, I can get lost in the crowd. His fingers wrap around my biceps just as I'm about to dart out into the street. "Audrey, it isn't what it looks like."

My gaze falls to his fingers around my arm, and just as

quickly, he lets go. I could run, but I need answers. "What does it look like, Dean?"

His face twists with emotion, as if he doesn't think I'll believe him. And maybe I won't. The sick feeling of seeing his hand in Jason's still hasn't subsided. "It looks bad, but I just need to make sure you're safe."

"By shaking his hand?" My voice betrays me and cracks over my question. It was too late, he could read me. So I just let it all pour out in a word vomit of hurt and pain for him to see. "Do you even know what those fingers did to me? What he used his hands for? What weapons he dragged over my skin to cut me open?" I swallow hard, dragging in a shaky breath.

Reaching for his hand, the same one that touched Jason, I spread his fingers wide, staring at the lines on his palm. I can't look at him as I admit my next words. "He is the worst of them all and a reminder of why I don't trust alphas. Why I shouldn't crave a pack."

I want him, though. Saint, Dean, whatever he wants to be called, the omega in me wants to roll over and submit, show him my belly and beg for attention. Every single part of me craves what I can't have. I drop his fingers and prepare myself for leaving him. We can't stay in the apartment. It is too close, and I'm too weak. So like a ghost, I'll disappear to protect myself this time. I won't make Sin come if he doesn't want to. He seems to have found his home, and I don't want to take it from him.

As I turn away, his fingers close around my upper arm, a magnetic force that draws me back. I'm compelled to follow, my heart quickening as I willingly melt into the contours of his embrace as if I belong in his arms.

"Don't," he whispers. He pushes back my hood so he can see my face better. My dark hair spills over my shoulders as he frees it from the confines of my hoodie.

His arm is like a band around me, holding me to him as if I would run. But I've almost lost myself in him. I'm not strong enough to fight him. I don't want to fight him.

"Dean," I say against his chest, breathing in his leather and lemon scent.

"Saint, call me Saint, spitfire," he murmurs into my hair.

Little kisses against my head are almost my undoing, but I give it one last hurrah. "Dean–Saint, let me go."

"No."

My heart thumps. He needs me as much as I need him. My fingers curl into his shirt, and I inhale deeply as I say, "No?" Afraid I've heard him wrong or that it means something else entirely.

"No," he repeats.

He holds me as if I'll run. When the car arrives to take us, who knows where, I submit. I let him carry me. I let him hold me. Why fight what I want? As the car buzzes across town, his fingers smooth down my back and over my hair, repeatedly. He murmurs soft words that mean nothing. The only thing that breaks the silence is the nonsense, soothing words.

Then we enter the garage, Mark parks, opens the door for Saint, and he is carrying me to the elevator. I glimpse Felix and Austin's surprised expressions as he passes through the living room and directly into the room that had been mine.

He drops me on the bed with no ceremony or warning, and I bounce on the soft surface as I stare up at him. "Don't come out until you understand that this is where you belong," he orders, and then he's gone.

I glance around at the room I thought I'd never see again. While listening to the timber of their combined voices on the other side of the door.

My fingers glide over the sheet as I take in the unmade bed. Is this where I belong? My heart is screaming, *yes, bitch, roll over and submit.* While my head is whispering, *'Run, all alphas are bad. It is only a matter of time.'*

As a reminder of how horrible alphas are, I lift my shirt and trace the faded scars from the thin slices that caused me pain but didn't kill. But they don't make me think of the three in the other room. Only the ones that caused them. For the first time since being tortured, I can't put the blame on all alphas.

And why should I? Even Austin forcing me into this situation hadn't been that bad. He could have done so much worse after catching me stealing from him. *I would have done so much more to myself.* But that is probably the De Luca in me talking. My dad wouldn't have gone as easily on me. I would have become a stain on his wood floor.

Pushing to my feet, I cross to the door and lean against it, attempting to hear what they are saying, but it is useless. They must have moved away from the door. If I were brave, I'd walk out and see what punishments Saint could think up. Instead, I turn back to the bed and decide to make it.

A soft knock sounds, but I ignore it, and they leave me alone.

Spending way too much time on making the bed, I finally cross to the windows. The sky is darkening, and night will fall soon. My stomach grumbles, protesting the fact I hadn't fed it anything after mentally promising it a feast. But I've gone hungry for longer, and it will be fine.

The door cracks open after another soft knock ten minutes later, drawing my attention to Saint as he steps into the room with a tray of food. Grilled cheese sandwich and tomato soup. A loud growl from my empty stomach sounds between us, and he crosses to the bed, placing the tray on the surface.

"Food," he grunts, sounding like a caveman and gesturing at the tray with enough sandwiches to feed an army.

I press my lips together and look out the window,

attempting not to smile at his effort at taking care of me. Felix must have told him I like grilled cheese sandwiches. The smell of the buttery toasted bread and creamy soup wins out, and I give in. Crossing the room, I perch next to the tray as he watches me like he's ready to feed me if I don't do it myself.

I lick my lips, lifting half of one of the gooey grilled cheese sandwiches and dipping it into the soup before taking a bite. Saint's gaze remains fixed on my face. I suppress the moan of appreciation as the food satisfies my hunger, although a small sound might have slipped out, judging by his expression.

But I don't care. I devour it while he watches, his eyes locked onto my every movement. The flavors explode on my tongue, comforting and indulgent, as if each bite is a small piece of heaven. I let myself savor the moment, relishing in the taste and the intensity of his gaze, a silent exchange of emotions passing between us.

Yep, the omega in me has utterly surrendered to this alpha. I'm a goner, caught in his grip, like a fish on a line. Reeling me in hook, line, and sinker.

"Thank you," I say, finally acknowledging his constant attention.

"Do you want more? Are you satisfied?"

I bite my lip and look up at him through my lashes, unable to stop myself from flirting a little. "Those are two different questions, Saint."

He clears his throat, and I watch as his hands fumble around, unsure of their purpose, eventually finding solace in his pockets. Suppressing the smile that tries to surface, it's amusing to witness his unease. This powerful man, usually so composed, rendered nervous by my presence, and I find it utterly endearing.

"I wasn't talking about–Are you still hungry? I can make more." He shrugs like it isn't a big deal.

"I'm full."

"You can come out and sit with us."

I glance at the door, mysteriously void of either of the other alphas. "Wouldn't that be admitting I belong here?"

"You *do* belong here," he replies.

I can't handle that kind of commitment right now, so I rise from the edge of the bed and return to the windows, my heart heavy. It's not about hurting him intentionally, but about being truthful. Allowing myself to love, to truly fall for someone, it's an overwhelming prospect. The fear grips me. Desiring something is a world apart from actually attaining it, and that distinction is never lost on me.

Absolutely, spending time with them shouldn't be a big deal, yet his message was crystal clear: remain here until I embrace the fact that being with them is my place. And maybe, on some level, I realize that truth, but I'm not prepared to fully acknowledge it. Despite the undeniable submission of my omega side to him, she's a needy bitch that will do anything for his validation.

As I gaze out of the window, I can feel his presence behind me. The tension in the room is palpable. He clears his throat, and I turn to face him, his eyes searching mine. "You're holding back," he whispers, his voice a mix of concern and understanding.

I swallow, my emotions caught in my throat. "It's not about you," I murmur, my fingers nervously playing with the sleeve of my hoodie. "It's about me. I'm not used to...this."

He takes a step closer, his expression unwavering. "I get it. Someone has hurt you before."

I nod, unable to meet his gaze. Hurt is a mild word for what happened to me, but he knows that already. "And I don't want to hurt you."

His fingers gently lift my chin, making me look into his eyes. "You won't hurt me by being honest," he assures me.

"We're in this together, whatever pace you're comfortable with."

I let out a shaky breath, feeling the weight of his words. "I'm not used to letting anyone in, it's just been me and Sin," I admit, vulnerability creeping into my tone.

He smiles softly, his thumb tracing my cheek. "I'm not asking you to let us in all at once. Just take it step by step, at your own pace. But don't leave. Don't throw this chance away."

I manage a small smile in return, feeling a glimmer of hope. "You're patient."

He chuckles, the sound soothing. "Well, you're worth the wait."

It's a simple sentence, yet it carries so much weight. I let his words sink in, the fear slowly giving way to a warmth I haven't felt in a long time. Maybe, just maybe, I can allow myself to open up, to take that chance on love again.

CHAPTER 39

Austin

I SENSE HER EVERYWHERE, her essence like an inescapable melody that keeps playing in the back of my mind. It's maddening how she effortlessly infiltrates my thoughts, my defenses.

Saint, well, he's taken to her presence like he was born to orbit her, and Felix... he is practically her personal hype man. Meanwhile, I'm wrestling with this infuriating contradiction, trying to convince myself that Audrey is really nothing like Sidney.

That I had trapped her, not the other way around.

But in reality, it's me who's trapped. Trapped in a whirlwind of emotions I tried so hard to deny. Deny that her laughter can light up a room, that the curve of her lips has become my personal North Star. I thought I could keep her at arm's length, protect myself from the chaos she brings.

I exhale a frustrated breath, my fingers clenching around the edges of the letter in my hand. A letter that ties us together, just like the contract I caught her in. The irony doesn't escape me—I, the person who took pride in avoiding attachments, have now become entangled because of my own actions.

Fate, it seems, has other plans for me. Plans that involve her—Audrey—and the wild, unpredictable path she's taking me on. And, for the first time, I'm realizing that maybe fighting this isn't worth it, a pointless fight when all I want to do is hold her.

I knew about the existence of this letter. The contract between our fathers naming her as mine, and me as hers. Audrey De Luca, the twin meant for my pack, the one my father had whispered about, his voice carrying a mix of hope and regret.

"Son, remember," he would say, a faint smile tugging at his lips, his eyes heavy with a knowing gaze. "Sometimes, the painting matters less than the artist behind it. Secure the future. It's the bond between the brush and the canvas that truly holds value."

His words echo in my mind as I stare at the inked lines on the paper before me, lines that outline a path we're meant to walk together. And as much as I've tried to resist, as much as I've fought against the pull that Audrey exerts over me, I can't deny the truth any longer. My father saw something, knew something I couldn't fully comprehend until now.

When she left, I started searching for this letter. The alpha in me determined to bring her back, even though I wanted her to make the choice to stay on her own. So Saint dragging her back is what I ultimately wanted if she didn't come willingly. He's right, I am a bastard, and I've accused him of doing exactly what I would have done.

I clench the letter in my hand, feeling the texture of the paper, the weight of the words. My father's wisdom lingers, a guiding force even in his absence. As much as I've tried to convince myself otherwise, this is bigger than Sidney, bigger than my doubts or fears. We can rewrite the story, to embrace the destiny that has been laid before us, to paint a future that is uniquely ours. If she will accept us.

And the stolen painting was only the bridge that brought us to this point.

Settling into my armchair, a tumbler of bourbon accompanies me in the late hours. The penthouse falls into a hushed serenity, the wall clock's rhythmic ticks serving as my sole accompaniment. The fiery liquid warms my throat, and I exhale audibly.

Another sip and my thoughts wander to tomorrow. The day I'd start on the mission to court Audrey—my father's last wish, a responsibility etched into my soul. Focusing on the painting had been a misguided attempt to remedy my guilt over his passing, my absence during his final moments. Yet, Audrey, like an unexpected revelation, emerged as the answer I have been blind to.

Just as I'm lost in my thoughts, the creak of the bedroom door announces Audrey's appearance. The surprise flickers across her face as she catches sight of me.

"Oh, I–" she says, gesturing at the kitchen.

I nod and lift my glass. In reality, I could press my advantage. She's left the room…one of Saint's terms.

My gaze sweeps over her delicate figure as she approaches the refrigerator, deftly retrieving a water bottle from within. This omega's presence grips me, ensnaring me in a way I can't fully fathom, and truth be told, I'm not even certain I'd wish to escape it even without that letter—an enigma that holds the last wishes of my father.

It arrived the week leading up to my dad's death. Back then, it had seemed inconsequential, as the De Luca twins were rumored to be dead. I had stashed it away, treasuring it as a keepsake of his last words to me.

"You can sit with me. I won't tell Saint you left the room," I suggest, my voice carrying an undercurrent of sincerity.

She snorts skeptically. "Why would you want me here?"

"Because perhaps I'm not the asshole you think I am," I reply with a wry smile, acknowledging my own flaws. "Well, I'm definitely an asshole, but I don't want you to have the wrong impression."

Her laughter punctuates the darkness, infusing it with a certain radiance. When her teeth graze her lower lip, it threatens to unravel my composure. "Maybe for a few minutes. I can't sleep."

Observing her, I witness as she curls her legs beneath her and gathers a throw pillow onto her lap. She avoids meeting my eyes, instead casting her gaze out of the window onto the vast, shadowy horizon.

"You're aware that just because Saint instructed you to stay, it doesn't mean you're obligated to if you don't want to," I remark, attempting to convey understanding. As she tenses, my words tumble over one another. "I'm not suggesting you leave. I want you here as well. But if this isn't what you want or—" I pause, grappling for the right words to conclude my sentence. Offering a shrug, I take another sip of my bourbon. "You don't have to stay. That's all I'm trying to say."

She studies me, her eyes momentarily tracing the rim of the tumbler in my hand. There's something in her expression —guarded yet intrigued—that makes my heart race faster. She shifts slightly, her fingers adjusting the pillow beneath her as if to buy herself more time.

"I appreciate that," she finally responds, her voice softer now, less defensive. "And I... I don't really know what I want. This whole situation is just...overwhelming."

I nod in understanding, my gaze locking onto hers. "Believe me, I understand overwhelming." I lean back in my chair, allowing the weight of my words to settle in the air between us. "But sometimes, even in the most tumultuous times, you find something unexpectedly meaningful."

Her lips curl into a small smile, a mixture of resignation and hope. "You think that's possible?"

I contemplate her question for a moment, feeling a strange vulnerability settling in my chest. "I do," I say finally, my voice quieter than before. "In fact, I think it's possible that the unexpected can be the most meaningful."

The silence stretches between us for a beat, charged with an unspoken connection. It's then that she shifts, her movements drawing my attention back to her. She pushes herself to her feet, her steps bringing her closer to where I sit. I'm not sure if she is going to throw my words back into my face and disappear into the room or crawl into my lap where I want her.

"I think I might stay a little longer," she confesses, her gaze meeting mine head-on. "If that's alright."

A sense of warmth unfurls in my chest, a surprising emotion considering my usual disposition. "It's more than alright," I reply, my tone steady. "I'm glad you're here."

Her smile deepens, and for the first time, I glimpse the unguarded woman behind the hard and bratty exterior. It's a small step, a spark in the vast darkness within, but it holds the promise of something more.

As she settles back into her seat, I permit myself a moment to simply observe her. We're two individuals brought together by chance and circumstance, each carrying our own burdens and secrets. Yet, in this quiet moment, there's an understanding that transcends words—a silent agreement to navigate the uncertainties ahead, together.

We are more than two heads of Mafia's, neither of us seem to really want. We are Austin and Audrey, fated mates. And I'm never letting her go.

CHAPTER 40

Audrey

THE WEIGHT of our conversation hangs in the air as I settle back into my seat, my fingers absently tracing the soft fabric of the throw pillow in my lap. There's something about the way Austin looked at me, his eyes holding a mix of understanding and vulnerability, that leaves a trace of warmth lingering within me.

I steal a glance in his direction, finding him lost in his thoughts, his tumbler of bourbon held loosely in his hand. It's strange, really, how the situation has shifted. From avoiding him to now willingly engaging in a conversation that goes beyond the surface. I can't help but wonder what has changed.

Lost in my musings, I almost jump when a soft voice penetrates the quiet. "Feeling any better?"

Startled, I turn to find Austin watching me, his gaze filled with a quiet concern that I hadn't quite expected. A small smile tugs at the corner of my lips, and I nod in response.

"Yeah, I think so," I admit, my voice softer than before. "Thanks for listening."

He offers a nod in return, a faint smile playing on his lips. "Of course. It's not easy, all of this."

I let out the breath I have been holding. It's a relief, really, to have someone understand the inner turmoil I've been grappling with since stepping into this tangled web of alliances and expectations. "No, it's not."

We lapse into a comfortable silence, and I find myself oddly content in his presence. The tension that had been hanging between us earlier seems to have dissipated, replaced by a shared understanding that transcends our roles and backgrounds. It's a rare moment of connection, and I can't help but cherish it.

The view from the window catches my attention. The darkness outside illuminated by the distant city lights. For a moment, I let myself become lost in the beauty of it all, allowing the weight of my responsibilities to temporarily fade into the background.

As I turn my gaze back to Austin, he's watching me with an intensity that sends a flutter of something unidentifiable through my chest. I catch the hint of a smile playing at the corners of his lips, and I'm struck by the realization that there might be more to him than meets the eye.

"You know," he begins, his tone almost contemplative, "sometimes life brings the right people into our lives at the right moment."

His words resonate deeply within me, a reflection of the thoughts I've been grappling with since our conversation. The unexpected, the uncertain—it's all a part of this journey I've embarked on, whether or not I wanted it.

"Yeah," I reply softly, my voice carrying a hint of hope. "I think I'm starting to believe that."

As the silence stretches between us once more, there's a sense of possibility that lingers in the air. One my inner omega rejoices in, her instincts sensing that this connection, however unexpected, might hold the promise of something more. And the part of me that has always wished for her happily ever after feels a flicker of hope.

Of course, a couple of sincere conversations don't make it a sure thing, but it is the first real glimmer of hope I've had since before Jason betrayed me and destroyed my entire life. It's like stepping out of the shadows and into the unknown, a territory I've been avoiding for so long. But with each word Austin speaks, with every unspoken understanding that passes between us, I wonder if maybe, just maybe, there's a chance for a different life.

The pack life I've avoided, the commitment and the bonds it entails, suddenly doesn't seem so daunting. With the three of them—Austin, Dean, and Felix—maybe I can have something real. A connection that's not built on obligations and politics, but on genuine understanding and shared experiences.

The thing about living in darkness for so long is that now that there is a sliver of light shining in, I'm not sure what it is. If it is an illusion, a fleeting mirage meant to deceive me once again, or if I can trust it to guide me toward a fresh path. But in this moment, as I sit here with Austin, one man I am inexplicably drawn to, I'm willing to take a chance. To step into that sliver of light and see where it leads, even if the road ahead is uncertain.

I set the throw pillow beside me and rise to my feet. Clutching the water bottle in my hand and meeting Austin's unwavering gaze, I offer a gentle smile. Then, I utter, "I'm going to catch some sleep."

Austin's eyes hold a gentle gleam as he offers me a tender smile. "Sleep tight, Audrey," he says, his voice a velvety murmur. "And if you need anything in the middle of the night, don't hesitate to wake me up. I'll be just a room away." His words carry a subtle hint of playfulness that makes my cheeks flush, and I nod in response, unable to suppress the small smile tugging at my lips.

The moment I step back into the bedroom, I slump against the door, my hand pressed over my racing heart. Austin's words, along with Saint's earlier ones, replay in my mind like a melody, and I can't deny the truth any longer—I'm falling for them, hard. It's as if they've walked right out of TV show *Omega in Paradise*, and I'm the omega they've come to claim.

Outside my room, Austin's footsteps pause for a moment before moving on. I hold my breath, a surge of anticipation coursing through me. If he were to knock, I know I'd invite him in. And whatever unfolds next would shatter the roles we've maintained until now. Emotions and touches would become a symphony that resonates deep within, staking a claim on my very soul.

But his footsteps continue, and I exhale, disappointment mingling with the flutter in my chest. Pushing the emotion aside, I chuckle softly and shake my head, determined to bury it. I slip under the covers, arranging the pillows and extra blankets around me like a nest, finding solace in the simple embrace of the bed.

Bright light pierces through the floor-to-ceiling windows, announcing the arrival of morning as I'm jolted from my dreams. I squint at the blinding whiteness of the ceiling above my bed, memories of how I reached this point and everything that's transpired since flooding back.

A part of me yearns to burrow beneath the covers, escaping into a world where my life isn't a whirlwind of upheaval. A place where I can continue to relish in normalcy. But that's not an option. So, I toss aside the blankets and swing my legs over the edge of the bed, making my way to the bathroom to attend to my morning routine. Then I head to the walk-in closet, opting for my usual attire—hoodie and leggings.

At least Austin got that part right when he coerced me into this living arrangement. If he had kept the closet stocked with clothes that didn't align with my style, I would've stubbornly clung to my old wardrobe.

A glance at the bedside clock tells me I'm up early, regardless of how late I stayed up the previous night. Crossing to the windows, I tuck my fingers into my hoodie and look out over the parts of the river I can see. A slight fog rises off the surface, seeping into the neighborhood. It looks peaceful. If I could go out on a boat, it would calm me, but maybe going down by the water would do the same.

With the decision made, I crack the bedroom door open, revealing an empty apartment and three closed bedroom doors. My heart flutters in my chest, a blend of anxiety and anticipation. Grabbing a pen and paper from a nearby desk in the living room, I scribble a hasty note: *'I'll be back soon. - Audrey.'*

After slipping my phone into my back pocket, I locate a pair of shoes Austin had bought for me neatly arranged by the door. With my feet snug in the shoes, I step outside, descending via the elevator. The brisk morning air graces my cheeks as I walk the short distance to the park.

The surroundings are quiet, a rare hush enveloping the usually bustling New York City. The park this early is adorned with a few joggers, a pair that exudes the air of a night spent awake, and elderly gentlemen engaged in feeding the birds. I lean against the railing, my gaze fixed on the river for an extended moment, absorbing the stillness of the morning.

The tranquility of the morning seeps into my bones, a calming balm that eases the tensions that have become an unwelcome companion. The fog ebbs and flows around me, stealing tiny distances of my vision before returning it. For a while, I allow myself to be present, absorbing the serenity of the scene before me. The water's gentle ripples mirror the newfound calm that I've been yearning for.

As I stand there, leaning against the railing, a whisper of hope tiptoes into my heart. It's been a while since I've allowed myself to dream of a future that doesn't involve constant struggle and fear.

The scars of my past, both physical and emotional, have held me hostage, trapping me in a cycle of survival. But the events of the last couple of days have offered a glimpse into a different life, one where I'm not just an omega on the run, but a part of something more.

Austin, Saint, and Felix. Three men who have barged into my life in the most unexpected way. Austin, with his determined gaze and a hint of vulnerability he tries to hide. Saint, the strong and silent protector who isn't afraid to let his emotions show. And Felix, the flirtatious spark that ignites laughter amid chaos. Each of them offering a promise of a future I never thought I deserved.

A soft sigh escapes my lips as I lean a little more against the railing, absorbing the warmth of the morning sun on my skin. In this quiet moment, surrounded by the simple beauty of nature, I allow myself to believe in the possibility of happiness again. The hope of a real future, one that includes love, laughter, and a sense of belonging that I thought was lost forever.

Feeling lighter than I have in years, I push off the railing. It's time to go back and admit that I belong with them. If I let this chance slip away, I'll forever be haunted by the nagging 'what if's.'

En route, I swing by the bakery close to our apartment and grab a selection of pastries. While waiting, I shoot a quick text to Sinclair, assuring him of my safety. He might not have even noticed my absence yet, but I want to spare him any unnecessary worry.

With the bag of pastries in hand, I make my way back to my trio.

My trio.

The phrase sends a warm flutter through my chest. As I stand there, thoughts racing, I nibble nervously on my lower lip. The elevator seems to take an eternity, but finally, it opens onto the penthouse floor. A smile tugs at the corner of my mouth as I realize I don't possess a key. A hesitant anticipation bubbles within me as I weigh the idea of knocking or waiting for someone to realize I'm here.

Unable to contain the building excitement, I raise my fist and knock. The door swings open as if Saint had been standing on the other side waiting for my knock. He has his keys in hand and is dressed in a pair of dark blue jeans, a robin blue henley, and a pair of Nikes. If he didn't also have his half a million dollar pair of sunglasses on his head, he'd look like a middle class guy going about a normal day.

"Audrey–"

I smile and hold up the pastry bag. "I brought breakfast."

CHAPTER 41
Felix

AUDREY'S scent envelops me as I emerge from my room. It's like stepping into comfort, into familiarity. The sight of her wide-open door tells me she's not in there. I search the living room next, but it's deserted, just like the kitchen. Disappointment tightens my chest, a heavy feeling I can't shake.

She's left, likely while we were all asleep.

It's only logical. If I were in her shoes, trapped somewhere against my will, I'd do the same. Deflated, I drag myself to the kitchen, my hope dwindling. But then a piece of paper on the island catches my eye. It's a note, simple and reassuring. She's gone for now, but she'll be back. She didn't run from us. Some of the tightness eases, maybe she just needed air.

Saint emerges from his room, his hair slightly disheveled the way I like it, his expression a mixture of confusion and concern. I have the note between my fingers, and the devil in me pops up, urging me to let him believe what he wants for a moment.

"She's not in her room," I offer, my voice casual.

"She left?" His face falls, and he draws in a breath. "I thought…I guess it doesn't matter what I thought."

I lean against the counter, studying him for a moment. "You know, for someone who can take down opponents in the cage like a force of nature, you've got quite the vulnerability when it comes to Audrey."

A faint blush dusts his cheeks, and he rubs the back of his neck. "Yeah, well… it's not like I planned on falling for her."

I chuckle. "Scent matching doesn't exactly come with a manual, does it?"

He huffs a small laugh. "No, I suppose not."

I push off the counter and approach him, my tone taking on a more serious note as I see his defeated expression. "Look, Saint, you're not alone in this. I know what Audrey means to you, and believe me, I feel it too. We can make this work."

He nods, his gaze falling to my hand. "What's that?"

"This?" I feign innocence with a smile. "Oh, just a little note."

"Felix," he growls, and I laugh.

"It isn't some declaration or anything, just that she will be back." I hold it out for his inspection. He snags it from between my fingers and reads the words the same as I had.

"Where do you think she went?"

I shrug. I couldn't even try to guess. It makes me realize how little I really know about our mate. I will rectify that as soon as possible.

"I'm going to get dressed and look for her," he says.

He disappears back into his room to do just that, I assume. I'm pretty sure that he'd have better luck looking for a needle in a haystack than he will in finding the omega in the city. So I pour a glass of water and curl up on the couch to wait.

Saint reemerges a few minutes later dressed like a model in his plain jeans and t-shirt.

"How do you think you'll find her?" I ask dryly.

"I'm not sure, but we're going to add a tracker to her ass."

I roll my eyes and mess with the ring on my eyebrow. "Right. I forgot you've turned into a caveman."

He tugs his fingers through his hair, somehow making it fall just right without a brush. "I'm going to do what needs to be done."

"You could text her," I suggest. I'm pretty sure I'm the only one with her number.

"I didn't get it from her, but I'm putting a tracking app on her phone the second I find her."

He snags up his keys and sunglasses just as a knock sounds at the door. He is across the room as if his feet are on fire, swinging open the door before I can move.

"Audrey–" he breathes like he's just seen the sun for the first time.

"I brought breakfast," she replies, her voice full of cheerfulness that makes me smile as I climb to my feet and approach the door.

"Mmmm, any chocolate donuts?" I ask, pushing past a still stunned Saint.

She grins, and I can't help but return the wide smile. "Maybe–" she says, her nose crinkling in the most adorable way. "I just told her to give me a variety."

I nudge Saint out of the way and urge her into the penthouse. Following her to the kitchen island. The door shuts behind us as Saint pulls himself out of whatever feelings he dived into.

"Where did you go?" Saint asks, his voice verging on bark.

I pull my lip ring between my teeth as I glance at him. Maybe I'm more at ease because she already wears my mark. Whatever it is, his tone makes me want to pull her into my arms and protect her from the big bad alpha. Which is silly because Saint will never hurt her.

Before she can reply, I say, "It doesn't matter. You're back with gifts of sweet bakery goods that smell as amazing as you."

I circle her with my arms, and when she practically melts into me, I sniff her hair as I lean around her to see the pastries. It is all the encouragement I need from her. She obviously decided what she wants while she was out, and it includes us in her future. When I nuzzle her neck, preferring the closeness with her over any food she could offer, she arches her neck and leans into me some more.

A low rumble from Saint brings my head up, and I smirk at him. Licking my lips, I nod at the donuts on the counter. "Looks like she got your favorite," I say. As if a donut will replace the feeling of not having her in his arms.

His gaze dips to the donut before coming back to us. "I'm more interested in the fact that Audrey is out of the bedroom."

She hums. "I've done some thinking."

"And?" he asks.

"Annndddd–" she draws out the word teasing him, "I've decided to see how the pieces fall. Which one is your favorite? The plain glazed? The cream-filled and chocolate-topped one? No, I bet it is the apple fritter. Perfectly pull apart cinnamon and apple yumminess."

It is amusing watching her try to redirect the conversation to the donuts after dropping the news that she is going to give our pack a shot because I'm positive that Saint only has one thing on his mind and it is locking it in with a mating bite.

"Brownies, that is my favorite pastry," he says. His gaze runs over her as his tongue wets his lips, and she inhales, picking up on his meaning.

Her perfume envelopes me in a haze of desire, drawing me in like the fucking pied piper playing his flute. I nip at her neck, and she mewls, pressing her ass into my front.

Saint circles the counter, his eyes on us, and I turn toward him, dragging her with me to face him. Then we are boxing her between us, and he is kissing her like a man drowning. It is erotic, and my cock strains in my pants, begging to be free. She whimpers, and I run my fingers down her sides before slipping my hands beneath her hoodie to pull it over her head. They break apart for a second as I toss the hoodie to the floor.

Saint palms her breasts, eliciting another half-whimper, half-moan from our omega. We have devolved into pure lust by the time Austin emerges from the bedroom. I sense him watching, but I don't stop kissing her neck or running my fingertips over her sides and down her stomach to the spot where her leggings begin.

"I'm suddenly regretting sleeping in," Austin says.

Audrey blinks over to him, her lips turning up into a mischievous smile that says she is going to say something that is going to press his buttons.

"Even daddies need to sleep in some time," she replies.

She gasps out a moan as Saint draws her nipple between his teeth and sucks. Her fingers tangle in his blond hair, holding him to her chest. "I've been a good girl and amusing myself–with help."

A purr rumbles my chest in agreement. She is a very good girl, deserving of all the best things that good girls get.

CHAPTER 42

Audrey

THIS RIGHT HERE IS FREEDOM. Why did I think a pack would make me feel trapped? Because with Saint's sinful mouth on me, Felix making me burn from the inside out with just his touch, and now Austin's fiery violet gaze fixed on us, I am floating with the stars as free from restraint as an asteroid floating through space. Yet still orbiting my suns, my alphas.

My pack.

It's time. I need all of their marks ringing my neck. Fuck, slow and steady. I need to dive directly into the deep end. They won't let me drown.

"Felix, bring our omega to the living room. We are going to need a lot of space to show her what good girls get," Austin commands. Saint's mouth and teeth leave me wanting as Felix sweeps me off my feet and carries me into the living room, placing me down on the couch as if I'm breakable.

Then Felix and Saint drop to their knees on the floor in front of me. Each of them takes a foot in hand and slips off my shoes. Once they are discarded, Felix dips his fingers into the band of my leggings, and I lift my hips to allow him to tug them down my legs. My slick has soaked through my panties, and all I can smell is my arousal as Saint spreads my legs wide and kisses up my inner thigh.

He presses his face to my soaked panties, inhaling deeply and sending a shiver through my whole body that pebbles my nipples and flips my stomach.

"I'm going to devour you. Every. Last. Bit."

Open the fucking flood gates because my body loves that idea. When he opens his mouth over the fabric of my panties and sucks, I arch into his mouth. My fingers going to his hair as I hold him to me. Not that I need to.

While Austin leans over the back of the couch, brushing my hair to the side and sucking on the sensitive area just below my ear and Felix runs his palm up my thigh, over my belly and palms my left breast, working the nipple between his fingers.

Saint hooks his fingers into the sides of my panties, and I know what he is planning before he does it. Is it an alpha thing? Before the question could fully form, he has the barrier between his lips and mine removed and his tongue diving into my folds.

"Audrey, I'm going to need you to come." Saint looks up at me, his mouth glistening with my slick, and I clench around nothing.

My body flushing as if I'm spiking into the starts of a heat. Pheromones bleed from my pores, eliciting purrs and low rumbly growls from my alphas that go straight to my clit.

When he sucks my clit into his mouth and swirls his tongue around my sensitive flesh, a breathless moan escapes my throat.

Felix moves up onto his knees and sucks my nipple into his mouth, his other hand finding my right breast and rolling the hard peak between his thumb and forefinger. Austin tilts my head back and captures my mouth with his. Nipping my lips and demanding more. As soon as I part my lips, his tongue is sweeping inside to tease me and swallow the constant flow of whimpers Saint is eliciting.

"Such a good girl," Austin says against my lips.

The couch is toast because I am drenching it in my slick. Towels. Next time we need towels.

Next time.

Fuck, I'm doing this again. Maybe for the rest of my life. The thoughts send a chain reaction through my body, and I explode on Saint's eager tongue, while my other alphas do anything they can to prolong the pleasure.

It isn't enough. I need a knot.

My pussy is pulsing around nothing, begging for completion, and all I'm able to get out is, "Knot."

But it's enough. Because Saint straightens, his fingers working the button and zipper of his jeans like a fucking pro. And he is commando. His dick bobs between us as he pushes his pants down, the knot heavy at its base. He's long and thick and everything my body is craving. A whine for him starts in my chest and works its way out of my lips. Austin nips at my neck, a promise of a bite, and I tilt my head to give him more access. Give me a fucking necklace of bites. I'm so far gone, I want it all.

"Protection?" Of course he still has his head.

The omega in me that wants to have a million babies with my pack wants to say no, but my practical brain wins out, and I nod. He drags out his wallet and pulls out a condom, dropping the wallet to the ground as he tears the package open with his teeth. And my heat is being so iffy, it is better to be safe than sorry.

How many omegas does he sleep with that he needs to carry protection in his wallet? The nagging thought is intrusive, and I push it away and hopefully off a cliff because what happened before me doesn't matter.

"It's new. For you. Only you," he whispers.

My stomach dips at his words as he reads my mind. *For me.*

Felix takes the condom from him and rolls it over Saint's length in a practiced move. Another insecure omega thought intrudes. And I need one of them to distract me with an orgasm, because this one wants to know how many women they shared. Fuck.

I'm a goner. Possessive omega, activated.

Just as Saint's tip is brushing my folds, Austin says, "Wait."

I hold my breath as he straightens up behind me and then circles the couch. He lifts me up as if I weigh nothing, then settles me on his lap, spreading my thighs wide. I can feel his hard length beneath me as Saint rises to his knees again.

"That's it. I want to feel every tremble that Saint works from your body while Felix and I watch."

Saint positions himself between my legs. His cock straining to be inside of me as he runs himself through my folds, the head catching at my entrance. He hisses as he pushes in a tiny bit. His enormous head filling me in the most delicious way, promising more with his knot.

He groans. "Audrey, fuck, I will not last."

A shiver works through me at his husky words. His leather and lemons musk envelopes me like a warm blanket and mixing with fall, spice, and the ocean on a perfectly sunny day.

"Saint, more," I say.

Another groan falls from his lips as he pushes in further, stretching me wider. Filling me in all the ways possible. Then he pulls back and strokes back in with a deliciously slow and measured thrust. He brushes a spot inside, and my head drops back to Austin's shoulder as I shudder.

Austin smooths his hands up and over my stomach, holding onto my breasts as if they are handles, his thumbs working the tight peaks. Felix leans forward and sucks an offered nipple into his mouth, and I'm positive I'm going to die. The sensations have another heat spike rising to answer them. As if my body wants to ensure we don't leave the apartment for the next few days.

I move my hips as much as I can, urging Saint to go deeper and give me what I crave. He moans and sinks another inch deeper.

"You are so fucking tight."

I don't tell him it's because, before them, I've only had one less than stellar experience by a man that then, tortured me a week later. I don't want to think about him. Not right now, in this perfect moment.

So I hum out my agreement, so I don't have to admit that I'm basically a virgin. Because we were interrupted before Jason could get that far. Thank whatever God that had been looking out for me that day, because being tied to him in that way would have been unbearable.

Saint captures my face in his palms, his movements stilling as he stares into my soul. "Stay here in this room, Audrey. I need you present. We will hunt down your monsters and kill them all, but right now, right here, it is about pleasure and connection. Not anyone else. No ghosts from the past are allowed in this room with us."

I stare into his brown eyes, letting him center me as a purr vibrates Austin's chest behind me, soothing me in only the ways my true pack can.

"I'm here," I promise. Then I wiggle my hips, drawing him further into my warmth, squeezing my muscles around him intentionally. When he hisses in pleasure before a moan flows from between his lips, I do it again. I love that sound.

He finds a rhythm and works all the way into me, except for his knot. He teases me and, before long, my hips are popping off of Austin's lap, attempting to take what I want. Each movement of my ass against Austin's length makes me want to be filled in two places.

That would be completely new, and I was pretty sure I should save it for another time if I want to walk tomorrow. Which, now that I'm thinking about it, maybe I don't want to walk tomorrow. I enjoy being carried. Held as if I'm a treasure worth more than any priceless jewel.

Saint presses into me, his knot slipping into me with ease, locking him to me and satisfying my greedy pussy. I clench around him, feeling his entire length in me. I can't help doing it again and again, as if I'm milking the seed from him. He moans, his forehead dropping to mine. His breath is ragged as he attempts to catch it.

My whole body feels flushed as all of their hands run over my sensitive flesh. Saint pulses his hips, moving as much as he can, hitting a spot that feels like he is stroking a flame, making it brighter and brighter with each movement.

Slipping my fingers into his hair, I bring his mouth to mine, kissing him in slow, sensual strokes that match the movements he's making. Need builds inside me, turning into a blaze burning me from the inside out.

Breaking away, I open my eyes to meet his gaze. "Bite me."

He sucks in a breath; his eyes dip to my neck. I imagine he is looking at Felix's mark. His would look amazing next to it. And at the moment is the only thing I want.

Encouraging him, I tangle my fingers deeper into his hair and tug his head to the nape of my neck. His tongue flattens against my skin, over my pulse, and he licks me. Then his teeth graze my flesh before he sinks his teeth into me, and I shatter into a million pieces, as it locks the link in place just as much as his knot. When he pulses inside of me, releasing and climaxing his own orgasm, I cling to him.

I'm not sure how long we are like that. Time passes differently, in a haze of pleasure and belonging. The best drug for my omega brain. I'm safe, secure, and wanted.

The three of them cuddle me until Saint slips from my folds and my legs are no longer weak. I know Austin and Felix deserve some kind of pleasure, too, and I'll make sure they get it, but my stomach rumbles, disturbing all three of them and making them spring into action to care for me.

Austin settles me gently on the sofa as all three of them care for me in different ways.

Felix disappears into my room, returning with an armful of blankets and pillows to make a nest in the middle of the living room. He makes a few trips, and by the time he is done, he's crafted a nest big enough for the four of us in the middle of the living room floor.

Austin disappears into the bathroom and returns with a warm washcloth and a bowl brimming with warm water. As he washes me with the utmost tenderness, ensuring every bit of stickiness is gone, and then massages my legs, stomach, and breasts with the gentlest touch of the soft cloth, I can't help but feel like I might just melt into a puddle of overwhelming omega bliss right here on the couch. His caring actions fill me with warmth and a heavy dose of desire.

As Saint works his magic in the kitchen, my stomach can't help but growl in anticipation. When he comes back with a plate piled high with eggs, potatoes, and one pastry I purchased earlier, I'm more than ready. As he sets the plate on the coffee table, which we had pushed to the side, I express my approval with a contented hum.

He selects a potato with his fork and offers it to my lips. I pause for just a moment, then open my mouth and grant him silent permission to feed me. Saint, his eyes filled with warmth, grumbles his satisfaction as he feeds me, and I can't help but feel a deep connection in that simple act of care.

Is this what it is to be an omega? They are treating me like a princess. And even the wary parts of my brain are craving them.

CHAPTER 43
Saint

SATISFACTION. That is the prominent feeling at the moment. Not even the asshole chained to the ceiling could bring me down. The bond created by the bite thrums inside my chest like a second heartbeat, reminding me of Audrey every second I'm away from her.

I pick up a scalpel. Stepping closer to the piece of garbage, I tsk when he attempts to swing away.

"Tell me. Did you think you would get away with your crimes?"

He whimpers, a darkness spreading over his pants as he wets himself. Of course. Once backed into a corner or hanging from a ceiling, all the monsters of the world turn into nothing but scared little boys. When they face their crimes, they snivel like wounded puppies, only not as cute and creating no urge to comfort them.

"Oh, you like to torture helpless omegas, but when it is you in their spot, you don't like it so much?"

With precision, because I want his pain to last, I slice a thin line down his side. He screams, and it is music to my ears. This isn't the same as being in the ring. In the ring, I can explode with my energy and pound into my opponent. Here it is slow and steady. But it's how I want it. Audrey deserves to be free of these monsters, these ghosts that haunt her dark eyes.

I'll take care of them one by one, like the Saint I am. Austin likes to tease and say my nickname came from doing good deeds, but really it came from exacting punishment for crimes. Which, in a twisted way, is a good deed.

I shrug off the thoughts as tears run down the coward's face. "Tell me, did you get off on her pain?"

"I didn't touch her." He uses his toes to swing away from me.

"No? Only her brother? Did you get off on his pain?" I growl, my voice low and menacing. He flinches as gravity brings him back in my direction, and I know I've hit a mark. He got off on it. Fucker.

It takes all my restraint when I slice into him again. He swings away from me again, squealing like a pig. Maybe I should get Audrey's brother up here to exact some of his own revenge. I'm sure the omega would want to. Maybe it would ease the darkness that clings to him. With that thought in mind, I pull out my phone and message Felix, asking him to see if he can bring him in.

Might be a long shot, but giving her brother his own revenge felt like giving Audrey something, and I want to give her the whole fucking world. But first, I need to remove all the monsters.

After a while, Felix arrives with Audrey's brother in tow. The omega eyes me as he comes into the room, hesitating only a moment, his gaze flowing from the red-tipped scalpel between my fingers to the man I've been slicing.

"This is Saint," Felix says through introduction. His face drains of color as he takes in the now unconscious man. The man was surprisingly weak, and it took little before he succumbed to the darkness.

"Sin," he says with a nod.

I grin because if I am going to team up with anyone, it should be a man named 'Sin'. "Well, Sin, this monster here is the first of many presents if you are so inclined. I believe he has a lesson to learn and thought you'd be the best teacher."

His gaze glimmers with the same darkness that lurks in his sister's eyes. And he steps forward, selecting a tool that removes nails from fingertips off of the tray.

"Let's wake him up," he purrs.

Felix drags a chair over the metal floor and sinks into it. "You don't have to stay for this. I know how you are with blood and torture."

"I'm staying. Watching the monsters that hurt our girl feel even the tiniest bit of pain is the highlight of my day."

"This is the highlight of your day?" I cock an eyebrow at him as a grin spreads over my lips. The highlight of my day was feasting between Audrey's legs, but that isn't something I will say in front of her brother.

He scoffs and meets my gaze. "Well–"

The monster's scream interrupts whatever he was going to say. And we both turn back to Sin as he tears off another fingernail. Where Audrey was quick with her anger and striking the man the other night down. Sin is methodical. Like he has dreamt of this moment since they escaped that hell.

"Wakey, wakey," he murmurs. "I've come to play."

If I thought the man tried to get away from me earlier, as soon as his wide eyes land on Sin, he scrambles away as much as he can. Sin just grins, perching on the edge of a chair he had pulled over to reach the man's fingers.

"Do you remember the day you caused this scar?" Sin lifts his shirt, and his finger traces a horizontal scar that could only mean one thing. They removed his ability to have children with an alpha. A shiver skates down my spine. What horrors did they face at the hands of these monsters? "Ah, yes, there is that recognition. The highlight of your fucking day, wasn't it?" He laughs. "Unfortunately for you, I wear a constant reminder, so I haven't forgotten either."

With that, he rips off the man's thumbnail. Blood drips from his fingertips as Sin removes one after another. When he's dropped the last nail to the floor, he hops down from the chair and places the tool back on the tray, picking up another one.

He slices his pants down each side, leaving them hanging from his ankles. "Do you want to know the true pain I felt?" he asks. Using the blade, he slices the boxers from the guy, baring him to the room. His dick shriveled and hiding like a fucking turtle. Sin reaches out and cups the monster's balls in his hand.

"No, man, don't do this. Christ. No," the coward begs.

It's useless. I can see it in the way Sin holds the blade, and I know what he is going to do before he even moves. The scream that echoes off the walls has me wincing as Sin slices the sack clean from his body. Blood flows down his legs, and he convulses.

Sin lifts a brow and turns back to the tray, reaching for the heat clamp, made for stopping blood and cauterizing wounds. "Can't have you die on me. Not when I'm just getting started."

The scent of burnt skin fills the air, and Felix looks green. I chuckle and lean against the counter, waiting to see what else Sin wants to do. The man blacks out as the bleeding stops. Sin purses his lips and puts the heat clamp back down.

Then he looks at me. "You smell like my sister. You both do, but you smell like you rolled around in her slick and didn't wash it off."

I laugh, the sound coming out in a surprised huff. "You are straightforward."

"If you hurt her, what I'm doing to this man will seem like child's play." The darkness, mixing with the madness, tells me he would follow through.

"Noted."

"We scent matched with her. We aren't going anywhere," Felix adds, and I'm not sure if he is saying that out loud so her brother knows we are for real or so he doesn't change his mind and torture us as soon as he is done with the guy.

"I bet she is hating that. Scent matching to three alphas. She didn't even want one."

"We know," I rumble, a slight growl coming out at the idea that she had tried to walk away.

"If I know my sister, she is planning her escape, so if you want to truly keep her, be ready when she runs."

A groan from the man as he wakes back up stops the conversation as Sin focuses fully on the guy again. The things he does to him make even me cringe, but he deserves them. I'm tempted to let the guy go to live whatever semblance of life he would have left as a sick punishment. But before I can voice it, Sin is playing tic-tac-toe with his chest and the last 'X' goes a little too deep.

When he stops breathing, the rest of his blood dripping from his limp form, I pull out my phone and call the cleaners.

As I hang up, I watch Sin as he stares at his masterpiece. I may have just created a monster, but at least he will only go after people that deserve it. The world could live with fewer rapists and murderers. Vigilante doesn't count. At least not in my book. The whole eye for an eye has merit.

"That was fun," Sin quips. "Almost better than feeling the pain myself."

"You like pain?" I ask.

He shrugs like it isn't a big deal. "Trauma response."

"From what they did to you?" I gesture at the dead guy.

"Well, considering before them I was a normal omega ready to find my pack, and they took not only my family from me, but my ability to match one. So I assume it stems from that, but I'm not a psychologist, and I'm pretty sure if I talked to one I'd be in a padded white cell some place."

I lick my lips, tasting his acidy and angry scent in the air. "I could get you into the fight rings. If you don't mind using your fists and earning some cash. Might be a good way to work out some aggression, and they allow beta and omega in the ring, although it is rare."

"If my sister knew you were offering to help me find pain, she would kill you before she ran." He flips a clean knife over his knuckles and leans against the stationary metal table the tools still rest on.

I glance at Felix, and he gives me a wane smile that says he is not hearing any of this, and he might just pass out. "I'll take my chances. Do you want an in? We can talk about it over dinner. There is a nice diner around the corner that won't judge the blood on your clothes.

"Or yours," he replies.

I glance down, and he's right; I got a few speckles over my white shirt. I shrug out of it and drop it on the floor. "We can get fresh shirts from Austin's office."

As I pass Felix, I give him a hand up and tug him along behind me, Sin following close behind.

After we've both got clean shirts, we head to the diner. The conversation flows, and the three of us share a few laughs as I give Sin the details of the fight club. I like Audrey's brother. He might be damaged but, in a way, I can see how he completes his sister, and the resemblance to each other, although she went the nurturing route, and he went deeper into the abuse. Maybe the fight club will help him find his center and a place in the world.

"Call me when you have the next one," Sin says as we exit the diner. "I'd love to see the fear in their eyes when they see me again."

"I'll be sure to include you," I promise. He gives us a chin raise and then strides away, in the opposite direction of the apartments.

CHAPTER 44

Audrey

THIS FEELING PING-PONGING around my chest is the worst. Saint and Felix have been gone most of the day. Austin is in his office, and I'm not sure if it would be too needy of me to interrupt whatever he is doing. But that is what I feel like. A needy fucking omega.

Two bites. One missing. Why didn't he bite me? He had a chance. But he clearly held himself back. I finger the two slightly raised patches of skin as I stare out at the darkening city. Even Sin has ignored my texts. Not even a reply; hell, I'm not even sure he read them.

I moved all of my blankets and pillows back to my room and made up my bed in the perfect nest, and even that isn't working to calm me. So, instead, I'm pacing in front of my window and fingering the marks that are ringing my neck.

Restlessness infuses every movement, and I can feel a heat coming on. The cramps tightening my stomach and my breasts heavy and achy. Whatever the doctor gave me is clearly wearing off. I need an alpha. Yet, I'm too afraid to just knock on the closed door. Not that I'm afraid of Austin. It's stupid. The lack of his mark is making me feel all kinds of insecure.

Stupid omega shit. If biology didn't have a chokehold on my fucking hormones, I would be fine.

As it is, my skin feels tight and tingly, like it doesn't fit correctly. With a deep sigh, I turn toward my door. Water. That is what I need.

Cracking the door open, I peek out as if Austin catches me I'd be in trouble or something. It is ridiculous. The hall is empty as I emerge and hurry to the kitchen. I'm half-way inside the freezer, cooling off my fiery face when Austin comes around the corner and comes to a complete stop.

Like a startled cat, I yelp, and if I had fur, it would definitely be puffed out right now.

He arches an eyebrow at me as he rubs the back of his neck. "You okay?"

He looks tense and tired, and suddenly, all I want to do is comfort him. Or climb him like a tree and beg for his mark. It is fifty-fifty at the moment.

I moisten my lips and nod. "I'm good. Just thirsty."

The corner of his mouth kicks up. "Well, you won't find anything in the freezer unless you're looking for the prepackaged frozen margaritas."

Nibbling on my lower lip, I shut the door as my face flushes hotter with embarrassment. Even my perfume gets in on it this time and spreads a sickly sweet scent between us that makes me cringe.

He says nothing though, just steps closer and opens the refrigerator door and snags out a bottle of water. He holds it out to me with a smile. Is almost melting a thing? Because I'm sure I'm so close to my heat that his insignificant gesture of taking care of me is going to push me into the lava, and I'd melt like magma.

Taking the cool bottle, I twist off the cap and down half of it. I'm sure if I actually was magma, you'd see steam coming off me. It helps a little to cool me down.

"Thanks."

"There is more where that comes from," he says, chuckling. The tension is easing in his shoulders, like just being around me is soothing him. It makes me want to nuzzle into his arms and listen to whatever caused it in the first place.

"Are you okay?" I ask.

"Fine." The way he averts his eyes tells a different story, but I don't press.

"Hungry?"

"Starving actually."

"I could make something," I suggest. Cooking is something I excelled at before my parents died. I have done little since, but it is like riding a horse.

The contents of the fridge are only good for making more grilled cheese or some sort of breakfast concoction. I frown before nibbling on my lower one some more.

"There isn't much in there," he admits as I close the door. "I can take you somewhere, get ready, wear one of the dresses."

I want to argue with his commanding tone, but curiosity gets the best of me, and I listen to him like a good omega.

A navy blue dress draws my attention once I'm in my closet, and I quickly change into it. The soft material hugs my curves in the best possible way, and it falls to my feet, almost puddling at the bottom, with a slit up the side of my right leg. A slight shimmer catches the light each time I move. Every part of me wants to please him tonight instead of taunting a reaction out of him. Although, maybe later pressing his buttons would be fun.

I pull out my boots, ready to put them on, but then I change my mind and scan the wall of shoes. He didn't miss a single thing when he stocked this room. A matching pair of heels calls my name, and I snag them off the shelf. They are Christian Louboutin's with an open toe and matte navy blue with a four-inch heel.

Slipping them on, I feel like Cinderella finding her glass slipper. They fit like they are made for my feet. And feel like walking on clouds. Probably not after a couple hours, but right this second, I love them.

When I return to the living room, his eyes sweep from my head to the tips of my Louboutin's. Appreciation gleams from his gaze as he returns it to mine. He doesn't look half bad himself. He changed into one of his suits, sans the tie, the white button up begging to be undone, and the blazer unbuttoned. His hands propped on the pockets of his slacks, he looks like a model right off the cover of GQ.

"Ready?"

I smile. Excitement corses through me, almost vibrating my whole body. I feel like I've stepped into *Omega in Paradise*. He closes the distance and offers me his hand before leading me from the penthouse and into the elevator. When he inserts a key and presses the button to take us up and not down, I tilt my head and look at him.

"What–?"

"A surprise."

Silence falls as we take the few floors before opening on the roof, and not the pool top roof but the top of what is probably the gym they showed me the first day we moved in. A helipad greets us with a sleek black helicopter, a soft whoosh-whoosh-whoosh fills the air front, the rotor blades turning above it. The sound captures my surprised gasp and his fingers tangled with mine urge me to move across to the gigantic machine.

He helps me into the helicopter like a perfect gentleman, making me feel like a princess and the most cherished omega in the world. Is this what those girls feel like on the show?

Even Jason hadn't done something like this, or really anything romantic, if I'm honest. How had I fallen for the guy?

I push the stray thoughts from my mind as he settles next to me and hands me a headset. After he puts his on, he helps me into mine. My dad had a helicopter, but it was for business, not pleasure, so I never rode in one.

"Can you hear me?" he asks. His husky voice sounding directly in my ear and making a shiver run down my spine. I nod, my head feeling heavy with the headset in place.

"I can. Where are we going?"

"You'll see," he replies with a grin.

This is a different side to Austin. He isn't the intimidating ex-mafia prince or multi-billionaire in this space. He is more like a boy on a date with a girl he likes. And it makes every single part of my omega heart sing. He may not have given me his mark, but he likes me as much as I like him. Just being next to him with his fingers tangling with mine again eases the oncoming heat, like it isn't looming around the next corner, and I'm able to just be in the moment.

We fly over the city, past the river, south over mountains until city lights shine on the horizon. It is magical and not something I'd ever thought I would experience after—I shake off the thoughts and smile over at Austin. He watches me, making me feel warm.

"Paparazzi won't be here expecting me, so we won't have to worry about them showing up."

Even more warmth spreads through my chest, making me realize I hadn't been worried about being seen, because the pack makes me feel safe. How the hell had that happened? I can't pinpoint when the shift occurred.

"Thanks, Daddy," I say through the mouthpiece. His pupils blow wide, and he growls softly.

"Play nice," he warns.

A wide grin pulls at my lips, and I'm half tempted to call him daddy again just to see his reaction. In an attempt to stop the smile, I clamp down on my lower lip and look at him from under my lashes.

His gaze rakes over me, and my stomach flips with excitement. I know it is all biology at this point and my body doing anything to encourage me to throw myself into his arms. But damn, when I say every part of me craves his bite, it is *every part of me.*

THE RESTAURANT he brought us to is elegant and expensive. The lack of prices on the menu gave that fact away the second I looked at it. I'm not sure how he managed it, but they led us to a private booth in the furthest corner away from the door and no one in the tables surrounding us when we first arrived.

Once the waitress strides away with our drink orders, I lean back in my seat, taking in Austin across from me. His foot nudges mine beneath the table, and when I arch my brow, he grins.

"Order whatever you want," he says, dropping his eyes to the menu on the table.

"You're different right now," I reply.

"How so?"

"Just lighter somehow."

He captures my fingers with his and leans forward, as if he is going to tell me a secret. "I just realized that it wasn't a painting that was missing. It was you."

The heat infuses my cheeks as I blush like a schoolgirl with my first crush. I have to remind myself even though he is saying flowery words; he didn't give me his mark. And before the other day, being marked by anyone sounded like a nightmare.

"You don't have to say that shit just because—"

His face smooths out and grows serious. "One thing you need to know about me, princess, is I don't just say *shit* I don't mean. I didn't want an omega. Not after Sidney."

Jealousy gnaws at my insides, and I chew on my lip before I say, "Who is Sidney?"

His eyes get a faraway look in them, and I want to call him back to the present with me. "She is an omega that pretended to want me, when what she wanted was money and power."

I stare at him. Blink once. Isn't that what happened to me? Only Jason was an alpha, and if he hadn't decided I wasn't worth the trouble and took out my parents at a bid to grab their power, he would have had it through me.

"How did you find out?"

He gives a tight smile. Before he can respond, the waitress is back with our drinks, setting his sipping rum down in front of him and my water in front of me. I know little about the cost of alcohol, but the way the waitress's eyes widened when he ordered the Legacy Rum told me it wasn't a normal drink.

We order, well, he orders, and from the sound of it, it is one of everything. After the woman walks away, he focuses on me again, our conversation right back to where we left off.

He runs a finger around the rim of the glass and inhales. "The Zade Mafia ten years ago isn't what it is now. We were profitable and strong, but other Mafia's like the De Luca Mafia–" he pauses and meets my gaze, "And Carmichael's were stronger, more power, more money. When Sidney saw her chance to bond to the head of the Carmichael empire, she jumped. She left me without so much as a goodbye."

"She is at the head of the Carmichael's?"

He chuckles, taking a sip of his rum. "For a year, until a

rival took her out, and Carmichael moved on to another omega. I'm not sure he ever really got over the death of his first omega, and Sidney was just a replacement, someone to help raise his daughter. His third wife's son is in charge now, taking his name. He is ruthless. But that is off topic."

"Well, at least she got what she deserved."

"Maybe you are the ruthless one," he says, arching his brow. He watches me over the rim of his glass, and I finger the side of my water.

"People like that, like her, they ruin lives. They take futures from you in their bid of a power grab."

He leans back, setting his tumbler back onto the table as he studies me openly. "Sounds like you are talking from experience."

I wet my lips. "Yeah," I say, the single word coming out like a dry croak.

"Is that who killed your parents?"

So perceptive. I nod because I will not force the words from between my lips. Reaching for my glass of water like it's a lifeline, I take a quick sip. Blinking back the emotion from my eyes, I say, "How much does this place cost, Daddy?"

He shakes his head, a mix between a smile and a frown at my change of topic. "More than the watch you swiped to get yourself here."

"How do you know I'm not here for the money and power?" I ask cheekily.

"Princess, you are the head of the De Luca Mafia. You have all the money and power you could ever want, you just have to claim it."

I shudder. I don't want it. Not the power, anyway. "Sin can have it all."

The topic switches again as Austin relaxes in his seat. "Felix said you like *Omega in Paradise*. The producers approached us to be on it a few years ago."

My eyes go wide. If they had accepted, would we be here right now? "And you didn't." Statement is not a question, I've watched every season.

"No. I didn't want an omega. Until now."

"Until now," I agree.

His eyes warm, the violet deepening as he watches me with a look of almost love in the depth of his irises. I am sure it is the scent matching talking or my oncoming heat, but I want it to be love. Which makes me certifiably insane.

The waitress returns with more food than we can possibly eat, and when she leaves, Austin insists on feeding me a bite of each dish and watching my reactions. After I finish chewing a bite of the last dish, he picks up the two I loved most and sets them in front of me.

"Eat. You'll need your energy," he says.

"For what?"

"For the punishment you are getting for calling me daddy in public."

CHAPTER 45

Austin

I DON'T REACT to the number at the bottom of the bill; only slide my black card into the waitress's fingers and focus right back on the only woman I can see, Audrey.

The guys are going crazy. My phone has been vibrating with texts I've ignored since before we arrived. And I know I'm being a selfish prick flying her away to have solo time with her, but I had held myself back all day. Locked myself in my office and avoided seeking her out, even though I knew she was in the penthouse only a few steps away.

She did something to my senses. Her perfume clung to me even when I wasn't in the same room with her, a phantom reminding me of the sweet taste of her skin.

My eyes drop to her neck, Saint and Felix's marks clearly leaving room for mine in the center. I want to give it to her, but first, I need to make sure it is what she really wants. No second guessing. No running. Once she wears my mark, she is mine. Fully and completely, forever. Because I won't let her go.

She captures her lip as I watch her, nibbling along the pink surface. And I can see the gears turning. She is about to say something that will make me instantly hard. Those kinds of words always follow her hesitance and holding back.

"What?" I arch an eyebrow.

"Just thinking of what my punishment could be–" she breaks off as the waitress comes back with my card, a slow smile working her lips. Then she stretches and lets out a yawn. "I'm so full, *Daddy*, I don't think I have room for anything else."

My blood runs hot. She has room for something else alright, and I'm going to prove it to her. I ignore the waitress as she openly gasps at my omega as a growl rumbles in my chest. How scandalized would she be if I laid Audrey on the table and partook in dessert for one? Audrey would let me, but giving the restaurant a show isn't in my plans. So instead, I slide out of the booth and hold out a hand for her. She shimmies her way over the leather booth and places her tiny fingers into mine.

The second we are out in the cool night air, I press her into the stone brick wall at her back, easily boxing her in and capturing her mouth like a man starving. As though I didn't just eat as much as she had. I can't get enough of her sweet taste, sweeping my tongue inside her mouth and deepening the kiss. She melts for me almost immediately, her fingers tangling into the hair at the base of my neck as I attempt to convince myself to take this back to the helicopter.

"Get a room," a man mutters as he passes by.

It reminds me we are out in the open, kissing like we are teens with no control. I pull back slightly, and she leans in, following me, not allowing the kiss to be broken. Groaning, I gather her closer again. She hums in satisfaction.

"Rutting in public is against the law," a woman complains, a man adding his agreement as they walk behind me.

Fuck. I'd go to jail for her. But I'd hardly call kissing,

rutting; they aren't the same. If I were in a rut, we'd be doing more than that. This time, I manage to break the kiss. She pouts up at me, her pink lips puffy and her chin red from the stubble of my day-old beard.

"Don't worry, princess, we will finish what we started." I thumb her lower lip and groan when her tongue slips out to taste my skin.

I thread my fingers through hers and lead her back to the helipad. The pilot is waiting, and he climbs in, starting his first checks as soon as he sees me. I help Audrey into the helicopter and follow behind her. My whole body is thrumming with need for her. I have wanted no one this badly, ever.

Busying myself with making sure her headset is on and she is secure in her seat, I try to ignore the lust flowing through my veins. She watches me, a mixture of the sub she pretends to be sometimes, and the brat swirling in the depths of her eyes, and I hope the brat wins. Once she is secure, I strap myself in and put on the headset.

"Is the pilot on this channel?" Her voice is like a soft caress along the shell of my ear, and any of the hardness that had gone down responded to her as if she reached out and cupped me through my pants.

I shift to give myself a little more room in my slacks, and her eyes drop to my hips. The heat in her gaze doesn't help, and I half-growl, half-groan when she doesn't immediately bring her eyes back up to mine.

"No," I reply.

"That's too bad." She looks over at the pilot as he completes his last checks outside before she returns her gaze to me. "I wanted him to hear what a good girl I could be, Daddy."

"How red do you want your cheeks, princess? You're earning quiet the punishment."

She presses her legs together in a move I wouldn't have

caught if I weren't obsessively watching her. Perfume, sweet and chocolatey, fills the small interior. If I had a divider to put between us and the pilot, I would. Next time we are taking the jet.

"But you like it," she protests.

I hum. Her eyes sparkle.

"Don't you, Daddy?"

Shit, she is going to be the death of me, or at least the death of my restraint. I'm not the kind that gives in to public displays, but I'm ready to tug her into my lap and have her demand her own pleasure from me on the way back home. Maybe I am entering a rut, but that would mean that she is releasing pheromones for a heat. Is that the extra sweetness of her perfume? Speaking to the alpha in me directly?

"I told you to knock the daddy shit off." I press my head against the headrest and roll my head to the side to look at her.

She grins. "Right, but I've found it gets me what I want."

"You want to be spanked?"

Her cheeks flush, giving me my answer. Why did I pick some place so far from home? My fingers curl into my palms as I imagine her over my lap, her round ass on display for me, my handprint a red mark that will fade on her skin. And most of all, her tantalizing scent wrapping around my senses like the pied piper calling me home.

I lick my lips and glance away. "Don't look at me like that, Audrey," I grind out.

She inhales, her breath catching as if my words do something to her. The mic picks up on her tiny whine as she exhales, and I snap my head back in her direction. I can barely hold myself in my seat as the pilot starts the helicopter running through the rest of his pre-check. The rotors thwomp-thwomp-thwomp a steady pulse through me, my need for Audrey growing the faster they turn.

The flight feels like it takes forever, and as soon as we touch down, I'm tearing off my headset and unstrapping, my eyes never leaving my omega. Her fingers fumble at the latches, and I reach over, easily releasing her, then I take off her headset and set it to the side.

I know the pilot will finish up and go home. He's not new to the position. So I tug her with me, wordlessly leading her to the elevator.

As soon as the doors slide shut, she's in my arms. I press into her, trapping her against the metal wall. Then I hold her there with my hips as I hit the button for our floor. My mouth is on hers before the elevator moves. I have half a mind to stop the elevator and give into this rut that has taken over. But the doors slide open on our floor, and I sweep her up in my arms, eager for more.

The penthouse door swings wide before we get to it, which is just fine with me. Saint and Felix stare at me, us really, as I pass them and head for my room. I'm not sharing. Not tonight.

"Where have you been?" Saint demands.

"We were worried." Felix shares a look with Saint that should make me feel guilty, and probably would if being inside of her wasn't the only thing my brain can think about.

I ignore them as Audrey gives them a lopsided smile and waves her fingers at them. "Daddy Zade took me out for dinner."

A growl rumbles my chest, and my cock pulses at the use of the nickname falling from her lips so easily. I twist her in my arms, throwing her over my shoulder at the same time as my hand smacks her ass. She yelps before a nervous laugh slips out.

"Now he's going to teach me a lesson," she says, lifting slightly to look at them, I assume. Her fingers wrapping around my belt and holding on.

I kick my bedroom door shut, cutting off the brief conversation. Then I set her on her feet and circle her, reaching for the zipper in her dress. It falls like a free-falling skydiver, and she lets the sleeves follow suit. The shimmery dress pools at her feet, leaving her in nothing but heels, thigh-high stockings, and a lacy pair of panties.

I drag my eyes from her head to her toes and back again. My blood heating even more, if that is possible. Then I sit on the edge of my bed and pat my lap. Her brows lift in question, and I can't help the wicked grin that pulls at my lips.

"Face down, princess," I order, my voice coming out gruff.

She comes willingly and stretches across my lap, her soft belly pressing against my hard length in the most delicious way. I run my fingers gently along the edge of her panties, before slipping them below the fabric and lowering them off of her ass. Caressing her skin with soft touches, I absorb the soft mewls coming from her as if they are the air I need to breathe.

Sucking in a breath, I lift my hand and smack her firmly. Her whole body jerks, and she whimpers. Her pheromones fill the space, and I do it again, brushing over the area my hand lands each time, soothing it before delivering another well timed spanking. My breathing becomes more ragged with each one.

"Is this what you wanted?" I husk.

She hums, her chest vibrating into my lap. I inhale deeply, reaching for the scraps of restraint I still have.

Then my hand lands firmly on her left ass cheek. The perfect hand print, and the slight sting I know she feels, followed by gentle touches that make her squirm.

"Words."

"Yes," she gasps.

I smack her again. "Yes, what?"

"Yes, Daddy," she whimpers.

Dipping my fingers between her legs, I delve into her slick folds. She becomes motionless as I swirl my thumb over her swollen clit and dip two fingers into her pussy.

"You're so ready for me," I groan.

She hums again.

"What do you want? Do you want my knot? Do you want to feel me deep inside you?"

"God, yes."

I press harder inside of her, adding pressure to her g-spot at the same time as I circle her clit. She moans loudly, so gone for me she would probably ask for anything I offer. Removing my fingers, I stand her up on wobbly legs and tug the lace panties the rest of the way off of her, kissing her stomach as I lean forward. She kicks them to the side, still in her heels and stockings. I run my fingers over the material on the way back up her legs.

Then I slip my arms around her and release her breasts, capturing one tight peak in my mouth and sucking until she gives me another moan. They are like a drug, making me lightheaded and unable to think straight.

With one hand, I undo my belt, releasing the button and dragging the zipper down. My dick strains against the thin material until I pull it out. The pre-cum gathers at the tip, and my knot is so large I'm surprised there is still blood flow.

Leaning back, I release her nipple, and she looks down at me with hooded eyes full of lust. I need her like this. Ready for me, so gone her pupils are blown wide, and her cheeks flush. My cock bobs straight up for her, and she eyes me like she didn't just help me finish multiple dinners. Then she is taking over, her tiny hands pushing me further back onto my bed and her legs straddling me.

"Protection?" I gasp.

She shakes her head, no. "Not this time."

"Use me, princess, take what you need."

She sinks onto me, impaling herself with my length. Stopping short of the knot before she lifts and starts short, teasing strokes. I arch my hips into her, and she groans as my knot slips inside, filling her up. Her walls grasp me, clenching and unclenching in the most sinfully erotic way.

I roll us, settling my full weight onto her and pressing her into the bed. Lifting her legs, I loop them over my shoulders as I pull out and thrust in repeatedly. Our cries of pleasure mix and mingle until I'm unsure whose is whose.

I can feel my orgasm building at the base of my spine, tightening my balls in preparation for release. Lowering my head, I lick and kiss her neck. The unmarked skin beneath my teeth tempting in a way I said I'd never be tempted again. Still, I withhold my mark, not because I'm unsure, but because I'm scared shitless. A coward. She squeezes me tight, and it is what I need because I explode into a million pieces, calling out her name as I come.

I'm so fucking lost to this omega, with or without my mark.

CHAPTER 46

Audrey

I'M a limp noodle as Austin drags me against his chest and cuddles me. But I still don't forget that I don't bear his mark. The pack leader still hasn't accepted me as his mate. And even through the euphoria of my most recent orgasm, a pang echos through my empty heart.

If he rejects me, I won't be able to stay, even with the other two marking me. And the crazy, impossible fact is I want to stay. I don't want to keep running. He snuggles into my neck, and a lone tear falls from the corner of my eye and soaks into the pillow.

It is clear he wants me. But I know that doesn't mean he wants to keep me, no matter how good the sex is. And with the most recent wave of heat satisfied by him now fading into the background, I feel rejected even though he didn't say the words. I know what they say, actions always speak louder than words, and he has told me I'm not the one by not giving me his bite.

Long after his soft snores fill the room, I lay in his arms, soaking up his alpha warmth, staring sightlessly out his large windows. I should go back to my room. He probably doesn't want me to be in here in the morning.

With that thought in mind, I attempt to slip from his arms, but he tightens them in his sleep, muttering nonsense as he holds me firmly against his chest. My heart races. It means nothing. Just alpha instinct. So I try again, this time finding success as I slip off the bed. My stomach feels hollow as I feel his cum leak from between my legs.

Pressing my lips into a tight line so I don't actually release the whimpering sob that wants to escape, I slip on my dress and grab up everything else to make the walk of shame back to my room.

The penthouse is silent as I slink to my door and close it behind me. Heading for the bathroom, I twist on the shower, to the hottest it can be, and then stand under the spray as it removes Austin's tantalizing musk from my skin and washes it down the drain. Only then do I feel like a semblance of myself, like I don't actually need an alpha to make my life whole.

Drying off, I slip into my bed, piling the pillows and blankets into a nest and sinking into them. Still, sleep doesn't come as I stare at the slowly lightening ceiling. I hate that I want him, that I want any of them. But what I hate the most is that he doesn't want me the same way. When sleep comes for me, it is filled with dark dreams.

Nightmares that pull me under.

I'm back in that room. Helpless. Strapped to a cold metal table, and Jason is grinning above me. A scalpel in-between his fingers promising pain. He slices me, and I bite my tongue to hold in the scream. But he keeps doing it, and finally, a scream tears from my throat as blood pools beneath me.

"Look at the princess, brought so low," he sneers.

"Stop, I'll do whatever you want. Whatever you need, I can give it to you," I plead, my voice broken and raw.

How had I fallen for him? Why wasn't I enough? If he wanted power, he would have had that once I took over for my father. He would have had that with me. But he was greedy. My parents' lifeless bodies flash into my head, the mental image as much of a torture as the knife he cuts me with, and I sob.

"Why would I want you? A spoiled omega? Nobody will ever want you once I'm done with you."

Then the scalpel finds my skin again, only this time it drags over my neck where the mate marks go. When he peels my flesh away, I scream. The sound wrenched from my body.

My gasps ring through the air as Saint gathers me into his arms, shushing me and running his hand over my hair. "You're safe, I'm here, I've got you," he promises.

The visage of the nightmare clings to me as I sob into his shoulder, making myself as small as possible as I curl into his lap. The safety he offers calms me.

As my heart rate returns to normal, slowing to an almost sluggish pace, I suck in a breath. That was a new nightmare. I run my fingers over the two bite marks on my skin. Of course, my brain would serve me up some portion of the truth of what happened. The words were real, an echo of a past I escaped, but the torture was a new twist to an old story that my brain dished out.

Brushing the tears from my face, I lift my head to look up at Saint. He isn't Jason, he could never be Jason.

"Nightmare?" he asks, his deep brown eyes darting between mine with concern making them even darker.

I sigh. "Yeah. I get them sometimes." I shrug, attempting to brush it off as easily as I had the tears.

"From what happened to you and Sin?"

I cock my head to study him. He is on a first name basis when talking about my brother, that—is—interesting.

I press my lips together and tug on my ear. "I really don't want to talk about it."

He rubs my back and nods. "Of course, I can just hold you."

"I'd like that."

He smiles softly and then guides my head to his shoulder, before reaching for a blanket to cover us with. His even breathing and calming purr seeps into my very soul. We fit so perfectly together that it puts me at ease. My thoughts drift to Austin and his avoidance of marking me. I am pretty sure during a rut that control is lacking, and he still held back.

"I don't think Austin wants me to be part of the pack," I whisper into Saint's chest.

"He does."

"I'm not denying that he wants me. I have physical proof of that fact. But he didn't claim me with his mark."

Saint's arms tighten around me, as if I would bolt for the door and run away again. But this time I'm only leaving if they make me. My heart flips at the thought, at the absolute pain walking away would cause.

"He'll come around," he says, ruffling my hair with his words, the ghost of a kiss against my head following.

"If he doesn't?" I want to groan. Why would I ask such a blatant 'pick me' question? I couldn't ever come between them.

"Audrey, I'm not letting you go, and I'm sure Felix feels the same. Austin will complete the bond."

I nod and press deeper into his arms, my fingers slipping over the skin on his abdomen and around his side. But it isn't sexual as he holds me. It is pure emotion and connection that blankets me as my eyes grow heavy, and sleep claims me once more.

I don't dream. When I wake, Saint is sprawled beneath me like a full size body pillow that I am wrapped around. I stretch over him with a full body yawn, and his palm settles on my lower back, holding me to him even in sleep.

It is tempting to stay right here, but nature calls, so I detangle from him and head to the bathroom. A night in my alpha's arms has completely refreshed me. My heat is no longer lurking at the edges, satisfied that I have an alpha in my nest, sure that my body will get what it needs. His knot.

I don't have pheromone blockers here, so I guess I'll be wearing my expectations all over my body, my perfume joining in just in case it isn't clear. *Fuck. Just because Saint is in my bed doesn't mean I get to have my way with him. Sure. Tell that to your body.* I huff out a half-laugh before swinging the door open and entering the bedroom.

Saint, looking adorably sleep-rumpled, leans against the headboard with a waiting smile just for me. "Hey, beautiful."

A flush races to my cheeks as I bite down on my lower lip. Compliments in my old life had been an everyday occurrence, but there is something about one coming from my alpha that makes me melt.

"You're not so bad yourself," I say as I crawl up the bed to him. He captures me and drags me closer.

His large palms frame my face, and he kisses me. A soft, panty-soaking kiss, that I lean into with a tiny moan of encouragement as he deepens it with a stroke of his tongue. But he breaks it off way too soon.

"I've got a surprise for you today," he whispers against my lips, pressing tiny kisses between each word.

"A surprise?" I breathe.

"Yeah, your brother is going to join us for a little vengeance."

Not the surprise I was thinking, but vengeance is always welcome. Maybe it will help me sleep better at night taking out the monsters that destroyed my family.

"But first, I'm famished. I need something to eat," he says. While flipping me onto my back beneath him and working his way down my body, dragging my sleep shorts and panties with him.

He wastes no time burying his head between my legs and sucking on my clit until my back arches from the bed and sounds I didn't know I could make echo around the room.

Then he gathers my slick on his fingers, working them inside me, his warm tongue making sweeping strokes through my folds, collecting every drop.

It's quick and no frills, but the orgasm that tears me apart before piecing me back together satisfies my tiny omega heart. And when his teeth sink into the sensitive flesh of my inner thigh, marking me again, my heart sings.

CHAPTER 47

Audrey

NOT EVEN THE glower on Austin's face as Saint and I emerge from my bedroom can bring me down. I may not have a single bite from Austin, but I have two from Saint.

And Saint doesn't seem to mind my constant need to touch him. He stays close as I make us a proper breakfast, brushing against him teasingly each chance I get. Finally, he boxes me in as I flip pancakes in the pan, the outline of his dick clearly pressing into my ass. He nips my ear, purring directly into the shell and making my nipples tighten in anticipation.

Elbowing him softly, I duck from under his arms and twirl to the opposite counter to cut up some fruit as the other side of the pancake cooks. He chuckles and leans next to me.

"I don't know why you are making so much food. I had my breakfast already."

My cheeks darken and ache as I smile so widely that I can't contain it. "Not everyone else did. I'm sure Felix and Austin are hungry. And I'm hungry," I say.

"Felix is still asleep, and Austin survives on bourbon and ice."

"Are you calling me an alcoholic?" Austin grumbles from his armchair, clearly listening to everything we say.

"I would never do that," Saint quips.

Austin glares. He seems like he woke up on the wrong side of the bed this morning. Still, I ignore it. He can work out his own issues.

I finish with the fruit and put it in a bowl, sliding it over the island, closer to the stools. Then I flip the pancakes out of the pan before creating new ones.

"Breakfast is served, Daddy," I say like the brat I am.

A full growl rumbles across the space between us that shoots directly between my legs. He slowly stands up and prowls into the kitchen area, and I have an irrational feeling he is hunting me. Like I should run and let him chase me. I'd like to be caught.

"You know what you get when you call me that," he says. The stool scraps across the floor as he drags it away from the island and sits down.

I grin widely and bat my eyes. "A few dozen orgasms?"

"Keep it up, and I'll edge the fuck out of you. You'll be begging for release when I'm done."

My skin feels tight and hot at the idea. But I focus on the pancakes before I burn them.

"I'll get Felix," Saint says before dropping a kiss to my temple.

Austin is around the counter, pinning me against the one at my back and looming over me the second Saint is out of sight. He sniffs my neck and nips my earlobe. The slight scent of maple syrup clings to him as he says, "If you start the night in my bed, I expect you to be there when I wake up, princess."

I catch my breath, holding it trapped in my lungs as his hands roam up my sides.

"Sharing you with those two is fine when it starts out that

way, but if you are mine for the night, that means the entire night. Do you understand?"

Pure molten lust flows through my veins. He rubs his chin and cheek over my neck, marking me with his pheromones. The same ones I washed off last night. His hands burn a path back down to my hips, where he grips me tight and pulls me flush against him.

"Tell me you understand, princess, before your pancakes burn."

I can barely think, let alone cook with his larger-than-life thickness pressed against my belly and his fingers digging into my hips with promising intent.

"Yes, Daddy," I whisper. Need for him fills each syllable, enough to satisfy him to step back, leaving me panting and on the edge of another fucking heat wave.

"That's a good girl," he replies, his voice husky and warm as it washes over me.

Like a robot, I move back to the stovetop and flip the pancakes before they burn. But my entire being focuses on Austin, exactly where he wants my attention. I'm like a live wire, flailing around, waiting for his next move.

He watches me as he eats, barely looking down at his food long enough to get it on the fork. Desire swirls in his violet depths that makes me want to hop up on the counter and crawl across it to him.

"The tension is so thick you can cut it with a knife," Felix says as he appears. He runs his hand through his hair before rubbing his stomach. "It smells amazing in here, and I'm not just talking about the pancakes."

He closes the distance between us and wraps me in a hug from behind. His brief kiss to the nape of my neck is enough to send goosebumps of awareness down my spine. I want to turn in his arms and climb him like a mountain.

"Mmm, Audrey, you smell fucking amazing," Felix murmurs. "A mixture of you and two of my favorite alphas."

I lean back in his arms as I flip his pancakes.

"Want to go to Central Park today?" he asks.

"She can't, I'm taking her to deal out some vengeance with Sin." Saint pops a strawberry into his mouth and leans on the counter next to us.

Felix shivers behind me. "Pass. Maybe after."

Saint chuckles, stealing another strawberry.

"When did you and my brother get on a first name basis?"

"When he let him take out his pent up darkness on one man that hurt you," Felix says into my shoulder.

I suck in a breath. Sin hadn't told me. Not that we've talked much lately. I need to fix that.

"He also set him up to fight in the ring," Felix adds.

"Saint—" I pin him with a look.

"He needs an outlet. I've been in that place before, and the ring helped me," Saint replies, shooting a look at Felix that says, 'stop spilling my secrets'.

Maybe it would help Sin to fight, maybe he would stop seeking pain in other ways. "Thank you."

Flipping the pancake onto the waiting plate, I slide it to the spot next to Austin, who has been devouring me with his eyes since both of them came into the room. Felix abandons me for the stack of carbs, and I pour a few more into the pan.

When Austin finishes his plate, he comes around the island and rinses it off before putting it into the dishwasher. So thoughtful. Sin would have left it on the other side of the island for someone else—me—to clean up.

His large palm lands on my hip, and he leans over my shoulder. "I don't have any meetings this morning. I'll come along to watch your vengeance."

"Probably for the best. Forewarned is forearmed after all," I quip.

He nips the side of my neck in warning, and it sends a shockwave to settle in my belly. "I'm not afraid of you, princess," he says, adding more softly, "Not in that way anyway."

I want to examine the words and pull them apart. What is he afraid of? Of course I'd never actually hurt him physically; he can be a prickly asshole sometimes, but the only thing he's ever done is spank me in a way I want to be spanked. So that doesn't count.

"Pancakes are ready to flip," he tells me.

I offer the spatula to him. "You want to take over?"

"Please, no, he isn't the best with pancakes," Saint answers for him.

Austin huffs out a laugh that flows over my skin, telling me there is more to that story. "That was one time, Saint."

"Once is enough."

"Agreed," Felix says, his mouth full.

"What happened?" Curiosity has a smile playing on my lips as I glance between the two that will tell me the story. And Austin buries his face in my neck, attempting to distract me from my question.

"So, it was a Saturday morning at his family's house," Saint begins, his eyes twinkling with mischief. "Felix and I were just minding our own business when Austin got the brilliant idea to make pancakes for breakfast."

Felix chimes in, a mischievous grin spreading across his face. "Oh yeah, it was a sight to behold. Austin fancied himself a bit of a gourmet chef back then, before he realized cooking wasn't for him."

Austin groans into my neck. His kisses pause as he listens to his pack tell the story.

Saint nods, continuing the story. "So, he rolls up his sleeves, grabs a mixing bowl, and starts whisking away.

Meanwhile, Felix and I are just watching, not wanting to ruin his culinary dreams."

Felix adds, "Yeah, we figured, 'How bad could it be, right?'"

"But here's where things took a turn for the ridiculous," Saint continues, trying not to burst into laughter. "Austin adds a little 'flavor' to his pancakes and pulls out a bottle of whiskey from the cabinet."

"Bourbon, it was bourbon," Austin says against my neck, sending goosebumps chasing each other down my back.

Felix leans over the kitchen island and whispers like he is imparting a secret, "Now, we're not talking about a dash of vanilla extract. No, he pours a generous glug of bourbon into the pancake batter."

Saint can't hold back his laughter any longer and erupts into adorable giggles, with Felix joining in. After a moment, they compose themselves and continue the story.

"So, Austin pours the boozy batter onto a sizzling hot griddle," Felix says, shaking his head. "The kitchen instantly fills with this weird, smoky aroma. And then, the pancakes flame up like they're auditioning for a circus act!"

Saint chuckles, "It was like a fiery pancake rebellion happening right before our eyes. Flames were dancing on the griddle, and we were just standing there, mouths agape."

Felix nods. "Exactly! And while Austin was panicking, he accidentally knocked the bottle of bourbon off the counter, and it shattered on the floor. Now, we have a flaming griddle, a bourbon-soaked kitchen, and a very alarmed Austin."

I smile, picturing the scene in my head. A younger Austin, who hadn't yet gained the rough edges and had been taught not to trust omegas, comes to mind.

"That's when Felix and I did the only sensible thing we could think of–we grabbed the fire extinguisher. Austin was frantically waving a kitchen towel at the flames while we sprayed foam all over the place." Saint shakes his head with a wide grin pulling at his lips.

Felix concludes, "Finally, the fire subsided, and it left us with a blackened griddle, a sticky floor, and a very defeated-looking Austin."

Saint laughs and grips his stomach. "And that's when we heard the sirens approaching. Austin had accidentally set off the smoke alarm, and his family had one of those alarms that automatically called the fire department if we did not shut it off."

Felix raises his eyebrows and smiles. "So there we were, standing in the middle of a pancake disaster zone, when the firefighters burst in, fully geared up and ready to battle a blaze."

"We had to explain the whole bourbon-infused pancake fiasco to them. They couldn't stop laughing." Saint chuckles.

"And the best part? Austin's pancakes, the ones that had survived the inferno, were so charred we could have used them as hockey pucks," Felix adds.

Saint and Felix burst into laughter once more, recounting the absurdity of that morning when Austin's wish to provide for his pack almost turned into a fiery spectacle. Austin joins in with their shared laughter, rumbling through my back.

"It really wasn't that bad," Austin mumbles.

"I thought your mom would beat us with a broom when she came home to find the destroyed kitchen," Felix replies.

Finishing up the pancakes and flipping the stovetop off, I turn in Austin's arms, loving the feel of them holding me. "They are right, no pancake making for you." I kiss the tip of his nose, and he gives me a droll stare.

"It really wasn't that bad," he repeats. He is adorable when all of his walls are down. I want to keep him like this forever.

CHAPTER 48

Audrey

NERVOUS ANTICIPATION BUBBLES inside of me as Saint, Austin, Sin, and I pile into the car for the drive to Zade towers. I'm not sure what I should be feeling right now, knowing that in less than a half hour, I'll be in that room with another one of the men that destroyed my family and tortured me and my brother.

Joy doesn't feel right. Neither does happiness. But it is akin to both. Slaying the real live monster and giving them what they deserve is a new addiction. That whole *let karma take care of them* doesn't always work and, in this case, change my name to Karma because I'm bringing it right to them.

I'll deal with the morality of it later. But for once, it feels right to release that darkness that builds inside of me. The darkness I've suppressed for so long.

I'm in a haze until the metal walls and the unconscious man strapped to a metal table that reminds me of the one they had us secured to before we escaped, comes into view. Then everything snaps back into focus. Time slows.

It is Thomas, the embodiment of every painful memory from my past. The beta that followed anything Jason told him to, no matter how cruel or vindictive it was. My heart gives a painful thump beneath my rib cage, not out of concern but out of the sheer irony of the situation. Fate can be a wicked jesteress.

My palms feel clammy as my fingers curl in, and my nails dig into them, though this time, it's not from anxiety or fear. It's from the surge of anger and resentment that bubbles up within me. I watch with a mix of disbelief and disdain as Thomas lies unconscious before me, his once-controlling demeanor reduced to vulnerability.

Memories of his torment and cruelty flash before my eyes. The relentless way he would drag the scalpel down my side or across my back. Or the way he would cause so much pain, the blackness would rise to claim me. He never showed an ounce of remorse, and I had to bear the scars of his actions long after we parted ways.

But now, the situation is reversed. My voice, surprisingly steady, calls out to him, "Thomas." There's no warmth in my tone, no affection if there ever was, just a cold and detached acknowledgment of his presence. "You're in quite a mess, aren't you?" I can't help but take a certain satisfaction in his misfortune.

Sin chuckles as he steps up next to me. The darkness flowing off him as if he wears it as a cloak. "I'm going to enjoy this one," he murmurs, cracking his knuckles.

Austin and Saint take up posts next to the door. Letting us seek our vengeance in our own way, but making it clear that they are here if we need them.

His eyes flicker open, and for a moment, they're clouded with confusion. It's clear he doesn't know where he is or what is happening. But there's a flicker of recognition in his gaze as it lands on my face, then even more as it darts to Sin, and he tries to sit up, wincing in pain. The straps hold him in place, and he groans.

"What happened?" he mumbles, his voice groggy.

"I'd say you messed with the wrong Mafia," Sin replies. "You should have killed us when you had a chance."

Panic flares in the depths of his eyes, and I feel nothing but an icy detachment. "Oh my God," he says as he struggles in earnest, and he wakes up fully to the situation he has found himself in.

"God can't help you now." I grin and pick up a short knife.

Sin adds, "And I'm pretty sure it won't be pearly white gates you see when you get to where you're going."

"Please—" he begs, his murky gray eyes pleading with me, as if I have mercy to show.

We take turns, bringing the flow of blood to the surface, waking him each time he passes out. It is the release I need. Maybe I really am meant to head the De Luca Mafia. Apparently, I have the stomach for it. At least for this part. Because no one hurts our family and gets away with it.

It feels as if the bindings that bound me and kept me trapped have been released. I feel free.

Saint comes over, his fingers gently wrapping around my wrist. "Sweetheart, he doesn't deserve this much attention from you. Finish it. Slay this monster."

Thomas whimpers, reduced to the same slave to pain as he made me. I share a look with my brother and without speaking, we slice his neck from each side. Blood splatters, and I blink at the mess we created. Sin grins. Droplets of Thomas's blood in an arc over his face, broken by his white smile.

"We should have hunted them a long time ago, sis." He drops the knife he'd been using as Saint gently takes the scalpel from my fingers and places it on the tray.

Slowly, emotion washes over me, a mixture of what I can only describe as sadness and the sense of security that one less monster roamed the streets. The sadness is for the fear I lived in for so long. Finally, being free of it, I can see how it held me back. It is time to take the head off the snake.

I fall into Saint's embrace as he and Sin chat. He runs his hands up and down my back in a soothing motion I've come to expect from him. Austin watches us from the wall next to the door. He pulls out his phone and sends a text before he drops the device back into his pocket and straightens.

"The cleaners will be here soon. We should go get these two cleaned up."

I nod. "I hope you have a fresh shirt for Saint, too."

"I'm always prepared, princess."

We follow him from the room and up the private elevator to his office. They must directly connect because both times, we never stopped at another floor. He strides out to the lobby and says something to the man behind the desk. The guy nods, his gaze barely flicking to us before he gets up and closes the second door behind him as he leaves.

Then Austin comes back and pulls out a book on the wall, and it slides open, revealing another room that looks more like a mini apartment than something that should belong in an office.

"Safe room," he says.

"Our father had a safe room in every place he spent a lot of time," Sin replies. "But none like this."

We step inside, and the door slides shut behind us. Monitors on the opposite side of the door light up, showing his assistant leaning against the wall next to the door he went out, an empty entrance, the boardroom from that first visit, each elevator that leads to this floor, and Austin's office.

"Wow," I say, taking it all in.

"Felix insisted on the surveillance. He said it was stupid to have a safe room if you can't see if it is clear to come out."

Austin shrugs. "The bathroom is through there. We have clothes that should fit you both in the connected closet."

Sin heads for the bathroom, and I'm left with Saint and Austin. As soon as my brother disappears, I turn to Saint. "Thank you for–"

"Letting you torture your monster?" He lifts an eyebrow, a smile playing on his lips.

"Yeah," I say.

"You have a knack for torture, princess." Austin leans against the back of the sofa that takes up much of the space.

"Apparently, I'm more like my father than I thought."

"Your father was a good man," Austin replies, his fingers gripping the couch.

I pause. Is this when he admits he remembers me, a gangly teenager found peeking into our father's meeting? Sneaking around in places I shouldn't have been.

Back then, Austin had been the son of a rival mafia, yet so attractive I was sure my teenage self would combust from just looking at him. But when he refused the deal, whatever it was and exploded out of his seat, stomping my direction, I froze in the shadows, seconds from being caught.

His eyes widened just enough to tell me he saw me. But he didn't say a word as he stormed from the room that day. I swallow, facing him now. "How do you know that?"

"I met him twice. My dad tried to make a deal with him prior to him dying."

"What kind of deal?"

"One that would unite our families."

Was that what the meeting was about? Had my dad been signing away Sin's or my future? "Because he had omega children–and you're an alpha." My heart sinks. I knew my father, and it was something he would have done.

Austin's mouth tightens, and I know I hit the mark.

"Was he offering me or my brother?"

His violet eyes swirl with an emotion I can't read. "My choice, if I wanted."

"But you refused."

"I was with Sidney. I didn't give it much thought," he admits.

Saint rubs my back, and I lean into the comfort. I'm at a loss for words. It's in the past, something our fathers tried to do. But it still feels like another rejection, which is stupid and totally my omega hormones talking. Yet I can't shake it. Paired with the fact he hasn't marked me yet, I want to curl up into a ball and cry.

As I nestle closer to Saint's soothing touch, my thoughts become a tumultuous whirlwind. It's as if time has folded in on itself, and the weight of our fathers' expectations from the past presses down on me like a heavy burden.

I can't help but wonder if there's something I'm missing, some crucial piece of the puzzle that could bridge the gap between us. The desire for Austin's approval, for his mark, gnaws at the edges of my consciousness. It's a primal need, a yearning deep within my very being, driven by these pesky omega hormones.

Saint's hand continues its gentle motion, and I let out a sigh, trying to find solace in his presence. But the tension lingers, and my insecurities refuse to fade away.

I turn my head slightly, stealing a glance at Austin. His expression remains enigmatic, a mixture of concern and contemplation. It's as though he's wrestling with his own inner demons, just as I am.

To top it all off, I can smell the bitter scent of my perfume in the air between us, so I know he can, too.

"What about now? What would you pick now?"

Stupid.

Just lay my heart open. Fuck. I want to snatch the questions back before he even opens his mouth to respond.

"Audrey—" he sighs, as if I'm a child that can't handle the truth.

My throat tightens, and my eyes burn, but I'm saved by my brother emerging from the steamy bathroom. I slip out of Saint's arms and pass Sin on my way to the safety of the bathroom. Where the water from the shower will hide my tears, and I can piece myself back together again. I knew this wasn't forever. Right? When had things gotten twisted? Why had I allowed hope to bloom?

A low argument erupts behind me, but I cut it off as I shut the door firmly between us. I don't want to know what they say. How Saint tries to convince Austin he wants an omega when he clearly doesn't. When Sidney has broken him too much for him to move on. If she wasn't already dead, I'd find her and kill her myself.

Inside the bathroom, the sound of running water from the showerhead drowns out the turmoil in my mind. I clutch the edge of the sink, trying to regain my composure. My reflection in the mirror stares back at me, my eyes red and puffy, a stark contrast to the facade of strength I've been desperately trying to maintain.

The steam wraps around me like a cocoon, offering a momentary escape from the chaos outside. I let out a shaky breath, willing myself to hold it together. I can't let them see me crumble, not now.

Stepping beneath the showerhead, I run a trembling hand through my wet hair, tears mixing with the water droplets. The muffled voices of Austin and Saint continue to drift through the bathroom door, their words unintelligible, but the tension unmistakable. Once in a while, I hear Sin add his two cents. I can't imagine what they are saying, and at this moment, I don't want to.

Pulling myself back together, I let the water run over my face. When I leave this bathroom, I will be composed. No crying for what can't be. Just enjoy the ride. Damn. If life hasn't taught me that, then I don't know what will.

I turn the water off. It is silent on the other side of the door as I dress in a pair of leggings minus panties because I guess Austin didn't think of that when he stocked the closet. And a t-shirt that hangs to just below my ass but is the softest material ever. I drag a brush through my damp hair. It hangs in limp curls around my shoulders. Once it dries, it will be a bunch of ringlets that are an effortless style.

Exiting the bathroom, the three of them watch me, and I suddenly wish there was a hoodie in the closet. My fingers curl into my palms, and I force a smile.

"All clean," I chirp. Fake it until you make it.

CHAPTER 49

Austin

AUDREY'S FACE FALLS, and I feel like garbage. She slips out of Saint's arms and past her brother. I step forward to follow her, but Saint slaps his hand against my chest, holding me back. The snick of the lock behind her would have stopped me, anyway.

"What the fuck, Austin!" Saint growls.

"I can't lie to her," I say, my voice raising to match his.

He growls low again, and if he were an animal, I would be afraid of having my throat ripped out. "What do you mean you can't lie to her? You want her! I can see it in the way you watch her. And it is more than that. You've fallen for her."

I shake my head, denying his words even though they are true. "It's complicated."

"The fuck it is!" Sin bites out, getting in my face. "Don't fuck with my sister. You either want her in your life or you don't. I will end you the same way we ended Thomas, if you string her along. Cut her loose or hold her close. There is no fucking in between. Do you understand?"

Saint attempts to pull him back, and he shrugs him off, staring relentlessly into my eyes. His burning with liquid fire in defense of his sister. It's good she has him. It is good they have each other.

"He's right, Austin," Saint adds. "But if you cut her loose, I'm going with her."

I suck in a harsh breath. Of course he would. I would too. My fingers curl into fists. "If I mark her and she leaves, it will destroy me. I can't live through that again."

"So, you are punishing her because you made a shitty choice the first time around?" Saint yells. "You think that if she leaves now, you'll come out the other side in one piece? Because I think you are so far fucking gone for her, you don't know which way is up. Shit, she even plays into your fucking kinks."

"I do not need to know that information," Sin replies, stepping back from me.

"You might be right, but Saint, you know what Sidney did to me–"

"God, just let it go. She is dead and gone and good riddance. She was a power climber. Her feelings for you were never genuine, there was no love for you. Audrey can and will if you just let her in. Jesus, man, you are so stunted emotionally."

"I don't know who this Sidney chick is, but my sister isn't a user. She would never use another person for personal gain." Sin crosses his arms and glares at me like I just killed a puppy in front of him. "But she will run if you push her away. She isn't without her own scars."

The sound of the shower turning off has all three of us facing the shut door. My heart is in my throat. Sin is right. I've connected with his sister in ways I never did with Sidney. Our times alone together have been so much more than my time with Sidney. But fear holds me in a choke hold. The great Austin Zade, ex-Mafia Prince, finally brought to his knees by an omega girl.

I shift on my feet as the door opens. A billow of steam preceding Audrey. Her gaze swings around us, barely touching on me, and I can tell she's been crying. It tightens my chest, and I want to go to her and apologize, crawl on my hands and knees begging for forgiveness.

"All clean," she chirps like a bird, a smile that doesn't reach her eyes pasted on her face.

Still, she doesn't look at me.

"Audrey–"

Like a squirrel on defense, her gaze flicks to me before she looks past me. "It's fine, Austin. We don't need to talk about it. A girl can only take so much—"

Rejection. That was what she was going to say, but she presses her lips together into a tight line and attempts to smile.

"Nevermind. I'm starving. The pancakes this morning are long gone," she says as she comes to a stop next to Sin, her hand over her belly.

"I'll get a fresh shirt on, and then we can grab some food," Saint says, playing into her pretending.

A growl starts low in my chest, but I hold it in. What am I going to do with her brother standing right next to her? If I throw her over my lap to spank her, he would probably knife me where I sit. And I don't really want to spank her. I want to beg her forgiveness from my knees in a very sensual way. If she'll let me.

Saint comes back with a blue button-up on, still buttoning it as he walks across the floor. The twins watch him, Audrey, with a look of pure desire that I want aimed at me because I'm a selfish, emotionally stunted, bastard. While Sin appraises him with a more clinical stare. As in, Saint is attractive, but he is only enjoying the view, not wanting to act on it.

"Can we go to that diner Felix likes?" she asks. "I'll text him, and he can meet us there."

She holds out her hand, and Saint drops her phone into her palm. Jealousy at my pack mate and *my omega* being so in tune. No words needed said for him to know what she wanted. I should be able to expect what she wants and needs.

If I had thought the torture she ensured that the man had suffered was bad, it is nothing to the painful way she ignores me. None of her bratty sub act or her soft calmness, nothing for me. It is like I'm a ghost for all the attention she sends my way.

Saint wraps his arm around her waist as we exit the building out onto the bustling street. Then he opens the waiting car door for her. She slides in and all the way to the opposite side, her brother follows, sitting across from her. And I nudge Saint out of the way and climb in next to her. It doesn't matter that facing the rear of the car makes me carsick. It's a short drive and being next to her means more.

Audrey tenses as I settle into the seat next to her. It is hard to ignore me if I'm right here. I run my hand down her arm, and she jerks as if she's been burned. Then she curls it around her body like an injury.

"Princess–Baby girl–" I try both, and the only sign she even heard me is the slight flaring of her nostrils and the bitter-sweet perfume she can't control. "We need to talk about this."

I pin my gaze to her lips as she rolls them together and looks across the seat at her brother and Saint like she is planning on crawling over there and taking up a position in Saint's lap rather than sit next to me.

It is here in my car that I see the full extent of how wrong I'd been. Audrey isn't even on the same level as Sidney; hell, I barely remember her name or what she looked like anymore. But I could conjure the image of Audrey without thinking.

"Audrey–" I beg.

She flicks her gaze at me, her lips parting, pink tongue

darting out to wet them. My heart gallops like a runaway horse.

"Mango."

Everything stops. Including my breath. Her safe word.

I blink once, twice, three times, then clamp my mouth shut and lean back in my seat.

I'm an alpha.

I don't cry or beg, and she has made me feel like doing both. And it is all my fault. Saint is right, I am emotionally stunted. All I want to do is order the driver to take us back to the penthouse, then fly her away to the house in the country and hold her there until we work this out. It worked for Saint. The idea has merit.

The car comes to a stop, and Saint opens the door, ending the thought before it can take root. The three of them slide over the leather and out the door before I move a muscle.

Felix greets them with his trademark smile, his gaze flicking to the darkened windows of the car when I don't follow. Saint says something following his gaze, and Felix lifts his chin in a quick nod. I rap the roof of the car indicating I'm not joining them, and Marcus closes the door and climbs back in. He lowers the shield between us a crack.

"Where to, Boss?"

"Just drive."

He shuts the shield and pulls away from the curb. I watch my pack and the twins until I can't see them anymore. I need to get my shit together before I lose them all.

CHAPTER 50
Felix

THE WALK to the diner was short, and I beat them here. Instead of heading in and getting a table, I pull up the phone tracker and see that they will be here in less than a minute. The sleek black car pulls up as I drop my phone back into my jeans. Saint pushes open the door and climbs out, followed by Sin and Audrey.

Audrey smiles and throws her arms around me, nuzzling my neck in the best of ways.

"I missed you," she murmurs.

"Not as much as I missed you." I press a kiss to the top of her head before she steps back.

Austin is notably missing, and I study the black windows of the sedan.

"He fucked up with Audrey," Saint leans in and tells me.

I lift my head in a curt nod. When Marcus gets out and shuts the door before getting back into the driver's seat, I know Austin has decided not to join us. I feel torn inside. I want to ease the pain I can feel from here, but at the same time, I want to knock some sense into him. He can't fuck this up. If we are all going to stay together, he needs to pull his head out of his ass.

As the car disappears down the street, I pull Audrey into my side and lead the way into the diner. I grab my usual spot, and Audrey slides in next to me. Saint and Sin share the opposite seat.

The conversation flows around us, as if the four of us have always eaten lunch together. It is easy and watching Audrey interact with her brother, seeing how different they are even while being twins, is interesting.

The only topic we all silently agree not to bring up is Austin. And for that moment in time, it is easy to forget that until Austin claims Audrey, none of this is real. It is all pretend. Unless we break our pack up.

Pushing that thought out, I focus on the way Audrey laughs, her head thrown back and carefree in a way she wasn't when I first met her. Is that the difference because of our pack? Had we helped to find her happiness again?

She smiles at me as if she can hear my thoughts and then leans into my side with a content sigh. "Felix, you are the best cuddler."

"Hey, I'm pretty sure you cuddled with me all night and didn't complain," Saint replies.

Sin chews his food and swallows before saying, "I really don't want to hear anything about my sister's sex life. Keep her happy. That is the only thing I need to know."

Audrey grins. "You mean you don't want to know how I took Felix's knot?" She leans across the table, her voice lowering to a whisper as Sin groans audibly.

"Aud, gross," he says, pushing his plate away.

She laughs, her eyes twinkling. "Pay back, Sin. I told you I didn't want to know a single thing about your…adventures."

"That is completely different. You never had to meet them

or carry on a conversation while imagining me with them. Whereas, right now, here, this thing between you and your guys seems like a pretty forever set up. I don't want to know what happens behind closed doors."

"What about the stuff that happens in not so private situations?"

"Aud," Sin groans.

"Okay, okay, I'll keep it to myself." She picks up her club sandwich and takes a bite, chewing slowly before she looks over at Saint. "Can you obtain Jason?"

Whoa topic shift. Tension fills the table, like an electric current.

"After the Valentine party. If I do it before, then he will be missed sooner."

"Is he going to the party?"

"He was," Saint admits. "He is on the security team for Valentine."

"Well, good thing it is a masquerade." She shrugs.

"You're not going," Saint says.

"I'm the thief. How are you stealing a painting without me?"

"We aren't," I say.

She pulls back to look up at me. "What do you mean, 'we aren't'? That is the whole reason I'm with you guys, is for the painting."

I know she doesn't mean it the way it sounds, so I ignore the way she phrases it. "Austin doesn't want it now."

Her mouth pops open before she clamps it shut. Still, she can't fight the words that flow from between her lips. "He went through a hell of a lot to just change his mind at the last minute."

"I'm on my sister's side on this one. What would make him change his mind?"

Saint sighs. "He hired Jason Vanross as the man to help with the job. He isn't willing to put Audrey into that situation."

"Funny fucking time for him to act like he actually cares what happens to me," Audrey replies.

"He is head over heels for you. He just doesn't know how to express his emotions," I say.

She snorts. "He desires me. He doesn't love me. Those are not the same thing. And I'm not letting a minor hiccup like Jason stop him from getting what he wants. Because I actually have fallen for him. As stupid as that is."

"A little hiccup like Jason?" Sin says, repeating her words slowly, like he hadn't heard them correctly. "Aud, you are not working with Jason to steal a painting. It will get you killed, or worse."

"I can handle it. If I don't talk and I wear the mask, he won't know it's me."

Her brother shakes his head, his jaw ticking. "No."

"No? You can't tell me no." Her voice raises, and I glance around at the other people in the diner.

"Maybe not the best place to have an argument," I caution.

"I can, and I fucking will. You think these three have you locked up? I will physically chain you to the motherfucking wall if you so much as think about going to that party." His voice rises to match her energy, and he leans across the table.

"She won't go to the party," Saint says calmly.

"Yes, I will!" she cries. "I'm getting that painting so he can finally find the happiness he craves."

"Whoa, guys, maybe take this someplace else?" I say, attempting to draw them all back down to a normal level.

Three sets of eyes pin me with a look that makes me want to sink into my chair. Instead, I straighten my shoulders and return their stares.

"Unless you want the entire city to know about the heist, lower your voices," I say. "But I still think we made this conversation for the penthouse, not the corner diner."

CHAPTER 51

Audrey

THE TOPIC IS DROPPED, but I can still feel the need to do what I agreed to do thrumming through me. It is stupid and petty. But handing him the painting and asking if he is happy now would make me feel better.

Is it completely irrational and a tad passive aggressive? Yeah, but I'll blame this one on the hormones.

Austin is absent when we return to the penthouse. Sin leaves us at his floor. I'm not sure when it became his apartment, but it no longer feels like home to me. Not that I stayed there much, anyway.

"Scrabble?" Felix asks.

Saint groans.

"What? It is fun!" Felix says.

Saint shakes his head. "Count me out."

"I'll play," I reply. We had a lot of fun the first time we played.

Felix pins Saint with a look that says he won. "We could make it spicy."

"Spicy?" Saint hedges.

"Strip Scrabble."

I choke on a laugh at Saint's incredulous snort. "How do you play strip Scrabble?" I ask.

"Each round the person with the lowest points for their word loses a piece of clothing."

"I would only last losing like four rounds," I say, mentally counting the items I could remove. Socks, leggings, and shirt. "Three if socks count as one."

"You're right, Saint, you don't want to play. You can leave us to manage on our own," Felix replies with a dismissive wave of his hand, his eyes heating on me. "We could make it *really* spicy."

Saint leans against the couch, clearly not leaving us alone, as Felix lays out the board on the coffee table.

"Really spicy how?" I question, but I know I'm going to do it, because the excitement thrums through me and getting naked with Felix isn't a bad thing at all.

"After all the clothing is gone, we finish the game... the new rule for the naked one," he pauses, fingering his eyebrow piercing, "Is allowing consensual touching of a player of her choice."

I choke on another laugh. "*Her choice?* It isn't a forgone conclusion you'll win."

He rakes his sparkling green gaze from head to toe and back again. "From where I'm standing, you are at a disadvantage. No jewelry to lose, and you took your shoes off already."

Saint straightens. "Jewelry doesn't count, and you should have taken your shoes off too."

"Oh, are you playing now?" he quips, raising his eyebrow as his tongue darts out to play with his lip ring. The undercurrent of flirting between them never fails to make my heart rate spike. The fact that they have been very hands to themselves around me so far has a hope building that Saint joins in and one of them picks each other, because that would be flaming hot.

"I agree. Jewelry doesn't count. But I'm confident enough in my spelling abilities that your extra shoes don't scare me." I settle to my knees on the opposite side of Felix.

"We need drinks if we are doing this properly." Saint heads for Austin's cabinet, where he keeps the good stuff.

"Fruity for me," I call after him.

He smiles over his shoulder and pulls out Grey Goose Vodka and Kirk and Sweeny Rum, then heads to the kitchen. "Lucky for you, I had a gig as a bartender before I found fighting in the ring pays more."

"Fighting pays more than getting people drunk?" I ask, leaning back against the bottom of the couch. I can't see him from here, only hear as he moves around the kitchen, pulling out things before the ice maker clacks into a plastic cup.

"Drunk people aren't normally the best tippers," he replies, his tone full of humor, and I can imagine the smile on his face. Felix laughs across from me.

"Tell her that one story," Felix says.

Saint chuckles. "Do you want to hear a story about a drunk?"

I nod and shift to watch him.

"It was a Tuesday night, quiet as a graveyard at the bar I worked for, until the door swung open, and in walked this guy."

"He was so drunk already," Felix adds, wobbling his hands in the air like someone trying to keep their balance.

"He was wearing a bright pink suit, I swear to God," Saint continues, chuckling at the memory. "And his hair—oh boy, his hair was a masterpiece. A neon pink Mohawk that practically glowed in the dark—Not even Felix has gone for that color—He sauntered up to the bar, all wobbly and disheveled, and he looked me dead in the eye."

I use my arms to prop myself up on the couch as he tells his story. "And then what?" I giggle, enjoying his storytelling.

"He orders a... wait for it..." he holds out his hand, a wide grin spreading over his face, "A glass of milk!"

I burst out laughing. "Milk? In a bar?"

"Milk," Felix laughs, "So, Saint pours him a glass, hands it over, and he raises it high in the air like he's toasting the milk gods. Then, he sings *'We are Never Ever Getting back Together'* at the top of his lungs."

I cover my mouth to stifle my laughter, but tears are forming as I imagine the scene playing out. "That is unreal."

"I wish it was. The entire bar goes silent, and this guy is belting out a Taylor Swift song like he is on stage. People were dying of laughter. The place went from quiet to loud in a matter of seconds." Saint shakes his head.

"Dang, what happened next?" I ask, propping my arm along the back of the couch.

Saint takes a breath, his gaze far away as he remembers. "Well, the guy finished his milk, set the glass down with a dramatic flourish, and declared, 'I've had enough for one night!' Then, he winked at me, tipped his imaginary hat, and waltzed out of the bar without a care in the world."

"That is nuts," I say with a shake of my head. "Did he ever come back?"

"Not while I was there. I think about him sometimes, he was completely sloshed and milk on top of that," he says with a shiver. "Coming back up would be gross."

He finishes making our drinks and brings them back into the living area, setting them down with a flourish. "Made especially for you, fruity for my little hellcat."

I sink back to the floor and curl my legs criss-cross in front of me, while Saint settles at my left, and Felix is across from me.

We pick our seven tiles, and I place mine on my holder,

barely controlling my squeal of excitement. There is no way I'm losing the first word if I can play it right. The guys grab their tiles, and the sigh from Felix tells me he didn't pick good.

"You can go first, Felix," I say sweetly.

"Yeah, Felix, you go first." Saint rearranges his letters, and I can imagine he is spelling a word he wants to use.

"I'll go easy on you two this first round," he says. Then he spells out I-N-E-R-T. "Six points."

I hold in a laugh, and he pins me with a fake glare.

Saint grins and uses the T to spell out his word. T-R-A-C-E-R. "Tracer, seven points. Looks like you are losing a piece of clothing." He wiggles his eyebrows teasingly at Felix.

"Audrey still needs to go," he grumbles.

I bite down on my lip, attempting to hold in my grin. My word is worth ten points, and if I was close to a triple square or a double square I'd hold it for them. But I'm not, so I lay out Q-U-I-Z-Z-Y.

"Quizzy?" Felix asks, disbelief in his tone.

"Yeah, super lucky this time." I push a strand of hair behind my ear and eye Felix. "Do I get to pick what you lose since I'm the winner this round?"

He chuckles. "Sure, if I get to pick what you lose when I'm the winner," he flirts.

Between their musk and my perfume, I'm in a haze of continuous lust. Riding that edge making inner promises to my omega that we'll be satisfied soon.

I lick my lips and eye his shirt. "I'd say your pants, but I know you wear boxers, and I can't see through the table, so your shirt."

He does that one-handed move, reaching over his back and magically removing it in one effortless movement. I want to tell him to put it back on and do it again just so I can watch the way his muscles move. Damn. Slick gathers between my legs, and I shift, so I'm on my knees. My gaze glides over his tattoos, wanting to run my tongue over them to trace each intricate line.

"Eyes up here, omega," he orders, sending a thrill through me. Who knew an alpha telling me what to do would ever have that effect on me, but here we are.

I pick up my replacement tiles, barely able to focus on them. Pheromones soak the air and at least a third of them are coming from me. I lose the next round with a seven point word. Felix has me take off my shirt. My girls pebble in the cool air of the apartment as both alphas stare at me openly as if they want to eat me up. *Please do.*

In rapid succession, we each lose our clothing, but I'm the first completely bare from the tips of my toes to the top of my head. So when I lose the next round, I nearly combust as I wait for Saint to decide what I need to do or have done. I get to pick the person to do it with, but the top scorer decides the deed.

Saint taps his lips, a smile on his face as if he is really thinking about it. "Hmmm," he hums, making me squirm. "Just a kiss."

My eyebrows raise. "Just a kiss?" I repeat.

"Yes."

A grin pulls at my lips. "Anywhere? Any kind?"

When he nods, I crawl around him to Felix. Saint's hand trails teasingly over the curve of my lower back and ass. I lean down and suck the tip of Felix's cock between my lips, slipping my tongue along the slit and swallowing the pre-cum. He groans and jerks in surprise at first, then his fingers find my hair and grip the base of my neck as I give him a *kiss* to remember. When Saint clears his throat, I pull back, letting Felix pop from my mouth with a loud smack. Then I move back to my side of the table as if I'm not as turned on as they both are.

The next round, Saint loses to Felix, and he orders him to touch one of us. Both hands run over my sides and massage my breasts until I feel like I'm going to beg for more. Then he is back in his spot, while I catch my ragged breath.

While we are creating our next words, I finger a tile without looking at either of them. "Do you two, ever–?" I trail off, flicking my gaze up to them.

Felix tilts his head, a smile playing on his face. "You're blushing."

His observance makes my cheeks flame more, and I duck my head.

"Don't do that. I've already told you I love it when you blush."

Saint shifts his weight onto his heels, his dick bobbing distractedly between his legs. "Are you asking if we have a sexual relationship?"

I nod as my face catches fire, and I swallow drily. My perfume flaring at the same time tells them both what I think about that possibility. Felix spells out his word A-N-A-L-S-E-X.

I point at the board. "I'm pretty sure that is two words."

"It is, but that's what you're asking, right?" Saint replies. "Does it bother you?"

"Does it smell like it would bother me?" I quip.

"We do all the things your mind is conjuring up," Felix says. "But since you moved in and created a tornado of chaos, we haven't."

"Because of me?"

"Once we realized you were our scent match, we paused our sexual relationship. Because our omega will call the shots, and if you don't like that or want that–" Saint replies.

"Then you won't?" That sort of hurt my heart. It was sweet but misguided. "You don't need to do that. Being an omega doesn't mean that I get to tell you what to do with your bodies."

"Audrey, we belong to you, body, heart, and soul," Felix says, his voice low and serious.

My stomach flutters as butterflies erupt and attempt to go braindead from his words. It isn't how I thought an alpha-omega relationship would be. The dynamics are not the alpha in charge of everything like I have imagined.

"Oh–" I manage to breathe. "It doesn't bother me. Not even a tiny bit."

Their faces light up with smiles that make me feel like the sun is shining down on me. How crazy is this conversation we are having, while we are all completely naked and bare to each other? Kind of poetic, really.

"But Felix, you can't have that whole word," I say, nodding to his most recent word.

He grins and removes 'sex'. "I'll take the loss this round."

Saint laughs and spells out his word, worth eight points only because it was on a double square. I follow with a nine point word and immediately lift my head to meet Felix's green gaze. I lick my lips and glance at Saint. My stomach does little flips in anticipation of what I'm going to tell him he has to do.

"Felix," I say and bite my lip. Letting out a breath, I add, "You need to make love to one of us."

My eyes dart to Saint as my cheeks pink again.

"But the other can join in," I say, adding that single qualification.

"I think I just won the game," Felix replies. Then he reaches for Saint, tugging him in for a passionate kiss, the kind that makes your toes curl and your heart try to escape your body. His fingers wrap around Saint's length, and he strokes him in practiced movements of his hand.

I lean down between them and capture the tip of Saint's

dick in my mouth, sucking as Felix strokes. Saint's hand buries in my hair as he moans into Felix's mouth. Slick is dripping down my legs, probably making a mess of the carpet, but none of us care. Besides, they probably have enough money to have the entire room re-carpeted if needed.

Saint curls his fingers at the nap of my neck, urging me to take more of him. Felix's hand wrapped around the base ensures I don't choke myself on his dick. Which is perfect. Oxygen being cut off is no big deal, but in a whole different way that does not involve tears and possibly snot from choking on a dick. I'm not a deep throater, what can I say? I've had no complaints, it is all in the tongue, anyway.

He pulls me up and breaks the kiss with Felix to kiss me, before it becomes a three-way kiss, and I'm pretty sure I'm going to combust. Felix breaks away and kisses down my neck, before he kisses down Saint's neck, too. He jumps up and runs butt naked to the kitchen, coming back with a bottle of olive oil. Then he moves around him, his hands gliding down his sides to his ass as he pops open the top. I stop kissing Saint as Felix gets into position behind him. Saint's pupils blow wide, making his already dark eyes darker.

Then he groans at the same time Felix does. "You ready to feel my knot for the first time, Saint?" Felix asks, his words choppy from the excitement at the thought of working himself into him. My pussy clenches around nothing, and I wrap my fingers around Saint's dick and stroke. Thoughts of climbing into his lap and sinking down onto him invade my mind, and it is an invasive thought that I act on. I wrap my right leg around him as I try to get into a suitable position. The table at my back tells me it's a long shot.

But Saint and Felix go up on their knees together, and Saint lifts me as if I weigh nothing and lays me back on the scrabble board, spreading my legs and nudging my opening with the tip of his engorged cock. I forget the word pieces beneath me as he slides into my folds in one smooth thrust.

I whimper at the amazing feeling of him filling me up, knowing he will be full too makes it even better. Saint pauses as Felix rubs the oil over his cock and works his way into him, both of them moaning in pleasure. We find a rhythm that works for all of us, and before long, I'm chasing that feeling that is building in my stomach like a storm. The release is teasing at the edges, threatening to drown me in intense pleasure. If I am going to die, this is how I want to go.

Clenching around him, I moan from my very soul when he works his full knot into me. It is all it takes, and I'm exploding into a million pieces and floating in the ether. I come back to myself, to the exquisite feeling of him pulsing inside of me, and the sound of Felix groaning his release. It is almost enough to send me straight into another orgasm.

We somehow end up in a pile next to the ruined scrabble game, my leg draped over both of them as Felix spoons Saint from behind. And Saint is still deep inside me, promising another round once we all recover. I drift into a relaxed sleep, the kind where you are just barely asleep but not quite awake either.

CHAPTER 52

Austin

IT'S LATE when I finally return to the penthouse. I have half a mind to just stay away. They would all be better off for it. I'm toxic.

I'm hit with a face full of their combined pheromones as soon as I push open the door. Then my gaze lands on the three of them, a tangle of limbs, sleeping on the carpet next to the coffee table.

I slip off my shoes and pad across the plush carpet to my armchair. I sink into it, my full attention on the three of them like a voyeur. Hell, I can even feel the blood rushing to my cock in response to the erotic scene. I'm pretty sure they are connected even in sleep, at least Saint and Audrey are from this angle.

Her pussy lips grip his half-hard dick, ready for more the second they wake up. I shift my growing problem down my leg to give it more room. And kick out my legs, spreading them wide..

By the time they move, I could paint them. The image is burned into my mind's eye. Art. Love. A mixture of both. Then the sense of longing growing in my chest with each passing moment. Saint is right, I'm emotionally stunted, but I want to change that. I want these three in my life.

If they will give me time to change, I'll do it for them, for me.

Saint presses a kiss to Audrey's nose, and she wrinkles it as she blinks her eyes open. "We have company, hellcat," Saint tells her, shifting his eyes down to mine.

I suck in a breath in preparation of her reaction to me being a complete stalker, watching them while they sleep.

She follows his line of sight to me, the only reaction her eyes widening slightly.

"Considering I live here, too, it shouldn't be a surprise that I've come home," I reply, holding her flashing brown gaze. My fingers curl into the edge of the arm of the chair when she slightly lifts her brows like she wants to say something but holds it back.

"What time is it?" Saint asks.

"After three," I say.

It is fascinating that Audrey doesn't pull away from Saint or try to hide her exposed skin. Saint's reaction is expected with our history of sharing, but she doesn't reach for the throw or cover herself in any way. In fact, I'm pretty sure she flexes her hips forward, drawing Saint further in as he hardens inside of her.

I've never thought of myself as a watcher. But I am prepared to watch them. I want to see what my brat has in store for me. She breaks eye contact with me and focuses on Saint. A hum of pleasure comes from her and shoots straight into my cock, turning me to steel.

Then she urges Saint to his back and straddles him. "It seems our company likes to watch, Saint. What do you think about that?" She moves slowly on him in a sweet torture.

"I think you should show him what he's missing," Saint murmurs, his hands running up her sides to cup her breasts in each palm, his long fingers working her nipples into tight peaks.

She moans and throws her head back as she rides him in the same teasing strokes. When she lifts her head, she pins me with her eyes. It spears me through the fucking heart, reminding me I messed up, and I have a lot of groveling to do before she'll let me back in.

She's worth it.

Her lips part as she breathes, her cheeks flush, and her eyes glaze as she uses Saint to reach an orgasm. Not that he minds one bit. In fact, he urges her on with his touches. Clearly not remembering or caring that I'm watching. Hell, if she was riding me, I wouldn't care who saw.

Felix stirs next to them, his eyes focus on Audrey as her climax rushes through her. It riveted all three of us on her. She is beautiful in her bliss.

She collapses onto Saint's chest, and his arms go around her, holding her close. It is where I want to be.

"Mmmm, that was good," she says, her voice husky with satisfaction.

"Quite the show, princess," I reply.

"That was just the encore." She glances at me. "But I'm not sleeping on this floor, so I'm going to bed."

"Alone?" I ask.

She presses a quick kiss to Saint's lips before turning to Felix and doing the same, then she pushes to her feet. "They can join me if they want. Not that it matters to you?"

"Tomorrow, Audrey, we need to talk."

Her lips form a flat line and some of the flush fades, my words chasing the afterglow away. "Right, talk." She uses her fingers as quotation marks. Then strides away like she doesn't have a care in the world.

I don't sleep. Instead, I'm out of the penthouse before the sun rises, and I pick up flowers, before heading to the local twenty-four-hour coffee shop and picking up pastries. Today is the day I fix the mess I created.

My steps are lighter than they have been in years, and I whistle as I make my way back to the apartment building. The penthouse is silent when I unlock the door and set my purchases on the kitchen island. I grab down a glass and put the flowers in water, then get a plate out and arrange the pastries before covering them with plastic wrap to keep them fresh. Then I pick up the Scrabble game that is strewn all over the living area, scattered around with their clothing. By the time one of their doors cracks open, the place is spotless again.

I know how omegas can be with messes. And I need Audrey to be here for what I have to say, not thinking about cleaning up the game they played last night.

Audrey steps out of her room, in a tank top and shorts. She silently walks over to the kitchen, and I watch as she fingers a petal and sniffs the flowers before turning to get a glass. She pulls out some O.J. to fill it up, and when she turns around and catches sight of me she yelps, her fingers losing their grip and the glass smacking the marble floor, glass shattering everywhere.

She gasps and immediately drops to her knees, picking up the larger pieces and putting them into the biggest shard. Concern has me moving into the kitchen. I kneel and pick up some of the bigger pieces before noticing that Audrey is bleeding.

"You're bleeding," I say.

She shakes off her finger and then sucks it into her mouth. "Just a tiny cut. I'll be fine."

"Let me take care of it," I reply. My single focus is on moving her to safety. I'll clean this up after she is okay.

"It's fine."

Ignoring her protest, I stand up and then sweep her into my arms and carry her over to the island stool. "Stay right here. I'll get something to bandage you up, and then I'll clean up the glass."

She huffs out a disbelieving laugh. "Now you care?"

I pause and cup her cheek, encouraging her to look at me, to see me at this moment. "Audrey, my perfect omega, I have always cared."

She sucks in a breath, her eyes widening, and I drop my hand to go do what I said, even though kissing her senseless has reached the very top of my list of things I want to do. I have a feeling plowing through all the steps of apology straight to that wouldn't have the same impact.

When I return with peroxide, some healing ointment, and bandaids, setting them all on the island, she is exactly where I left her. I reach for her hand. Her finger is still bleeding, proving that it wasn't just a minor cut. I clean it off and bandage it up, then press a soft kiss to the bandaid.

"All better."

She pulls her eyebrows down, making a little crease appear over them as I stand up and head around the island. Being careful not to step on the remaining glass. I pull down a fresh glass and fill it with O.J., setting it down in front of her.

"What–Why–?" She shakes her head. "You're being really nice."

I sweep the shards into the dustpan. The small shards of glass clings to the broom, but I don't worry about it.

"I can't be nice?"

She takes a sip of the juice as she thinks about her answer. "I've seen you be nice," she admits. "But this is a different level. Almost a, 'what have you done with Austin?' level."

I chuckle. "I'm still an asshole. That will probably always

be true, but I don't want to be that person with you. I want to be better. For you."

She shakes her head. "Be better for you, Austin. That is the only way a change will ever stick, is if you are doing it for yourself."

"I'll work on it."

Silence falls as I finish cleaning up the accident. After I put the broom away, I stay on the opposite side of the island from Audrey. The space allows me to think about things other than touching her.

"I bought you flowers," I say with a nod at the flowers in the glass. "I'll have to buy a vase, we never needed one before–" I stop when I realize I'm rambling.

She eyes the flowers again like she isn't sure they won't launch across the space and bite her. "They are pretty. Thank you."

"And pastries." I slide the plate to her.

A soft smile plays on her lips. "Have you slept? When did you have time to clean the apartment and go shopping for pastries and flowers?"

"I did it this morning." I ignore the question about sleeping. Who needs sleep when their future could be slipping through their fingers?

"Austin, it is six-thirty," she says, something akin to concern playing over her face, as she runs her finger along the edge of the pastry plate.

I glance at the clock. "It is."

She swallows. "You don't have to do all this because you feel guilty about—"

"I do."

She inhales and focuses on the marble countertop, shielding her eyes and emotions from me with the move. Even her perfume doesn't give her away.

"I need you to know…" she says and lifts her eyes up to

mine. The emotion swirling in their depths freezes the breath in my chest. "I will not take your pack from you. That isn't what I'm doing."

Not even cement shoes would keep me on my side of the island. I'm around it to her side before she can blink. Using the motion of the swivel stool, I twist her toward me, cradling her face in my palms.

"Audrey, you aren't understanding. It is me who will not take your pack from you. You belong here with them. And if I've crossed lines and done unforgivable shit, it will be me that leaves." I pause and swallow, my chest tightening painfully. "But–I hope you give me a chance to beg for your forgiveness." She gasps as I drop to my knees at her feet and bow my head. "I've been an emotionally stunted alpha, and I'm sorry I've caused you pain because of it. Audrey, my omega princess, can you ever forgive me?"

The moments that pass feel like eons. I keep my eyes on the bottom bar of the stool. Her toes curl around the metal bar as she shifts and drops her feet to the floor next to me and sinks to the floor with me. Her soft touch lifts my face, sending electric awareness through every part of me.

Her eyes are damp as mine meet hers, and she blinks. A smile tries to show itself on her lips, almost like the sun trying to break through the clouds. "All of this," she says, gesturing at the counter above us, "is to ask my forgiveness for what?"

My tongue wets my lips before I part them to answer. "For making you think I don't want you as pack. Because I do. I can't imagine my life without you in it. It wasn't you. There were things I needed to come to terms with."

"And you think you have?"

"I think the thought of losing you hurts more than anything I've ever experienced, and if you try to walk away–I can't promise my alpha wouldn't find you and lock you up until you change your mind."

She huffs out a surprised laugh.

"Without you, I would cease to exist, Audrey. Bratty omega and all. I need you in my life to push me and challenge me."

"Saint and Felix…"

"Are not you," I say, stopping whatever she was going to say.

A flurry of emotion plays over her face too fast for me to pick up on all of them. She settles with a mixture of hope and trepidation. A crease between her brows wrinkles her nose ever so slightly, while her brown eyes brim with expectancy.

"I know I'm not a prize, and I'll be more work than I'm worth. But every part of me is in love with you. I fell as soon as you signed that contract without reading it. And each moment since has only made it grow. Fear held me back, but not now."

She swallows. "I think I'm going to need some actions to back up these words," she replies, her eyes dipping to my lips as she licks her own.

I sway toward her, unconsciously closing the distance between us, and her hands drop to my shoulders. Her chin tilts up, and her mouth parts on a soft breath. It is all the permission I need before I'm kissing her, or she's kissing me. I'm not sure who moved first.

The soft slide of our lips against each other lasts for a moment before her tongue delves into my mouth, seeking mine out. They tangle as my arms draw her closer. Soon, she is in my lap, and we are kissing like teenagers between two stools beneath the kitchen island.

CHAPTER 53

Audrey

"I **THINK** the thought of losing you hurts more than anything I've ever experienced and if you try to walk away–I can't promise my alpha wouldn't find you and lock you up until you change your mind."

Austin watches me, his face dead serious, and I can't help the laugh that burst from my chest. It isn't a laughing matter, but the fact he is admitting all of this to me, it is bubbling many emotions to the surface.

"Without you, I would cease to exist, Audrey. Bratty omega and all. I need you in my life to push me and challenge me," he says. His voice drops with his emotion, and it grabs hold of my heart and squeezes. I'm not the only one to challenge him. I've seen Saint and Felix do it.

"Saint and Felix…"

"Are not you," he cuts me off.

And I believe him. I want to believe him, anyway. But it is like I'm two halves of the same person. One part wants to dive headfirst into this second chance for us, and the other is afraid he will rip it all away once he gets between my legs again. His violet eyes swirl with intensity as he watches me. It makes me feel like the only person in the world.

"I know I'm not a prize, and I'll be more work than I'm worth. But every part of me is in love with you. I fell as soon as you signed that contract without reading it. And each moment since has only made it grow. Fear held me back, but not now."

My heart attempts to jump through my throat. He *loves* me. He has loved me since the start. I want to throw myself into his arms and jump headfirst into the hope that is blooming like a rare flower inside of me. I hold myself still as my gaze drops to his lips.

"I think I'm going to need some actions to back up these words."

His eyes hood as he looks at my lips and moves closer because of my words. I can barely catch my breath as I run my fingers over his shoulders and press my lips to his. This moment is everything. His thumb glides over my jaw, and I part my lips, seeking more.

A whimper builds in my chest, and I wrap my legs around him, climbing into his lap to get the closeness I crave. He's hard beneath me, and I move over him, seeking friction. The sinful groan that flows from his lips gives me life. If I could record that sound, I could definitely get off on it when I am alone. But who needs to get off on it alone when the real thing is running his large hands over my back and pulling me closer.

His hands find skin between the bottom of my tank top and the hem of my shorts, and he drags his warm palms up my sides beneath my shirt. All while nipping my lower lip with soft love bites. Before he can work my tank top over my head, a throat clears, and I'm jerked straight back to reality.

Our kiss ends, and I'm left staring at Austin, my chest rising and falling with rapid breaths. His warm hands are still beneath my shirt, fingers flexing into my skin as if he is debating carrying me from the room and away from whoever interrupted us.

"What are you two doing on the floor beneath the island?" Felix asks, his voice full of humor.

Austin groans, but not one of his pleasure-filled ones I am addicted to. "What did it look like we were doing?" he asks as he leans his head back against the counter, pulling me with him as he shifts.

"I wasn't asking why you were going at it like a couple of horn dogs. I was asking why you were doing it there," Felix clarifies with a laugh.

"You're right, we will take this some place more comfortable."

I yelp in surprise as he unfolds and misses knocking his head on the countertop by inches while still holding onto me, my legs wrapped around him and my arms clinging to his shoulders. He strides toward the hall without another word, and I peek over his shoulder at a grinning Felix.

My stomach tumbles as Austin kicks his bedroom door shut behind us and carries me to his bed, laying me down before following. He presses his weight onto me, and I arch up into him, needing more.

"Is this okay?" he whispers.

"Yes, more than okay," I whisper back.

He kisses my nose, then my cheek, followed by just beneath my ear, and down my neck. He licks the unmarked skin between Saint and Felix's marks, breathing his warm breath over after. "This spot is mine, just like you are mine," he growls.

And just like that, I'm fire. My blood is lava, and the rest of me is ready to set fire to a forest. I'm not sure if my clothes just combust or if I'm just that far gone. But when his thick head settles between my legs, I'm more than ready.

I arch my hips up, taking him in and eliciting a moan from him that mixes with my own.

The need builds until I'm seeing stars, then he sinks his teeth into my throat, giving me his bite, marking me as pack. And I'm gone. I've died. Electricity flays me alive, as if I've touched a live wire and can't let go. Pieces fit together and fall into place, my pack. My place. I belong. I'm wanted.

Tears flow freely down my cheeks as I notice time again. Austin has stopped moving and is staring down at me with concern. His thumb wipes a tear away.

"Did I hurt you? I've never–uh–you are the first omega I've marked."

I pull in a steadying breath and swipe at the tears. "That was intense."

He nods. "It was like I felt you inside of me. It lodges some piece of you deep in my heart."

"Yeah." I have no words. It was bliss, but more.

"I love you, Audrey," he tells me, and I feel his words at the soul level.

I reach up and smooth my fingers over his brow. "I love you, Austin Zade."

THEY SHOWERED me with whatever my heart could desire over the next couple of days. It was nirvana transcending from the bliss. A new level of acceptance and family. But the need to get the painting for Austin only grew. In the quiet moments, I mentally planned how I would do it.

I am a thief. I don't really need anyone's help, but I can wear the mask and use the men Austin has in place to help. Including Jason Vanross. He won't know it is me. Not with my hair color and the mask. And I would walk through hell to make my guys happy.

Absentmindedly, I finger the marks that ring my neck, as I stare out at the river in the distance, caught in my own thoughts in the quiet apartment. I want to show them off to the world. It is a giddy feeling. Sin continues to tease me relentlessly for doing the one thing I swore I would never do, but he's happy for me.

Austin and Saint had to go to the office today, so it's me and Felix for the day, which I kind of adore. He is always easy to be around with the added benefit of making me feel safe. Was he the first to joke and tease? One-hundred percent, but I loved that about him.

"Earth to Audrey," Felix says, waving his hand in front of my face. "You spaced? Where did you go?"

Blinking, I smile at him. He hadn't been on the other side of the couch a moment ago, and I completely missed his arrival. "Just thinking about making you guys happy."

He snorts. "We're guys. It is pretty simple."

"Not like that," I say, rolling my eyes. Although my body warms at the idea.

He tries to contain a grin as his teeth capture his lip ring, but his green eyes sparkle with mischief I've grown accustomed to.

"What?"

"You still owe me that date to Central Park," he says.

"Date, huh?" I tease. "Is 'hang out and take a walk in the park' the new way of asking someone out?"

He blushes. "I preceded it with 'do you want to'."

"Are we going to have a picnic?" I ask, letting him off the hook with a laugh.

"What is a date in the park without a picnic? We can pick it up on the walk over. Unless you want to drive there."

"Walking is good." Uncurling from the couch, I drop my feet to the floor and stand up. He smacks my ass playfully as I pass by him, and I shake my head ruefully. "Really?"

"You like it. I've seen the way you squirm when Austin deals out his punishments," he says.

I shake my head again. He isn't wrong. "I do enjoy that. I'll be back in a minute. I'm going to get ready."

I grab out a pair of distressed jeans and a soft blue t-shirt followed by a black hoodie, the kind that has the pre-made holes for my thumbs, from my endless closet. There are seriously more clothes in here than I could wear in a month. Maybe two months.

Sliding my feet into a pair of sneakers, I lace them up and join Felix back in the living room. He drags his fingers through his tousled hair as he runs his eyes over me.

"You are so beautiful," he breathes as he meets my gaze.

I laugh, feeling warm all over again. "I'm just wearing jeans and a hoodie, not a dress."

"You could be wearing a trash bag, and you'd still be the most beautiful woman I've ever laid eyes on."

I close the distance and link my arm with his. "You're not so bad yourself."

"Mmmm, yeah, but I have competition, and I know how sexy Saint and Austin are." He leads out of the apartment, locking it behind us, and to the elevator.

"The three of you combined are nothing short of gorgeous. They splashed you guys all over newspapers and magazines as the most eligible pack for a reason. It has nothing to do with your money."

He chuckles as the elevator comes to a stop on the first floor. "Maybe a little something to do with our money," he says, holding his fingers an inch apart after sliding the metal grate to the side to let us out. "Not that we would ever look for a different omega. You are it for us, sweetheart."

"Good, because you're stuck with me," I say, bumping his shoulder as we walk across the lobby.

If there are other people watching our exchange, I hardly

see them. None of them really matter. The walk to the park is peaceful, and the streets only start to get busy when we get closer. We picked up our picnic from the diner Felix loves, basket and all, and then found a spot in the park to lay out the checkered blanket.

It is the stuff movies are made of. A romantic picnic in central park, the bustling city just moments away. Kids playing, people flying kites, couples flirting, and families enjoying the day. The perfect sort of adventure.

I lean back on the blanket, taking it all in while Felix sorts out the contents of the basket. "She went above and beyond for us," he says. "Chocolate covered strawberries and everything."

"Do they serve chocolate covered strawberries at the diner?"

"I don't think so."

"That waitress is just in love with you," I say.

He huffs out a laugh. "That waitress is in love with Vinny. But Vinny is clueless."

"Oh, I see. If she sugars you up, she has a better chance," I laugh.

He blows a raspberry at me. "Vinny is his own man. He can figure it out himself, just like Austin did with you. Now, let me feed you strawberries," he says, holding one out for me to take a bite of.

His gaze fixes hungrily on my mouth as I take another bite. He purrs his pure alpha sound as his musk fills our space.

"Mmm, you are going to tease the shit out of me."

A laugh pops from my lips. "Me?" I raise my eyebrows. "I haven't even tried to tease you yet."

"Here, try some cheese," he holds the cube between his fingers, and I swipe my tongue over his thumb as I take it from him.

He groans, his eyes rolling back, and shifts his weight, adjusting himself at the same time. "Fuck, that was sexy. Do it again."

I repeat the motion when he holds another cube of cheddar out.

He leans forward and captures my lips in a claiming kiss that lights up my blood and makes me forget where we are. His fingers dive into my hair, and he cradles the back of my neck as he explores my mouth with his tongue. I whimper and press closer. Damn. Fuck the consequences and public indecency laws, because I need this man.

"Felix James Parker!" A shrill voice breaks us apart and leaves me gasping for air. "What are you doing? Some harlot offers herself, and you just disgrace your family by taking her in the middle of Central Park! As if being a beta wasn't bad enough."

I swallow as my heart beats fast for a completely different reason than what we were doing moments ago. My gaze settles on an older woman with an equally older man. They are both scowling at Felix like he is nothing but the dirt on their shoe, and I growl as I quickly get to my feet.

"Who the fuck do you think you are?" I demand, placing myself between him and whoever these people were. Assholes for sure, and someone he'd rather not see if the way his face paled meant anything.

"Are you that omega whore that has wormed her way in with his pack?" the lady sneers. "At least he had the pack, but now you are moving in, trying to steal that from him. You are such a disgrace, Felix."

I step closer, getting into her face and blocking her view of him completely. "You are not allowed to talk to him, and if you don't back off and leave us alone, you will regret it."

The man rakes me with a disgusted look. "You have an omega standing up for you, son?"

My breath shudders in my chest as rage takes over my entire body. I'm vibrating with it.

"It's okay, Aud," Felix says, stepping next to me, half shielding me with his body. He faces his parents with a sneer of his own. "Don't talk to my omega that way. I don't care who you are. You lost the right to judge my life when you tossed me out for being a beta."

"Your omega," his mom scoffs, as if she is talking to a child. "Son, betas don't get omegas."

"Then it is probably a good thing he is an sigma, you judgemental sacks of shit," I growl, attempting to push past Felix. "You want to see my marks? I've got three of them, one from each of my *alphas*."

The two of them pale, their attention fixing on their son. Not that I think they have the right to call him that.

"You presented as an sigma?" his father asks.

"Son, you're an alpha?" His mom presses her hands to her mouth as tears gather in her eyes like it is the happiest day of her life.

I force myself between them. This is not happening. "Fuck you both. You lost all of your rights when you were piece of shit parents and kicked your kid out because he wasn't what you thought he should be. And it was for something he couldn't control, so fuck you both to hell and back. Come on, Felix, let's get out of here. The park has lost its appeal."

I tangle my fingers with his and tug, but he stays rooted to the spot. Turning slowly, my heart breaks for him as he takes in his parents. Pain shines clearly from the depths of his soul.

"Audrey is right. You two aren't my family. I have a new family now, and it will never include you two. Who does that? Kicks their teenage son out when he can't give them what they want. You were supposed to take care of me and love me unconditionally," he pauses, his fingers flexing in mine. "Being a beta isn't a bad thing. I did it for years. It is a little freeing if I'm honest. No restrictions or expectations placed on you. And I had the support from my pack that the people that were supposed to care for me the most didn't even give me. Now I have the best of all three worlds. So whatever relationship we have with blood, that is broken. There are no second chances, or tentative relationships. And when I become a father, my children will never know the pain you inflicted on me."

Their mouths hang open as we stride away, leaving everything behind. I hold Felix's hand as we move in silence. I feel a sadness inside for him. If I could, I would put him back together and make sure he never hurts again.

We walk around a building further into the park, and he catches me off guard as he presses my back to the stone wall. Then kisses me hard. "You were fucking amazing back there, like an avenging angel ready to defend me from the monsters in the dark," he says, breaking away a little with panting breaths. "It was so damn sexy."

I grin into another kiss as he deepens it, pressing his hips into mine as his fingers dig into my ass, holding me close.

"Audrey, you are everything."

My stomach flips. He kisses down my neck in a frantic, wanton, wet presses of his lips. And I arch my neck to give him better access.

"Mmm, I've wanted to say that to them for years," he says, pulling back with a grin. "*Judgemental sacks of shits*, God, I can't wait to tell Saint and Austin about this." He laughs and kisses my nose.

"You're okay?" I ask. I squeeze his shoulders as I watch his face.

I mean, it is clear he is okay, but he's Felix, and he hides behind humor, so maybe he's hiding.

"I am. I promise," he says, dipping his head to meet my eyes directly. "Are you okay?"

"You mean them calling me names? I'm fine. I was madder about how they talked to you."

He chuckles, his eyes crinkling as amusement fills his green eyes. "I was pretty sure you were going to go all Saint on them and beat them into the ground, defending my honor."

"The thought crossed my mind," I reply with a laugh.

He threads his fingers with mine and then turns from our tiny hiding place, leading me behind him. "Come on, my little firecracker."

I snort. "Firecracker?"

He shrugs and tugs me under his arm and close to his side as we walk. "I'm trying out nicknames. That one was a six."

I hum happily. He can call me whatever he wants.

CHAPTER 54
Saint

AUSTIN LEANS BACK in his office chair, a tumbler of bourbon in his grip, his face serious. I look up from the contract his father had laid out, naming Audrey as Austin's property, basically. She wouldn't like that one bit, even if Austin is a scent match.

"Why do you have this?" I ask, holding it out.

He sighs and rubs his forehead. "I found it when I was looking for something else. I didn't even know it existed."

"You should burn it." I toss it back onto his desk. "Your dad is dead. Her dad is dead. No one would even know."

"But I would know. You would know." He takes a long drink of his bourbon.

"Yeah, thanks for that, asshole."

He swivels in his seat, facing the glass and looking out at the darkening city. "What if we show her? Tell her it means nothing."

I lean forward, my elbows on my knees, hands loose between my legs. "If she runs–"

He turns back slightly, half his face cast in shadow. "She won't."

There is a threat in his tone, one I know well. If she thinks me kidnapping her and putting her back into her plush room in the penthouse was bad, what Austin would do would be more extreme.

"You know that just because she wears our marks doesn't make it a done deal, right?"

"I know all about the birds and the bees talk. It will be permanent with her next heat. And since she has been riding the edge of one since that injection, I'm sure it will be soon."

"Don't fuck this up for us, Austin," I warn.

"Our omega is just that, *ours*. Nothing and nobody will change that."

I hope he's right, but I can't shake a feeling in my gut that the letter on his desk is going to ruin everything.

FELIX AND AUDREY are cuddled on the couch, watching a movie when we finally get home. Take out litters the table in front of them. I flick my attention to the TV for a moment as the sappy romantic Christmas movie plays on it.

A small town romance, the omega probably left her big city job to rescue a town from some terrible alphas. Then they all fall in love and live happily ever after. Christmas is saved.

"Hey, don't judge my choice of movie," Audrey says, picking up on my opinion pretty easily. She tosses a kernel of popcorn at me with a giggle. "I'm in a sappy *everyone lives happily ever after* kind of mood."

Austin settles in his armchair without a word, a besotted look on his face. He is as far gone for Audrey as Felix and I are.

"Sounds fun," I say and drop to the seat next to her after lifting her legs up and placing them on my lap. I absently massage her feet as her attention turns back to the screen.

She is captivating as she watches the movie play out. Emotion dances on her face, as the credits roll along with the happy tears down her cheeks, she looks around at us and realizes that none of us paid the movie any attention.

She wiggles her toes in my grip, and I move my hand to her calve muscle, massaging her lower leg for a moment.

"How was work?" she asks, glancing between us.

Austin sighs. "Terrible without you there to push my buttons."

"Awe, does Daddy Zade want his omega at work with him?" She fake pouts and bats her eyes at him.

I chuckle when a low growl emanates from his direction. "Careful or you'll end up draped over his lap getting his special sort of discipline."

She arches her foot and rubs her toes over my dick, ensuring that it wakes up and takes notice. "Maybe I like spankings."

I'm sure she does.

"I want you with me in my office," Austin admits. "But you'd probably be on your knees, under my desk."

She hums, a smile playing on her lips. "Your dirty little secret? Hidden away? Would you be meeting people?"

Felix snorts. "I'd like to see you meet people with her under your desk. I'm sure you wouldn't be able to do one bit of business."

"Who says the object would be to do business?" Austin raises his eyes to mine. "Maybe I just want to feel her mouth around me while we both know they could catch us."

"We all have fantasies," I agree.

Audrey pins me with a look. "What's yours?"

I rub my bottom lip as I think about it. "Probably taking you right after a win in the ring, with the same energy."

Her eyebrows go up into her hairline. "Like in front of the crowd?"

"No, for my eyes only, in the dressing room." Just the thought has me expanding in my pants, and I tug at the fabric to ease some of the growing pressure.

"That's lame," Felix says.

Audrey swats his chest. "It's hot, not lame. What is your fantasy?" She rolls her head up to look at him.

He laughs. "I like the idea of being caught, too. But actually being caught and not stopping," he admits. "Like today, if we ignored my parents and just kept going."

"What do you mean, your fucking parents?" Austin demands, tense for a brand new reason. And I don't blame him. After what they did to Felix, neither of us can even tolerate the idea of them.

Felix waves him off. "Don't worry, I had my omega with me, and she protected me from them." He rubs her shoulder and grins down at her.

"How did our little hellcat do that?" I ask as a wide smile pulls at her lips.

"I was pretty sure she was going to beat them to the ground, like someone else we know, but she used her words."

"My words?" She snorts out a laugh.

"She called them *judgemental sacks of shit*," he chortles out a breathy laugh. "You should have seen their faces. Priceless. And when they found out I was an alpha, God, I wish you two were there to see it. It felt so good."

His words ease the growing tension, and both Austin and I settle back into our seats.

"I'm glad you finally got to tell them where to go," I say.

"Me too. It feels like a weight that had been holding me down has been lifted. It is freeing in a way I didn't know I needed."

Audrey runs her fingers over the side of his face, adoration painted on her features. "You were so strong."

He shakes his head, capturing her hand against his skin.

"You were the strong one, and it allowed me to be what you needed."

"Okay, enough of the sappy shit. I need to hold my omega for a while. It was a long day," I say and drag her from Felix's arms. She nuzzles into my neck and molds to my body in the most perfect way.

"A long day?" Austin scoffs. "Who is the brains of the operation? All you had to do was put an offer on a building."

"And deal with your shit all day," I add.

"Was Daddy Zade awful today?" she asks.

"The worst," I say.

He growls, and we both laugh.

CHAPTER 55

Felix

WHEN THEY DISAPPEAR into Saint's room for some alone time, I heave a heavy sigh. Today was a lot. I hadn't lied earlier when I said I felt relief. But there is a sort of sadness and guilt at the feeling of freedom.

Who knew finally being free from their overbearing judgment would bring either emotion to the surface?

Austin eyes me from his chair. "Are you really okay?"

A smile briefly tugs at my lips before disappearing. "I am."

"None of us would think differently if you weren't."

I huff out a half laugh. "Do you want someone to take care of? I think Audrey is right, and you have that daddy vibe."

He shakes his head. "Don't start that shit."

"You love it."

"You're avoiding," he sighs, redirecting the conversation again.

"Fine. I feel guilty for finally feeling free," I say, crossing my arms. "Are you happy now?"

"It is strange how the people that raise us can have such a heavy hold on us. My dad is dead, and all I could think about was getting that painting to make him happy." He laughs and shakes his head. "Do you think the feeling will go away?"

"Eventually. The pain of them rejecting me faded, or at least scabbed over, and even that didn't hurt nearly as bad this time when I ran into them. And if you can forget about a painting, then I know I'll get over these feelings."

He nods and runs his fingers along his jaw. "There is something you should know–"

When I remain silent, he pulls out a folded envelope from his back pocket and holds it out. I reach for it and take out the contents. I scan the words before looking back at him.

"What's this?"

"A contract, written by mine and Audrey's father prior to their deaths."

"Why the fuck does it make it sound like Audrey and Sin are property to be traded? Did her dad think so little of them?"

"I don't think it was like that," he says, denying my words with a shake of his head. "I was at the meeting. They drew this up as a sort of back-up plan to keep both Mafia's strong. But I left the table like a child throwing a tantrum before it got this far."

I shift on the couch. "Did you show her?"

He presses his lips together in a tight line. "Not yet. I'm trying to figure out how to do it."

"I'd take her someplace she can't run, like an airplane."

He snorts, a smile pulling at his lips. "She would probably jump."

"Only if parachutes are handy," I reply with a grin.

"I want you and Saint there too."

I push off the couch and put distance between us as I circle the kitchen island and fill up a glass of water. "You might need the backup. But I think she will understand, really. Unless you tried to put the contract into place, then she might run. I don't think belonging to an alpha is at the top of her list of things to do."

"Maybe we should do it when we get Jason for her, then she has an outlet for her anger," he chuckles.

"He is the asshole that hurt her most," I agree. "But then it might remind her why she didn't want a relationship."

He stands and joins me in the kitchen. He leans against the island as I pull out stuff for a sandwich.

"You want one?"

"Starving actually." He rubs his stomach, and I pull out more bread to make two more sandwiches.

"It's because you think bourbon is a food group, and it is definitely not."

He brushes his fingers over my cheek. "You are too good for me. I don't think I tell you enough. But I'm pretty sure you saved me back then, as much as I saved you. And you are always the voice of reason for our pack. I don't know what I would do without you."

"Did you bump your head at work today? You aren't normally sappy," I say, pushing a plate with two sandwiches toward him. Even though my stomach is flipping at his words.

"I'm trying to acknowledge my feelings. I've been told that I'm emotionally stunted, and I don't want to be that way anymore."

"Well, what you're saying is a good start and will definitely get you laid tonight."

A purr rumbles from him, and I smile. I've never had an issue with the way Austin shows his love. Sure, he wasn't as soft as Saint, but I always still knew he cared. If he wants to make this change, though, I'll welcome it.

I eat my sandwich slowly as he devours his as if he hasn't eaten all day. "Maybe you should work on feeding yourself, too. You could be an asshole all the time because you're hungry," I tease as he licks his fingers.

This all feels like a dance, as if now that we have an omega, we are finding our places again. And the fact that I'm an alpha now has changed dynamics a little. The only thing that hasn't changed is our mutual feelings for each other. Eventually, we'll find a rhythm that will work for us all.

"I could use another sandwich," he admits.

Dragging his plate back to me, I pull out the stuff to make him another one. He circles the island and steps behind me, enveloping me in his musk of a late autumn day and spice. He presses a kiss to my shoulder as I prepare the sandwich.

"You're too good to me," he whispers.

I shrug. "I take care of the people I love, Austin. Just differently than you do. You bulldoze things to give the people you love what they want. Very caveman of you, by the way. I make sandwiches, because God knows I can't cook much else."

I turn in his arms and hand him the plate, putting it between us.

"Eat up, Boss."

He quirks an eyebrow and takes the sandwich off the plate to devour it like the first two. I place the plate on the counter as he finishes his last two bites. Then he lifts my chin, and I stare into his swirling violet eyes.

"Time for dessert," he says and then kisses me with the same enthusiasm he had for his food.

I melt as he does what he does best, dominates me. It is a unique feeling with him than the other two. All of them are amazing. But there is something about giving up any power I have to him that never fails to zip through me like an electric current, washing away any negative feelings, and replacing them with the promise of a sated body.

Sex with Austin is always like that. He is as demanding as a lover as he is an alpha business man.

Any lingering feelings of guilt or sadness flee as his fingers find the button of my jeans and pop it open. He palms my bare cock and strokes as he pushes my pants down my hips with his other hand. All the while, neither of us comes up for air, and he captures my moans with his mouth.

"Your knot is so large," he murmurs against my lips. All I can do is moan in response as he circles my cock and squeezes the base before pulling all the way to the tip. "Turn around."

He keeps hold of me as I turn and face the island. My palms meeting the cool marble counter as he undoes his slacks and releases himself with one hand while giving me a hand job with the other.

When he presses against my ass, rubbing some olive oil along his shaft before pushing in, I shift to give him better access, needing to feel him inside of me. It is our first time since Audrey has come into our lives, and as much as I love Audrey, I missed this too. Knowing she is okay with it is as freeing as not worrying about the judgment of my parents.

It doesn't take long for either of us to reach a climax as the sounds of Audrey and Saint flow to us from the closed bedroom door. It only adds to our heightened arousal. He bites my shoulder as he comes, and I erupt all over the kitchen island as the pleasure and pain mix.

Once we are done, we tuck ourselves away and clean up the mess I made, both wearing similar satisfied grins.

"I think I needed that," Austin says.

"I think I'm the luckiest alpha in the world," I reply.

"How?"

I straighten as I look at him. "I not only have a beautiful omega that I can't get enough of, but I also have two willing alphas that help me get off when she's busy."

He snorts. "I'm just a stand in, then?"

"Well–" I tease.

He laughs. "We do have the best of both worlds now, don't we? I don't know why I was so afraid of completing our pack."

CHAPTER 56

Audrey

TIME FLIES when you're happy and having so much sex your head spins. I adjust the dress on my hips, allowing it to fall just right, the slight sparkle catching the light. The week went by fast. No one tells you that being in love and happy makes time move in hyper-drive.

I slide my feet into the heels that probably cost as much as rent in a normal suburb of America. At least they fit like they were made for my foot. It will make sneaking around easier. I appraise my make-up in the mirror, wiping a bit of the lipstick from the corner of my mouth. The gloss shines, making my lips look plump and sexy.

Then I pick up the mask I chose for the party. Large feathers crown the top, which will cover my forehead completely, and it obscures my nose, leaving my brown eyes lined in charcoal and my pink lips the focal point of my face. Black feathers with a mixture of blue pull out the little green that is naturally in my brown eyes. The blue matches my guys' ties.

Straightening from the mirror, I turn toward the door and find Saint standing there watching me get ready. I flush as a smile pulls at my lips at the appreciative look shining in his eyes.

As he steps back into my room, he glances at my nest of pillows and blankets, then back at me. "We could stay in. No need to go talk to people we don't care about."

It had taken all week to get them to cave and say I could go to this thing. There is no way I'm backing out now. Not being this close.

I stride to him and lay my hand on his chest. "This is important for Austin's business. All of us can suffer for a little at least."

He snorts. "Austin is a big boy."

"And we are his pack." I lift an eyebrow in challenge. Not going to the party isn't an option. It is my chance to finally finish the job they hired me for. Even if that contract is null and void.

He sighs, acting more like Felix, and relents. "A brief appearance then—"

Austin props his hand at the top of the door frame as he pops his head into the room. "Saint, as much as you hate parties, this one will be fun."

"Fun," Saint repeats like it is a bad word.

"I had no idea you didn't like these things," I say.

"Too many people in one space. They get too close and nosy." He shivers dramatically.

My nose crinkles under the mask. "But you can fight in a ring with hundreds of people focused on you."

He shrugs and glances at Austin. "That's different."

I brush past Saint and head for the hall and Austin. His eyes run down me from my head to my toes, and it makes me feel warm all over.

"You are stunning," he says as he brings his violet eyes back to mine.

"I have to be if I'm going to be surrounded by you three."

"I think you outshine us all," he replies.

He backs out of the room as I approach, and I can feel myself blush from my chest up. Felix's eyes light up when he catches sight of me, and he bounds over and sweeps me into a hug.

"My moonbeam, you look beautiful, as always." Felix drops a kiss to my lips.

A laugh pops free from my throat. "*Moonbeam?*"

"Yeah, you're right. Not that one either," he exhales.

Austin and Saint follow us as Felix leads me to the door. My stomach flutters with excitement and a bit of trepidation that I ignore.

The drive takes a half an hour before we are pulling up outside of the Central Park Towers, the tallest building for residential homes in the United States. Also known by me as Suit tower, because every single multimillionaire and billionaire in New York City wants an apartment in this place. Well, except for my guys, I guess.

I look up, and up, and up as Saint helps me out of the car. The building towers over the ones surrounding it and has picturesque views of Central Park just a block over.

"I thought you said Valentine was having this at his house?" I ask.

"His penthouse, maybe," Felix replies.

Austin steps out of the car and fixes his suit, his gaze running up the building in the same way mine had. "It is the club on the 100th floor."

"Oh. And Valentine owns the penthouse?" I ask. I totally dropped the ball on doing recon, I've done jobs on less.

"No, he doesn't have enough money for the penthouse," Saint chuckles. "But I bet he is salivating at the mouth with just the idea of ever having enough money to buy it."

"He is on the 17th floor."

My stomach dips. The heist is feeling like a failure, and I

haven't even tried yet. I nibble on my lip as we cross the courtyard that leads to the entrance. A door man stops us and checks for our names on his list before he steps out of the way and lets us in. My heart beats loudly in my ears as we ride the elevator up to the 100th floor.

The doors slide open to reveal a lavish space already full to the brim with party goers. I run my hands over my dress as if I am smoothing it down, when in reality my palms feel clammy. Austin's hand lands on the small of my back, and it steadies me as he guides me through the space effortlessly.

"Nervous?" he whispers next to my ear.

"Is it that obvious?"

He chuckles. "You keep smoothing out your already smooth dress." He nods at my hands that are currently doing just that.

I shake them out and cross them lightly over my stomach. "It's a lot."

"Yeah. But imagine how much you could lift here. You'd be set for years. A watch here, a necklace there," he whispers as he nods at a woman wearing a line of diamonds around her neck.

I laugh. "I think I learned my lesson on that one."

He rubs a circle on my lower back. "It didn't turn out so bad."

When I look up at him, he's smiling. Adoration shines from his eyes and makes me melt. That look. That is the reason I'm still going forward with this crazy plan.

"Yeah, not that bad at all," I agree. "But are you suggesting I trade up?" I tease, and a growl rumbles in his chest, making my nipples hard.

He slides his hand around my side and pulls me close just as Saint returns with our drinks.

"Where is Felix?" I ask, glancing behind him.

Saint gives me a lopsided smile. "Doing what he does

best, flirting with the millionaires so they invest in Zade enterprises."

"And we are okay with that?" I ask, a twinge of jealousy rattling in my chest. I might be a little possessive of my guys.

Austin presses a kiss to the side of my head as my fingers curl around the stem of the glass Saint hands me. The bubbles rise to the top, and I swirl the liquid around the edge.

"Come on, you can see him in action yourself. No reason to be jealous," Austin says.

He guides us through the room until I spot Felix. He's chatting with a group of people. Smiles are all around, and he is clearly the center of attention, but the flirting he is doing is subtle and clearly not sexual. He meets my stare, and his gaze softens for me, telling me everything I need to know. He might play a part, but he is mine.

It relaxes me, and I finally take a sip of the bubbly in the glass. The champagne tingles as it slides down my throat. Austin excuses himself, and Saint takes his place at my side. We watch from the sidelines, where I'm most comfortable, as Austin and Felix work their magic.

"Are these parties just for making connections?" I ask, tilting my head up to Saint.

The corner of his mouth lifts, and he nods. "Basically. They are so boring."

"Definitely not like the clubs my brother frequents," I agree. Not that those are fun either.

We circle the outside of the room, coming to the large floor-to-ceiling windows that have a view over the park. It is so far down I feel slightly dizzy looking out over the sprawling park. I take a few more sips of the champagne. It is slightly sweet on my tongue, and the bubbles are pleasant as they travel to my stomach.

I switch out my glass for a full one as a waiter passes. The liquid isn't like whiskey that burns a path down your throat and makes you aware it is there, settled in the pit of your stomach before it roars through you like a storm. This one is unassuming and soft as it eases your muscles and bleeds into your bloodstream. One minute I'm sober, and the next I can't stop the giggles at apparently nothing.

Saint smiles indulgently down at me as I cover my mouth as a hiccuping laugh escapes. "Look who's a lightweight with champagne. I've heard of that, but never seen it in person."

I shush him as he plucks my empty glass from my fingers. *Huh, when did that happen? I just picked it up. Didn't I?*

He leads me to the appetizer table, and I load a tiny plate with donut holes and cheese. Saint eyes the plate and shakes his head. Ignoring his judgment of my choices, I head to a tall table and pop a cinnamon and sugar donut hole into my mouth. I hum around the sugary goodness, closing my eyes with pleasure.

"So good," I say, pressing my fingers to my lips.

Saint chuckles and shakes his head. "You keep making those noises. I'll give you a lifetime supply of those things."

I follow with a cube of cheese, which isn't a normal accompaniment of donuts but isn't horrible either. The burst of cheddar on my tongue is so sharp compared to the sugary mess I just had. It would pair well with the bubbly. I search the room for waiters, and as one comes close, I snag another glass. And I'm right. It is amazing.

I am the embodiment of distracted. My plan to steal the painting that wasn't really much of a plan slips slowly away. Austin will understand. Right?

After a while of the crowd watching, Felix appears next to me, and I throw my arms around him and give him a very public kiss before he can say a word. He laughs as he pulls away, his eyes going to Saint.

"Is now the time to play out your fantasy?" I stage-whisper as he smiles down at me.

"Did you drug her?"

"Champagne lightweight, apparently. She only had three glasses." There is a pause, and then he adds, "I need to use the bathroom. Don't let her out of your sight."

I bite my lip as I gaze up at Felix. His piercings and hair are at odds with his suit, the combination surprisingly sexy. Or maybe he is just sexy.

"Did you enjoy flirting with other people?" I ask.

"No. I never do." He tucks me under his arm, and we start the circle around the room again.

"Good."

"Jealous, little rabbit?"

I snort loudly, drawing attention to us. *"Rabbit? And no."*

"I'll find some kind of nickname."

"You really don't need to." I laugh, enjoying his determination.

He grins down at me before changing the subject. As we circle the room, he points out different people, telling me about them. Or at least telling me the gossip about them. We spend the next half hour like that, in our own little world, taking in all the guests.

Then my eyes land on a tall, lanky man from behind. My breath shudders in my chest as I catch sight of Jason. Even from behind, his frame is hard to miss. Involuntarily, my fingers tighten into Felix's biceps. He's instantly on alert, scanning the crowd for the danger. Seeing my worst nightmare in the flesh, breathing the same air as me, cements my heels to the ground and sobers me up in less than three seconds.

"Are you okay?" Felix's voice drops low with concern as he scans the party goers again.

I don't know why I thought I could face Jason and use him to steal the painting. Seeing the back of him in that restaurant with Saint had only been a tiny taste of the negative effects he brought to my body. As it is, my whole body trembles as a clammy sort of sweat breaks out on my hands and neck. My heart feels like someone has a vise around it as fear rises to choke me. I rapidly blink, faced with him ten feet away.

Then he turns, and he's not wearing a mask. He might be tall and lanky, but his face is handsome in a way a monster shouldn't be. But as much as I used to think that, it does nothing that it used to do to me. Now it is a shot of terror straight into my bloodstream, as I imagine him making me beg for his mark to save my brother. Not that it was good enough, he still cut Sin open and took who he was as an omega from him.

His cruel laughter crosses the space between us as he laughs at something the man next to him says, cutting straight through me. My perfume sours as I inhale through my nose.

The next thing I know, Felix has my face in his hands, blocking the view of Jason. And I can breathe again. He grounds me, and I realize my face is damp beneath the mask, but I can't take it off, not out here.

"Are you okay?" he repeats, dipping his head to catch my eyes with his.

Time starts again, and my pulse, although still rapid, no longer feels like my heart is going to explode.

"I–" I say and then swallow before clearing my throat. "Jason Vanross," I barely whisper, afraid it will bring him to us. What if he scents me? Breathing through my nose again, I take calming breaths. I can do this.

Felix swears and looks over his shoulder, catching sight of him. "We can leave. Austin will understand."

I shake my head. "No, after tonight I won't have to worry about this ever again. Right?" I attempt a smile, but it feels brittle and fake on my lips.

"If Saint or Austin sees your reaction to him, you won't have to worry about it in two seconds," he mutters.

My eyes widen as I search the crowd for them. I don't see either of my guys, though, so I'm sure they missed the melt down.

"Then I guess we should head the other direction, because I want the pleasure of taking him out."

He drops his hands to my shoulders, squeezing softly. "You are the most stubborn omega I've ever met. We can leave."

"And let him win?" I say, not expecting an answer. It isn't really a game for either of us to win, but mentally, if I run, who am I?

"If that is what you want, let me be your anchor tonight. I'll keep you steady." He wraps his arm around me again, effortlessly turning us in the opposite direction. "I know what it's like to be cornered with seemingly no escape. Especially at parties."

CHAPTER 57
Saint

WHEN I RETURN from the bathroom, Felix and Audrey have wandered off. I scan the area and don't see them. Before I can do a search, Melody Lynn steps into my field of vision. She smooths her gloved hands down her pink dress, looking like a vision for any omega searching for an alpha.

"Saint, where is your lovely omega?" she asks and looks around as if Audrey will pop up from behind the table and say, 'here I am'.

I press my lips together. Melody Lynn isn't a bad person. She is a big personality that I don't have time for at the moment, though, so I give a noncommittal shrug.

"Oh, have you lost her?" She pouts. "Or are you setting up for the heist?" she asks, lowering her voice as if she was part of the plan.

"There is no heist." I slip my hands into my blazer pockets and rock back on my heels, flicking my gaze over the party goers nearby.

She throws her head back and laughs. "Maybe not for you, but I've met that omega of yours. I'll bet even if Austin canceled it, she is still going to make a play for it."

I snap my eyes back to Melody Lynn. "Why do you think that?"

"Love makes you do dangerous things. Don't you think?" She cocks her head to the side. Propping her hand on her waist, she glances around like she is ready to spill a secret, she licks her glossy lips as she parts them, then adds, "A birdie told me she is a long lost De Luca princess, and her dragon that needs slayed is Jason Vonross. Well, he's here, and he knows she is too. You really should keep better track of your omega."

The blood drains from my face, making me feel light-headed. "Who told you that?"

"It doesn't matter, Saint, find your omega," she replies and steps out of my way. "Good luck," she calls to my back as I stride away, searching the area.

I don't see either of them. But there are other rooms, other areas, so I barely contain my strides, so I'm not all out running as I enter the next one. Austin is in the middle of a group of old money business men schmoozing away, but one look at me, and he stops mid-sentence and breaks away from them.

"What happened? Where is Audrey?" he asks as soon as he reaches me.

"Felix has her, but Melody Lynn just basically said she is in danger. We have to find her."

I'm sure we look like a pair of charging bulls in a china shop as we search the next room. People move out of our way, and all eyes seem to watch us as we come up with no sign of them again. Once we reach the last room, I'm on edge. I can feel it in my stomach that something is wrong.

Felix stands alone near the window, and every single one of my fears grows wings and batters my stomach for release.

"Where is Audrey?" I ask as we stop in front of him. It feels as though the air is being cut off, and I crack my knuckles as I tighten them into fists. I need to fight something.

Felix looks between us, the smile on his face fading. "She went to the bathroom a couple of minutes ago." He gestures to the bathroom not even five feet from where he is standing, and I relax slightly.

"We have to go," I say.

"Yeah, probably for the best. She caught sight of Vanross, and she—I don't know, shut down. She was terrified. That bastard did some horrible shit to her if just the sight of him brought on her reaction."

"You saw Jason? Did he see you? Did he see Audrey?" I ask, my muscles tensing all over again.

Felix rolls his lip ring between his teeth, trapping the ball. "I don't think he did."

I tug my fingers through my hair and look at the bathroom door, tempted to go inside to make sure she is okay. Austin looks the same.

He glances at his watch. "Was she just using the restroom?"

"Washing her face," Felix says.

Austin heads for the door, coming up short as a woman exits. "Was there a tall brunette in a blue dress in there?" he asks.

The woman looks back at the door and shakes her head. "No, just me."

My heart drops out my ass, and I'm right behind Austin as he tears the door open. Felix is at my heels. The room is empty, but there is another exit that leads to the first room.

"Shit."

"She's gone."

A startled beta jumps out of our way as we fly out the other door. Austin stops a few people asking if they saw her. An older man points to the elevators and says something I don't catch. But Austin is heading that way, so we follow.

"What did he say?" Felix asks.

"He saw her head this way, took the elevator down."

"Was she alone?" I ask.

"Yeah."

"She's going after the painting." It was the only possible thing, and after Melody Lynn's observations, I am almost one-hundred percent certain that is where she went.

The elevator dings open on the 17th floor, and I head down the short hall. A door hangs open. It looks like someone rammed it with a log it is so splintered. There is no way Audrey did that.

Austin toes the door open, and a piece of wood falls to the ground. He steps into the apartment, the plush carpet silencing any of our footsteps. A safe hidden behind a painting is wide open, jewels and cash piled inside. The first bedroom is empty, the second equally vacant.

Felix walks to the floor-to-ceiling window, and a gasp steals his breath as he looks down at something.

"We have to go. He has her," Felix says, and he is running past me, pushing past Austin and out of the apartment before I can move to the window and see what he did.

Jason Vanross has Audrey by the neck, out on the pool deck on the next floor down. She looks terrified as her feet dangle off the ground. Then he drops her into the pool, pushing her back under the water when her head bobs up.

It is more than enough before I'm out of the apartment, tearing after Felix, Austin now following us. I take the emergency stairs down, missing the last four steps completely as I jump to the landing. Then I burst out of the stairwell and into a community area, the pool deck straight through the windows.

Felix stops as he catches sight of the scene in front of us. I tumble into Felix's frozen form, and Austin barrels past us. Jason's head snaps up as Austin flies out the door, and Jason drags Audrey out of the pool by her hair, quickly dragging her limp body after him closer to the ledge. She is still. Not even a breath raises her chest, and it freezes my heart inside my own.

An evil grin lifts the corners of his mouth as he watches us. His eyes dance with a sick satisfaction in the low light of the patio.

"About time you came for her, I thought she'd die with no witnesses." He shakes her, and her head lulls to the side like a rag doll.

"Stop right there," Austin commands.

"You're not the one in charge of this situation right now," Jason taunts him. "How does it feel to spiral?"

"You're a dead man walking."

It isn't an idle threat. Austin doesn't play a bluffing game. He lays all of his cards out and tells you exactly how you are going to die.

"The only thing that would make this sweeter is if her brother was here," Jason continues, as if Austin is not pulsing with rage less than ten feet from him. Audrey sputters, coughing up water after another jerk of Jason's arm. "That a girl, get that water out of your lungs so you can see your death coming."

Audrey struggles weakly against his hold, her fingers digging into the back of his hand. He laughs cruelly, and I watch as he curls his fingers into her stomach, causing her to whimper.

I take a step, ready to pounce across the distance, and he shakes a finger at me. "Ah-ah, stay where you're at or she doesn't last until Sin gets here to watch."

She fights harder, screeching at the mention of her brother. "No!"

"Don't worry, sweets, I'll make it fast," he says. Pressing his lips to her temple, he adds, "For old times' sake."

He drags her closer to the edge, stepping onto a raised step overlooking the sheer drop. Then he gestures at Felix. "Call her brother, tell him where we are. I've made sure he's on the guest list. Then the real fun can begin."

Felix hesitates, looking to Austin for direction.

"Now!" Jason barks and dangles Audrey over the edge, his hand gripped around her neck.

Austin holds out his hand and nods at Felix, giving him the go-ahead. The conversation that follows is low and short. My ears are ringing, so I don't pick up what they say, but I can hear the urgency in his tone.

"Look at that–your alpha listening like a good boy," Jason purrs, while Audrey gasps for air.

A growl rumbles out of Austin.

"You got what you want," I say, and the words are almost pleading. Why did I leave my gun at home? We didn't bring any weapons, and it is the stupidest move we've ever made.

When Audrey's feet find purchase on the stone wall and his arm is wrapped back around her waist like an iron grip, I try to breathe again. My mouth is dry, and I've got tunnel vision. But the second Audrey slams her heeled foot down on Jason's, and he releases her with a curse, she tumbles to her knees, barely missing the fall.

"Audrey!" Austin shouts as he lunges for her. Jason grabs for her at the same time, yanking her back by her hair.

Panic blooms like a poisonous cloud inside of me as he moves her closer to the edge again. He's too far away. We can't reach her before she plummets sixteen stories to her death.

"We can talk about this," I say, reaching an empty hand out in their direction.

He throws his head back, laughing like an insane hyena. "That's funny coming from the guy that uses his fists to talk."

My knuckles crack as I close my fists, digging my nails into my palms, imagining doing exactly that as soon as Audrey is safe. A muscle pulses in my jaw as I grind my teeth together. He catches both movements and chuckles. He knows he's not walking out of here. That's dangerous.

She goes still when he holds a switchblade to her neck. "Did you tell your alphas you begged for my mark, *princess?*"

He presses the blade firmer against her skin, and she whimpers, tearing my heart and soul out while boiling my blood all at once.

He continues with a sneer. "That you were on your knees for me?"

Her mouth trembles as tears streak dark lines down her face. The mask hangs around her neck, forgotten and out of place with the wet feathers. Her dress is torn up the side, blood from her knee making a path to the strap of her heels.

"Tell them!" he shrieks, his hand dropping from her neck as he shakes her again, clearly walking the thin line of completely insane and unhinged.

"I did," she sobs. "I begged him to save my brother!"

"That isn't why!" he yells.

I share a look with Austin and Felix. We can't wait for her brother to get here. This is only getting worse. He's spiraling down a dark hole. There is no talking him out of this.

"You're right," Audrey gasps. "I wanted you. I've only ever wanted you."

I hate the lies she is throwing out, but I recognize them for what they are—a way to talk him down.

"You can have the mafia and the money, Jason. I've never cared about any of it. I'll give it to you."

His face flushes, and he gentles his hold on her, bringing

her into his chest. "It means nothing without the De Luca name backing me. I didn't know that before."

I can feel my pulse pounding in my temples as he seems to calm down, if only slightly.

"You can't be marked," he says, his gaze dropping to our marks ringing her neck. He fists her hair and yanks her head roughly back, holding the blade to her throat again, at our crescent marks. "I'll cut them off."

CHAPTER 58

Audrey

HE PULLS MY HAIR BACK; the roots burn from the pain, then he slides the cool metal of a knife over my skin.

"Did you tell your alphas you begged for my mark, *princess?*" he whispers into my wet hair.

I can't help the whimper that releases when he presses harder with the blade, and I feel it cut into my flesh. My guys look helpless as they watch us up on the ledge.

I glance down at the street below. It is a dizzying height that no one would survive.

The next floor down has a patio that is out a little further. If I fall just right, I have a chance of living. But I can't think as my knee pounds with its own pulse where it slammed into the concrete when I was almost free. Slamming my heel into his foot again probably wouldn't work. He has me to the side of him, and I'd most likely miss.

I don't even attempt to hide my tears or my fear. It is what he wants to see. He wants to think he broke me, so I let him. But inside, I feel my emotions shutting off, the same way they did when he tortured me. The same way they did the last time he made me beg.

Sin. He is on his way. I need to get out of this before he shows up. Nothing will stop Jason from tossing me like yesterday's trash and then getting a hold of Sin.

"That you were on your knees for me?" he hisses, his fingers tighten on my sore neck again. If I survive, it will be black and blue. "Tell them!" he demands as he shakes me again, rattling my brain in my head.

"I did," I cry, playing into the fear. "I begged him to save my brother!"

Bastard. He vibrates with rage and shakes me violently.

"That isn't why!"

My guys look at each other, and I know they are about to do something reckless to save me. I can't let them get hurt. Jason is like a cornered and injured animal right now.

"You're right, I wanted you. I've only ever wanted you."

God, please let this work. I squeeze my eyes shut, praying to a God I don't believe in. That he will finally show some sort of grace and save me. But it is his son that loved the sinners, and I definitely am no angel. So maybe I should pray for his son.

"You can have the mafia and the money, Jason. I've never cared about any of it. I'll give it to you."

"It means nothing without the De Luca name backing me. I didn't know that before," he whispers, his arm becoming softer around my stomach.

I want to throw up. His palm flat against my abdomen makes the skin below feel like it is being eaten away by acid.

"You can't be marked," he says. My roots burn as he yanks my head back, arching my neck, and pressing his knife to my throat. "I'll cut them off."

It is my nightmare. My breath catches, and I can't get more oxygen into my aching lungs.

"They'll fade," I choke. "If they don't complete my heat with me, they will fade."

He pauses and sniffs at me. I'm thankful the chlorine from the pool clings to my dress, hiding my true scent. Because it is not brownies baking in an oven. It is probably sour and tart like rotten milk.

"Your heat?"

I feel him running his nose over my neck to my ear, and my gag reflex is almost triggered.

"Any day now," I admit. Hell, it is already seeping from my pours right now. If he had run with me and locked me up, instead of whatever this was, he would have had me completely without my choice.

"Then let's get started now," he says before he is dragging me to a lounge chair and tossing me down. When his suffocating body covers me, I freeze. I can't think. I can't breathe. He doesn't notice as he undoes his belt and uses it to latch me to the top of the chair. "Tell the alphas to stay back, sweets, if they come closer, I won't hesitate to slit your throat while I come inside you."

I quake with fear. My lower lip wobbles as I wet them, attempting to say the words. Felix looks wrecked on the other side of the pool, Saint not much better standing next to him. While Austin is a barely contained storm.

"Don't–" I say and catch my breath.

Austin shakes his head, and I'm not sure if he is saying okay, he won't do it or no, he can't listen.

"You don't have to see this," I say, meeting Felix's sorrow-filled stare. "Please," I beg, and I don't even know what I'm begging for.

Saint shuts his eyes and draws in a steadying breath, then resolutely opens them.

"If you try to take what isn't yours, Jason, I will kill you slowly. One finger nail at a time, one toe nail at a time, I'll carve the flesh from your body and keep you alive while I do it. You will feel every slice of my blade. And you'll beg for death. But not even then will it come, because I will let you heal, and I'll do it all over again," Saint says, his voice is even, and there is no threat in his words, only promise. "You will feel every ounce of pain you have ever given to Audrey or her brother, but I will be the karma that brings it to you."

My heart leaps. And really, that should not make it flutter like he just declared his love for me, but just imagining Jason squealing and begging brings me happiness.

Jason ignores him, the sound of his zipper lowering filling the pool patio. He lets his pants hang open and then takes the knife and slices my dress up to my waist before using it to slice my panties off me. This is it. I squeeze my eyes shut, unable to face what is about to happen, completely helpless to stop it.

Two breaths in, less than thirty seconds pass, a popping sound like a firework goes off as if it is in a distant hall. Then Jason's weight is on me. But it is dead weight, and he's not moving. Warmth soaks into my dress, and chaos erupts.

Someone pulls him off me, and I hear Sin at my side, pressing cool hands to my cheeks, begging me to open my eyes. To tell him I'm okay. But I can't. I'm shaking and shivering and probably in shock.

"Audrey, you're safe, it's okay, baby, open your eyes," Felix pleads. Someone undoes the belt holding me to the chair, and my arms slump to my sides. But finally, I blink open my eyes.

Sin hovers next to me, a gun on the lounge chair at his side. Felix is on my other side. He smooths my hair off my forehead and pulls me in for a hug.

"You're okay," he says, and I'm not sure if he is telling me or himself.

"Baby?" I croak into his warm chest.

He pulls back and attempts to smile. "Simple and natural.

But I'll make up more nicknames if they make you smile, one for every day of the rest of your life."

"No, baby is perfect."

Soon after, I'm a sandwich with my alphas as they each reassure themselves I'm still breathing and okay.

Jason's body is discarded to the side like the trash he was. There is a perfect bullet hole in the back of his head. I didn't even know Sin was that good of a shot. When they pull me up, I stare down at the painting I stole. It lays at the bottom of the pool. The old paint is already swollen and cracking. Austin will never have it now.

Austin follows my gaze. "Is that?"

"I'm sorry, Austin–"

He turns me in his arms and cradles my face until I look up at him. There is nothing but love shining from the depths of his perfectly violet orbs. "You are the only thing that matters to me, and we will discuss your *punishment* later for going after the painting after I said that was no longer the plan."

My stomach flips as butterflies erupt. I like his punishments, and the slight smile on his lips as he promises pleasure does things to me, even after what just happened. Although spankings may need to wait until the rest of me isn't bruised.

"How about you don't talk about your sexual preferences in front of me," Sin says. "As much as Aud doesn't want to know about mine, I definitely do not want to know about hers."

RECOVERY TAKES DAYS, the stress has my heat subsided for now, and although the threat to my life is gone, sometimes in the dark, in the middle of the night, I wake up from nightmares. The therapist Saint found for me assures me it will get better.

But even the omega in me has had enough pampering for a lifetime. My nest has gone from comforting and safe to stifling and annoying.

Kicking off my blanket on the third day, pushing the wall of pillows to the floor, I climb out of my bed. My muscles only protest because they haven't even let me walk to the bathroom.

As if he senses my rebellion, Saint comes flying into my room.

"What do you need?"

I growl low in the back of my throat and swat his hands away as he reaches for me.

"Different scenery," I grumble.

Saint holds his hand up and backs away. Austin leans against the doorframe, the corner of his mouth kicking up.

"Looks like our omega is almost back to herself," he says, earning another growl from me.

Concern deepens the lines on Saint's face as Felix pushes past Austin into the room.

"Am I a prisoner?" I take in all three of them and prop my hands on my hips.

"No, of course not." Felix moves in front of Saint. "We just wanted to let you heal."

"Well, I'm done. My therapist said I needed to get back to normal. I'm going to see her at her office." I take a deep breath, ready to fight them.

Austin straightens. "Okay."

I continue, "And none of you can stop me—wait what?"

"He said okay," Saint says.

My mouth pops open around a silent 'Oh'. I really expected an uphill battle to get them to agree to me leaving the room, let alone the penthouse.

"And I want ice cream–" when no one says anything I add, "and pancakes at the diner."

"I'll get ready," Felix says before disappearing as fast as he appeared.

I'm left with Austin and Saint watching me. "What?"

The corner of Austin's mouth kicks up, his eyebrows lifting slightly, and he licks his lips. "Are you ready to talk about punishments yet?"

I swear my whole body flushes at his words. My belly flips, and I sink my teeth into my lower lip. "After my errands, Daddy," I reply.

A grin slowly spreads over his face, and my scent blooms strong and ready. "Well, then I guess I need to get ready, too. Have to make sure you don't take your time."

I shake my head as he backs out the door, leaving me with my concerned alpha. "I'm okay, Saint."

He steps forward, his hands coming up to cradle my face. His rough thumb strokes my cheek bone as he stares into my soul. "We need to talk about why you left the party to get that painting. Austin is letting it go, but Audrey, you can't put yourself in danger like that."

My stomach dips like I'm on a rollercoaster as I think back on that night. I hadn't planned to steal the painting. Seeing Jason had messed with my head. I felt off and had the stupid idea of stealing the painting and hiding it somewhere I could return for it later. When I saw the back exit in the bathroom, it was like I was possessed. I needed to get it.

And it went off without a hitch. I knew what floor Valentine lived on, so I took the elevator down. I passed a guy in the hall and made up some story about surprising him, and he told me which door was his. All of that was perfect. I had all I needed to pick the lock in my hair, and I had done it before. It just wasn't my preferred method of stealing.

Then fate showed her hand. Painting in hand, I headed

back to the elevator. I didn't think about taking the stairs, which may have avoided everything that followed.

The doors slid open, and Jason was there, standing in the middle of the elevator. I froze. The same way I did when I saw him at the party. But this time, it was only us, and I was stupid to think a mask and different hair color would prevent him from knowing me the second he saw me.

"Little sweets, I was looking for you," he said. His words washed over me like a cold shower, and before I could move, he snagged my arm and pulled me into the elevator.

"Let me go! What do you think you are doing?" I struggled against him as the metal box moved again.

He chuckled. That sure of himself sound, the one he used to do when he knew he had me where he wanted me and it soured my stomach.

"Did you really think I wouldn't find you? That I wouldn't come for you?" he asked, but he wasn't looking for an answer.

The doors slid open on the next floor, and he let me go. I bolted. Running for freedom. All I had really done was make his job easier. He wanted me on the pool deck. It was a game for him. He blocked the stairs before I could get to them, leaving me on the patio beyond the doors. If I could get out and block them somehow, someone would come for me eventually. Right?

How wrong I'd been. I tripped as one of my heels broke. The painting went flying across the cement, stopping right next to the pool. But my fall was what he needed. He yanked me up by my hair and then dragged me to the edge of the pool. He laughed when he looked down at the painting.

"If I knew they would deliver you straight into my arms, I wouldn't have spent the last few weeks following the crumbs you've left to your location. Did you really think you could keep running? That I wouldn't track you down? We found the warehouse, the pawn shop, a few gangs in the area were way too willing to give you up. Then it went dry. Until two nights ago, after yet another one of my men showed up tortured and dead, I knew we were close, and Saint," he laughed like a madman, "He was the common denominator. Your down fall."

I wrapped my fingers around his hand that was pulling my hair, trying to get myself free. He kicked the painting into the water, and it sank to the bottom. Then he kneed me in the back, and I tumbled in after. As I came up and sputtered the water from my mouth, he shoved me back under, holding me there.

"Hey, Audrey, come back to me," Saint says, tugging me from the nightmare of a memory. Tears roll down my face, and I blink up at him.

"I thought I was doing what was right. But I should have told you and Felix."

He shakes his head and pulls me into his chest. "I didn't mean to push. Any one of us would have done the same if we had your skills. And none of us knew you were in danger until it was too late."

"I should have known," I say and swallow. "I knew we weren't safe, and that he was still coming after us. I just grew comfortable and secure with you guys. It felt like nothing could hurt me if I had you three watching my back. Only I left a party without telling any of you–"

I let out a self deprecating laugh and shake my head against his firm body. I had been stupid. Not that I was some girl that needs rescued, well, clearly I was, but not normally. Normally, I can hold my own.

He shushes me as his hands rub my back soothingly. "Let's get you ready so you can get that ice cream and pancakes."

CHAPTER 59

Austin

THE NEXT DAY, I finally go into the office. I'm reluctant to leave Audrey and almost demand that she come with me. But I've grown. At least I'm telling myself I have.

I run my finger around my tumbler full of water, watching the clear liquid like it can tell the future. It turns out it isn't any better than the bourbon that I've been cutting back on.

Almost losing Audrey right after admitting I need her had been like an arrow through the heart, and it took every part of myself to hold back the need to lock her up in a padded room to ensure her safety. Even emotionally stunted, I am pretty sure that wouldn't equate to love. So I tease and fall back into the Dom role play; at least it is one I know. And I'm positive she likes it, too, even if she isn't exactly a sub, we both like the pretend.

I rotate my chair and stare out the window, watching the clouds for who knows how long. Someone cracks open my office door, but even though I'm at the office, I'm not really here. I'm ten miles away in a little penthouse on the Lower East Side.

"I'm busy," I call out.

The door shuts, and I breathe a sigh of relief until I hear someone walking across the floor to my desk.

"I said I'm busy," I bark.

"Yeah, I'd say, it is hard work deciding what kind of cloud animal is outside the window," Audrey says, her voice full of humor.

She strolls around the desk and leans against it, her eyes on me as she smiles. "I escaped my jailer."

I snort. Saint has been completely over-protective. He's slipped right into my normal roll. "He just blames himself for not taking care of Jason as soon as he found out."

"Well, he can stop."

I study her. "I think you enjoy it."

She presses her lips together, withholding another smile. "Maybe a little, but I will not tell him that."

"What brings you here, baby girl?"

She shrugs, her fingers lightly curl around the dark wood of the desk. "It was the one place I knew I could go to give the other two a break on babysitting duty."

I raise my brow. "I am pretty sure that being around you is the highlight of their day. I know it's mine."

She blushes and averts her eyes. "I don't think I'll ever get used to this."

"This?"

"Alphas."

I choke out a laugh. "Alphas?"

"Yeah, making me feel like I'm the center of your world. Like the sun orbits around me, and the moon and stars wouldn't exist if it weren't for me."

"It does, and they wouldn't," I say, turning and capturing her between my legs.

She shifts her weight and faces me, her hands falling to my shoulders like they belong there. "Austin–"

I press a finger to her lips, stopping her from saying more.

"Audrey De Luca, you are our everything. There is no air without you, no sun, no warmth, no light or dark. It is nothingness expanding forever. So get used to it, because that feeling, it's real. It isn't your mind playing tricks on you. It isn't any of us playing a part. You complete each of us and make us whole."

"You really know how to make an omega melt, don't you, Daddy?"

Before I can respond, another knock sounds at my door, and she drops to her knees and scurries under my desk, dragging my chair after her.

"What are you doing?"

"Seeing how well you concentrate," she says.

Her fingers go to my belt loop, loosening my belt and popping my button, sliding the zipper down and reaching inside my slacks. Her warm palm strokes my length, and I groan.

"Come on, Daddy, call in your meeting."

My fingers tangle into her hair as I look from her to another knock on the door. Her lips pull my head into her mouth like a lollipop, and I call out, "Come in."

The door snicks open, and Gary Price strolls into the room. The old beta is a part of a business deal I have in the works.

"Mr. Zade, sorry for coming by unannounced. My boss has agreed to your terms for the building project. He agrees that a sanctuary for omegas is a good idea."

I swallow as Audrey twists her fingers and palm around my shaft, and she squeezes my growing knot while bobbing her head up and down on my dick.

I can barely form a thought, let alone respond, but when Gary stares at me expectantly, I cough and hold Audrey still by her hair. "That is fantastic news. Omegas should have safe havens from alphas."

She rolls my balls into her palm and massages them as her tongue works along my slit, sucking my head like a blowjob expert, and I groan, covering it with another cough.

"Absolutely. My mother would have loved to know that I'm a part of something so good for omegas. And it will help your image with the media like you wanted."

"Oh God," I moan as my balls tighten in her hold, and I feel my climax coming on. "Yeah, that is exactly what I wanted. A good media presence."

Gary's eyebrows raise as his eyes drop to my hand gripping my desk. "Are you okay?"

"Just excited," I croak as Audrey drags her teeth along my head before slipping my dick all the way into her mouth, hitting the back of her mouth, her hand still around my knot. "Can we take this up tomorrow morning?"

"Uh, yeah," he says slowly. Then he stands and steps forward to shake my hand before he turns to leave. "I'll come around ten?"

"Perfect," I bite out a little too quickly.

As soon as the door shuts behind him, I slide back, pulling her with me. Giving her a hungry look, I tug her up off the floor and swipe my arm across the top of the desk, laying her on her back on top of it and pulling off her leggings all in one smooth motion. Dipping my fingers between her folds, I groan.

"Fuck, Audrey, you are so wet for me."

"Mmmm," she hums. "My heat is coming. I'm going to need lots of knotting."

"Maybe I'll be rescheduling that appointment tomorrow then. He'd understand."

She moans as I swipe over her clit with my thumb before circling the swollen nub until her hips arch off the desk, silently begging me for more.

"You were a naughty girl," I murmur, my gaze on her slick folds.

"So bad, Daddy," she pants as I dip a finger into her cunt. When she arches into my touch, I hold her down with my other hand on her stomach.

"Mmmm, sweet little omega, I think it's time to pay for that." A satisfied smile spreads across my face as she attempts to move again. "Imagine what Gary would have thought if he knew you were on your knees beneath my desk? Your sweet lips wrapped around my cock."

I groan at the idea of him knowing. Fuck, that is a turn on. I flick my finger over her clit again and sink two fingers deep inside of her, her silky walls clench around me, seeking what I have between my legs. And I curl them up, pressing against her g-spot, and she whines low and needy.

"Austin–" she breathes. "Please."

"Please what?"

"Make me come."

I laugh. "Not yet, you naughty girl."

Ever so slowly, I finger her, filling her with another finger as her slick coats my hand, and her fucking delectible brownie scent fills my office. Her breathing is ragged as she clenches around my fingers even harder than before. I ease off, leisurely rubbing her clit until her breathing evens out, and she whines again. Her body is vibrating with the need to come, and I love it. My perfect omega falling apart all over my desk.

"Please, Daddy," she begs.

Relenting, I move her to the edge and spread her legs wide. Then I'm knot deep but not locking, instead I give her just enough to stretch her before pulling back and slamming back into her. If I knot her like I really want to, I wouldn't get any more work done today, and as tempting as that, is the anticipation of later will hold me over. She gasps and moans as she grips me so tight I can't hold back and explode inside of her as our mutual orgasm crashes over us.

I pull out and help her sit up. She stands on shaky legs that make the alpha in me happy, before padding over to my office bathroom, her ass swaying on her way. Maybe we should go into the safe room and make use of the shower in there. Provide a little aftercare and cuddling on the couch while we're at it

Ignoring my baser urges, I tuck myself away and put myself back together before she returns. She eyes me with a pout as she comes back to my desk and pulls on panties and leggings, and slips on her shoes.

"Guess I need to get back to my jailer." She presses a soft kiss to my lips, and I reluctantly let her go when she pulls back. "I'll see you at home, Daddy."

I love the sound of that. *Home.*

CHAPTER 60

Audrey

FELIX HAS his feet propped up on the couch when I return. Saint stops pacing near the door and wraps me in his arms.

"Austin said you went to see him," he mutters. "We could have taken you."

I pull back and frame his face with my palms with a smile. "You needed a break from omega sitting. I think you are going as crazy as me."

"We almost lost you," he says.

"But you didn't."

"If your brother—"

"Who is also an omega," I point out.

He sighs and drags his fingers through his hair. "I just wish I could have brought Jason back to life so I could torture him."

I snort. Who knew I'd fall for someone exactly like my father? He always wanted to protect us, only his way of protecting was a little extreme. Scaring away all the boys he thought weren't good enough was a sport for him back then. And maybe if it hadn't been, he would still be here. I shake myself out of the morbid thoughts and focus on Saint.

"Me too," I admit. "But can we stop this mother hen hovering?"

He wraps his hands around the back of my neck and presses a kiss to my forehead. "No promises, but I'll try to ease up."

Felix laughs, and I pull away from Saint to look at him. "Saint doesn't know how not to be protective, and you've activated the alpha protection mode in him. It is a good thing he didn't promise."

"Where is your alpha protection mode?" I ask, propping my hands to my hips I lift my eyebrows as he toys with the ring in his lip.

He twists his lips as he holds in a grin. "I'm sure it will activate at some point, but right now, all I can think about every time you are around is stripping you naked and knotting you."

My stomach flutters at his crass words as slick prepares for just that between my thighs. "Well, that is perfect then, because I'm pretty sure my heat is almost here."

He pops off the couch like an excited puppy and bounds over to us. "Then it will be official." He fingers the ring of marks on my neck, and I nibble on my lip at the anticipation coursing through me.

I yelp when his arms sweep my feet from under me, and he carries me back to the couch with him. He settles back on the soft surface with me in his lap. Saint follows and sinks to the couch next to us.

Felix points the controller at the tv stand, and the TV slowly drops from the ceiling. The *"Omega in Paradise* finale was the other night. You want to watch?"

I smile into his neck. I have my own sort of omega paradise right here, but I would never pass up my favorite show. We settle in for the next two hours watching the perfect ending. Grace came out the winner, and her pack adored her.

I'm not sure why I had always been so blind to that result, that it wasn't just the omega who was head over heels, it was the entire pack too.

As the credits roll, I nuzzle into Felix's neck, inhaling his salty ocean breeze musk. Mixed with the leather and lemons of Saint's was almost perfect, I was only missing Austin's fall scents. As if my thoughts conjured him out of thin air, the door swings open, and he strides in with a grin on his face.

"I couldn't work. So I'm taking the day, and I've cleared the entire week of appointments, including the one with Gary, he was understanding, said first heats are special and to take all the time we need. A plane will be ready to go when we make it to the airport." His words are a whirlwind, and I sit up watching him as he comes around the couch. "Why are you three just watching me? We are going someplace warm with crystal blue water and private over the water huts for Audrey's first heat."

I clamp down on my lower lip as excitement rushes through me. "You don't have to do that, the apartment is fine, more than fine."

"As much as Saint plans on protecting you, I am going to pamper you, and you're going to humor me and let me do it. After coming into my life and bulldozing every single one of my fears, taking you someplace nice for your heat is the very least I can do. I looked it up, a lot of packs go to the resort for heats, it is secure and discreet."

Finally allowing the grin out, I climb off Felix's lap and throw myself into Austin's arms. He catches me, holding me close.

"Let me get some clothes," I say.

Austin nips my neck. "You won't need many outfits, just your birthday suit."

I swat at his chest as a laugh bubbles up. I am living the show, fairytales are real, happily ever after is actually a thing.

WE ARE ready and on our way to the airport in record time. The car goes through a private entrance, and we are driving next to the huge planes to a small hangar. A luxury jet just large enough for us is waiting, and they lead me on board.

I want to pinch myself. This is my life, spur of the moment trips and three sexy alphas. Settling into one of the soft plush cream colored chairs, I buckle as the guys do the same. The four large chairs sit facing each other with a table between them. There is a couch running the opposite length and another row sits behind us with four chairs. It is large enough to fit two packs.

The pilot climbs on board and disappears into the cockpit, and before long, we are airbound. I love flying. There is some-thing about being thousands of feet above the ground. It puts life in perspective, the world so big in comparison to the self. We are like ants on the surface, each of us living our lives, unaware of the bigger picture.

Austin draws my attention away from the window when he pulls out an envelope. The guys tense, and it makes me wary. I swallow and eye the paper he is unfolding. What is this? Is this where it all tumbles down and shatters on the ground?

"Audrey–" Austin begins, and I blink up from the old piece of paper to his swirling violet eyes. "Before you accept us fully…there is something you need to know."

My heart hammers inside my chest, and I swallow again, not that it does any good, as my mouth is bone dry. My lips part as I glance at Felix and Saint. Both of them look uncom-fortable, Saint looks like he wants to rip the paper away from Austin and shred it into tiny pieces.

"What is it?" I croak.

Austin presses his lips into a tight line and holds out the

letter. I take it, hesitating only a moment, before my eyes fall to my father's signature at the bottom. My breath catches, and I lift my gaze to the start of the letter, or contract really.

My dad had been so sure he knew what was right for his children, and he was half right. Because I was here with the men he wanted me to be with, the men he arranged for me. But my pack, they weren't for Sin, maybe before everything he would have fit, but now he had his own path. A bitter-sweet sadness fills me as I read the words.

I can see the care he put into them, the way he wanted to make sure both the Mafia and his children were protected. A tear slips out, and I brush it away as I finish reading.

"Princess, it doesn't mean anything. I would never–"

My fingers tighten on the letter as I bring my gaze back up to Austin. "It means everything, Austin."

"You are your own person, I just didn't want any more secrets between us. The contract was just between our parents."

A chaotic jumble of emotions bounce through me. He is trying to reassure me, but I'm not sure why.

"No, it is between us. I belong to you, just as you belong to me. Fate would have brought us together either way."

"You're not going to jump out of the plane?" Saint asks.

Felix cracks a smile and tugs his lip ring between his teeth. "Austin made sure to lock up the parachutes."

My nose crinkles as I realize they thought I would be upset or try to run. And maybe before I knew them I would have, but now, I can't imagine my life without them. I slowly fold the letter and bring my gaze up to Austin's uncertain one.

"If you think you can scare me away before claiming me, with this–" I laugh. "Daddy, you're going to have to do more than that to get rid of me."

A low growl emanates from Austin, and I grin.

The click of his belt as he undoes it sends a thrill of excitement through me. He stands up and motions Felix out of the way. "Our princess apparently wants to be reminded about who she belongs to."

I clamp down on my lower lip as I watch him. If this is the way he shows me I belong to him for the rest of our lives, he can tattoo his name on my ass for all I care. I don't help him as he unbuckles me, then he is sitting on the couch, me draped over his legs. Swapping my leggings in for skirts might be a real thing soon.

Brownies and cream fills the space, mixing with all three of their musks, and I groan before he even runs his fingers over the curve of my ass. Anticipation for joining the mile high club with them settles in my belly, making me feel flush and warm.

"I bet you're slick between your legs already," Austin says. He caresses my ass cheek, and his fingers run over the fabric between my legs, pressing into my warmth. "Mmm, yeah, our pretty little omega doesn't need any encouragement. What do you want, princess?"

"You, all of you." I lift slightly, my palms flat on the floor to look up at him.

Two more clicks sound, and it is music to my ears. Before long they have me spread out and bare on the table. Felix works his magic between my legs, devouring my pussy like he is starving. I thread my fingers through his hair holding him to me as I am violently thrown into the first of many orgasms. They don't let up as Saint drops to his knees and takes Felix's place, three fingers working inside me as his tongue swirls my sensitive nub.

I gasp and clench the table as he holds my legs wide. Then another orgasm tries to drown me in pleasure. The third comes quickly when Austin trades places with Saint. My body is so spent after the third that I lay there panting as I come back down. The slight uncomfortable feeling the heat was bringing with it eased, but it is still there like a lion ready to pounce.

I am not going to survive my heat.

CHAPTER 61

Audrey

FOUR DAYS LATER.

The small hut over the crystal blue water smells like sex. Which in my opinion is the best smell in the world, at least ours is. My heat has eased. Although, I wouldn't mind staying here for a whole month pretending it hasn't.

The warm breeze caresses my skin as I stand on the porch. The whole place is over water, a long bridge connects us to the beach. There are seven other huts all for the same purpose, with privacy walls on the sides of the porches that face the ocean, the clear white sand of the shore behind us.

Saint comes up behind me, his arms circling my waist. The bond between the four of us is complete, making me feel like a brand new person. I run my fingers over the now perma- nent marks that ring my neck. It was intense at first, right after Austin pack bonded me with his bite, ensuring it would never fade as he was knot deep inside of me. His rut and my heat worked like a seal, forging us together in an unbreakable bond. I had read about it, but feeling what they feel through our link, adds to everything. Knowing the love they feel like a gentle touch on my soul has healed me in ways I never thought were possible.

I've convinced Austin to frame our contract, we will hang it on the wall at the penthouse. He was reluctant, but I managed to get him to agree.

Fate, destiny, the powers that be, it didn't matter–we were meant to be.

"What are you thinking, hellcat?" He presses a kiss to my bare shoulder.

I twist in his arms and wrap my arms around him. "Just about how loved I feel."

He hums, his brown eyes glowing with that love. "You have really made our pack whole."

"Well it is the least I could do," I reply. "The three of you picked up my broken pieces and put me back together."

Felix steps out onto the porch. "Austin has decided he can cook again."

Saint and I share a look, and then we are following Felix back into the hut. Austin is at the stove top, pancakes in the pan already.

"Don't worry, no bourbon this time," he says over his shoulder.

I come up behind him and sliding my fingers over his bare stomach, peeking around him at the pan. The pancake has been flipped already, the done side up. He purrs as he flips it out and onto a plate.

"I need to take care of my princess, and cooking for you is part of it." He pours more batter into the pan before he turns toward me. He smooths stray hairs behind my ear and smiles softly down at me.

"Saint is a pretty good cook," I say.

He growls and puts the spatula down before he wraps his arms around me. "But I *want* to care for you."

I smile into his chest as he hugs me tight.

Felix clears his throat. "Uh, food is smoking."

I laugh as Austin swears and pulls away. "Felix, take care of the omega, she's a distraction."

He sounds grumbly and gruff, but I catch the smile on his lips as Felix tugs me away. I settle in Felix's lap as he sits at the breakfast nook.

"Just where I like you," he rumbles.

Once there is a pile of pancakes all golden brown and perfectly cooked, Saint preps a plate for me while Felix takes my fork and proceeds to feed me, unwilling to let me go. My stomach full and heart overflowing, I groan as he tries to bring another bite to my lips.

"No more," I beg.

He smiles and takes the bite instead before putting the fork down.

Austin leans against the counter with his legs crossed at the ankles and a mug of coffee in his grip. "I received news this morning."

I twist on Felix's lap to face Austin and the guys watch him too. "About?"

"The painting."

Saint groans.

"The one that went into the water was a fake. A decoy. Valentine knew we were coming and moved it. But Carmichael got to it first."

"Austin–" Saint says.

He holds up a hand. "But it's okay. The only treasure that matters is in this room with us. Audrey, I could never live without you. I just wanted you guys to know that the painting is still out there in the world somewhere. That knowledge is enough for me."

"I am a thief."

Three resounding, "No!" echoes back at me. I grin. I know how to play the long game. Someday I'll be in a position to get it back for him.

"I won't put myself in danger," I promise.

"Muffin, pretend you didn't hear what Austin said," Felix says into my ear.

I choke on a laugh. "*Muffin*?"

"You're right. Doesn't make sense with your brownie scent." He taps his chin. "What about donut? It is perfect, and I am as addicted to you as I am donuts."

Austin snorts, and Saint laughs. This is my life, and I wouldn't trade it for anything else in this world. I'm finally an Omega in Paradise.

$$Epilogue$$

AUDREY

Sin leans against the chain link fence of the fight ring, with the crowd around us growing louder as we wait for Saint's fight to start. Felix wraps an arm around my waist as he and Austin carry on a conversation of their own with an associate.

Sin nods across the space at Carmichael, his step-sister, and a friend of Carmichael's who looks like he is going to fight in the ring tonight too. "Do you remember him? From when we were teens?"

I shrug. Not really.

"He was a jerk."

"Well, that jerk is the one that stole Austin's painting. He's having a party next weekend, you need to go and see if you can find it."

He lifts a brow and glances back at them again. "I hate parties."

"You party every night, you used to come home smelling like booze."

"That's different."

"Is it?"

He rolls his eyes. "Who's the omega?"

"That's his step-sister, he keeps her close."

Sin hums.

"So will you do it?" I press.

"Of course I will. You are the reason I'm still here," he says with a half-hearted shrug.

Our conversation is cut short as Saint enters the rings and the crowd goes insane for him. I understand the obsession. He is a work of art. Butterflies batter my stomach as I watch him bounce on the balls of his bare feet and shake out his arms.

I smile. Tonight is the night we both live out a fantasy. My perfume blooms and he shifts his attention in my direction as he inhales picking up my scent in the crowded room. He pauses on the other side of the chain fence, his fingers threading through as he watches me.

"I'll make this quick," he says.

"Not too quick I have money on three rounds," Austin replies.

"Kiss for luck?"

I lean forward and press my lips to his, and he pulls away grinning.

"You know he doesn't need luck out there right?" Sin asks shooting me a look as he twists around to watch his new mentor. "He is really good."

"Then you have a good teacher, and you can win next week." I link my fingers through the holes as I press as close as I can to the ring.

The announcer recites the rules he does every match and then steps out of the way as the bell sounds. Saint dodges a right hook, before landing a firm fist into the alpha's ribcage, doing his dance of figuring out the weaknesses. Before I know it the round is over, the second beginning after the small break.

After the second he leans against the fence and looks over at my brother. "You see how he drops his elbow? When he does that he is opening up his opposite side. Overcompensating. Whoever you fight next week will have the same kind of tells. If you pay attention you can catch them." He wipes his arm over his sweaty forehead and heads back to the center of the ring again.

My brother would hate it, but every single time Saint cares enough to teach Sin something I want to reward my alpha in the bedroom. My whole pack has taken Sin in as a family member, and it has really helped him heal a little.

"Sin, I'll be back, in, uh a little, stick with Felix," I say as Saint knocks out his competition.

I GIVE Austin and Felix quick kisses and then dance through the crowd as I head for the backrooms. Slipping into Saint's dressing room I perch on the small table in the center of the space. My stomach flips and my pussy clenches around nothing as anticipation has my hormones kicking into high gear.

AS THE DOOR swings open I bite my lip and watch Saint as he catches sight of me. He grins, the door slapping shut behind me as he prowls across the room. His musk is heavy in the air, mixing with my perfume.

HIS HANDS LAND on my hips gathering the thin material of my dress in his fingers. "Is this what I think it is?" he husks, pressing his forehead against mine.

* * *

I walk my fingers down his slick chest to his fighting shorts. "That depends on what you think this is," I reply.

It doesn't take more for his lips to crash into mine, and him to pull me into his arms, wrapping my legs around him and exposing my bare core to him as my dress rides all the way up.

"Fuck, you planned this didn't you?" He growls low in his throat, nipping at my lower lip as he walks me into a wall, pressing my back against the firm surface. He slips his hand between us as he frees his length from his shorts, the hot press of him against my already heated folds has me panting, a small whimper coming out freely.

"If I did, I expected you to be knot deep inside of me already," I say against his lips.

He groans. "Fuck, you have a mouth on you, I love it," he says between kisses.

Then he slips into my pussy with a fast thrust, his fingers going into my hair as he single-mindedly thrusts into me. He nips at my skin as he kisses his way down the side of my throat, his hot pants of breaths against my flesh are everything.

With one arm securely around my waist, he steps away from the wall and turns, aimlessly finding the table again. He presses me into the solid surface, dragging my knees up so he can go deeper. His knot almost pushes inside my pussy with each stroke.

"Saint, harder," I order. I love him like this, on the verge of losing control. I can see it flash in the depths of his eyes, as his inner alpha takes over completely.

The table scrapes across the floor with every forceful meeting of our bodies. The slapping of skin, moans and gasps of pleasure, and Saint's harsh breaths the only sounds between us as he destroys me from the inside out.

His fingers dig into my hips in the best possible way as I tumble into the abyss of pleasure. He pulls out, without knotting me, his seed making a mess of the floor and table.

He leans over me, pressing his forehead to mine again. "I'm going to expect this going forward," he says before pressing his lips to mine.

I huff out a happy laugh. "That makes two of us," I reply.

"I'll clean this up, and we can join the others," he says as he tugs me to a sitting position and fixes my dress the best he can without me sitting up.

OUR LAUGHTER RINGS out over the empty diner. We are the only late-night customers, and we are piled into one booth. Sin and Saint sit across from Felix, Austin, and me. The table has all of the guys' favorite foods and I can't think of a different life.

After everything that happened to us, I had lost hope. But now I'm living proof, anything is possible. If I found my pack and the loves of my life, then my brother, my twin...he will find his.

Sin relaxes in his seat, completely at home with our new family. Who knew stealing a watch would lead to this?

"You with us?" Austin murmurs, brushing a strand of my hair over my shoulder and kissing my temple.

"Always and forever," I reply.

"Good."

I tuck into his side with a content sigh. This is love, and it drowns out the darkness within, casting it away as the final chapter of our happily ever after unfolds.

THANK YOU FOR READING! Reviews are highly appreciated and so helpful to an author. Reviews for The Darkness Within can be left on Goodreads, Bookbub, and other retailers.

Gabriella's story will be coming out in February of 2024. Called 'The Darkness Appeal' and Sin will find his happily ever after with his new found harem. Join my Facebook group A.J. Moran Sweethearts for sneak peeks along the way, or be some of the first to join my brand new discord A.J.-Moran's Sweethearts. Xoxo

Afterword

I hope you loved Audrey's story as much as I loved writing it.
I never really imagined writing an omegaverse, but I found
that once I started it flows so easily from my fingertips onto
the screen. Expect more to come. Including - The Darkness
Appeal - Sin's journey to happiness with a pack of his own.

Xoxoxo

A.J.

Acknowledgments

This one is for Jenni. Girl, this book wouldn't have happened if you didn't encourage me (boss me around) to write this story. It is my first venture into omegaverse, and I went in completely blind with just the descriptions of what it was from web searches. And it worked! So thank you so much for that encouragement! You are an amazing friend and editor.

Fawn, gosh, I need to impress you more. I'm so happy you are one of my alphas and someone I can call friend. I enjoy our random talks and hearing how much you enjoyed this story. You're the best!

Carol, I know your live is busy!! And I appreciate you taking time out to alpha for me. Just always remember family comes first! Anytime you can spare is amazing, but I would hate for you to miss out on memories while your kids are smaller. (Well, smaller than my four at least.)

ARC readers! You guys are fantastic. I couldn't ask for a better group of readers. Even if I am the worst at posting in the group, you are all still willing to read and let me know what you think.

And finally, although definitely not least, family. Eric, my everything, thank you for supporting me in all the ways. And my children, thanks for all the love and support even though you'll never read these stories. But Bb, if you do, I told you that you'd love them if you just pretended it wasn't your mom that wrote them. Lol

Also by A. J. Moran

Fae Warriors Series

Creation

Destruction

Salvation

Brookview Academy Series

Splintered

Unbreakable

Fractured

Orion's Daughter Series

Playing with Fire

Flirting with Death

Gambling with Time

A Brookview Academy Story - Revisit Brookview with all new characters

Conjuring: A Bully Romance (part 1)

Dream Walking: A Bully Romance (part 2) (coming soon)

Omegaverse - The Sins of Darkness Duet

The Darkness Within

The Darkness Appeal (coming soon)

YA BOOKS (Not spicy or Reverse Harem)

Royal Pain: A Step brother romance

PenPals